Praise for Yesterday's Embers

"Deborah Raney writes from the heart with a story that probes the depth of human sorrow, the grit of endurance, and the ability of love to rescue us when we've forgotten how to dream. *Yesterday's Embers* will leave you warmed long after the last page."

—Harry Kraus, MD, bestselling author of *Perfect* and *Salty Like Blood*

"With characters so real they feel like family, *Yesterday's Embers* will stir your heart with sorrow, compassion, and joy as you journey with the characters down a road too many have traveled. More than just a good read, *Yesterday's Embers* offers greater understanding and insight to the challenges of others. A must read!"

—Diann Hunt, author of *For Better or For Worse*

"Deborah Raney weaves a tender story of love, loss, sorrow, and reconciliation that will remain with you long after you've read the final page. *Yesterday's Embers* expertly unfolds to reveal engaging characters and a compelling story of difficult choices and determined commitment. This is a book filled with warmth and hope that you'll recommend to all your friends!"

—Judith Miller, author of the Postcards from Pullman series

"Deborah Raney has done it again . . . made me want to pack up and move to her fictional town of Clayburn, Kansas. *Yesterday's Embers* is a powerful story of love lost . . . and found, but not at all in the way you expect. A surprising and touching story. Kudos."

—Roxanne Henke, author of *After Anne* and *Learning to Fly*

"*Yesterday's Embers* took me through a roller coaster of emotions with the characters tugging at my heart throughout. I wanted so badly for things to turn out well for Doug, Mickey, and the children. I should have known that Deborah Raney wouldn't fail her readers—or her characters. *Yesterday's Embers* is another winner."

—Robin Lee Hatcher, bestselling author of *When Love Blooms* and *A Vote of Confidence*

"I sat down to read just a little, and then allowed myself the luxury of reading a little more. Before I knew it I had turned page after page of this satisfying story about the intersection of love and commitment and how our God gives, and takes away, and then unexpectedly gives again."

—Sandra Byrd, Christy award finalist for *Let Them Eat Cake* and its sequel *Bon Appétit*.

"Deborah Raney has truly captured the emotional turmoil of love lost and the struggle to move on—and that each step forward is only possible by placing one's trust in God. A powerful, touching read."

—Linda Windsor, author of *Wedding Bell Blues* and *For Pete's Sake*

"*Yesterday's Embers,* with its realistic, emotionally engaging characters, is a book that will linger in the back of one's heart long after the final page is turned. Anyone who has loved and lost . . . and dared to love again . . . will celebrate Doug and Mickey's journey."

—Kim Vogel Sawyer, bestselling author of *My Heart Remembers*

"I couldn't put this story down. When the highs of new love translate to poor decisions, the innocent suffer until God extends an invitation to love. We all can see ourselves in this powerful story of tragedy turned to unexpected blessings."

—DiAnn Mills, author of *Breach of Trust*

"*Yesterday's Embers* makes a powerful impact with its message of not just second chances, but endless chances, to renew our lives. What hope lies within these pages for all of us! Thank you so much for a great read!"

—Hannah Alexander, author of *A Killing Frost*

"Deborah Raney masterfully draws us into the lives of two people searching for love through some of life's most difficult circumstances. These are not just characters in a novel—they're real people, and I walked every step of their journey with them. *Yesterday's Embers* is a poignant story of mistakes, restoration, and the thread of grace that can fan dying embers into triumphant flames."

—Virginia Smith, author of *Age before Beauty* in the Sister-to-Sister Series

"Deborah Raney depicts the innermost human emotions with poignant realism. *Yesterday's Embers* is a stimulating, thought-provoking read that kept me turning the pages—at times wishing I could give a character a good scolding and, at other times, a comforting embrace. Prepare to be hooked!"

—Kathy Herman, author of the Baxter, Seaport, and Phantom Hollow Series

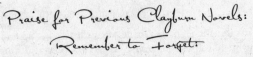

Praise for Previous Clayburn Novels:

Remember to Forget:

"Deborah Raney has done it again! *Remember to Forget* is a wonderful, heartwarming story about learning to trust . . . and love. Yes, I loved it."

—Roxanne Henke, author of *After Anne* and *The Secret of Us*

"I was enthralled from start to finish. *Remember to Forget* took me to deep places of the heart and touched the spot where we all long for unconditional love. I wanted to stay in Clayburn, Kansas, forever. Raney's best book yet!"

—Colleen Coble, author of *Midnight Sea*

Leaving November:

"Faith and love triumph in this small-town story of overcoming the past and finding hope for the future. *Leaving November* gently plays the heartstrings and embraces the spirit in the name of love."

—Linda Windsor, author of *Wedding Bell Blues* and *For Pete's Sake*

"Deb Raney's books have been an enjoyment and inspiration for me since her first, *A Vow to Cherish*. She has again touched my life with *Leaving November*. A gifted storyteller, she also has a way of having her characters learn to lean on God that causes me as a reader to relearn that same lesson. I highly recommend *Leaving November*."

—Yvonne Lehman, author of 46 novels and director of the Blue Ridge Mountains Christian Writers Conference

Yesterday's Embers

a clayburn novel

Award-Winning Author

Deborah Raney

HOWARD
Fiction
A DIVISION OF SIMON & SCHUSTER
New York   London   Toronto   Sydney

Our purpose at Howard Books is to:
- *Increase faith* in the hearts of growing Christians
- *Inspire holiness* in the lives of believers
- *Instill hope* in the hearts of struggling people everywhere
  Because He's coming again!

Published by Howard Books, a division of Simon & Schuster, Inc.
1230 Avenue of the Americas, New York, NY 10020
www.howardpublishing.com

Yesterday's Embers © 2009 by Deborah Raney

In association with the Steve Laube Agency

Library of Congress Cataloging-in-Publication Data

Raney, Deborah.
    Yesterday's embers : a Clayburn novel / Deborah Raney.
        p. cm
    ISBN 978-1-4165-9309-6 (tradepaper : alk. paper)
    I. Title.
    PS3568.A562Y47 2009
    813'.54—dc22

                                        2008033836

0837

ISBN-13: 978-1-4165-9309-6
ISBN-10:   1-4165-9309-8

10 9 8 7 6 5 4 3 2 1

HOWARD and colophon are registered trademarks of Simon & Schuster, Inc.

Manufactured in the United States of America

For information regarding special discounts for bulk purchases, please contact: Simon & Schuster Special Sales at 1-800-456-6798 or business@simonandschuster.com.

Edited by Dave Lambert and Ramona Cramer Tucker

Interior design by Tennille Paden

Acknowledgments

I wish to offer sincere thanks and deep appreciation to the following people for their part in bringing this story to life:

For help with research, proofreading, and "author support," I am forever grateful to my dear friend Terry Stucky; my parents, Max and Winifred Teeter; my daughter, Tobi Layton; and my amazing Club Deb gang.

I appreciate the kind folks at The Swedish Country Inn in Lindsborg, Kansas, where the ideas for the Clayburn novels were born.

To Mary, Ariana, Christy, and the rest of the gang at Lincoln Perk: you make my Tuesday mornings special (and a Very Vanilla Latte to die for).

I'm not sure I could ever finish a book without the collective wisdom and brainstorming of the ChiLibris Midwest contingent. I love you guys.

To my critique partner, Tamera Alexander, thanks for your eagle eye and creative mind. Thank you for injecting your critiques and our conversations with a dose of your wonderful sense of humor. But most of all, thank you for the gift of your friendship.

A long-overdue word of appreciation for Father James Hoover and the late Reverend Harmon Lackey, whose words of wisdom when my husband and I were about to marry have never been forgotten and have often found their way into my stories in one form or another.

Deep appreciation to my agent, Steve Laube, who knows how to make me feel like his one and only client; and to my talented editors Dave Lambert and Philis Boultinghouse at Howard Books; and also to Ramona Cramer Tucker, who is such fun to work with, even on a killer deadline.

To our incredible, supportive kids and our extended family: what a gift from the Lord you all are. I am blessed beyond description.

And to my husband, Ken . . . I can't ever say it enough: I love you, babe. Still.

Hear my prayer, O Lord;
let my cry for help come to you.
Do not hide your face from me when I am in distress.
Turn your ear to me; when I call, answer me quickly.
— Psalm 102:1–2

Be glad, O people of Zion,
rejoice in the Lord your God,
for he has given you the autumn rains in righteousness.
He sends you abundant showers,
both autumn and spring rains, as before.
The threshing floors will be filled with grain;
the vats will overflow with new wine and oil.
"I will repay you for the years the locusts have eaten. . . ."
— Joel 2:23–25

The woman was
right about one thing:
she knew how to keep
a fire going.

Prologue

Thanksgiving Day

You sure you guys'll be okay?" Doug DeVore leaned over the sofa to plant a kiss on his wife's lips.

But Kaye turned her head, and his lips landed somewhere in the vicinity of her left ear.

"Sorry, babe." She wrinkled her nose and put a hand over her mouth. "You'd better not kiss me. My stomach's feeling a little woozy this morning. I never should have shared that milkshake with Rachel. I'm afraid I'm coming down with whatever she has." Kaye looked down at their six-year-old, asleep in the crook of her arm.

The car horn tooted from the garage, and a second later Sarah appeared in the kitchen doorway. "C'mon, Daddy, hurry

1

up! Landon's bein' bossy, and Kayeleigh says she's gonna walk to Grandma's if you don't get the lead out."

"You tell Landon to cut it out, and tell Kayeleigh to hold her horses and quit sassing." He gave Kaye what he hoped was a desperate frown. "Sure you don't want me to stay home with you?"

She narrowed her eyes. "Don't even think about it, buster." She turned her pretty face to the hearth, where the first fire of the season crackled like brittle leaves underfoot. "But, hey, thanks for the fire."

"Yeah, well, I just wish I could be here to keep it going." He wriggled his brows, making sure she got his innuendo.

She laughed. "Real subtle . . . and I'll take you up on that offer once I get rid of whatever this crud is I'm coming down with. In the meantime, I think I know how to keep a fire going." She imitated his eyebrow gymnastics.

He smoothed a hand over her tousled hair. "I had Landon bring in some wood, but if you run out, there's a dry stack on the porch." He went over and checked the damper. Man, what he wouldn't give to call Kaye's mother and bow out of Thanksgiving for all of them. Sit here by the fire with a good book and watch the game later without Kaye's brother giving his obnoxious play-by-play.

He sighed. That would never fly. Kaye's mom had no doubt been cooking for days. And Thanksgiving was always the last time they got together with Harriet before she headed to Florida for the winter. Besides, if he stayed home, dinner was likely to be a sleeve of stale saltines and a can of Campbell's tomato soup that he heated up himself.

With visions of the usual dinner-table mayhem, Harley in her highchair flinging soup all over the kitchen—and Kaye too sick to supervise—he reconsidered. "I'll bring a couple of plates home for you two."

"Uh-huh . . . that's what I thought." Kaye laughed and he knew she'd read his mind. As she always could.

He reached down to brush a wisp of hair off Rachel's forehead. "Man . . . she feels hot."

His wife gave a knowing nod. "I don't think this little angel is going to be eating anything any time soon. But bring a plate home just in case."

Kaye had been up all night with Rachel while Doug played possum through the sounds of his daughter's retching. A twinge of guilt nipped at his conscience now.

Kaye tugged at his sleeve. "Make sure Harley wears her hat if the kids take her outside. I don't want her getting sick, too."

"I will." He grabbed his jacket off the back of a kitchen chair and started for the garage.

"Hey, you . . ."

He turned back at Kaye's voice.

"I like lots of whipped cream on my pumpkin pie." She dared to wink at him.

"Excuse me, I thought you were sick."

She smiled. "Not that sick."

The door to the garage opened again, and Sadie, Sarah's twin, popped her blond head in. "Da-aad, hurry up. Harley's fussin' . . ."

He gave Kaye a hopeful grin. "You *sure* you don't want me to stay home, babe?"

Pulling Rachel closer, Kaye cocked an eyebrow his way. "So you can help me clean up vomit, you mean?"

He stuffed an arm through his coat sleeve. "I'm going, I'm going." Talk about the lesser of two evils.

"Love you," Kaye called after him.

Her soft laughter followed him out the door, and he couldn't help but smile to himself.

The woman was right about one thing: she knew how to keep a fire going.

What would
she say? What could
anybody say to make
what had happened
be all right?

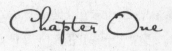

Chapter One

The parade of taillights smoldered crimson through the patchy fog hovering over Old Highway 40. Mickey Valdez tapped the brakes with the toe of her black dress pumps, trying to stay a respectable distance from the car in front of her.

The procession had left the church almost twenty minutes ago, but they were still barely two miles outside Clayburn's city limits. The line of cars snaked up the hill—if you could call the road's rolling incline that—and ahead of her, the red glow of brake lights dotted the highway, flickering off and on like so many fireflies. Cresting the rise, Mickey could barely make out the rows of pewter-colored gravestones poking through the mist beyond the wrought-iron gates of the Clayburn Cemetery.

She smoothed the skirt of her black

crepe dress and tried to focus her thoughts on maneuvering the car, working not to let them stray to the funeral service she'd come from. But when the first hearse turned onto the cemetery's gravel drive in front of her, she lost it. Her sobs came like dry heaves, producing no tears, and for once she was glad to be in the car alone.

The line of cars came almost to a standstill as the second hearse crept through the gates.

The twin black Lincolns pulled to the side of the gravel lane, parking one behind the other near the plots where two fresh graves scarred the prairie. The drivers emerged from the hearses, walked in unison to the rear of their cars, and opened the curtained back doors. Mickey looked away. She couldn't view those two caskets again.

When it came her turn to drive over the culvert under the high arch of the iron gates, she wanted desperately to keep on driving. To head west and never turn back. But Pete Truesdell stood in her way, directing traffic into the fenced-in graveyard. Mickey almost didn't recognize Pete. He sported a rumpled navy double-breasted suit instead of his usual coveralls. How he could see through the tears welling in his eyes, Mickey didn't know.

Her heart broke for the old man. She wondered if he was related to the family somehow. Seemed like everybody in Clayburn was related to at least one other family in town. Everybody but the Valdezes.

Pete waved the car in front of her through the gates and halted her with his other hand.

Maybe if she stayed in the car until the procession left the cemetery. She didn't want to walk across the uneven sod. Didn't want to risk the DeVore kids seeing her . . . risk breaking down in front of them. What would she say? What could anybody say to make what had happened be all right?

She didn't know much about carbon monoxide poisoning, but she'd heard that Kaye and Rachel had simply drifted off to sleep, never knowing they would wake up in heaven. She wondered if Doug DeVore found any solace in that knowledge. Maybe it was a small comfort that his wife and daughter had left this earth together.

But on Thanksgiving Day? What was God *thinking*?

She'd never really gotten to know Kaye DeVore that well. They'd exchanged pleasantries whenever Kaye dropped the kids off at the daycare on her way to her job at the high school, but usually Doug was the one who delivered the children and picked them up at night when he got off work at Trevor Ashlock's print shop in town.

The DeVore kids were usually the last to get picked up, especially during harvest when Doug worked overtime to keep his farm going. But Mickey had never minded staying late. It wasn't like she had a family of her own waiting for her at home. And she loved those kids.

Especially Rachel. Sweet, angel-faced Rachel, whose eyes always seemed to hold a wisdom beyond her years. Mickey had practically mourned when Rachel started kindergarten and was only at the daycare for an hour or two after school. Now she forced herself to look at the tiny white coffin the pallbearers lifted from the second hearse. She could not make it real that the sunny six-year-old was gone.

Through the gates she watched Doug climb from a black town car. One at a time, he helped his children out behind him. Carrying the baby in one arm, he tried to stretch his free arm around the other four kids, as if he could shelter them from what had happened. How he could even stand up under the weight of such tragedy was more than Mickey could imagine. And yet, for one shameful, irrational moment, she envied his grief, and would have traded places with him if it meant she'd known a love worth grieving over, or been entrusted with a child of her own flesh and blood. She shook away the thoughts, disturbed by how long she'd let herself entertain them.

She dreaded facing Doug the next time he brought the kids to the daycare center. Maybe they wouldn't come back. She'd heard that Kaye's mother had cancelled her plans to winter in Florida like she usually did. Harriet Thomas would remain in Kansas and help Doug out, at least for a while. Wren Johannsen had been helping with the kids and house, too, when she could take time away from running Wren's Nest, the little bed-and-breakfast on Main Street. Wren was like a second grandma to the kids. Thank goodness for that. Six kids had to be—

Mickey shuddered and corrected herself. Only five now. That had to be a handful for anyone. The DeVores had gone on vacation in the middle of April last year, and with their kids out for a week, the workload was lighter, but the daycare center had been deathly quiet.

Deathly. Even though she was alone in the car, Mickey cringed at her choice of words.

She started at the tap on the hood of her car and looked up to see Pete motioning her through the gates. She put the car in gear and inched over the bumpy culvert. There was no turning back now. She followed the car in front of her and parked behind it next to the fence bordering the east side of the cemetery.

A tall white tombstone in the distance caught her eye, and a startling thought nudged her. The last time she'd been here for a funeral had also been the funeral of a mother and child. Trevor Ashlock's wife, Amy, and their little boy. It would be five years come summer.

As if conjured by her thoughts, Trevor's green pickup pulled in beside her. Mickey watched in her side mirror as he parked, then helped his young wife climb out of the passenger side. Meg walked with the gait of an obviously pregnant woman, and Trevor put a hand at the small of her back, guiding her over the uneven sod toward the funeral tent.

Mickey looked away. Seeing Trevor still brought a wave of sadness. Because of his profound loss, yes. But more selfishly, for her own loss. She'd fallen hard for him after Amy's death—and had entertained hopes that he might feel the same about her. That she might be able to ease his grief. But he was too deep in grief to even notice her.

Then Meg Anders had moved to town and almost before Mickey knew what happened, Trevor was married. He and Meg seemed very much in love, and Mickey didn't begrudge either of them an ounce of that happiness. But it didn't mean she was immune to a pang of envy whenever she saw them together.

This day had to be doubly difficult for Trevor. It must be a comfort to Doug having Trevor here—someone who'd walked in his shoes and still somehow managed to get up the next morning—and the next and the next.

Again, she had to wonder what God was thinking. Where was He when these tragedies struck? How could He stand by and let these terrible things happen to good men . . . the best men she knew, next to her brothers? None of it made sense. And the only One she knew to turn to for answers had stood by and let it all happen.

Everyone else had gone home, back to their normal lives. Decent lives they failed to appreciate and griped about for no good reason. He knew, because he'd been just like them.

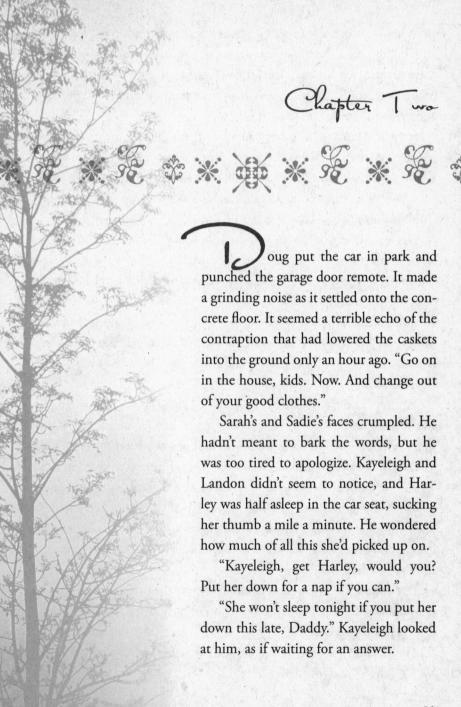

Chapter Two

Doug put the car in park and punched the garage door remote. It made a grinding noise as it settled onto the concrete floor. It seemed a terrible echo of the contraption that had lowered the caskets into the ground only an hour ago. "Go on in the house, kids. Now. And change out of your good clothes."

Sarah's and Sadie's faces crumpled. He hadn't meant to bark the words, but he was too tired to apologize. Kayeleigh and Landon didn't seem to notice, and Harley was half asleep in the car seat, sucking her thumb a mile a minute. He wondered how much of all this she'd picked up on.

"Kayeleigh, get Harley, would you? Put her down for a nap if you can."

"She won't sleep tonight if you put her down this late, Daddy." Kayeleigh looked at him, as if waiting for an answer.

When he didn't say anything, she reached to unbuckle the baby.

He didn't have the strength to argue, or to hurry her along. What was there to hurry for anyway? The funeral was over. Everyone else had gone home, back to their normal lives. Decent lives they failed to appreciate and griped about for no good reason.

He knew, because he'd been just like them. Taking for granted the blessing of a cup of coffee and the morning paper at the kitchen table. While in the bathroom down the hall, your wife stood under the shower for a few extra minutes, and your kids slept that serene sleep that only children could.

His kids would never sleep that way again. Two nights in a row, Landon had dragged his bedding downstairs at two in the morning, knocking on Doug's half-closed door, whimpering that he heard somebody trying to break in.

Doug slammed the door to the old Suburban and prodded the twins toward the house. Out of habit he started a head count. The twins were here . . . Kayeleigh had Harley, Landon was already in the house. That was five. Who was miss—?

His knees nearly buckled as it hit him afresh. *Rachel.* His sweet girl was missing from the lineup. Forever. It was bad enough losing Kaye, but Rachel, too? How long would he look for that sixth, sweet blond head, feeling restless until all his little towheads were accounted for?

But he hadn't been able to keep them safe. For all his training as a volunteer firefighter and certified EMT, for all the talks he'd given at parent-teacher meetings about the dangers of carbon monoxide poisoning—none of it had saved Kaye and Rachel. He was the *last* man this should have happened to.

But nobody ever thought it could happen to them. You never thought it would be your wife, your child they were carrying away in the ambulance. And then a hearse.

How would he bear it? He couldn't imagine going back to work, back to any kind of normalcy.

But he had no choice. He had to think about the kids. He was grateful for his job at the print shop, glad to have paying work to return to. Still, he'd begged off his volunteer EMT and firefighting duties indefinitely. Right now he didn't trust his own judgment—even though Blaine Deaver, the fire chief, assured him there wasn't anything he could have done to prevent what had happened to Kaye and Rachel.

At the end of winter last year, Kaye had called a chimney sweep from Salina to come and clean out the fireplace and flue, but apparently with several freezes and the spring thaw since then, crumbling mortar and bricks had blocked the flue again.

"Daddy?" Sadie and Sarah sang out in unison, their voices identical even if the girls were not. "What're we havin' for supper?"

It seemed like they'd left the funeral dinner only minutes ago, but a glance at his watch told him little bellies would be hungry again. An odd sense of panic enveloped him.

He was doing well to get the coffee maker going in the morning. Kaye always teased him that if it weren't for her, he wouldn't know how to boil water. Sadly, boiling water was as far as he'd gone in Kaye's school of culinary skills. How was he going to fill his kids' bellies tonight, let alone tomorrow and tomorrow and tomorrow after that?

He opened the door to the din of utter silence. For four days the house had swarmed with family and friends. This was the first time he'd been alone, just him and the kids, since he'd come home to find—

He wouldn't let his brain finish the sentence. He groped for the switch on the kitchen wall and flipped on the lights. The sight of countertops littered with cake stands and pie tins and plates full of cookies came as a strange relief. On one end of the counter, a stack of empty dishes Kaye's mom had labeled for return reminded him that the refrigerator was still packed tight with casseroles that neighbors and church friends had brought in. He didn't have an appetite for any of it, but his kids needed to eat. And he was grateful someone had provided.

Somehow he got all the kids out of their coats and dress clothes and into jeans and T-shirts. He scooped spoonfuls of some cheese-laden casserole onto plates and put the first one in the microwave. "How long should I nuke this, Kayeleigh?"

His oldest daughter looked at him like he'd grown another head. "For real? You don't know?"

"A minute, you think?" He punched the quick-minute button like he'd seen Kaye do whenever he'd worked late in the field or got called out on an ambulance run and she had to reheat his supper. He watched the digital numbers count the seconds off, wanting only to crawl in bed and pull the covers up over his head.

Behind him, he heard Kayeleigh sniffling. *Please don't let her cry, Lord. Please.*

He couldn't look at her but kept punching the quick-minute button until steam came off the lump of food in the middle. He heated one plate after another, thankful for the mindless task.

"This one's cold, Daddy."

Coming out of his fog, he saw Sarah beside him, jostling a plate in her pudgy hands. "This is still cold," she said again, sliding the plate to the back of a counter she could barely see over. He opened the microwave, and the empty turntable came to a halt. He slid the plate in, trying to force his thoughts to the present.

At the table Kayeleigh sat in front of Harley's highchair doing the airplane-spoon thing, trying to get the baby to eat. So like Kaye.

He put a hand on Sarah's head. "Okay, honey. Go sit down. It'll only take a minute."

He finished heating the food, set a plate in front of Kayeleigh, and also one at his place. Then he sat down, feeling queasy just looking at the food. Careful not to meet any of his kids' eyes, he stabbed a glutinous glob of casserole with his fork.

"Aren't we gonna say the blessing, Daddy?"

He looked up. Sadie's doleful blue eyes, so like her mother's, bored into his.

The blessing. The irony pierced like a sword. With effort he bowed his head. He sensed the kids following his lead. "Heavenly Father, bless this food to the nourishment of our bodies. In the name of Christ our Lord . . ."

It was the rote prayer his own father had prayed. He didn't know where he'd pulled it up from, but he lifted his head to see the kids gaping at him as if he'd prayed in Chinese.

Sarah broke the silence. "Why are you prayin' like that?"

Sadie's crinkled brow matched her twin's. "Does Mommy's body get food in the ground?"

"Sadie!" Kayeleigh hissed.

Sadie ignored her big sister and cocked an eyebrow at him. "Does it, Daddy?"

"What are you talking about, honey?"

"What you prayed . . . 'bout the food and 'nurshment' for our bodies. Is that what Mama's body gets?"

Maybe he'd been wrong to let the kids view Kaye's and Rachel's bodies. The twins especially had seemed obsessed with the topic since that night at the funeral home. He shoveled tasteless bites of casserole into his mouth, afraid he'd choke. "Eat your supper, girls. It's almost time for bed."

Landon twisted in his chair and stared out at the pinkening sky beyond the bank of windows on the west wall. "It's not even dark outside."

Doug looked past Landon out the window, at the line of trees in the distance, tracing the banks of the Smoky Hill River, and between the house and the river, acres of rolling farm ground his father had entrusted to him. Land he'd always hoped to someday pass on to Landon. With Kaye gone, it seemed a paltry promise to make his son.

Kaye's cheery red and white cherry-dotted curtains framed the view. She'd sewn those curtains right at this table on a little Singer sewing machine that had been her grandmother's. He'd always meant to buy her a new one. One of those fancy machines that cost as much as a good riding lawn mower—and that Kaye declared would be worth every penny.

"It'll be dark soon." Doug gestured with his fork. "Eat."

Kayeleigh scraped her chair back. "I'm not hungry."

"Sit down, Kayeleigh." He stared her down.

But she dipped her head and mumbled, "Can I be excused, please?" Without waiting for a reply, she pushed away from the table and rushed down the hallway to the room the girls shared.

He let her go. He didn't have the energy—or the will—to argue with her. Not tonight.

Somehow he managed to clean up the kitchen a little bit and get the kids in bed. Even Kayeleigh was in bed—or in her room anyway—by eight thirty.

Now the evening stretched out in front of him. The silence of the house echoed through his head, and he rubbed away the beginnings of a headache. He should have taken Kaye's mom up on her offer to come and stay with them tonight, to be here for the kids. But that would have meant making Harriet sleep on the sofa—or giving up the bed that smelled like Kaye.

Besides, they'd been surrounded by people for four days. He was ready to be alone. He huffed out a breath. What was he thinking? He would have done anything, given anything, to *not* be alone right now.

At ten o'clock he locked up the house, checked on the kids one last time, and crawled under the covers. In the crib at the foot of his bed, Harley's deep, even breathing brought a pang of envy. The baby couldn't understand that Mommy was never coming back, but she'd seemed to accept the kids' matter-of-fact explanation—"Mommy's not here, Harley. She's in heaven now"—as if they'd said, "Mommy went to the grocery store."

He wondered if his baby girl would carry any memories of Kaye and Rachel. His own earliest memories didn't begin until he was about four, when his grandfather had moved in with them after Grandma died.

He had hazy memories of Grandpa lying on his bed in this very spot, making a strangled, pitiful sound as he wept, not knowing Doug was listening at the door.

He hadn't understood the old man's loss then. Now he pulled the covers up and rolled away from the empty side of the bed to face the wall.

He wanted to weep the way his grandfather had. But the tears would not come.

For the first time
in a long time, Doug
remembered what it was
like to be an ordinary
man having an ordinary
day. It was a
good feeling.

Chapter Three

Doug unlocked the back door to the print shop and let himself in. Flipping on the lights, he waited for his eyes to adjust, inhaling the smells of the pressroom . . . paper, ink, dust, and yesterday's coffee.

It was a relief to leave the kids with Kaye's mom each morning and escape to the print shop. Today, like every Thursday, would be slow. The weekly *Clayburn Courier* was printed and mailed on Wednesdays, and the mad rush to get next week's thin issue out didn't start in earnest until Monday—at least for him.

He traded his coat for a printer's apron on the hook by the door and slipped the canvas strap over his head. Tying the ink-stained apron at his waist, he walked past the layout banks where next week's pages were already beginning to take shape. The *Courier* staff—Trevor, Dana Fremont, and a couple of part-timers—still put the weekly paper together the old-fashioned cut-and-paste way, although much to Dana's dismay, Trevor was working with a program that would soon move it all to the computer.

Doug flipped through a fresh copy of yesterday's edition, surprised to realize that for the first time in almost three weeks, the paper was void of news about his tragedy. Instead, Christmas ruled the headlines, and cheery ads proclaimed only twelve more shopping days. A strange mix of relief and disappointment infused him. He'd hated seeing Kaye and Rachel smiling back at him from photos he'd supplied at Trevor's request. At the same time it pierced him to see how the rest of the town could move so casually into celebration.

He shook off the resentment that tried to attach itself to him and went back to clean off the desk everyone called his. His wasn't exactly a desk job, and his desk usually ended up collecting odds and ends that no one knew where else to put.

He was about to finish the job when the lights in the front office flickered on. Through the half-mast blinds he saw Dana moving about in the front office. A minute later the alley door opened, and Trevor backed in, a stack of boxes balanced in his arms.

Doug hurried to hold the door for him, but Seth Berger, the kid who'd started working for Trevor on Saturday mornings, came in behind Trevor and beat him to it.

Doug nodded good morning.

Trevor set down the boxes and put a hand on Seth's shoulder, steering him over to Doug. "Seth, this is Doug DeVore, my pressman."

Seth shifted from one foot to the other. "Yeah . . . I know."

Doug put out a hand and, for a few uncomfortable seconds, was afraid Seth was going to ignore it. Finally the kid offered a brief, sweaty handshake.

"Besides his Saturday hours, Seth's going to try to pick up some extra hours a few days a week before school," Trevor explained.

Seth was in Kayeleigh's class at school, but Doug remembered Kaye saying he'd been held back a year. Maybe two, by the looks of him. The seventh-grade boys Doug knew were pencil-armed shrimps, but this kid was a full foot taller than Kayeleigh and had a good start on some rather impressive biceps. He was apparently proud of them, too. Who wore a muscle shirt in the dead of December?

Doug glanced up at the clock over the door. "Aren't you supposed to be in school now?" Doug hadn't made Kayeleigh and Landon go back to school yet, but he was pretty sure there weren't any school holidays this close to Christmas.

"The second bell doesn't ring till eight-ten." Seth jerked his head toward the clock and lifted one cocky shoulder. "It's only a quarter till. Besides, it's no big deal if I get a tardy."

The little smart aleck would be lucky if he got in twenty minutes of work before he had to clock out. But Trevor didn't say anything, so Doug bit his tongue, stifling the lecture he would have given if Seth were his kid. Shaking his head, he went back to his desk.

Around eleven thirty Trevor came back to where Doug was cleaning the old Heidelberg press. "I'm heading over to the coffee shop to get a sandwich. You want to come?"

Out of habit he started shaking his head.

"Come on," Trevor said. "I'm buying."

Doug took a deep breath. He'd kept a low profile since the funeral, and he wasn't up for the load of sympathy he was sure to get if he went downtown. "I think I'll pass."

Trevor cocked his head and studied Doug. "Hey . . . I know what it's like. I remember how hard it was to get out there—to go out in public—after I lost Amy."

Watching Trevor, Doug tried to imagine himself four or five years out. Would he look as normal, as happy, as Trevor did?

Trevor took a step backward toward the door, his smile a challenge and a warm invitation at the same time. "Come on. It helps to just

21

get it over with, you know? People mean well, no matter what they say, and after a while they start acting normal again. Quit crying when they talk to you. And hey, I can run interference. You see somebody coming you don't want to talk to, just give me a high sign and we're outta there."

Doug hesitated for a moment, then slipped the knot from the apron and ducked out of it. "You're buying, right?" he joked.

Trevor laughed. "You bet. Get your coat."

Doug hung up the apron, grabbed his jacket off the hook, and slipped an arm through the sleeve. "Lucky for you, Vienne doesn't sell T-bones at the coffee shop."

Trevor clapped him on the back and followed him through the front office and out to Main Street. It was only a block up the street to the coffee shop, the former Clayburn Café. The owner's daughter, Vienne Kenney, had recently turned it into an upscale coffee bar and renamed it Latte-dah. Most people still called it the café, even though Ingrid Kenney's home cooking was sadly absent from the menu now that she'd moved to the nursing home. But they served a decent sandwich, and the soup they served through the winter months wasn't bad. Soup sounded good about now. The wind was bitter cold, and he was grateful for a reason to pull his collar up around his face as they walked up Main.

There were only two people in line at the counter, and they didn't seem to notice him. But when it was Doug's turn, Vienne gave him that smile and the mournful, dropped-head "Hey, Doug" that seemed to be part of a new language everyone suddenly spoke around him.

Trevor stepped up to the counter, fishing his wallet out of his pocket. "How's it going, Vienne? Wedding plans going okay? That's coming right up, isn't it?"

Doug took a step back and breathed easier, grateful for Trevor's deft deflection.

Vienne beamed. "Two and a half months. But tons to do still. What'll you guys have this morning?"

Trevor eyed a tray of wrapped sandwiches in the deli case. "I'll have the turkey. And a bowl of soup."

"Sounds good," Doug said, glad to have the choice made for him.

"Two turkeys with minestrone, coming up." Vienne arranged the sandwiches on trays and hooked a thumb at the microwave behind her. "You guys want those sandwiches nuked?"

"No, it's fine like this," Trevor said, touching the plastic wrapper.

Doug agreed and eyed a table in the back corner near the fireplace. But after Trevor paid, he headed for a table near the front door. Doug followed and took the chair that allowed him to sit with his back to the door.

They talked shop while they ate, and as the noon crowd trickled in, Doug was grateful for Trevor's casual greetings, bringing him into the lighthearted small-town chatter, but again, warding off any undue attention.

They were finishing thick slices of apple pie that Vienne had talked them into, when Phil Grady, the pastor of Community Christian, the church Doug and Trevor attended, came in with the new youth minister from Clayburn Lutheran. Doug recognized the man from a photo that had been in the *Courier*. Pastor Grady went from table to table, introducing the new guy around.

Doug had always liked Phil Grady. His sermons were laced with humor but hard-hitting and straight from the Bible. He'd been a steady rock in the storm of that terrible Thanksgiving Day, and the aftermath of the funeral.

Doug hadn't been in church since the funeral. Even if he could have managed to get five kids ready for church on time, it was too hard to think about facing everyone. Too hard to think about sitting alone in a pew after the kids all went off to children's church.

From the corner of his eye, he saw Phil and the young man headed their way. Trevor apparently saw, too, for he scraped his chair back and rose to meet Phil. Doug followed suit.

Phil smiled and made introductions. An ornery glint came to his eye, and he put a hand on Doug's shoulder. "Now listen, John, Doug here has a whole passel of kids, and Trevor's got one on the way, but just so you know, I've got dibs on every last one of 'em."

They all laughed and for the first time in a long time, Doug remembered what it was like to be an ordinary man having an ordinary day. It was a good feeling.

They left the coffee shop and headed back to the print shop. "Thanks, man . . ." Doug unexpectedly choked up. "For lunch. But for getting me out, too. It . . . wasn't as bad as I thought."

Trevor shook his head. "Hey, I remember what it was like. It's not easy." His Adam's apple worked in his throat.

Doug could almost see the memories swirling in Trevor's head. He could picture that little boy—a miniature of Trevor, but with Amy's coloring. He'd forgotten Trevor's son's name already, and he felt awful about that. Because it meant people would forget Rachel's name. And Kaye's.

Trevor put a hand briefly on his shoulder. "Just . . . get through this first year. Be glad you can get this first Christmas without them over with right away. Next year will be a little easier. And the one after that. I know that doesn't seem possible right now. Right now you maybe don't *want* it to ever get easier. But trust me. It's a terrible cliché, but it's true. Time helps. It really does. I think that's the way God intended it."

For one moment Doug could almost believe him.

How many nights
would this go on
before Harley got used
to her mommy being
gone? Before he got
used to it?

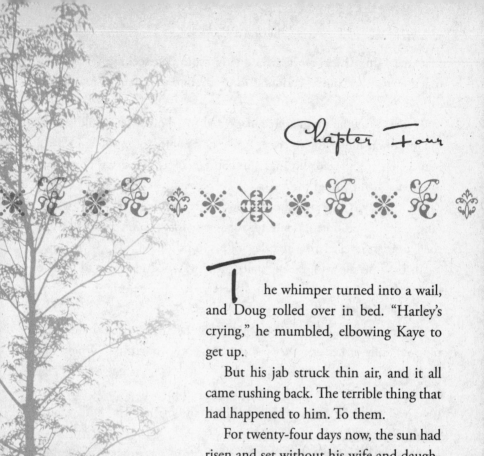

Chapter Four

The whimper turned into a wail, and Doug rolled over in bed. "Harley's crying," he mumbled, elbowing Kaye to get up.

But his jab struck thin air, and it all came rushing back. The terrible thing that had happened to him. To them.

For twenty-four days now, the sun had risen and set without his wife and daughter. It seemed like an eternity. Christmas was still ten days away, and he wore Trevor's "just get through it" as if it were a life jacket.

He tried to push away the awful images . . . calling home after Thanksgiving dinner that day to check on Kaye and Rachel. Not getting an answer. Leaving the kids—*thank God*—with Kaye's mom and running home to check on his sick girls. Pushing open the door between the kitchen and the garage . . . the odd silence that met him. Then entering the living room and seeing them curled together on the couch, cuddling, the way he'd left them a few hours earlier.

His relief at the poignant sight turned to a horror he would spend the rest of his life trying to erase. When he'd come closer, spoken Kaye's name, he'd recognized the angry, unnatural color the poison of carbon monoxide had painted their skin. . . .

He threw his legs over the edge of the mattress and sat there, struggling to catch his breath. He stayed that way for a while, trying to wipe the haunting images from the slate of his mind.

In the dim glow of the night-light, he watched Harley pull herself up on the crib mattress and stand there in her flannel nightie, whimpering.

He rose and stumbled to the end of the bed, where she stood gripping the rails of her crib, her pudgy face shiny with tears. "What's the matter, punkin?"

She raised her arms, begging to be picked up. He scooped her into his arms, relishing her warmth, relishing the *life* in her. "You want a drink, sweetie?"

"Mama?" Harley looked over his shoulder to the empty bed, a question in her sleepy eyes.

Doug's knees went weak. He slumped into the rocking chair beside the crib. "You wanna rock with Daddy?" he murmured, trying to ease her head onto his shoulder, praying she would go back to sleep.

She pulled back and smiled at him, reaching again for the bed. "Mama?"

Kaye was always the one who got up with the kids when one of them had a tummy ache or needed a drink. But he worked two jobs, getting up at the crack of dawn to work for Trevor in the pressroom—earlier on the days the *Courier* came out, or if they had a contract job to fulfill— then home and to the fields till dark. And if that wasn't enough, he'd been a volunteer firefighter and EMT for the fire department.

I'm sorry, Kaye. He whispered into the dark, "Oh, God, I am so sorry." If he could only have her back, he would spend a lifetime making up to her what he'd not been able to provide in the thirteen years she'd been his. She'd deserved so much more than this little rundown farm. He'd hung on to it out of pride. It was where he'd grown up. The only inheritance his parents had left him.

And though it took a second job and Kaye going to work to do so, he'd managed to hang on to the 240 acres his father had left him. Dad had always believed times would get better. Doug chose to believe the same.

But for most of their marriage, what the crops brought in barely paid the bills, and he'd had to work "a real job," as Kaye's mother called it, to make ends meet. For a long time now, it had been his day job and Kaye's that supported them, with an occasional dip into the small trust fund Kaye's father had left.

Harley squirmed in his lap and tried to get down. He carried her back to the crib. "It's time to go night-night, Harley."

The second her feet touched the crib mattress, she let out a wail. "Mama!"

"Harley. Stop it. Lay down, and Daddy will pat your back." It was a trick he'd heard Kaye use, but the baby was having none of it tonight.

She toddled across the mattress to the far corner of the crib, turning up the volume. "No! Mama. Want Mommy."

"Mommy's not here, Harley." He scooped her out of the crib again and started down the hall. "Let's go get a drink."

In the kitchen he got her sippy cup from the refrigerator, but she knocked it out of his hand and shook her head like a rag doll.

He took her back to the bedroom and eased into the rocker with her again. "Come on, Harley. Shhh . . ."

Any other night the whole routine would have merely frustrated him. Tonight her cries broke his heart. How many nights would this go on before Harley got used to her mommy being gone? Before *he* got used to it?

He blanched at the thought. Trevor had been right. He didn't *want* to get used to it.

He held his daughter to his chest, even while she struggled, and rocked her the way he'd seen Kaye do. After a while she stopped fighting him, her sobs changing to stuttered whiffs. The sound did something to him. Paralyzed him. How would they ever make it without Kaye?

There was no way by himself that he could keep the farm afloat, keep his pressroom job, keep the kids fed and clothed.

His strength drained out of him, and he held on to the baby as if she might somehow support him.

�֍ ֍ ✕

Kayeleigh lay flat on her back, staring at the ceiling fan as it turned languidly overhead. *Languidly.* She'd come across the word in the library book she'd been reading before turning out the lamp tonight. For once she hadn't hurried over the sentence, trying to figure it out in context. It wasn't a word they'd had in seventh-grade spelling yet, so she'd gone to Dad's computer to look it up. *Drooping, sluggish, listless, flagging.* Then she'd had to look up *flagging.* She hated it when the dictionary used one hard-to-understand word to define another. Tonight, at least, it kept her from thinking about Mom and Rachel.

She rolled over on her side. In the matching double bed on the opposite side of the room, she heard the twins' even breaths. But the empty space beside her felt like a black hole. Rachel's side of the bed.

Grandma said they should talk about what happened. Remember stories about Mom and Rachel so they'd never forget them. Like *that* was going to happen. Sometimes she wished she *could* forget. It hurt too much to keep remembering. Most of the time she didn't know who to cry for. When she thought about Rachel and sobbed for her, she felt like she was betraying Mom. And when she cried over Mom, she worried that Rachel would feel jealous. It helped a little to picture them together in heaven. At least they weren't lonely up there.

Or were they? She still had Dad and Landon and her other sisters down here, but if anything, that made what had happened seem worse. It killed her to see the faraway look in Dad's eyes, to never see him smile. To see Landon curling up into himself. To hear the twins constantly asking questions about Mom and heaven.

Could Mom see them from up there? She couldn't be happy in heaven if she saw how sad they all were down here.

She wondered if Mom had remembered her birthday. Nobody else had. Kayeleigh Jane DeVore had turned twelve three days ago, and still no presents or balloons or the usual birthday girl treatment Mom had always been in charge of. Grandma brought over a card with a check for ten dollars, and Dad had pulled a twenty-dollar bill out of his wallet and handed it to her the morning of her birthday.

Maybe there'd been a big celebration in heaven. Mom always said the angels in heaven had a party when it was your birthday. But it would have been nice to have a cake down here.

A noise from downstairs made her sit straight up in bed. Harley. Crying for Mommy. Kayeleigh held her breath, waiting. Dad would get up with her.

She put a pillow over her ears and drifted back to sleep. But a few minutes later, she started awake to a low-pitched wail. Harley was still crying. Why wasn't Dad getting her? He had to hear her. The crib was two feet from his bed.

She slid from beneath the quilts and sat on the edge of the mattress. The moon outside the second-story window cast a wedge of light on the wood floor, and Kayeleigh followed its path, picking her way through the maze of stuffed animals and Barbie dolls littering the floor.

She tiptoed down the stairs, avoiding the places where the old steps creaked. But there was no need to tiptoe. Harley was crying loud enough to wake up the whole house.

Crossing the living room, she tried not to think about the empty corner where the Christmas tree should have stood. They'd always put up their tree the Sunday after Thanksgiving. She knew there would be no tree this year. No Christmas. She didn't want one.

The door to Mom and Dad's room was ajar, and from the hall she could see the empty crib. She stopped for a minute, suddenly feeling the way she had that early morning last summer when she'd walked in on Mom and Dad kissing and giggling, their shoulders naked above the sheets while Harley snored softly in the crib right next to their bed. A flush of heat crept up her neck at the remembrance.

But Mom was gone. Something made her stop and listen harder. Her breath caught. It wasn't Harley making that awful sound. Her little sister had stopped crying.

Trembling, she peeked around the corner. Dad was sitting in the rocking chair with Harley on his lap. She was cuddled up against his chest, sucking her thumb like she did when she was about to go to sleep.

The sound, the terrible sound, was Dad. He was crying. Sobbing and moaning—like the noise Frisky had made when he got hit by a truck out on the highway. They'd had to put the puppy to sleep after that.

Kayeleigh's heart was beating so fast she was afraid she was dying. In all of her eleven years, she'd never seen Daddy cry. She wanted to fall into his arms and cry herself. But her legs wouldn't work right.

She stumbled backward. Would Dad be mad if he knew she'd seen him? Breathing hard, she stood there, frozen to the spot, terrified he'd see her, and yet, wanting him to see her—wanting him to *stop*.

But he stayed, clutching Harley to his chest, his sobs coming like hard hiccoughs.

"Dad?" she whispered.

He didn't seem to hear her.

She choked out his name again.

This time he stopped crying, lifted his head, and stared out into the hallway. Even in the dim yellow glow of Harley's night-light, she could see that his eyes were red and puffy. But he looked past her, and she somehow knew he didn't see her. Something in his face frightened her.

She slunk farther into the shadows of the hallway, trying to figure out what to do.

Everything was quiet in the house now. Kayeleigh stood in the darkness, her shoulder blades pressed against the cold doorframe, knees locked. She waited. For what, she wasn't sure. To hear Dad put Harley back to bed? To hear him crawl back into his and Mom's bed?

But the only sounds now were the baby's ragged breathing and the creak of the rocking chair. Back and forth. Back and forth.

Finally, careful to avoid the creaky boards again, she crept back up the stairs and crawled into the empty bed. But sleep never came, and she lay there until the sun rose, red and bright, over the top of the white eyelet curtains Mom had sewn for their room.

She knew then that nothing would ever be the same.

There was something exciting about the start of a brand-new year. But the tragic events of the holiday season tempered her enthusiasm this morning.

Chapter Five

Mickey scurried around the classroom, taking down the last of the Christmas decorations and watering the jungle of plants on the sunny windowsill that spanned the width of the room. She'd neglected them over the Christmas break, but a little water and some fertilizer and they'd bounce back.

There was something exciting about the start of a brand-new year. But the tragic events of the holiday season tempered her enthusiasm this morning. Keeping one eye on the window to the street, she put away the watering can and laid out paper and supplies for a finger-painting project.

The DeVore kids would be back today, and she was nervous about how to help them adjust. She hadn't talked to Doug DeVore since before the funeral, although he'd left a brief message on the answering machine at the daycare, asking her to hold the kids' spots.

Mary Harms, the librarian, told Mickey that Doug had pulled the kids out of school for the whole month of December, and Kaye's mother had not gone to Florida, where she wintered, so she could stay with them.

What a sad Christmas it must have been at the DeVore house. And today, while everyone jumped into the new year, Doug and the kids were learning to go on without their mom and sister. She shook her head. Sometimes life didn't make sense at all.

Pushing a toddler-size chair under the puzzle table, she recited the feeble words in her mind once more. A dozen times she'd rehearsed what she would say to Doug and to the kids when they came back. But now nothing sounded right. How could she offer anything that didn't sound trite and hollow?

She looked up to see the door open and a ball-capped head bobbing above the bookcases that hid her view. A current of nerves shot through her, then subsided when she realized it was just Mike Jensen, dropping his kids off.

She'd dared to hope the DeVores might get here before the other children arrived so she could spend a little time with them and assess how the kids were adjusting.

She stopped to greet Brett Jensen and his little sister, Hallie. They gave their dad distracted good-bye hugs, then chattered to Mickey about the presents Santa had brought them. She steered them toward the reading corner and helped them settle in with some books and games.

By the time she got back to the front, Brenda Deaver, her main teacher, was making coffee.

"Hi, Mickey. How was your New Year's? You do anything special?"

"Not really . . . same as every year . . . went to my brother's." She knew Brenda's real question was "Did you have a date?" She was getting tired of disappointing everyone with her love life—or rather the lack thereof. She might be forced to deck the next person who felt the need to tell her, "You're so beautiful . . . I can't believe you're not married." As if beauty were some magic key to wedded bliss.

Time to change the subject. "Listen, Brenda, would you mind doing story hour this morning? The DeVore kids will be back today, and I want to stick pretty close."

Brenda frowned. "Of course. Those poor kids . . ."

The door opened again and Doug walked in, a bundled-up Harley in his arms. He herded the twins toward Mickey and Brenda, nodding a greeting, then lowering Harley to the floor.

Mickey wiped her palms on the knees of her pants and went to greet them, watching the children closely. The twins seemed cheerful, like it was any ordinary weekday morning. They shrugged out of their coats and followed Brenda to the reading corner.

But Harley stood there, droopy-eyed, trying to put a mittened thumb in her mouth.

Doug squatted and pulled off her mittens, then sat back on his haunches and went to work at the knotted strings tied under the toddler's chin. He glanced up at Mickey. "She's not quite awake yet."

"Here . . . let me get that." Mickey knelt beside him and reached for the dingy white laces, asking permission with her eyes.

"They make these stupid strings too short. Or else my fingers are too big." He inspected his hands as if he'd never seen them before. Dark circles rimmed his eyes, and his face looked thinner than she remembered.

Mickey swallowed hard and busied herself with the soggy knot, training her attention on the toddler. "How are you this morning, Miss Harley? We missed you. Did you have a good Christmas?" Her heartbeat faltered, and she silently begged the thoughtless, stupid words to evaporate.

Instead, they hovered between her and Doug. *Did you have a good Christmas?* Was she a complete idiot? Somehow her carefully rehearsed speech had disintegrated, and she'd spouted the same lame greeting she'd given her other students as they came in.

Her cheeks burned while she finished working out the tangled ties on Harley's hood. She unzipped the little coat and slipped off the hood to reveal blond curls in dire need of a comb. She rose to find herself eye level with the collar of Doug's flannel shirt.

Her throat swelled. Forcing herself to meet his eyes, she croaked out an apology. "I'm so sorry," she muttered, then realized he probably thought she was apologizing for her thoughtless comment. She couldn't leave it at that.

Clenching her fists, she started again. "I'm so sorry about . . . what happened. We've been praying for you and the kids. We'll—miss Rachel so much. And Kaye, of course," she added quickly.

Words that had sounded compassionate in her head came out clunky and cold. *Shut up while you're ahead, Valdez.*

She recognized his effort to paste on a smile, but it didn't work, and for a minute she was afraid he might break down.

His jaw worked and he bent to pick up Harley again. "Thanks." He hitched the little girl up on his hip and kissed the top of her blond head before setting her back down.

But she scrambled after him, lifting her hands. Her face crumpled. "Daddy!"

"Bye-bye, Harley. You stay with Miss Mickey. Daddy will see you tonight." Doug gave Mickey a pleading look and backed away. He turned and walked purposefully toward the door, but Harley toddled after him, sobbing now.

It broke Mickey's heart. She raced after Harley. "Come on, honey. You come with Miss Mickey. Let's go find your sisters." She scooped the toddler into her arms, but Harley only screamed louder.

"Daddy!"

The shrill cry pierced Mickey's eardrums and she winced, but Doug kept on going. With one hand on the door, he turned around and gave Mickey a look that said, "Help me out here."

But she'd never seen Harley like this. Usually the little girl was all sunshine and giggles. How could he walk away from her like this, after all she'd been through? She hurried to the door, Harley screaming in her arms. "Are . . . are you sure you want to leave her like this?"

Doug stared at her. "I don't have a choice. I've missed enough work as it is."

She nodded. "All right, then."

Poor Harley. Her face was rosy and tear-stained, but her crying subsided a little. Sniffing, she looked between the two of them, suddenly interested in their conversation.

Mickey bounced the toddler on one hip. "She does seem to be calming down a little. Maybe I can distract her. I'm sure she'll be fine." She nodded in the direction of the reading corner, where Sarah and Sadie were sitting quietly. "How are the girls doing? Is there anything I should know . . . anything they're especially struggling with?"

His expression was dull. "You mean other than the obvious?"

His caustic tone sent her reeling, and she looked away. This was a side of the man she'd never seen in the five years she'd had his kids in daycare. Tears pressed at her eyelids, but she blinked them back. The last thing he needed was to feel guilty about hurting her feelings.

But he didn't seem to notice. "I've got to get going." He pushed the door open.

She nodded and started back to the reading corner with Harley. She worked to keep her voice from trembling. "Let's go see what your sisters are doing, okay?"

Harley pointed toward the dayroom and gave a shy smile. Mickey sighed. She should simply have dealt with Harley the way she did with any child who didn't want to be left. Still, this was different. Harley might not be old enough to understand the tragedy her family had experienced, but she'd been exposed to their grieving. That had to have an effect.

Mickey left Harley ensconced between her sisters, sucking her thumb and looking at a picture book, but she fretted over the exchange with

Doug. He was understandably not himself, but he could have been a little more helpful. Under the circumstances, she wouldn't have been wrong to insist he stay until Harley calmed down a little.

Turning to go back to her desk, she looked up to see Doug peering over the bookcase. She hurried to where he was.

"I guess . . . she settled down okay?" Worry etched his forehead.

She forced a smile and found that it diminished some of her ire. "She's fine. I'm sorry I—"

He held up a hand. "No. I'm the one who's sorry. I—I shouldn't have snapped at you like that." He dipped his head.

"It's okay. I understand. This has to be terribly hard . . . for all of you."

He nodded. "I think she's a little afraid of being left. She doesn't want anybody else to disappear out of her life."

"Of course." She could have kicked herself. She was the one who was supposed to be the expert on childhood development. "Don't worry. We'll reassure her that you'll be back soon."

"Thanks." He glanced at his watch. "I need to go."

She lifted a hand. "Go. She'll be fine. They all will."

Doug gave his girls one last longing glance before he turned and walked out the door.

She'd been ready to punch the guy a minute ago. But now the hunch of his shoulders made Mickey want to give him a hug. Poor guy.

Mickey hung back.
It felt awkward to
just barge into
the house.

Chapter Six

Mickey zipped up Timothy Plank's coat and sent him out the door with his mother. That was everybody except the DeVore kids. She waved a hand toward Brenda Deaver. "You might as well go on home. I'll wait with the kids."

The teacher rolled her eyes. "The kids have barely been back for three weeks, and he's been late every single night, Mickey."

"Not that late. I feel for the guy."

"Are you going to talk to him?"

"How can I, Brenda? He's trying to be mom and dad both." The puff of air Mickey blew out ruffled too-long bangs off her forehead. She'd missed a hair appointment Tuesday, thanks to Doug being late. "It's not like he can help it."

Brenda propped her hands on her hips. "So you're going to start keeping the center open till seven every night, then?

Because if you are, you'd better think about hiring another worker."

"I know. I know. But what am I supposed to do?" Mickey threw up her hands. Brenda was her only full-time employee, and as it was, Mickey struggled to pay her after-school help and the substitutes, and still pay herself and Brenda a salary with benefits.

"I thought Kaye's mom was staying with the kids." Brenda glanced toward the playroom.

The children's laughter filtered through the wall of windows that separated the reception room from the rest of the center. Kayeleigh and Landon had come from school and managed to turn "I Spy with My Little Eye" into a rowdy game for their siblings. Mickey smiled. She might have tried to settle them down . . . before. But it was good to see them having fun. They'd been glum for too many days of this new year.

She turned back to Brenda and lowered her voice. "Kayeleigh said Harriet went back to Florida for a few days to close up her condo. She's apparently going to stay in Clayburn for the rest of the winter. I sort of got the impression she's not a whole lot of help, though."

Brenda nodded. "I could see that. She's not exactly Mary Poppins. But at least there'll be somebody to—"

The phone on Mickey's desk rang. She held up a hand. "Hang on. . . . Clayburn Day Care, this is Mickey."

"Mickey, it's Doug. I'm sorry, but I'm running late again. I had to deliver some printing to Ellsworth. Are the kids doing okay?"

"They're fine." She waved Brenda out the door and took the phone to the entrance of the playroom. "You can probably hear them."

"I hear them." There was a smile in his voice. Too rare these days for a man who used to always be laughing. "It's probably going to be another twenty minutes. I just left town, but I'm in the van, so I'll have to stop by the office and switch vehicles."

That meant a good twenty-five minutes. "Let me bring the kids home. I'll meet you there. There's no sense in you having to back-track."

"You don't need to do that." But his voice sounded hopeful.

"I don't mind. I'm not doing anything else. I'll meet you there."

"Can you fit everybody in your car?"

"I can take the center's van. Hang on. Let me make sure there's a car seat here."

She carried the phone to the closet and found the car seat under a box of Christmas decorations she hadn't gotten around to putting up on the shelf yet. "Okay," she told Doug. "We're good to go."

"Thanks, Mickey. I really appreciate it. I'll add some gas money to your next check."

She went to help the kids into their coats. She truly didn't mind. It wasn't like the extra trip was keeping her from a hot date or anything.

Twenty minutes later she pulled the minivan up behind Doug's Suburban in the DeVores' driveway. She never would have found the place if Kayeleigh and Landon hadn't told her where to turn. The two-story farmhouse stood in the center of the section facing east, but it was set back from the road about a thousand yards, hidden behind a thick shelterbelt of red cedars. An overgrown, tumbledown barn north of the house appeared faded and scoured by half a century of summers.

Bicycles in an array of sizes littered the front yard, and three tiger-striped cats perched on the porch railing. The house looked as if it had been added on to numerous times over the years, but a fresh coat of white paint unified the patchwork of rooms tacked to the house.

She unbuckled Harley from the car seat while the kids piled out of the car. With the toddler on her hip, she followed the older kids up the porch steps. They jostled to be first through the front door, but Mickey hung back. It felt awkward to just barge into the house. "Wait. Kayeleigh, is your dad home?"

45

"His truck's not here," Landon said.

Kayeleigh motioned her inside. "He's probably parked in back. Come on in."

Mickey shook her head. "I need to get home. But I want to make sure your dad's here before I leave."

Kayeleigh shrugged her narrow shoulders. "It's okay. I can babysit until he comes in."

Mickey hesitated. "I'm sure you can, but I should wait and make sure . . ." She cleared her throat and started again. "I should stay until he gets home."

The living room was a pigsty. There was no polite way to put it. And the house smelled musty—like a basement that had been closed up for a long time. The coffee table was littered with dirty dishes, and she had to pick her way around toys and stacks of newspapers and magazines before she found a place to set Harley down. She helped the twins out of their coats and gloves while Kayeleigh did the same for the baby.

With the matching coats draped over one arm, she turned to Kayeleigh. "Where should I hang these?"

Kayeleigh looked around the room as if she hadn't lived here her whole life. "Um . . . you can just throw them on the couch."

The sofa was already piled high with a laundry basket and a load of white clothes in various stages of folding. She tucked the girls' gloves into the pockets of their jackets, moved a stack of unopened mail off the arm of the sofa, and placed the coats there.

"Come see our room, Miss Mickey!" Sarah grabbed her hand and Sadie took the other, and they started tugging her across the toy-littered living room.

She wriggled out of their grasp. "Not tonight, girls. I'm sure your dad will be here any minute. It's late and I need to get back."

"Hows come? Is your husband waitin' for supper?"

"Stop it, Sadie." Kayeleigh looked embarrassed. "Miss Valdez isn't married."

"Yeah, dummy," Landon piped up. "Why do you think she's called *Miss* Valdez?"

Sadie gave an impish grin that said she did, indeed, know.

Before she could think of a comeback, Mickey heard the front door close behind her. She turned, still with a twin attached to each arm, to see Doug duck through the doorway.

Relief shone in her blue eyes. He'd never noticed before that she had such blue eyes. Liz Taylor eyes, violet almost.

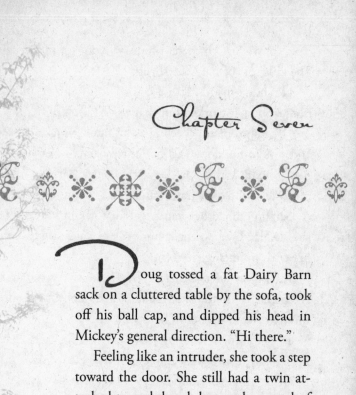

Chapter Seven

Doug tossed a fat Dairy Barn sack on a cluttered table by the sofa, took off his ball cap, and dipped his head in Mickey's general direction. "Hi there."

Feeling like an intruder, she took a step toward the door. She still had a twin attached to each hand, but at the sound of Doug's voice, they let loose and made a beeline for the door. "Daddy!"

Harley squealed and toddled toward him, too.

Even Landon jumped off the sofa where he'd plopped in front of the TV with the remote. "Hey, Dad."

Doug squeezed his shoulder, patted the girls' heads one by one, and scooped Harley into his arms. But he kept his eyes on Mickey. "Hope you haven't been waiting long. It took me a little longer than I thought."

"No, we just got here. I hope you don't mind that I . . . came on in. The kids sort of . . ." She shrugged.

He shook his head. "Of course not. I appreciate you bringing them home. Sorry it worked out that way."

"It's no problem." Feeling awkward, she picked her way through kids and toys to the door. "I'd better get back . . . let you guys eat your dinner." She looked pointedly at the Dairy Barn sack, which masked the mustiness with a fragrant burger-and-onions-and-fries aroma.

Sarah grabbed her hand again. "You can have supper with us. Can't she, Dad?" Like an eager puppy, she wagged her blond head, sending her curls bouncing.

Mickey avoided Doug's eyes. "That's sweet, Sarah, but . . . I need to get going." Reaching past him for the doorknob, she glanced up and thought she saw relief in his eyes.

But he surprised her by picking up the Dairy Barn bag and giving it a little shake. "Sure. Stay. There's plenty." He tousled Landon's hair. "That is, if this little wolfhound doesn't get carried away."

"We'll share. Won't we, guys?" That was Sadie, always the mediator.

Mickey held up a hand and opened the door, shaking her head. "Thanks, but I couldn't."

"Stay." Doug beckoned her and carried the Dairy Barn bag to the adjoining dining room.

She traipsed after him and stood by dumbly while he moved mounds of junk-mail catalogs and a stack of what looked like sympathy cards off the tabletop.

"This'll be your reward for hauling the kids home. It's the least I can do."

She felt trapped now that she'd followed him back here. It was awkward, being here with him and the kids. But the burgers smelled good, and it would be more awkward to bow out now. "You're sure there's enough?"

"Oh, yeah. No problem." He set Harley on the floor and clapped his hands. "Kayeleigh, you and Landon get the paper plates and napkins." He turned to Mickey, looking sheepish. "We avoid dishwashing at all costs around here."

She laughed. "Hey, I hear you." But looking through to the kitchen behind Doug, it was apparent he wasn't kidding. The sink was piled high with dirty dishes, and the countertops were strewn with cereal boxes and empty juice bottles.

Doug pulled out a chair. "Here. Sit."

She did as she was told while the twins vied for chairs on either side of her. Kayeleigh and Landon put slightly crumpled paper plates at each place. Doug got the toddler settled in the highchair with a handful of French fries. Stuffing her mouth full, Harley banged on the tray for more.

Doug obliged, then disappeared into the kitchen. He came back with a half-empty bottle of ketchup, a two-liter bottle of store-brand pop, and a stack of plastic cups.

Kayeleigh doled out burgers and fries, putting two on every plate except her own. "Tear some of yours off for Harley," she told the twins.

"Thanks, honey, but I can't eat two. Here . . ." Mickey handed back one of her burgers.

The twins looked relieved, but she felt bad that Kayeleigh had still ended up with only one hamburger.

Without prelude, everyone bowed their heads around the table and recited a blessing Mickey had sometimes used at the daycare center.

> "Thank You for the world so sweet.
> Thank You for the food we eat.
> Thank You for the birds that sing.
> Thank You, God, for everything."

✳ ✣ ✳

Doug's "Amen" seemed to be the signal for everyone to snarf down the food in front of them. Kayeleigh unwrapped her burger, tore off a hunk for herself, and put the rest on Harley's highchair tray. Trying to be discreet, Mickey winked at Kayeleigh and followed suit.

They ate in silence for several minutes, everyone's chewing noises magnified.

Landon elbowed Sarah, eyeing her second burger. "You gonna eat that?"

"Yes, she is," Doug answered for her. "If you're still hungry, there're some apples in the fridge."

"No. They're gross, Dad. They're all squishy."

"Oh. Well, maybe Grandma can make a pie out of them."

Harley grunted for more to eat, and Kayeleigh put another handful of fries in front of her.

Doug took a swig of pop and offered Mickey a crooked smile. "It's kind of like watching a bunch of pigs at a trough, isn't it?"

"Actually, I feel right at home." Mickey grinned. "This is pretty much what lunch at the daycare is like every day."

Laughing with him, she relaxed a little and listened to the kids' banter, no longer feeling like she had to make conversation.

✳ ✣ ✳

When the last fry had been polished off, Doug rose and started collecting paper plates and cups, hoping Mickey would take the hint and go home. She got up to help, but he held out a hand. "Don't bother. I'll handle this."

She followed him into the kitchen, rolling up the sleeves of her shirt as she went. "Let me help with the dishes."

He decided to aim for levity and turned his back to the overflowing sink, stretching out his arms as if he could hide the pathetic mess. He made his voice deep. "Close your eyes and back away. There's nothing to see here, folks."

"Too late," she said, laughing. She had a nice laugh.

"You don't need to get involved."

"I don't mind. I'm not easily intimidated." Her expression turned serious. "Let me help. It's always easier with two." As soon as the words were out, she cringed.

He remembered the day at the daycare when he'd snapped at her. He felt bad now.

"I'm sorry," she said. "I didn't mean—"

He waved her words away. "Don't worry about it. I-I've noticed everybody seems to think they're putting their foot in their mouth around me these days."

She nodded.

"It's not you. Everything seems to have . . . double meaning, you know?"

"Exactly." Relief shone in her blue eyes. He'd never noticed before that she had such blue eyes. Liz Taylor eyes, violet almost. Striking with her olive Latina coloring. He shook his head, trying to banish the thought. What was he doing? Kaye wasn't dead two months, and he was mooning over a strange woman's beautiful eyes? *Knock it off, DeVore.*

He grabbed the bottle of dish soap off the counter and squirted a stream into the side of the sink with the fewest dishes in it, then turned the water as hot as it would go.

Mickey nudged into the space beside him at the sink and went to work on a pot with macaroni and cheese cemented to the bottom.

Doug grabbed a dishrag and rinsed it in the soapy water. He headed back to the dining room, where the kids were arguing about what to watch on TV. "Huh-uh. Turn it off. No TV until your homework's done," he said.

"Da-ad," Landon started.

Doug cut him off. "End of discussion." He handed Kayeleigh the soggy dishrag. "Please go wipe off the table so you and Landon can get going on your homework." He put a hand on each twin's head. "You two go get your pj's on . . . and take Harley with you."

When he was sure the kids were on task, he came back to the kitchen to stand beside Mickey at the sink. She'd already emptied one sink and was starting on the other side.

"Wow. You're fast."

"I'm running out of room."

"Huh?"

She nodded toward the precarious stack of dishes drying in the rack on the drainboard.

He rolled up his shirtsleeves and grabbed a couple of wilted dishtowels from the back of a kitchen chair. He took a covert sniff, hoping they weren't sour, before he handed one to her. They worked in silence side by side for several minutes while he scrambled for something to say.

"I hope the kids were good today," he came up with finally. "I'm sorry about being late again."

"Your kids are always good. They've never been a bit of trouble."

He put the dishtowel down and looked askance at her. "Are we talking about the same kids?"

That musical laugh again. "Yeah, I get that a lot. I think we get to see kids at their best because they're not tired or hungry or being told to do their chores. Kids are pretty good at playing Mom and Dad against each other. They know they won't get away with quite so much in an environment like the daycare setting." She sounded like a professor giving a lecture on childhood development, and he scrubbed hard at an already-dry frying pan, trying to keep a straight face.

She seemed not to notice but rinsed the last dish, setting it in the drainer. "Where do you keep your dishtowels? Mine's a little soggy." She held it up as if he'd need proof.

"Oh, they're in the laundry room. Here . . . I'll get you one." He ducked through the doorway of the enclosed porch that served as the back entry and utility room, praying he could unearth a not-too-wrinkled dishtowel from the clothes dryer.

"Who's the artist?" Her voice behind him startled him. She'd followed him to the door and stood looking past him at the easel with his half-finished canvas perched on it.

He shook his head. "That would be me—using the term *artist* very loosely. I thought I wanted to try my hand at oils. Took some art classes Jack Linder was teaching last fall. Discovered I probably wouldn't want to quit my day job."

She laughed, and he appreciated that she didn't try to dispute him— or comment on his work at all. He didn't know why he'd told her all that anyway. She probably didn't give a rip.

He brushed past her, and she followed him back to the sink. Together they finished drying the dishes and she wiped off the few empty spaces on the kitchen counters. He desperately needed to recruit the kids to clean this place up. Maybe Saturday.

Harley toddled into the kitchen, looking cherubic in footy pajamas a couple sizes too big, thumb suctioned to her mouth. She popped her thumb out, though, when she saw Mickey, and came at her with her arms up.

He quickly intervened. "Here, Harley, let Daddy—"

But Mickey lifted the baby into her arms as if she were on daycare duty. "Well, don't you look cozy. Are you all ready for bed, sweetie?"

Harley started wagging her head back and forth. "Uh-uh. No bed. No bed."

"We'll see about that," Doug said, reaching out for her.

"Uh-oh, I guess that was the wrong thing to say." Mickey gave Harley a hug before she handed her over to Doug. "I'll see you tomorrow, sweetie. You'd better go to Daddy now. Miss Mickey needs to go home."

Harley came to him happily, and Mickey looked thankful for a graceful exit.

He walked her to the door, suddenly embarrassed that she had to pick her way through a minefield of toys and junk in the living room. Six kids—*five* kids—could mess up a house in nothing flat, but Kaye would never have let things get this bad. Saturday, for sure. They'd get this place whipped into shape.

"Landon, turn down that TV. Are you done with your homework?"

"I have all weekend, Dad."

Doug held the door for Mickey with one hand and snapped his fingers at Landon behind Mickey's back. "See what I mean?" He gave her a sheepish grin.

She shrugged. "They're angels for me." Then looking uncomfortable, she took a step backward. "Well, good night."

"Yeah, good night. Thanks again. For bringing the kids home . . . for helping with the dishes. I appreciate it."

"Thank *you* for supper." She waved over his shoulder. " 'Bye, kids."

They turned away from the TV long enough to return her wave. "'Bye, Miss Mickey."

Doug waited at the open door until she was safely off the porch and in the van. The car engine revved, and her headlights flashed across the driveway.

He closed the door and leaned against it, surveying the mess that was his home. A wave of longing—for Kaye—rolled over him, pulling him into its undertow.

He looked across the
room at Kayeleigh's
bed and stopped in
his tracks. There were
two forms beneath the
fluffy comforter.

Chapter Eight

Harley had kicked her blankets off and Doug tucked them over her sleeping form. She was on her belly, thumb in her mouth, her round little bottom hiked in the air. Kaye always called her Mount Saint Harley when she slept in that position.

He pulled the door shut and went upstairs to check on the other kids. Landon was sprawled diagonally across his twin bed, the covers tangled between his lanky limbs. When had he gotten so tall? The kids had all grown and changed in the two months since he'd lost Kaye and Rachel. A vivid image formed in his mind of Kaye walking through the door, like she was coming home from a week in Florida with her mom. "Oh, my goodness," he heard her say as clearly as if she were standing in the room beside him. "They've all grown a foot since I left."

Doug shook off the vision, unsettled, yet strangely comforted by the memory of Kaye's voice. It had started to bother him when he couldn't remember what her voice had sounded like.

He disentangled Landon from the blankets and covered him back up, then scraped a path through the toys so the kid wouldn't kill himself when he got up to go to the bathroom at 5:00 a.m. like he always did.

He went down the hall to check on the girls. Sadie and Sarah were curled in the middle of their bed, back to front like teaspoons in a drawer. He envied them each other's warmth. It struck him that, in a house of six, they were the only two who had the comfort of the warmth of another body now.

He looked across the room at Kayeleigh's bed and stopped in his tracks. There were two forms beneath the fluffy comforter. The image dragged him two months into the past, when their sweet Rachel had been Kayeleigh's bed partner. For a minute he was disoriented. Had Kayeleigh invited a friend to spend the night? He didn't remember that. But then, his memory hadn't been exactly trustworthy lately. But surely he would have remembered an extra person at the dinner table.

Maybe one of the twins had crawled in bed with Kayeleigh. But a glance at their bed confirmed that he'd indeed seen two curly heads on twin pillows. He'd just seen Landon and Harley in their beds. Everybody was accounted for.

She'd better not have snuck one of the muddy dogs in to sleep with her. Squinting through the dim light that spilled into the room from the hallway, he tiptoed to Rachel's side of the bed, trying to figure out who was in bed with Kayeleigh. Whoever it was had burrowed deep into the quilts.

Gingerly he pulled the covers back. An empty pillow. He pulled the quilts down farther. Another pillow—this one turned the long way in the bed. Kayeleigh breathed deeply, asleep beside the row of pillows. Doug pulled the blankets back up over the Rachel-shaped form, then snugged them around Kayeleigh's shoulders, aching for the daughter he'd lost. And, for the first time, realizing the depth of *Kayeleigh's* loss.

She'd been so morose lately, and distant. It seemed he had to repeat everything he said to her at least twice because she was off in some la-la land daydream. He didn't know whether to chalk it up to grief or simply preteen hormones. Kaye had been warning him for a year now that Kayeleigh would soon hit puberty and that they might be in for some rocky times with their sweet firstborn.

With a king-size lump in his throat, he crept back downstairs to his own bed. He didn't want to lose another daughter. He had to find a way to reach her.

Harley stirred when he came into the chilly room, but she stilled and her breaths came evenly again after he put another quilt over her.

He turned out the lamp on his nightstand and settled under the blankets, trying to get warm. He rolled onto his back and lay staring at the ceiling, then flipped to his belly, punching his pillow into shape, unable to find a comfortable position. After ten minutes of tossing, he crawled out of bed and went into the living room.

He grabbed a bolster cushion off the sofa and carried it to his room. Throwing back the bedspread, he laid the cushion on Kaye's side of the bed, gently bending it into a fetal position—the way Kaye slept on cold winter nights. He tucked the blankets around the lifeless form and climbed into bed beside it.

※ ❀ ※

Kayeleigh hunched over in a back-row seat of the school bus. The yellow bus bounced over the county road Mom always called Washboard Lane. She put her hands over her ears, trying to tune out Landon and the other rowdy elementary kids in the front of the bus. She didn't know which was worse—having to go to daycare after school like a little kid, or riding the bus home to be babysat by Grandma Thomas. Why couldn't Dad just let her be home alone for a few hours?

Okay, she knew why. He was afraid the same thing might happen to her that happened to Mom and Rachel. He was only trying to protect her, and she loved him for it, but come on. She was responsible. She wasn't stupid. Besides, she was almost a teenager, and he couldn't protect her forever.

It seemed like Dad spent every spare minute these days fixing stuff. Since the day after the funeral, he'd come home nearly every night to march through the house on a mission, looking for something that wasn't working right. Loose hinges, closet doors that didn't shut right, the electrical short in the medicine cabinet in the bathroom. All the stuff Mom had always been nagging him to fix. Well, it was too late now. He could fix everything in the whole stupid house, and it wouldn't change anything.

The bus eased to a stop in front of their driveway. Landon jumped up from his seat behind her and smacked the back of her head. "Come on, dopey. Get your nose out of that book. We're home."

"I'm not reading, dummy."

"Well, then wake up from your nap."

"Shut up."

"You shut up."

Landon ignored her and dragged his oversized backpack past her down the aisle. She watched through the window as he bounded across the front yard. Probably thought he could beat her to the last pack of Pop-Tarts in the cupboard. What he didn't know was that she had her own secret stash in the laundry room. And she didn't feel one bit guilty. It was the only way to make sure you got a snack around this stupid place.

She gathered her things and climbed down from the bus, waving over her shoulder at Mr. Turner, the bus driver. She stopped by the mailbox at the end of the driveway, but it was empty. Grandma must have already gotten the mail.

When she got inside, Landon had already parked his butt in front of the TV. He waved a shiny, empty foil wrapper in the air. "Ha! Too bad they're gone."

"So? Who cares? I didn't want a dumb ol' Pop-Tart anyway. I hope you get food poisoning."

"Kayeleigh." Grandma's stern voice came from the kitchen. "That's no way to talk to your brother."

Landon stuck his tongue out at her.

She returned the favor and went out to the kitchen. "Hi, Grandma."

She braced for a lecture on getting along with Landon, but Grandma only smiled and asked her how school was.

Kayeleigh shrugged. "It was okay, I guess. Did I get any mail?"

"Why, were you expecting something?"

"No . . . not really. Can I see what came?"

"It's in on the dining room table. But there's nothing there for you, honey. It's all important stuff for your dad."

"I know . . . I'm just going to look."

"Well, don't lose anything."

"I won't." She went to the dining room table and found the newest stack of catalogs and envelopes. She riffled through the envelopes. A bunch of stupid credit card offers and what looked like bills. There was a card in a lavender envelope, too. Probably another sympathy card. The cards had come in an avalanche at first, mixed in with Christmas cards that were sometimes addressed to Mom, too. Some people—the ones who lived far away—hadn't heard about Mom and Rachel yet. Those always made Dad sad. She could tell because he would read them, then sit there for a long time, staring at nothing.

But the cards had pretty much quit coming after New Year's. She glanced over at the mile-high stack of opened envelopes and cards on the highboy. Dad kept saying he needed to answer them, but he never did. She'd heard him hint at Grandma to do it. But Grandma said she had her own stack to answer.

"Can I open this sympathy card, Grandma?"

Her grandmother appeared in the doorway, dishtowel in hand. "I don't know . . . who's it addressed to?"

Kayeleigh read the front of the envelope. "Doug DeVore. It's probably a sympathy card."

"Let me see it." Grandma took the card. "Hmmm . . . no return address. It doesn't look like a sympathy card. Looks more like an invitation."

"Can I open it?"

"It's not addressed to you, is it?"

"No, but Dad lets me open the cards," she said hopefully. She could tell Grandma was dying of curiosity. She was, too, now that it might be an invitation.

"Well, I guess . . . if your dad lets you open the cards. But don't you tell him I let you."

"I won't." She ripped into the envelope with her grandmother's hot breath on her neck.

Inside the envelope was another smaller envelope. This one simply said *Doug DeVore and Guest.*

"And guest?" Grandma huffed. "That's hardly appropriate."

Kayeleigh didn't know what she meant by that. She slid a glossy cream-colored card from the second envelope. "It's a wedding invitation."

Grandma peered over her shoulder. "Who is it from?"

Kayeleigh read the fancy printing. "Oh, it's Vienne—from the coffee shop. She's marrying that artist guy Dad took lessons from."

"Jackson Linder. That's right. I remember seeing their engagement in the *Courier.*"

"Mom said Dad probably saved Jack's life when he fell off the roof of the coffee shop."

Grandma nodded. "I was in Florida when it happened, but your mom told me. Your dad has saved a lot of lives."

Except Mom's and Rachel's. Kayeleigh ignored the accusing voice in her head and turned the inner envelope over to read the address. "Why does it say 'and guest' on it?"

Grandma sniffed again, like she was disgusted. "It just means your dad can bring whoever he wants to the wedding."

Kayeleigh gave a little gasp. "Me?"

Grandma's frown turned into a chuckle. "Or me."

"Grandma . . ." For a second Kayeleigh thought she was serious. She let herself breathe again when she saw the twinkle in her grandmother's eyes.

But Grandma quickly turned serious again. "You let your dad decide about going, Kaye. He might not be ready for . . . something like that."

Kayeleigh didn't bother to point out that Grandma had called her by Mom's name . . . again. Dad did that, too, sometimes. Instead she let herself daydream about going to the wedding with Dad. She could wear her pink satin dress. The one Mom had sewed for her for the Christmas Eve program at church. She'd never gotten to wear that dress. The program was only three weeks after Mom and Rachel died, and Dad didn't think it would be right for them to go. She still wasn't sure why.

It didn't matter. She probably wouldn't have been able to sing without crying anyway. But she'd tried the pretty dress on half a dozen times since then, dancing around her room in it after the twins were asleep, pretending everything was the way it was before the accident. Pretending Mom and Dad had come to the Christmas program to hear her sing "Lo, How a Rose E'er Blooming." She could picture them side by side in the middle-school gym, Harley standing on Dad's lap, clapping. She shook the fantasy away. She was starting to get mixed up about what had really happened and what she'd only wished for in her imagination.

What really happened was that Dad called Miss Gorman and told her Kayeleigh wouldn't be back in school till after New Year's. Her friend Rudi told her that when Miss Gorman found out she wasn't going to be in the program, she'd given Kayeleigh's solo to Lisa Breck. At least Lisa hadn't rubbed it in the way she usually did.

She read the invitation again. The wedding was March 10. She would ask Dad if she could tack the invitation on the bulletin board above her side of the bed. But she'd take it to school to show off first. She bet Lisa Breck wasn't even invited.

By March it would be spring. And surely by spring Dad would be ready to start going places again. Maybe a wedding was exactly what he needed to remind him how much he used to like being around people, how much fun he used to be.

For as long as she could remember, Mickey had dreamed of having a big family like the one she grew up in. . . . And prospects in Clayburn were "slim to none," as her brothers liked to say.

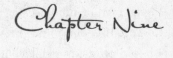

Chapter Nine

Mickey filled the watering can from the kid-height sink in the corner of the playroom and looked out at the blustery March sky. She'd be glad when she could get some of these plants back in the ground in her garden. Plucking off the yellowed leaves of a leggy philodendron, she eyed the rest of the plants. They were starting to look a little peaked. She'd neglected them over the winter.

She soaked the soil in the clay pot and moved on to the next plant. Brenda teased her about babying her plants as much as she did the daycare kids. It wasn't true, of course, but Brenda probably didn't understand how much it meant to her to be surrounded by the leafy curtains of greenery—especially when the winter days grew short and sunshine was all too rare.

Brenda had kids of her own. She'd been a mom since she was twenty-one.

69

She couldn't know what it felt like to long to hold a baby of your own in your arms, but to have that wish denied year after year after year.

For as long as she could remember, Mickey had dreamed of having a big family like the one she grew up in. When she was in high school, it never crossed her mind that she might still be single at thirty.

And prospects in Clayburn were "slim to none," as her brothers liked to say. Even though her brothers and their wives had all moved out of Clayburn after both parents had died, the Valdez clan still managed to get together the first Sunday of every month—usually at Rick's house in Salina. She doted on her nieces and nephews. She had four of each, and Rick's wife, Angie, was expecting another little girl any day now. But it wasn't the same as having her own babies.

She pinched out a spiky flower from a coleus she'd brought inside for the winter. It was tempting to let the flowers bloom, but the colors of the leaves—the true beauty of the coleus—were more vibrant if the flowers were pinched off as soon as they appeared. That was one question she would ask God her first day in heaven. Why would He create a flower that was meant to be pinched out before it reached full bloom?

She wasn't sure she could be happy if she had to go through life alone, never knowing what it was like to give birth, to nurse a baby at her breast. She wanted to look into her babies' eyes the way her brothers and their wives did, and see Dad's Cuban heritage in a little girl's brown eyes and coal black hair, or their mother's Swedish blood in the blue eyes and stubborn jaw of a little boy.

Mickey had inherited equal doses of her parents' blood. She had her father's thick dark hair and warm olive skin, and Mama's crystal blue eyes. It was a combination her high school friends had envied, but sometimes she would have preferred Mama's silky white blond hair and Dad's rich brown eyes. But even if that might have helped her fit into Clayburn's Euro-American population, the Valdez name—and the Catholic faith that came with it—would still have set her apart from a phonebook full of Andersens and Petersens, Schmidts and Johannsens.

She would die before she'd tell her brothers, but truth was, a chance to change her name was just one more reason she'd always longed to find a husband. Her brothers had all married nice Latina girls—never mind they were Mexican, not Cuban. They'd joined their wives' churches and settled down to raise large, noisy families. And they were happy. Nauseatingly happy. They didn't seem to feel out of place in the Midwest. Of course, they hadn't stuck around Clayburn. Rick had headed to college, and Tony and Alex to trade school, straight out of high school. And they'd never come back to Clayburn except to visit her.

She wasn't ashamed of her Cuban ancestry, but Mama's Swedish blood was in her, too. Pure native Clayburn blood. Why did people have trouble remembering that?

She would never deny her surname, but she wouldn't be sad to shed it someday. Maybe then everybody wouldn't automatically assume that her father had worked the railroad (which he had) and against Grandpa Swenson's will, Mama converted from her Lutheran faith so she and Dad could be married in the Catholic church (which they had).

Dad had been a good man and a good provider, and Grandpa Swenson mostly forgave all when Mickey's brothers started coming along. But Mama always said it was Mickey who finally melted his heart. She was christened Michaela Joy, after Michael Swenson, and that sealed the deal.

Grandpa died when Mickey was ten, but she had happy memories of the white-haired man with twinkly blue eyes like Mama's.

She missed her parents and ached to think her children would never know their Papa and Nana Valdez the way most of her brothers' kids had. She looked into the playroom and saw the DeVore twins playing with Harley. Sometimes it made no sense that God allowed someone like Kaye DeVore to die while Mickey Valdez, who had no one who depended on her, no one who waited for her to come home at night, went unscathed.

Dad and Mama had raised their four children to believe that life wasn't fair, wasn't *supposed* to be fair, but that didn't keep Mickey from wondering *why*. If God was omnipotent, as she'd been taught to believe, then he had the power to balance the inequities in the world. Why didn't He just *make* things fair?

She glanced at the clock. Doug would be here any minute. He'd been much better about picking the kids up on time since that night she'd had to bring them home. Mickey suspected Brenda had said something to him, though she denied it. At any rate, neither of them had stayed late waiting for Doug for several weeks now.

She'd thought often of her time at the DeVores'. Kayeleigh and Landon hadn't been in daycare since the end of January, since Kaye's mother was back and helping out with the older kids after school. The twins and Harley seemed to be getting along okay—they laughed and played like the other kids, though they seemed to stick together and play apart from the other children more than before. She had to wonder what kind of lasting emotional damage they would have. Even as an adult, you didn't lose your mother without it affecting you deeply.

She heard the front door open and looked up to see Doug making his way through the maze of toddler-size furniture and bookshelves to where she stood.

He nodded at the watering can in her hand. "Trying to keep a little green in your life?"

"Trying. I haven't done a very good job lately. Things are looking a little wilty."

He pinched the leaf of a hibiscus between his index finger and thumb. "A good watering, they'll spring back."

She winced. "I just hope I haven't waited too long."

He gave her a sympathetic smile, digging in his back pocket for his wallet. "I want to pay my bill."

"Oh . . . okay. Let me get you a receipt." She set the watering can down and crossed to the file cabinet.

Doug followed her and straddled a chair in front of her desk. He pulled a blank check from his wallet and selected a ballpoint pen from the pencil holder made by some long-ago daycare child.

The scratch of his pen stopped, and she realized he was waiting for her to tell him the amount. "Oh, sorry." She checked the hours and read off the amount.

He filled it in and handed her the check, looking up at the bulletin board behind her. "I see you're invited to the big wedding, too."

She turned to follow his gaze to the invitation tacked up on the bulletin board. "Oh, yeah . . . Jack and Vienne's. Are you going?" she asked. She hadn't decided yet if she was or not. Probably the wedding, for Vienne's sake. But there was a reception and dance at Latte-dah after the ceremony, and she wasn't sure she wanted to subject herself to that.

"I suppose I'll go. It's all Kayeleigh's talked about since the day the invitation came."

Mickey smiled. "I loved weddings when I was her age, too." It was true, but she refrained from telling him that lately they only served to emphasize what she didn't have.

Doug became preoccupied with a loose thread on the carpet, rubbing at it with the toe of his boot. "What do you think a guy's supposed to wear to something like that? I'm not going to have to rent a tux or anything, am I?"

She curbed a grin. "No, you can just wear a regular suit. A tie would be nice."

He tugged at the collar of his chambray shirt as if the mere thought of putting on a tie made him claustrophobic. "Okay, then. Well . . . maybe I'll see you there. See if I can remember how to dance." The sheepish grin he gave her did something funny to her insides.

Maybe she'd go to that dance after all. Her invitation said "and guest." Maybe she could borrow one of her brothers to chaperone her for the evening. It would beat sitting home moping.

Doug wished
desperately for
a glimpse into
his own future.

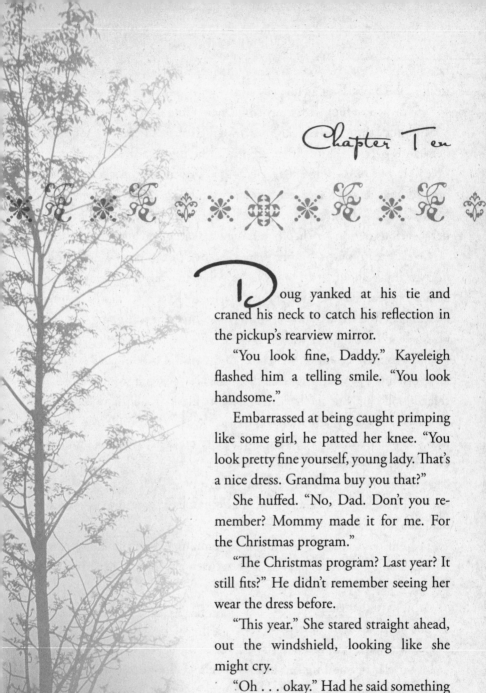

Chapter Ten

Doug yanked at his tie and craned his neck to catch his reflection in the pickup's rearview mirror.

"You look fine, Daddy." Kayeleigh flashed him a telling smile. "You look handsome."

Embarrassed at being caught primping like some girl, he patted her knee. "You look pretty fine yourself, young lady. That's a nice dress. Grandma buy you that?"

She huffed. "No, Dad. Don't you remember? Mommy made it for me. For the Christmas program."

"The Christmas program? Last year? It still fits?" He didn't remember seeing her wear the dress before.

"This year." She stared straight ahead, out the windshield, looking like she might cry.

"Oh . . . okay." Had he said something wrong? It didn't seem to take much to set her off these days. How did he always manage to say exactly the wrong thing? "Well, you look awful pretty."

She turned to him with a shy smile, her chin quivering. "Thanks."

They rode the rest of the way into town in silence. Kayeleigh smoothed her hands over the skirt of her dress until he thought she'd flat wear a hole in it. She must be feeling as nervous as he was. He'd never been big on weddings, but if Kaye were here, he would have simply followed her lead. Kaye was the life of any party, and wherever they went together, her vivacious personality had paved the way and made him look good.

Over three months—more than a quarter of the year—and it still hurt to think about her. How was he going to walk into that church alone? He reached over and patted Kayeleigh's knee. He wasn't so sure he was glad he'd let her talk him into going, but if he was going, he was glad he had his daughter with him.

He watched her out of the corner of his vision. When had she gone and gotten so grown up? Like all their kids, Kayeleigh had her mother's thick blond hair. But she had more DeVore blood in her than Thomas. Her features were sharper than the delicate Thomas profile the other kids had inherited. Still, Kayeleigh was every bit as pretty as her mother, even if she was in that gawky preadolescent stage. He'd noticed with chagrin that her figure had begun to take on the slightest of womanly curves. He didn't even dare to ponder how he'd face *that* aspect of raising daughters without Kaye.

He pulled into the parking lot of Community Christian Church and parked beside Pete Truesdell's truck. Kayeleigh already had her hand on the door handle.

"You have that card?"

She held up the oversized—and overpriced—wedding card she'd helped him pick out. Shoot, the card cost almost as much as the crisp twenty-dollar bill he'd tucked inside. He could almost hear Kaye chiding him for being such a cheapskate, but he had his kids to think about and money was going to be tight until after harvest. Assuming his wheat didn't get hailed out. He climbed out of the pickup and peered up at the sky. Clouds swirled threateningly overhead. "Let's go . . . before we get rained on."

He went around the truck and grabbed Kayeleigh's hand, and they ran across the parking lot. He opened the door to the church and followed her inside. The vestibule was all decorated in candles and ribbon. Kaye would have been in hog heaven. Kayeleigh *was*. She looked up at him, beaming.

A girl in a fancy dress handed each of them a program, and a tuxedoed usher—one of the Brunner boys, he thought—met them inside the sanctuary. "Friends of the bride or groom?"

Doug shrugged. "Both, I guess."

The usher held out his arm for Kayeleigh. Snickering, she took it, but had to practically run to keep up with the long-legged fellow. He stopped at a pew five rows from the front and motioned for Kayeleigh to go in.

Doug followed her to the middle of the pew, feeling the eyes of the guests in the pews in front of them turn to gawk. He was grateful when they were seated and the rows behind them began to fill up. Two empty spaces separated him from the aisle to his left, and he settled in to the padded bench, grateful for room to stretch his legs. It didn't last long. He had to straighten in his seat when another Brunner brother deposited Mickey Valdez beside him.

He smiled and mouthed a hello. Mickey cleaned up mighty nice, if he did say so himself. Instead of her usual ponytail, her dark hair fell around her shoulders in waves, and she wore sparkly earrings and a little lipstick or gloss or whatever the shiny stuff was called. Kaye had always said lipstick was the one makeup she could never live without.

Kayeleigh leaned around him and waved to Miss Valdez. He noticed Mickey was doing that same skirt-smoothing thing Kayeleigh had done all the way into town. Maybe it wasn't just nerves. Maybe there was a reason behind it.

A minute later Jack Linder stepped out from a door behind the choir loft, followed by Trevor Ashlock and another man Doug didn't know. He felt a tug on the sleeve of his suit coat and turned to find Mickey eyeing his wedding program. "Can I look at that for a minute?" she whispered.

He handed her his program and motioned to the one Kayeleigh was studying. "Keep it. We have another one."

The organist held a long note and switched the sheet music with one hand. The very air in the room seemed to change, and he recognized a song he'd heard at weddings before. Maybe even his own. He glanced over Kayeleigh's shoulder at the program. "Trumpet Voluntaire," it said. She squirmed in her seat until she was facing the back of the room. Everyone else seemed to be looking there, too.

Suddenly, as if to some invisible cue, everyone stood up. Doug nudged Kayeleigh, and they stood with the rest, turning toward the back of the sanctuary where a very elegant Vienne Kenney floated down the aisle on Pete Truesdell's arm. She wore a radiant smile, but she had eyes only for Jack.

Doug remembered that same look in Kaye's eyes when she'd marched down the aisle of that big church in Salina. He thought she'd never looked so beautiful . . . until the day she held a newborn Kayeleigh in her arms. And then sweet Rachel—

His eyes stung and he had to look away.

Kayeleigh tugged on his coattail, her voice a stage whisper. "Daddy, I can't see."

Mickey must have overheard, for she motioned Kayeleigh to come and stand on the other side of her in front of the seat on the aisle. Doug put his hands on Kayeleigh's shoulders and eased her past him and Mickey, giving the teacher a grateful smile.

Vienne stopped at the front pew where her mother hunched in a wheel-chair. It was sad to see Ingrid Kenney so frail, but she beamed a crooked smile at her daughter and raised her head to receive Vienne's kiss.

Pete turned the bride over to Jack and the couple moved to the altar. While the congregation took their seats, Kayeleigh scooted back in front of Mickey to sit beside Doug again. He put an arm around his daughter, relishing the feel of her warmth against him. Nothing like a wedding to remind a guy how lonely he was.

Jack repeated his vows, his voice strong and clear as he echoed the pastor. Doug felt genuinely happy for him. The poor guy had weathered some tough times, and it was good to see him finding happiness. How much more quickly might Jack have overcome his addiction to the bottle—or even avoided it altogether—had God only allowed him a glimpse of this day?

For a moment Doug wished desperately for a glimpse into his own future. If he knew for sure that the sentiment of all those sympathy cards was true, that someday time would dull the edge of his agony, maybe he could start living again. He pulled Kayeleigh closer.

Every morning he went through the motions, punching the clock for Trevor, doing the farmwork, picking the kids up from daycare.

He couldn't allow himself to think too hard about what his life had become, because he wasn't sure such a life was worth living. And for his children's sake, he *needed* to live.

She kept dancing with
Seth, but she wasn't
thinking about him so
much now. She felt torn
up inside. She wanted
Dad to be happy . . .
but she hadn't counted on
this sick feeling in the
pit of her stomach.

Chapter Eleven

Kayeleigh sat by the front window of Latte-dah, saving Dad's seat with her little pink wallet and her wedding program. The coffee shop didn't even look like the same place Dad had brought her and Landon to for hot chocolate a couple of weeks ago.

Today, all the tables had been cleared away and chairs were lined up around the room, leaving the shiny floor in front of the fireplace clear for dancing. Dad came back from hanging up their coats just as Jack and Vienne cut into their three-story wedding cake. With a gleam in his eye, Jack smashed a hunk of the white cake into Vienne's waiting mouth. Chewing and laughing at the same time, she tucked her veil behind her shoulders and did the same to Jack. Cameras flashed all over the room, like those strobe lights Seth Berger had at his birthday party last summer.

Kayeleigh wrinkled her nose. "Did you and Mom do that?"

Dad got a faraway look in his eye. "Yeah, we did. It's tradition."

Watching the bride try to pick icing out of her curly hair, Kayeleigh decided then and there that she didn't want that tradition at her wedding. But she did want to have a toast with grape juice in fancy glasses and pretzel her arm through the groom's to take sips as they looked into each other's eyes.

"And now, ladies and gentlemen . . ." A DJ in the corner by the door got everyone's attention. "The bride and groom will share their first dance as man and wife. Allow me to introduce Mr. and Mrs. Jackson Linder."

Everybody clapped and whistled while Jack and Vienne took the floor. Kayeleigh let a sigh escape. She hoped she looked as beautiful on her wedding day as Vienne Kenney. And that God put her with a husband as handsome as Jackson Linder. They danced like there was nobody else in the room. When the music died down, Jack kissed Vienne—and not the quick, soft kiss he'd given her when the minister pronounced them man and wife. This time his kiss made all the people clap and cheer. Kayeleigh felt her face grow warm.

The DJ invited everybody to dance. Dad grabbed her hand. "Come on . . . you want to dance?"

She hung back. There were only a few people on the floor, mostly grandmas and grandpas dancing the old-fashioned way. "Not yet, Dad. Wait till the next song."

"Chicken," he said. But she liked the way he winked at her. He tapped the seat of his chair. "Save my place. I'll be back for the next dance."

She nodded and watched Dad cross over and shake some guy's hand. Probably somebody he worked with at the print shop. When Dad's face got that sad look, she could tell the guy was saying something about Mom and Rachel. But then they talked more and Dad even laughed at something he said. That made her feel better.

Dad turned around and started back across the dance floor, but

Wren Johannsen stopped him. Still smiling, he gave her a hug. She said something, then pointed her way.

She waved at Wren and Wren waved back, but then Wren led Dad over to where Miss Valdez was sitting. Dad shifted from one foot to the other, looking kind of embarrassed. She couldn't hear what they were saying, but Wren was pointing to the dance floor like she wanted them to dance together.

Out of the corner of her eye, she saw Seth Berger coming her way. She looked away, but not before he caught her eye. Her hands started sweating. He was going to ask her to dance. *Come on, Dad. Hurry up . . . hurry up . . .*

But even as she thought the words, another part of her prayed she would get to dance with Seth. She wiped her hands on her skirt and licked her lips.

"Hey, Kayeleigh . . ." Seth's voice cracked and he cleared his throat. "You wanna"—he swung his head toward the dance floor—"you know . . . dance?"

He had on a white shirt with a tie. His dark hair had gel in it, and he'd gotten it cut since she'd seen him at school Friday. He looked really good.

She leaned around him to look for Dad. She spotted him in the middle of the dance floor. He was dancing with Miss Valdez. They were standing kind of far apart and not talking, but still, it made her feel funny seeing him touch her like that.

"Who are you looking for?"

She looked back at Seth. "My dad. I was gonna dance with him."

Seth followed her gaze to the dance floor. "Hey, he's dancing with that daycare teacher. Man, she's hot."

"Seth!"

"Well, she is."

"She's like, old enough to be your mother."

Seth raised an eyebrow. "Or yours."

She didn't like the way he said it. Like Dad had a thing for Miss Valdez or something.

Seth put a hand on her shoulder. "Come on. You wanna dance?"

"Okay." Her tummy felt a little fluttery as she followed him to the edge of the dance floor. It was crowded now and she lost sight of Dad.

The song was a slow one. Seth put a hand on her arm. "Ready?"

She nodded and as he moved his hands to her waist, she placed her hands on his shoulders, almost around his neck, the way she'd seen the high school girls do. His collar was damp. Maybe he was a little nervous, too.

They turned a slow circle, staying in one spot. She kept her eyes glued to the floor, scared she'd step on his feet. But after a few minutes she didn't feel so nervous. She even looked up a couple times to see Seth smiling at her. She liked the way it felt to be dancing with the cutest guy here.

Looking over Seth's shoulder, she scanned the crowd for Dad. She wondered what he would do if he saw her with Seth. She would dance with Dad on the next song. It wasn't so scary once you were out on the floor. Besides, almost everybody was dancing now, and nobody was paying any attention to them.

The song ended and another one started. She pulled away. But Seth grabbed her in a one-armed hug. "Let's dance one more."

"I promised my dad I'd—" She saw him then, dancing with Miss Valdez again.

"Okay." She let Seth pull her back into his arms. He held her a little tighter this time. But even though she almost had to tiptoe to see over his shoulder, she couldn't help watching Dad and Miss Valdez.

They were dancing closer together on this song, too. And they weren't only dancing. They were talking to each other, putting their mouths close to each other's ear because the music was so loud. They were laughing. A lot.

She'd never seen Miss Valdez look so pretty. Instead of the ponytail or bun she usually wore at the daycare, she had her hair down long and smooth, skimming her shoulders. She was laughing in that flirty way Lisa Breck laughed when she was trying to get some boy to pay attention to her.

The DJ had put on Natalie Cole's "This Will Be." Mom used to play that song on the CD player all the time. Kayeleigh knew the words by heart. "*An everlasting love . . . together forever . . .*" Counting down to the last verse, she tried to catch Dad's eye. But even though it was a fast song, he was dancing close to Miss Valdez, whispering close to her ear and laughing with her. The only time she'd seen Dad laugh like that was—when he was with Mom.

She kept dancing with Seth, but she wasn't thinking about him so much now. She felt torn up inside. She wanted Dad to be happy. She'd hoped this wedding would remind him how to smile again. But she hadn't counted on this sick feeling in the pit of her stomach. In all her daydreams about this night, she'd pictured Daddy dancing with *her*, not Miss Valdez. He wasn't really doing anything wrong. They were only dancing and talking. But for some reason, she felt like she should look away—pretend she hadn't seen them laughing and smiling with each other.

And Dad seemed to have forgotten all about his promise of dancing with her. She was going to sit down when this song was over. If Dad kept dancing with Miss Valdez, she'd come up with some excuse to go out on the dance floor and get him. Maybe she'd tell him she was sick. Her stomach *was* feeling kind of funny.

Before she could rehearse an excuse, the song ended. She pulled away. "I'm . . . going to go sit down for a while."

Seth's face fell. He shuffled his feet. "Okay. But maybe we can dance again later . . . after you're rested up?"

"Maybe." She turned and hurried over to where she and Dad had been sitting. She saw him making his way back through the crowd. She

85

smiled, but then she saw that Miss Valdez was right behind him, smiling that great big smile.

"I'm going to get some punch for Mickey—for Miss Valdez." Dad seemed a little breathless. "You want some, Kayeleigh?"

"Yeah, I guess." Sure enough, he'd totally forgotten about the dance he promised her.

He came back a minute later, juggling three plastic cups of peach-colored punch. But Dad and Miss Valdez barely took two sips from their cups before they were back on the dance floor again.

When that song was over, the DJ said something about the next song being for young lovers. Before she lost her courage, Kayeleigh drained her punch cup, set it on the chair beside her, and threaded her way through the dancers to where Dad was. Some slow, mushy song started playing, and Dad and Miss Valdez stood facing each other, looking like they weren't sure if they were going to dance this time or not.

When Miss Valdez saw her, she brightened. "Hi, sweetie. I'm going to turn your dad over to you while I go see if they need any help in the kitchen."

Dad put out a hand like he might try to get Miss Valdez to stay, but she was already sidestepping the other dancers and heading over to the counter where people usually ordered. Kayeleigh turned to watch her.

She felt a tap on her shoulder. She felt Dad's warm breath on her neck, and his aftershave tickled her nostrils.

"Excuse me, miss. May I please have this dance?"

She giggled, then tried to make her face serious. "I'm not allowed to dance with strangers."

That made him laugh. He scooped her into his arms and twirled her around. Her cheeks flushed. If Seth saw her, he'd think she was a baby. Daddy brought her down until her feet found his shoes and she forgot about Seth. Just like when she was a little girl, Dad led her in a circle around the floor. Holding him tight around the waist, she buried her face in his chest.

She closed her eyes and pretended Mom was sitting in one of the chairs along the wall. She pretended that when the song ended, Dad would escort her off the floor. Then he and Mom would dance the rest of the night while she watched them smile into each other's eyes the way he and Miss Valdez had.

Across the room he spotted Mickey leaning against the wall talking to the man she'd been dancing with. Now he didn't want to leave, either.

Chapter Twelve

Doug looked over Kayeleigh's head and scanned the chairs along the far wall. They were mostly empty now and the dance floor was full. He spotted Mickey slow-dancing with a man he didn't know. His stomach knotted. Had she come with a date? And here he'd been hogging her on the dance floor.

But when her partner twirled Mickey, he saw her face and the way she held herself—stiff and a little apart from him. Then he knew, somehow, that she wasn't with the guy.

She waved over her dance partner's shoulder at Doug and smiled down at Kayeleigh, giving him a thumbs-up.

Part of him was grateful for her graceful exit before the "young lover's dance," but he hoped this guy wouldn't horn in on his chance to dance with her again later.

He was glad Kayeleigh had talked him into coming. It was good to not be sitting home alone. Good to be among friends, laughing, celebrating life. The winter had seemed like an eternity, but tonight he could finally believe there might be a spring to come.

The dance ended and he kissed Kayeleigh on top of the head and guided her over to the chairs where they'd left their punch cups. Mickey's cup was gone, and Tom Bengstrom had plopped his ample backside in the seat where Doug had left his wedding program, hoping to save a place for Mickey. He looked around for her, but she'd disappeared in the mash of dancers.

They were breaking all kinds of fire codes here this evening. As a former volunteer firefighter, he probably should do something about it, but Blaine Deaver, the fire chief, and Sheriff Hayford were both standing by the refreshment table and obviously turning a blind eye, so he let the thought go.

With Kayeleigh tagging behind him, he worked his way through the crowd to the front door. He put a hand to the window and shaded his eyes. The afternoon's clouds had grown heavy and now spilled out rain. The gutters on Main Street ran swift with it. Thunder rumbled in the distance. He made his way over to where Blaine and the sheriff were standing. "We're not in a storm watch, are we?"

Blaine waved a beefy hand. "Nah. They've got some weather over in Ellsworth County, but nothing too severe on our radar."

Doug looked around again for Mickey. Not seeing her, he gave Kayeleigh a sidewise glance. "Maybe we ought to get going. You know Grandma. She'll be worried."

"Daddy . . . no! We just got here. I only got to dance with you one time."

He had a feeling he wasn't the one Kayeleigh wanted to dance with. Seth Berger prowled at the edge of the dance floor, eyeing Kayeleigh like a hungry cat. All the more reason to leave. But across the room he spotted Mickey leaning against the wall talking to the man she'd been dancing with. Now he didn't want to leave, either.

He sighed and slipped his cell phone out of his pocket. "Okay, just a while longer. Let me call Grandma, though." Harriet was watching the kids at her house tonight, since there was a show on cable she wanted to watch. Kaye had never wanted cable in their house.

Kaye. He'd hardly thought of her tonight.

He looked up from punching in Harriet's number to see Mickey coming toward them, her purse clutched under one arm. She gave a little wave and reached for the door. He waved back and started to ask if she was going home already, but Harriet answered the phone just then. He heard Harley crying in the background.

"Harriet? Is she okay?"

"Harley? Oh, she's fine," Harriet said quickly. "Landon accidentally knocked her down. Nobody's bleeding. How's the wedding?"

Harriet must not be able to hear the thunder over the kids' noise. "It's all right. I just wanted to make sure things are going okay for you. We should be home before long."

He tousled Kayeleigh's hair and turned to look out the window. Mickey was standing under the narrow awning outside Latte-dah. Like she was waiting for the rain to let up long enough for her to make a dash for her car. It didn't appear that was going to happen anytime soon.

"I need to hang up, Harriet. Call my cell if you need me." He closed the phone without waiting for a response.

"Stay here, Kayeleigh. I'll be right back." He opened the door and told Mickey the same thing—"Stay here."

He dashed to the back room that tonight was serving as a coat check, grabbed his suit jacket from the rack, and ran back to the door.

Mickey was right where he'd left her, but Kayeleigh wasn't there. He panned the room, looking for her. His breath caught when he saw her dancing with Seth Berger at the edge of the dance floor. He had her wrapped in his clumsy paws like prey.

Doug didn't know the kid that well, but the older Berger boy was trouble, and judging by the attitude Seth had sported that morning at the print shop, he was a tiger of the same stripe. Doug wasn't a fan of the boy, and he for sure didn't like the way the guy was clutching his daughter right now.

He pushed his way through to where Seth and Kayeleigh were. When she saw him, she wriggled out of Seth's arms. The look she gave Doug said, "*Please* don't embarrass me."

He worked to keep his voice even. "Hey, kiddo. We need to get going."

"Da-ad . . ."

He put a hand on her shoulder and gave Seth a dismissing nod. "Sorry, but we need to go. Come on, Kayeleigh." He herded her toward the door.

"I don't have my stuff, Dad." She shrugged out from under his arm and started back toward the row of chairs.

"Well, run and get it quick, then meet me outside. And hurry up."

She turned and gave a little growl, but she must have seen the determination on his face because she quickly wove her way back to the chair where her jacket was.

He sighed and went out to the sidewalk in front of Latte-dah. Mickey stood a ways down under the awning, looking out at the storm. "Mickey!" He had to shout over the rain hammering the awning.

She smiled when she saw him. She was already soaked, her hair forming soggy ringlets around her pretty face.

Slipping off his coat, he jogged toward her. He held the coat up over her head. "Where are you parked? I'll walk you to the car."

Her expression turned sheepish. "Actually I . . . I walked."

"Good grief, you weren't going to walk home, surely?"

She shrugged. "I'll wait till it lets up a little."

"Here." He stepped from under the tent of his coat, transferring it to her. She raised goose-bumped arms and accepted his offering, and they walked back toward the door together.

Just then Kayeleigh stepped from the coffee shop, wearing a scowl she made no effort to hide. Seeming not to notice, Mickey swooped in to take her under her wing, holding the makeshift umbrella over both their heads.

Doug pretended not to see the disappointment in Kayeleigh's eyes. "You two stay here. I'll bring the truck around."

He'd have to do damage control with his daughter later, but she'd thank him in the long run, and he was not going to let Mickey Valdez walk home in this downpour. It would soon be dark.

Jogging around the side of the building to where his truck was parked, he somehow managed to hit every puddle in the uneven sidewalk. His socks squished inside too-tight dress shoes. Climbing behind the wheel, he caught a glimpse of his reflection. A drowned rat in a dress shirt and tie. He raked his fingers through his thinning hair, but it remained plastered to his scalp.

But in spite of the rain shower and his wet clothes clinging to him in the March chill, he felt elated. Truly alive for the first time in so long. And just a little guilty for having so much fun.

For the first time it hit him that maybe he hadn't behaved tonight in a way that honored Kaye. It had barely been four months. Maybe it was too soon for him to be smiling and laughing and dancing with other women—another woman.

But he was sick to death of crying himself to sleep. Sick to death of being a single parent, of being alone everywhere he went. Tonight had been nice. And Kayeleigh enjoyed it. He'd mostly done it for her anyway. She was the one who'd talked him into going to the wedding in the first place. He winced inwardly, remembering the disappointment on her face when she realized they were leaving the dance. He'd only danced one dance with her.

He pulled the truck around in front of Latte-dah and parked as close to the curb as he could. Mickey helped Kayeleigh over the running gutter and clambered in after her, laughing.

She laid his suit jacket neatly over her knees and pushed the damp curls off her face. "I don't know that I could have gotten much wetter walking home. And now I've made you get out in the rain and probably ruined your suit."

He flipped the heater on high. "Don't worry about it. At least you won't freeze to death." He pulled away from the curb. "Let's see . . . you live over on Pickering, right?"

She nodded. "Last house on the left. Thanks. I really appreciate it. You didn't have to leave early on my account."

"We—" He gave Kayeleigh a sidewise glance. She sat with her arms folded over her chest. His daughter was not a happy camper. "I needed to get home anyway. Kaye's mom has the kids."

"Oh. I heard she was back from Florida. It's nice she can be here."

"It is. I'm hoping she can move back here permanently—to help out with the kids. But we'll see. She can't seem to let go of her condo." He knew Kayeleigh wasn't missing a syllable they were saying, but he lowered his voice as though he could protect her from the pain in his words. "Kansas winters are tough on Harriet's arthritis, and it's not easy for her to be here. There are a lot of . . . reminders."

Mickey nodded soberly. "I can understand."

He sighed. "I don't know what I'm going to do if she goes back." He hadn't let himself think about it. There were too many other things to worry about. But now panic moved into his chest. He had roughly ten days to find somebody . . . or change Harriet's mind. And he hadn't changed the woman's mind once in the twenty years he'd known her. He turned onto Pickering Street and flipped the wipers on high.

Mickey pointed through the windshield. "A couple more blocks. There . . . it's that one right up there with the garden cart in the front."

The house was set back from the street. A high picket fence enclosed the backyard and the lawn in front was tidy as a pin. Already the grass was greening up with the day's rain.

Mickey unfastened her seatbelt and opened the pickup's heavy door. "Thanks for the ride." She laid his jacket on the seat between her and Kayeleigh and gave a little wave in the girl's direction. "See you two later."

She started to climb out, but Doug motioned for her to wait. He grabbed the jacket, jumped out of the truck, and came around to help her out.

"You don't have to do that. Seriously, I'm fine."

"I don't mind." He spread the sodden jacket over their heads again, and they huddled under it, making a run for the house.

Under the cover of the front porch, she dug through her purse. "I know my keys are in here somewhere. You really don't need to stay." She gestured toward his truck. "Kayeleigh's waiting. You go on."

He felt himself grasping for a way to prolong their time together. An idea sparked. A thin warning followed, but he quickly dismissed it.

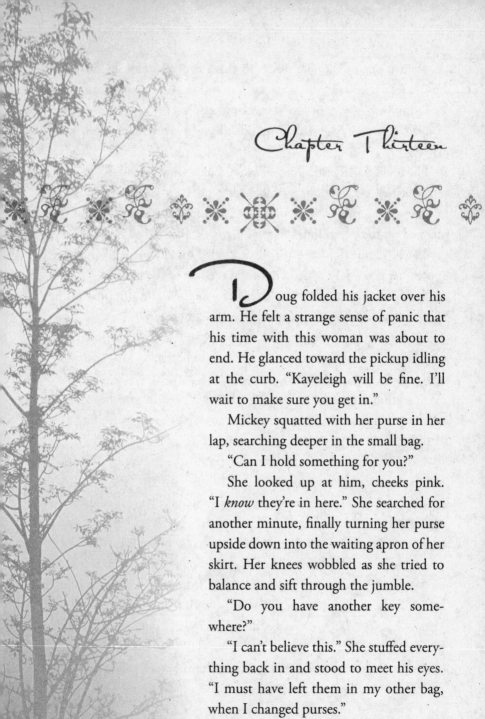

Chapter Thirteen

Doug folded his jacket over his arm. He felt a strange sense of panic that his time with this woman was about to end. He glanced toward the pickup idling at the curb. "Kayeleigh will be fine. I'll wait to make sure you get in."

Mickey squatted with her purse in her lap, searching deeper in the small bag.

"Can I hold something for you?"

She looked up at him, cheeks pink. "I *know* they're in here." She searched for another minute, finally turning her purse upside down into the waiting apron of her skirt. Her knees wobbled as she tried to balance and sift through the jumble.

"Do you have another key somewhere?"

"I can't believe this." She stuffed everything back in and stood to meet his eyes. "I must have left them in my other bag, when I changed purses."

"You're one of the rare ducks in this town who actually lock their houses."

"I know. By order of the Valdez brothers."

"Wise men all," he said. "You don't have an extra key hidden somewhere?"

She looked sheepish. "Sure. Two of them—in the house."

"Maybe the back door is unlocked?"

"No. But I might be able to pry a window open in the back." She stepped off the porch into the rain.

"Well, I hope not." He quickly unfolded his jacket again and tented it over her head, following her around the side of the house.

She looked askance at him over her shoulder, rain dripping off her eyelashes and sliding down the bridge of her nose.

"Listen, if *you* can pry a window open, think what some boogeyman could do. If that's the case, you don't need to bother locking your doors anymore."

She grinned. "Good point. Don't worry. I'll get in somehow. You go on now. You've wasted enough time. Kayeleigh's going to think you've abandoned her."

He waved her off and opened the gate to the backyard. "You don't have a dog or anything, do you?"

"Nope. A pussycat. She's in the house, though." She raised his jacket higher over her head. "You want back under here?"

He turned his face to the sky. The rain had let up a little—or else he was so wet already he just didn't feel it as much. "I'm fine."

She led the way around to the back of the house. "You might be able to get in a basement window if I didn't—" Her words were cut off by a yelp, and before Doug could reach her, she went down hard in a flooded patch of grass.

She scrambled to her knees, and he offered her a hand up. "Are you okay?"

She brushed at two muddy spots on the front of her skirt, her cheeks flaming again. "I'm such a klutz."

"You didn't look like a klutz out on the dance floor tonight. Of course, you weren't trying to dance on wet grass." He tried too late to edit what had come out sounding like a pathetic pickup line. "You didn't hurt yourself, did you?"

She covered her eyes with one hand. "Only my pride. You really don't have to do this. I can call one of my brothers to help. You've gone way beyond the call of duty."

He ignored her and took in the lay of the yard. For the first time he noticed the landscaping and shrubs. "Wow! You've got your own secret garden back here."

His comment seemed to please her. Even this early in the year, before anything was in bloom, it was obvious the garden would soon be an oasis. A narrow rock garden snaked along the border the fence created, and near the house a flagstone patio was flanked by a low waterfall and an elaborate hedge made up of rose arbors. He could imagine the transformation that would take place over the next few weeks as spring came to Clayburn. Kaye would have loved it. She'd been after him for two years to replace their rotting deck with flagstone.

He let a wave of guilt roll off him and went to rattle a basement window near Mickey's garage. He could break the glass, but that would be a last resort. Too bad he'd taken the toolbox out of his truck to make room for the kids' bikes last time they stayed at Harriet's.

He went to inspect the back garage door. Maybe he could jimmy it. He checked the doorknob. It turned half a turn and the door swung open.

Behind him, Mickey let out a little gasp. "How did you do that?"

"Um . . . it wasn't locked."

She put a hand to her mouth. "Oh good grief. I must have forgotten to lock it after I put Sasha in this morning. My cat . . ."

She was saying something about her cat and he was listening, but all he could think about was how nice it had been to laugh and talk with her at the dance. How carefree and *normal* he'd felt being with her. He didn't want to go home to the solitude that had been his constant companion in recent days.

He felt himself grasping for a way to prolong their time together. An idea sparked. A thin warning followed, but he quickly dismissed it.

Mickey pushed open the door and stepped into the dimly lit garage. He followed her inside. She turned to hand him his jacket, but instead of taking it, he grabbed her other hand. "Do you want to go to a movie with me? Tomorrow afternoon?"

A hesitant smile painted her face. "Are you asking me on a date?"

He grinned self-consciously. "I . . . guess I am. That's sure what it sounds like, doesn't it?"

"Doug, are you sure . . ." Her smile faded and she pulled her hand away from his, thrusting his jacket at him. "Are you sure you're ready for this?"

Did he dare tell her that he hadn't really thought through the invitation he'd rattled off so easily? But no . . . he wasn't sorry. He was glad he hadn't had time to talk himself out of it. He wanted to see her again. "I had a good time tonight. And that's not something I've been able to say very often lately. I . . . I'd like to see you again."

She bit her bottom lip and tossed her damp curls. She looked down, and he followed her line of vision to his hands, clutching his jacket. He could almost read her thoughts as she eyed his left hand—where his wedding band caught a glint from the single lightbulb overhead. But he ignored his better judgment that told him to back off and give her an out.

She eyed him for a minute, then exhaled. "That new Disney movie is playing in Salina. We could take the kids."

He could have kissed her. But his better judgment won out. He backed toward the door. "We'll pick you up at noon. Fine dining at Mickey D's okay?"

"Hey!" She tossed him a mock glare. "Don't denigrate my name."

He held up both hands in defense. "Oh. I didn't think about that. No insult intended, though. It's more like honoring your name. . . . At least my kids would think so."

"As long as you don't mean Mickey V's."

"Huh?"

"V . . . Valdez . . . Mickey V. Get it? I am *not* cooking on our first date."

It felt so good to laugh again that he wanted to cry.

She'd had an absolute blast. And Doug DeVore was mostly the reason why. Scratch that.

No ~~mostly~~ about it.

Chapter Fourteen

Mickey changed out of her wet clothes and dried her hair. Belting a fluffy white bathrobe around her, she padded out to the kitchen and loaded the few coffee mugs and silverware that had collected in the sink into the dishwasher. She wiped off the counters in her cozy kitchen and watered the plants in the bay window behind the sink.

Sasha jumped up on the counter beside her, purring in anticipation of Mickey's touch. She stroked the silky calico's fur. "You know you're not supposed to be up on the counter, little princess." She scooped the cat into her arms and carried her to the sofa. "What did you do all day, huh?"

Sasha kneaded broad paws on Mickey's knee, revving her feline motor.

"I bet you didn't have as much fun as I did." Mickey felt like an idiot grinning at a cat who couldn't understand a word she was saying. But she couldn't seem to quit smiling. Weddings were usually pure torture for her, a colossal reminder of everything God had said no to over and over again for almost a decade now, ever since she'd brought the request for a husband before Him as a serious college grad dating a man who didn't love her as much as she loved him. Jon Lundholm had kept her hanging on to the hope of a diamond for two years while he played the field at college. The handful of other guys she'd dated had been immature, cocky jocks interested in only one thing—a thing she wasn't willing to give.

Jon was a nice enough guy, but she'd been stupid enough to try to force him into the "perfect husband" mold she'd patterned after her brothers. After he dumped her, she realized she couldn't have wedged him inside that mold with a shoehorn. But love was blind and all that.

The chorus of "This Will Be" ambled through her mind, shoving the gloomy thoughts out. She smiled to herself and hummed along. To think she'd almost skipped Jack and Vienne's reception this afternoon. She shot up a prayer of thanks that she hadn't. She'd had an absolute blast. And Doug DeVore was mostly the reason why. Scratch that. No *mostly* about it.

If she closed her eyes, she could picture those blue eyes as he'd laughed down at her while they were dancing. He was a fine, fine dancer, too. And easy on the eyes, with skin bronzed by the sun and his hair bleached to the color of wheat.

She'd never once thought of Doug in that way before today. Of course, until now she'd only known him as a married man—just another father of her daycare kids. She'd always been impressed with the kind of father he was, but seeing him at the dance with Kayeleigh as his date, she'd been charmed all over again. He was so sweet with the gangly almost-teenager. Mickey knew how much that had to mean for a girl who'd lost her mother at an age when mothers were crucial.

Doug had seemed so different tonight. Even though things were a little awkward at first with Wren practically pushing them together, they'd ended up having a great time dancing together. It was fun joking and talking out on the dance floor with him. Not just talking about his kids, either, but real conversation, getting to know each other better than they ever had.

Doug was doing well by his kids. He was exactly the kind of man she wanted to find someday. It bothered her a little—okay, a lot—that he still wore his wedding ring. A recent widower with five kids was not exactly on that list she'd given God for the man of her dreams.

She rubbed her hands together, remembering the warm urgency of Doug's hand on hers when he'd invited her to go to Salina with him tomorrow. Somehow she didn't think he'd planned to do that. A warning light went on—again—somewhere in the back of her brain. Maybe she'd been wrong to say yes. She did the math and it shocked her a little to realize that it hadn't been even four months since Kaye died.

A knot twisted in the pit of her stomach when she thought of what her brothers would say if they found out she was going with Doug tomorrow. Well, she wasn't stupid. And she wasn't naive enough to discount that Doug had a lot of grieving left to do. Years' worth probably.

But it wasn't like they were talking about getting married here. Surely it couldn't hurt anything to go to a movie with a friend. It wasn't like it was a date. After all, they were taking the kids.

Except that had been her idea. And Doug had called it a date. But that was only after she'd made the suggestion. What else was he going to say after she was so coy with him?

She looked out the kitchen window toward the north end of town. The rain had stopped, but the night sky was inky. She couldn't see beyond the trailing verbena that hung under the porch eaves. Maybe Doug was regretting his invitation by now.

Sighing, she closed the curtains. It was too late to back out now. She'd go with him and the kids tomorrow. McDonald's and a movie. And they'd probably have a great time. Tomorrow would be about being a friend to Doug and an encouragement to his kids. Nothing more.

It was too soon for anything else—if "anything else" was even a future possibility. And she doubted it was from Doug's perspective. He was lonely. That was all.

A veil of melancholy settled over her. Why couldn't the men she was attracted to ever be *available*? Was that too much to ask?

※ ❀ ※

Doug squirmed in the pew and folded the bulletin in half and then into quarters. If he was nervous yesterday, before the wedding, he was in full panic mode now. What in the world had he been thinking when he asked Miss Mickey on a date? Good grief. Suddenly he couldn't even think of her outside of the name his kids called her by?

Twisting his wedding ring, he shifted in the pew again. He might technically be a widower, but he couldn't have felt more married if Kaye were sitting here beside him. So why did he have a date this afternoon?

He'd watched grieving people do stupid things before and wondered what they were thinking. Well, now he knew. They *weren't* thinking. Last night he'd been caught up in the relief of the moment—a chance to smile and forget for a few hours about the tragedy that had cut him down.

Kayeleigh had moped the rest of the night over having to leave the dance early, but despite her efforts to ruin the evening, he'd gone to bed last night excited about the plans for this afternoon.

But the minute he'd come awake this morning, he'd begun to second-guess himself. Well, it was too late to back out now.

When the pastor spoke the benediction, he quickly herded the kids out to the foyer. He sent Kayeleigh to pick up Harley in the nursery and hurried the rest of the kids out to the car. His purposeful stride apparently worked. At least no one tried to stop him to offer condolences.

Maybe he'd finally reached some magical point in the mourning period where people felt they'd said enough.

Good. Though he knew they were well meaning, he'd grown a little weary of being the object of the town's sympathy.

He'd asked Harriet to keep Harley again this afternoon. He and Kaye had learned the hard way that a two-year-old was impossible to keep quiet in a movie theater. Even if the film was geared toward kids, Harley would rather make friends with the people in the row behind them. Or, like their last disastrous trip to the movies with her, see how much popcorn she could toss into the pouffy hair of the woman in front of them. The memory made him smile . . . and caused a fresh wave of longing for the way things used to be.

He forced his mind to shift gears and concentrated on getting everybody buckled into the Suburban. Nowadays, Kayeleigh sat up front with him and the twins shared the backseat, while Landon rode with Harley in the middle bench. He'd have to warn Kayeleigh that she'd be giving up her seat today.

He hadn't told the kids yet that Mickey was going with them. He hadn't wanted to answer a bunch of questions. But now that they were minutes from picking her up, he pictured himself answering hard questions in front of her.

Not a pleasant prospect.

As soon as they pulled out of the parking lot, he plunged in. "Listen, guys, as soon as we drop Harley off at Grandma's, we're going to go pick up Miss Valdez—Miss Mickey—and she's going with us to the movie."

In his rearview mirror the twins exchanged wide-eyed looks and started bouncing on the seats. They clapped and squealed, "Miss Mickey! Miss Mickey!"

"Why's *she* going with us?" He barely heard Landon's low voice over the twins' noise.

"I invited her. Thought she'd enjoy . . . the movie." He met Landon's skeptical expression in the mirror and turned to Kayeleigh, hoping for support. "Won't that be fun?"

She leveled a suspicious glare at him. "You have a *date* with Miss Valdez?" She wrinkled her nose and dangled the question before him like it was one of Harley's dirty diapers.

He shook his head and glued his eyes to the street. "It's not a date exactly." But what if Mickey referred to it as that? "We just thought it would be fun to do something together today."

Kayeleigh twisted in her seat, suddenly allies with her brother. "Dad danced with Miss Valdez half the night last night at the wedding."

"Gross!"

"Cut it out you two. And be nice to Mick—Miss Valdez. I mean it."

"You're taking her to McDonald's? Oh, that's real cool." Kayeleigh rolled her eyes in full, sassy-preteen mode—a mood she wore quite regularly lately.

He tried for levity, using a term he'd heard Kayeleigh toss out. "It's not like it's a hot date or anything."

"Daddy, please. Stop talking about it. I don't even want to *think* about it." Kayeleigh shuddered.

This was going to be tougher than he thought.

He made the kids stay in the car while he took Harley in to Harriet's. Kaye's mother was still in her church clothes. He set Harley on the floor and she toddled over to the basket of toys Harriet kept by the sofa.

Handing Harriet the diaper bag, he backed toward the door. "She'll probably take a long nap this afternoon. We should be back by six or seven at the latest." He patted his pocket. "Call my cell if you need me."

"We'll be fine." Harriet spoke in clipped tones and avoided his eyes. If he hadn't had such a warm conversation with her when he picked up the kids last night, he would have thought she was mad at him.

"Is everything all right? I-I hope I'm not taking advantage of your offer to keep the kids. If I am—"

"I'll tell you what you're taking advantage of." Kaye's mother straightened to her full five-foot-nine height and looked him in the eye. "My daughter's reputation."

Uh-oh. This couldn't be good. "What are you talking about, Harriet?"

Harriet's moods had always kept their lives interesting, but she was beyond moody right now. Propping her hands on her hips, she let him have it with both barrels. "Rumors are flying all over town about you and that Valdez girl at the reception last night."

He steeled himself for the worst. "Exactly what kind of rumors?"

"Did you take her to the dance?"

"No, Harriet. I took Kayeleigh. I took my daughter to the dance."

"But you danced with Mickey Valdez." It wasn't a question.

"I did." His defenses shot up, but he worked to keep his voice even. "I wasn't aware it was a crime to dance with a friend."

"Well, from what I've been hearing, you two were"—her face flushed crimson and she looked away—"you were all over each other."

"What? Who in the Sam Hill did you hear *that* from?" This was crazy. But then, he shouldn't have been surprised. He'd grown up with the rumor mills of small-town life.

"I heard it from *everybody*, that's who." Harriet's voice rose. "The phone's been ringing off the hook ever since I got home from church this morning."

That probably meant she'd had one phone call, but Harriet wasn't going to let this go. "Not to mention the way people were looking at me during the service this morning. I've half a mind to take the phone off the hook."

He resisted the urge to expound on her half-a-mind comment. Still, even if she'd received one call, it was one too many. "Who called you? I want to know what's being said, because if it included that Mickey and I were 'all over each other,' I can put that rumor to rest right now."

"I'm not going to say who it was, Douglas, but it was somebody who was there and saw it with her own eyes, and Clara does not—" Harriet clapped a hand over her mouth.

He rolled his eyes. Clara Berger. He should have figured as much. Kaye always said Clara's motto was: Spread the gossip first, verify later. Well, if that was the juiciest morsel the old bag could come up with, she needed to move out of Clayburn.

"Harriet, I don't know what that woman told you, but I assure you nobody was all over anybody. I had Kayeleigh with me, for Pete's sake. You think I'm going to act like that?" Shaking his head, he let his words trail off. It didn't pay to argue over something like this. But he also needed to do some major damage control.

He took a deep breath. "I danced with Mickey a couple of times. And you may as well know that she's going to Salina with the kids and me this afternoon."

"She's *what*?" Harriet put a hand to her throat. "You mean, you have a *date* with her?" Her face went pale, and for a minute Doug thought she might faint.

"We're grabbing lunch at McDonald's and taking the kids to see a movie. That's it. For crying out loud, she's the kids' daycare teacher." Why did he feel compelled to reassure everyone that this was not a date, when he'd conceded to Mickey that it was?

Harriet looked at the floor and shook her head. "I can't believe you would do this to Kaye. She's barely been *gone*"—she choked on the word—"a few months and you've already moved on. I simply cannot believe you would behave like this. Disgrace the mother of your children this way."

"Harriet. Stop it."

Harley looked up from the plastic toy she was chewing on, her little blond eyebrows knit. "Da-da?"

"It's okay, sweetie." He forced his adrenaline to a noncrisis level and reached to put a soothing hand on Harriet's arm—more for Harley's sake than Harriet's. But she jerked out from under his touch.

He took a step back. "I'm sorry you feel this way. We can talk about it later, if you like. The kids are waiting in the car. . . ."

Did other people think he'd made a fool of himself at that dance? Certainly, if Mickey had been Kaye, there would have been nothing whatsoever to be ashamed of. But maybe others saw things differently. He gestured weakly toward the driveway, where the Suburban idled. "I need to get going."

She turned her back on him. "Go, then. Just go."

Doug wasn't sure which was more difficult: resisting the urge to haul his daughter out to the car for a good talking-to or resisting the urge to hug Mickey.

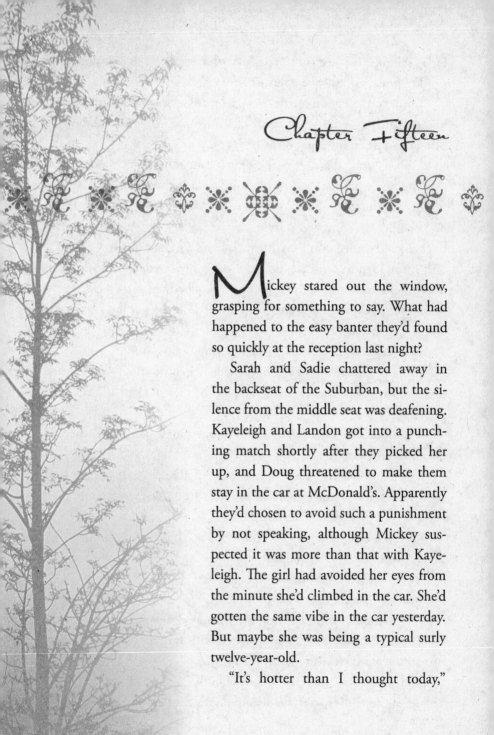

Chapter Fifteen

Mickey stared out the window, grasping for something to say. What had happened to the easy banter they'd found so quickly at the reception last night?

Sarah and Sadie chattered away in the backseat of the Suburban, but the silence from the middle seat was deafening. Kayeleigh and Landon got into a punching match shortly after they picked her up, and Doug threatened to make them stay in the car at McDonald's. Apparently they'd chosen to avoid such a punishment by not speaking, although Mickey suspected it was more than that with Kayeleigh. The girl had avoided her eyes from the minute she'd climbed in the car. She'd gotten the same vibe in the car yesterday. But maybe she was being a typical surly twelve-year-old.

"It's hotter than I thought today,"

Doug said. He reached for the dashboard controls. "You cool enough?"

"I'm fine, thanks." She adjusted her seatbelt and crossed her legs.

"I hear this is a good movie. Reviewers are saying it's even entertaining for parents—adults, I mean." His Adam's apple bounced, and he turned and glued his eyes on the highway.

"Yeah, I heard that, too." She didn't want to tell him she'd already seen the film with her brothers' kids in Salina last weekend.

"Are you hungry?"

"I could eat." She was starving. She'd been trying to drop the five pounds she'd gained over the Christmas holidays, but right now a cheeseburger sounded like just the ticket. If she really cared about making an impression—or losing those extra pounds—she'd opt for a salad.

In the McDonald's parking lot, she helped Doug get the kids inside and settled at a table.

"Everybody want the usual? Mickey, how about you?"

"I'll have . . . oh, make it a salad with Ranch dressing." She'd make up for it with popcorn and Milk Duds at the movie. "And a Diet Coke, please."

"You got it. Be right back." He motioned for Landon. "Come and help me carry stuff, buddy."

While they waited, the twins doled out the ketchup packets and straws and napkins Kayeleigh had collected from the counter.

"How's school going, Kayeleigh?"

Not meeting Mickey's eyes, she gave an abbreviated shrug of her slender shoulders. "Okay, I guess."

"You sound like you're ready for summer."

Another shrug.

Mickey took the hint and quit trying to spark a conversation. Thankfully, Doug and Landon soon appeared with trays piled high. Mickey helped the twins with straws for their drinks.

Doug hadn't finished the "amen" of his blessing when the first Coke spilled. It was Sadie's, and she dissolved into tears.

Mickey jumped from her seat and started sopping up the icy mess with her napkin. "It's okay, Sadie. Nothing to cry about. Come here. Did your shirt get wet?"

She quickly cleared off one of the trays and scooped the spill off the table. The mess was mostly cleaned up when she became aware of Doug watching her. At first she was worried that his expression was disapproval for her usurping his authority.

But his frown quickly turned into a grin. "Nicely done. Thanks."

"Hey, this is what I do for a living."

"Well, I didn't invite you along to clean up our messes."

She returned his smile. "It's instinct. I can't just turn it off when I walk out of the daycare, I guess."

He held up his hands in mock surrender. "That's fine by me. Swab away."

She laughed, happy a spilled Coke had broken the ice.

But a few minutes later, when they were clearing off the table and getting ready to leave, she picked up a table tent advertising the movie they were planning to see. The illustration on the placard brought a scene from the movie to her memory—a scene of a family of mice losing their mother to a raging forest fire.

Only the week before, her four-year-old nephew had wept on Mickey's shoulder in the theater. She'd been a little choked up herself. Glancing at the colorful illustration again, she realized why. The scene had made her think of Kaye and Rachel—of how the DeVore kids had lost their mother.

Why hadn't she thought of this when Doug invited her? This was not a good movie for these kids right now. Or for Doug.

The kids climbed into the Suburban, chattering with excitement over the upcoming movie. Mickey scrambled to think how she could arrange a detour. Doug began to steer the Suburban across town to the mall where the theater was.

Halfway there, she reached to touch his arm.

He looked her way, a question in his eyes.

"Doug, I-I think we need to . . . change our plans."

"Our plans? About the movie?"

She nodded, sure her sheepish grin would give her away.

"Why? What's wrong?"

"I sort of saw it last week and . . . well, it hit me at lunch that it might not be the best choice." She tried to get the point across with her eyes, aware that Kayeleigh and Landon were all ears behind them.

"You've seen the movie already?"

She nodded.

"So you'd . . . rather not see it again?"

"Oh, it's not that." Did he think she was that selfish? "I don't think it would be a very good movie for . . . for your kids. There's a—situation with . . ." She took a deep breath and started again. "You remember Bambi?"

"Bambi's mother died," Sarah piped up from the back of the vehicle. "It was sad."

Doug looked at her. "Oh . . ."

She nodded.

He shook his head. "I don't think *I* want to go there. Never mind the kids."

"What if we went bowling?"

"Bowling?"

"Sure," she said, suddenly enthused about the idea. She'd bowled on a league team until a couple of years ago. "Do you ever bowl? Starlite Lanes is right behind the theater."

He shook his head. "Not in a long time."

Landon leaned as close to the front seat as his seatbelt would allow. "I went one time. For Eric Feldon's birthday party. It was cool. Let's go, Dad."

Doug craned his neck to check the rearview mirror attached to the windshield. "Everybody okay with that? The bowling alley?"

Kayeleigh just shrugged, but the other kids cheered.

"Good call." Doug held up his right palm for a high five.

Mickey obliged him, feeling oddly proud that she'd come up with what he thought was a good idea. It felt good to think maybe she'd had a little something to do with the gorgeous smile he was wearing right now.

※ ※ ※

Doug watched the heavy marbled ball leave Landon's hand and wobble down the alley. It landed with a thud on the veneered lane, then veered dangerously close to the gutter before curving back on track. In slow motion the ball struck the front bowling pin. One after another, like dominoes, the other pins fell.

"Strike!" Mickey yelled, jumping up and down. "You got a strike, Landon!" You would have thought it was her own throw that felled the pins.

She jumped up and motioned Sadie over. "Your turn, sweetie."

She put her arms around Sadie, showing her how to hold the ball and walking her through the approach. When it was Doug's turn again, he dumped his first ball in the gutter inches before it reached the pins and picked up only one pin on the next roll.

Mickey followed him with a strike.

She turned around with a triumphant cheer and swaggered back to her chair to exchange high fives with the kids. Well, with all the kids except Kayeleigh, who sat at the console with her arms crossed.

Doug rolled his eyes. "You didn't tell me you were a professional bowler."

She giggled. "And you didn't tell me you've never bowled a game in your life."

"I'm a little rusty, that's all." He made a show of rubbing his hands together. "Wait till I get warmed up a little."

But by his next turn, he was beginning to think there was a factory defect in the wobbly ball he'd chosen. He inspected the ball, then put it back on the ball return. Rubbing his hands together, the fingers of his right hand met the smooth gold of his wedding band. Remembering Mickey's pointed look at his left hand last night, he turned away and worked the ring off his finger. He tucked it safely into the pocket of his jeans—along with the twinge of guilt that niggled at him.

Landon threw a spare on his turn. Mickey gave Doug a sidewise grin and pointed to Landon's score on the overhead. "You're about to put your dad in last place, buddy. Your turn, Kayeleigh."

Kayeleigh had been sullen all afternoon. She slouched off the bench and picked up the hot pink ball she'd claimed as hers. She picked off two pins on her second throw.

"Great job, Kayeleigh," Mickey crowed.

Kayeleigh acted like she hadn't heard and brushed by Mickey to sprawl on the bench.

Mickey seemed not to notice the slight but came over and sat down beside her, patting her knee. "You're a natural, girl. Seriously, you've got great form."

It startled him to realize that in some ways Mickey knew his kids better than he did. She somehow managed to offer each of the kids what they needed most, stroking Landon's ego, cheering the twins on, and trying to coax Kayeleigh out of her funk.

But Kayeleigh shrugged out from under Mickey's touch and bored a hole in the floor with her eyes.

Doug wasn't sure which was more difficult: resisting the urge to haul his daughter out to the car for a good talking-to or resisting the urge to hug Mickey for the way she handled Kayeleigh.

He managed to resist both, and by the end of the day, Kayeleigh had lightened up a little and Mickey had made them all laugh. She'd helped him see that they were still a family, and for a few hours Doug had felt a slender ray of hope. Maybe there would be patches of happiness in his life again someday.

They got back to Clayburn as the sun was setting. The twins were asleep against each other in the back when he pulled up in front of Mickey's house. He put the Suburban in park. For some odd reason, he was reminded of his courting days with Kaye. Their first date was the summer after their sophomore year in high school. He had a brand-new unrestricted driver's license and an attitude to go with it. Trying to look cool, he'd pulled in to the Thomases' driveway and tooted the horn.

Kaye had come out with Harriet tagging close behind, hands on hips. She had informed him in no uncertain terms that there would be no more honking for her daughter. He would come to the door like a gentleman, or he would find some other girl to date. But as far as he was concerned, there *was* no other girl for him. From that day on he'd happily abided by Harriet's rules, coming to the door for Kaye and walking her to the porch whenever he brought her home. Of course that was only so he could claim a quick kiss before Kaye's dad came out to play chaperone.

Mickey put a hand on the door handle. "Thanks for the afternoon. It was fun."

"It was. Thanks for going with us."

She turned and waved to Landon and Kayeleigh. "Will I see you guys after school tomorrow?"

"Will we, Dad?" Landon asked.

"No, not tomorrow. You'll go to Grandma's after school. But probably Tuesday."

"Tuesday, then," Mickey said. "Thanks again, Doug." She climbed out and shut the door behind her.

Doug caught Kayeleigh's eye in the rearview mirror. "You guys wait here while I walk Miss Mickey to the door. I'll be right back."

He had to run to catch up to Mickey.

She jumped when he came up beside her. "Did I leave something in the car?"

"No. Just walking you to the door."

"You don't have to do that, Doug."

"Yes, I do." He opened his mouth to tell her about Harriet's edict all those years ago, but thought better of it. That made him remember Harriet's tirade this morning. Neither would he tell her about that. He wasn't going to let anything ruin his last few minutes with Mickey. He followed her up the walk. "I may not be much of a bowler, but I am a gentleman."

She laughed. "That you are."

"Tell you what . . ." Thoughts of Harriet's rumor mill made him hesitate. But no. It had been a wonderful, healing day for him and for the kids, and he wasn't going to let a bunch of gossips dictate his life. Beaming at Mickey, he issued his challenge. "How about a rematch? Same time, same place, next Sunday?"

"Sunday? Um, I really—" She bit her bottom lip and blew out a breath.

For a minute Doug was afraid she was going to turn him down. But a second later her voice exuded confidence. "Sure, I'd love to. But don't get your heart set on winning."

He wiggled his eyebrows. "I'm going to practice all week, you know."

"I don't think a week is gonna cut it, buddy," she teased. "I'm pretty good, in case you hadn't noticed." And with that she turned her key in the lock and disappeared into the house.

Doug smiled all the way back to the car.

That's all we
are . . . . friends.
She had to keep
reminding herself
of that.

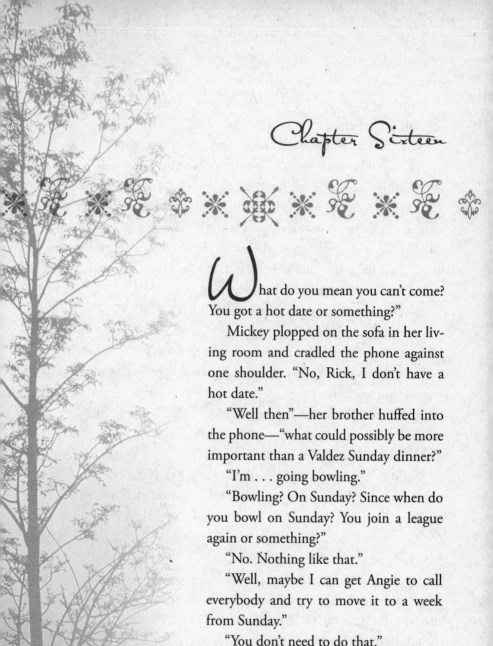

Chapter Sixteen

What do you mean you can't come? You got a hot date or something?"

Mickey plopped on the sofa in her living room and cradled the phone against one shoulder. "No, Rick, I don't have a hot date."

"Well then"—her brother huffed into the phone—"what could possibly be more important than a Valdez Sunday dinner?"

"I'm . . . going bowling."

"Bowling? On Sunday? Since when do you bowl on Sunday? You join a league again or something?"

"No. Nothing like that."

"Well, maybe I can get Angie to call everybody and try to move it to a week from Sunday."

"You don't need to do that."

"You're not going to make a habit of this, I hope?"

"No. Just this once."

He was silent on his end, waiting, she knew, for an explanation. Finally he said, "Don't go all Mystery Woman on me here. What gives?"

"Nothing gives, Rick. I'm taking . . . some kids. From the daycare." It wasn't a lie exactly.

"On Sunday? You know, I haven't seen you at mass forever."

"I'll be there next month. I promise. And for dinner, of course." She'd had no idea her brother would give her the third degree like this. Their monthly family get-togethers were important to her. In fact, she'd almost told Doug no when he asked her to go bowling again. But something about his boyish eagerness hadn't let her turn him down. She'd had a great time with him and his kids last Sunday, and she was eager for a rematch, in more ways than one.

"Well, okay." The pout was evident in Rick's voice. "We'll miss you."

"Yeah, right. You'll just miss that apple pie I was going to bring."

He laughed. "What? You mean you're not dropping a pie off on your way to the lanes?"

"Ha! You wish. Tell Angie and the kids hi. How's she feeling?"

"Fat."

"Rick!"

"I didn't say she *was* fat. You asked how she's feeling. I'm just telling the truth. The doctor says the baby probably won't come for another week or two."

"Give her my love. Everybody else, too. And call me the minute you have baby news. I'll miss you guys."

She would miss them, too. Maybe she shouldn't have made plans. Family was important. But she was looking forward to Sunday, too . . . maybe more than she cared to admit.

"Well, stop by after if you can," Rick said.

She smiled at the sulkiness in his tone. For a minute she considered calling Doug and canceling. But the minute quickly passed.

"Don't hold your breath," she told her brother. "We probably won't be done till late. Talk to you later." She hung up before he could grill her further.

✳ ❀ ✳

Doug's Suburban pulled into Mickey's drive Sunday afternoon at twelve thirty on the dot, and she ran out to meet him before he could get out of the car. He waved through the windshield and reached across the seat to open the passenger door for her.

He was a gentleman. She had to give him that. He'd stayed and talked to her twice at the daycare when he picked the kids up last week . . . stayed for half an hour while the kids hung out in the playroom. He was easy to talk to, and he seemed to think the same about her. She could almost see his heart healing as the days went by. And even though it was mostly his kids they talked about, it felt as if she'd made a new friend.

That's all we are . . . friends. She had to keep reminding herself of that.

She crawled into the Suburban and turned in her seat to greet the kids.

The truth was, she slipped too often into imagining what it would be like if she and Doug were dating for real. Of course, he couldn't possibly see her that way, but she hoped for a day when he might.

Out of nowhere an image of Trevor Ashlock formed in her mind. And a cloud of doubt enveloped her. Was there something wrong with her that she was attracted to the widowers of Clayburn? There was some story or legend about that, wasn't there? A black widow who latched on to men who'd lost their wives. She shuddered. Even she could see how creepy it sounded.

But she'd been young—barely twenty-five—and still licking her wounds over the breakup with Jon, when she developed a king-size crush on Trevor shortly after he lost his wife. He'd never reciprocated her feelings—probably never even known how she felt about him. It wasn't like she'd pursued him. And Trevor was married again now . . . happily. And with a baby due any day.

And this wasn't some schoolgirl crush she had on Doug DeVore. She was wise enough to know that it was too soon for him to even consider another relationship. Besides, the feelings she had for Doug were more akin to compassion and sympathy than romantic love. She was merely imagining what the future *might* hold for them. Not like the unhealthy fantasizing she'd done over Trevor. And this friendship went two ways. After all, Doug was the one who'd invited her to go with him to Salina. Not the other way around.

Still, she couldn't help trying to view Doug through her brothers' eyes. Would they approve? Tony and Alex maybe. They didn't dote on her quite as badly as her oldest big brother. Rick would be a tough sell. Especially if she missed any more family dinners because of Doug.

Harley bounced in her car seat.

"Miss Harley gets to come this time, huh?"

Doug shrugged. "Not by choice exactly. Harriet was busy this afternoon. I figured she'd do better at the bowling alley than a movie theater. We'll see."

"Oh, she'll have a blast." Mickey waved at the other kids, then settled in her seat and buckled her belt.

Landon leaned forward with a wide grin. "Dad says he's gonna whoop you today. He got a new ball and everything."

"Landon! Don't give away my strategies, buddy."

That only egged the boy on. "Yeah, he borrowed Uncle Brad's lucky bowling ball and he's been practicing in the upstairs hall."

"Hey! Hey!" Doug looked sheepish and gave Landon the evil eye in the rearview mirror. "Come on. You're killing me here, bud."

Mickey bit her lip, holding back a smile. "Practicing, huh?"

"Yeah, he 'bout blew a hole in the sheetrock throwing gutter balls." Landon was on a roll.

She couldn't hold it in another minute. Her spirits fluttered and took wing, and all doubts about missing a Valdez get-together went out the window. "Well, this ought to be good."

※ ▓ ※

When they walked out of the bowling alley a few hours later, Doug's hangdog face and slumped shoulders told the story. He managed to laugh at the sound thrashing she'd given him. "Okay, maybe you did beat me, but I came in a strong third."

Mickey hitched Harley up on her hip and feigned a disapproving frown. "It's pretty pathetic when you have to brag about scoring better than small children to feel good about yourself."

That left him speechless for a minute. He reached to ruffle Landon's hair. "You know, if my kids *really* loved me they would have seen to it that I at least came in second."

"You only beat me by two points, Dad," Kayeleigh reminded him.

Landon, who'd nabbed second place, ducked out from under Doug's grasp and gloated. "Yeah, that lucky ball wasn't so lucky, huh, Dad?"

"No, it wasn't. And I'm going to have a word with that brother-in-law of mine. Lucky ball indeed," he muttered under his breath.

Mickey laughed again, and Harley joined in as if the joke was on her. Mickey turned to make sure the twins were behind them. "Hurry up, you two."

She looked over their heads and caught the reflection in the front window of the bowling alley. The sun's angle turned the plate glass into a mirror, and the image reflected there made her catch her breath. They looked like a family. The family she'd always wanted. Doug had a kid under each arm, the twins were skipping hand-in-hand behind them, and she—she had a baby in her arms. They were all smiling, looking like they belonged together. It was like a murky video image of her dream come true.

"You okay?"

She looked up to see Doug watching her, waiting for the twins to catch up.

She shook off the fantasy. She had no business entertaining such thoughts. *We're friends,* she reminded herself again. They'd gone bowling a couple of times. Big deal. She was thinking crazy thoughts.

"Mickey?"

"I'm fine." Embarrassed, feeling like he'd read her mind, she turned away and made a show of hurrying the twins along.

The drive back to Clayburn was rowdy, but she was grateful for the kids' noise that prevented her and Doug from having to talk.

When the Dairy Barn came into sight just inside Clayburn's city limit, Doug gave in to the kids' pleas for ice cream. "Is that okay with you?" A rhetorical question if ever there was one, since there was no way she was going to disappoint his kids now.

"Sure. We could even take it to my house if you want." She looked up into the cloudless blue sky. "Take advantage of this gorgeous weather." The sun was sinking fast, and the sixty-degree temperature would be history by the time they got to her house, but she could make a fire in the pit Rick and Tony had built for her last summer. She felt elated at the prospect of extending the evening.

"Sounds good to me." Doug nodded. "We'll get a half gallon to go."

"Chocolate!" Landon shouted.

Kayeleigh punched his arm. "No way! You always get chocolate. Vanilla, Dad. He always gets to choose."

"Cut it out, you two."

Mickey raised her hand, playing referee. "How about we get a quart of each? My treat," she added quickly.

"Ever the diplomat." Doug held up a palm for a high five.

She slapped her hand against his, grinning.

Twenty minutes later she and Doug were huddled in Adirondack chairs by the fire, their ice cream dripping down the cones faster than they could eat it. Out in the yard the kids played a game of tag in the waning spring sunlight.

"It was a fun day," Mickey said, attempting to rein in her enthusiasm. In truth, it had been one of the happiest days of her life. But she could hardly tell Doug that.

He hadn't counted
on leaving his arm
around her. But there
it was. And now it
seemed awkward for
him to move away.

Chapter Seventeen

Doug swaggered out to the truck, relishing Mickey's side-splitting laughter as she herded the kids behind him. He'd finally, finally beaten the woman at her own game—bowled a 236. And he was going to milk it for all it was worth.

While she pulled seatbelt duty with the kids, he sat behind the wheel gloating.

She finished buckling Harley in and climbed into the Suburban beside him.

"Let's see," he said. "Now, what did you bowl again? I forgot."

"Oh, brother." She rolled her eyes at him. "I suppose I'm never going to hear the end of this, am I?"

"Not unless you somehow manage to get the championship title back. And by the way, as I recall, the rule was, loser buys dinner. Am I right?" He wiggled his eyebrows, which earned him a punch on the bicep. "Ow!"

"Okay, okay. Dinner's on me."

He could tell she was having to work hard not to crack a smile. And he was loving every minute of it. Somehow, Mickey had returned to him—to all of them—the gift of laughter. For a few hours every Sunday, she helped them to forget the terrible thing that had happened to them. And he adored her for it.

So did the kids, though they probably didn't think about it in such concrete terms. But Mickey had endeared herself to them even more than she had as their daycare teacher, if that was possible.

Sometimes when he picked the kids up from daycare and stayed to talk to Mickey, they talked about how he and the kids were coping with the tragedy. Sometimes they talked about Rachel, with Mickey helping him to remember sweet things his daughter had done and said.

But by unspoken agreement, Sundays were strictly for fun. It was the best therapy he could have hoped for. For the whole family.

"Mickey D's again?" he said, putting the car in gear.

"No . . ." She thought for a minute, and then a spark came to her eyes. "How about Mickey V's tonight?"

He laughed, remembering her warning the first time they'd gone bowling. "Sounds good to me."

"My brother butchered last week, and they brought me a bunch of hamburger steaks. We can grill those outside."

"What's this 'we' business?" he teased. "I thought dinner was on the loser."

"I'm providing the food, buster. I'm not playing chef and dishwasher, too."

He held up a hand in surrender. "I know, I know. Just kidding." His mouth was already watering at the thought of a thick, juicy burger.

"You man the grill and I'll take care of the rest."

"Deal." It sounded like a very good deal. . . .

❋ ❀ ❋

An hour later he watched the kids play in Mickey's spacious yard while the two of them enjoyed the meal she'd "whipped up."

The sun had gone down. The night air was chilly and laced with the lingering scent of grilled beef.

"You want some ice cream?" Her teeth chattered and she shivered.

"You crazy woman . . . offering me ice cream while you sit here shivering." He looked up at the graying sky. "It is almost cold out here, isn't it?"

"No almost about it. And I thought it was shorts weather." Mickey pulled shapely legs up onto the wrought-iron bench where they were sitting and wrapped her arms around her knees. "You want to go inside?"

He looked out over the yard where the kids were turning cartwheels on the grass. "I'm not sure I trust the kids not to tear up your flowers."

"I'm not worried about that."

"Do you want to go in?"

"I'm fine."

He could almost see the gooseflesh rising on her bare arms.

"Here." It seemed the most natural thing in the world to slip off his windbreaker and drape it over her shoulders. He hadn't counted on leaving his arm around her. But there it was. And now it seemed awkward for him to move away.

Mickey leaned into him ever so slightly. Enough that he realized she'd been anticipating the possibility. For a long minute he struggled with the implications of his simple gesture. All the while they'd worked together making dinner, he'd found excuses for their fingers to touch, or to put a gentle hand at the small of her back as he slipped by her to reach for something. If he left his arm around her now, let her respond to him as he knew she would, they would automatically move to a new level in their friendship.

He was acutely conscious of the warmth of her arm beneath his hand. Her hair barely brushed his shoulder, and the scent of her shampoo filled

133

his nostrils. Desire swept over him in a way it hadn't since Kaye. . . .

He desperately wanted to draw Mickey close, feel her weight against him. Run his fingers through her silky hair. Make love to her—

He cut the thought off, not wanting to, but knowing he needed to. It felt like forever since he'd known the touch of a woman. *The touch of his wife.* Mickey was a beautiful, terrible reminder of that.

Knowing there would be a price, yet not caring to count it at the moment, he slid closer to her until their hips were almost touching on the bench. He tightened his arm around her. "Mickey . . ."

She moved closer still, leaning her head back on his shoulder. She rested one dainty hand on his knee, her fingers drawing gentle circles in the denim.

"It's been a good day, Doug. Thank you." Her breath tickled his neck.

She shuddered, and he didn't think it was from the cold.

"It was a good day. Mickey—" Something told him to backpedal. Stop, before they traversed a line they could never cross back over. "I-I've enjoyed our Sundays together. It . . . it's helped a lot."

She leaned heavier against him. *Oh, dear God. I don't know what to do. Kaye* . . . His wife's presence seemed so strong. Guilt pressed in on him. But Kaye was gone. She was never coming back. And he felt something—something powerful for this woman who'd made him laugh again. Made him hope again.

But surely it was too soon.

He looked down at Mickey. Long, thick lashes lay against the curve of her olive cheek. She was a beautiful woman. Kaye had been pretty in a girl-next-door, all-American-cheerleader sort of way. But Mickey Valdez was a beauty by anyone's standards. With her wavy, almost-black hair and those violet eyes, she was no doubt accustomed to turning heads. He knew strangers assumed she was his girlfriend—or his wife—when they were out in public together. He enjoyed being the envy of other men when he and Mickey were out on one of their Sunday dates.

Dates? The word rolled so easily from his thoughts. Well, what else were they? *C'mon, DeVore. Be honest. You may as well be dating her.* And what was wrong with that? No one expected him to grieve forever, to stay single forever.

He squeezed Mickey's shoulder and brought his hand to her head. She put her hand over his and stroked his fingers. He gave a strangulated laugh. "I suddenly don't feel cold anymore."

She smiled up at him. A smile that let him know she was feeling the same things he was feeling. He planted a kiss on top of her head, brushed a wisp of hair away from her face.

From the yard Harley's squeal of glee jolted him to his senses. With a gentle nudge he lifted Mickey away from him and rose, moved away from her to look out over the deck's railing. "Landon, don't get her all worked up." *You ought to listen to your own advice, DeVore.* "It's almost time to go. You guys need to start gathering your stuff up."

They hadn't brought a thing with them, but it was all he could think to say.

He leaned to put a hand on top of Mickey's. She was still sitting where he'd left her. Her head was bowed, and he couldn't tell if she was embarrassed or hurt . . . or praying . . . or what.

He cleared his throat. "Thanks for everything. We . . . we really need to go. Got to get the little squirt in bed."

She lifted her head, and somehow he read every nuance of her smile. It told him that she knew he wanted to stay, knew he wanted more of what they'd dabbled at. Maybe even knew that it *would* happen. Soon enough.

Well, maybe she was right. But for now he was done. He rubbed his hands together. He hadn't meant for any of this to happen, and he wouldn't let it go any further. Not tonight. Not until he had a chance to think things through.

She unfolded herself and glided toward him. For one terrifying moment, he was afraid she was going to kiss him good night. But she brushed by him and started to clear the dishes off the patio table.

The kids made a stink about leaving so soon, and he had to get on their case. By the time he finally got everyone rounded up and strapped into the Suburban, the enchantment of earlier had dissolved. Though it certainly left an imprint.

Mickey seemed to be herself again, helping him buckle seatbelts, chattering with the kids, and dishing out challenges about their next bowling night. She didn't seem to notice when he didn't offer to walk her to the door.

Driving home, he wondered if he'd imagined the whole thing. Dreamed up the electricity that had arced between them back there in her yard. But no. His fingers still tingled where he'd touched her. His lips still burned where he'd kissed her fragrant hair. He'd only known her—like this anyway—for two weeks. But there was no denying that he was falling for her.

And he had no idea what to do with that fact.

She was perfect.
So perfect, it moved
Mickey to tears. But
there was regret—and
fear—mixed in those
tears as well.

Chapter Eighteen

ome on in, stranger." Rick opened the door wide and tipped an imaginary hat.

"Well, look who decided to come back into the fold," Tony called from his roost on the recliner in front of the TV.

"Shut up, you two." Mickey seared her brothers with the fiercest look she could feign and carried 'the Boston cream pie she'd made back to the kitchen.

Angie and Rita were at the counter in Angie's tidy kitchen chopping vegetables for the salad.

"Mmmm . . . something smells good."

"Rick made barbecue."

"Yummy." She slid her cake-taker onto the counter and exchanged hugs with her sisters-in-law. "Alex and Gina aren't here yet?"

"They just called," Angie said. "They're on their way."

"The important question is, where's that baby? You look terrific, Angie."

"Thanks, hon. I feel good." Angie glanced at the clock. "The baby's sleeping, but you can go get her if you want. It's about time for her to nurse anyway."

Mickey washed her hands at the sink and headed back to the nursery. She'd held Rick and Angie's little girl in the hospital two weeks ago, but she was eager to get her hands on the little doll again.

The nursery smelled of baby powder and Lysol. Angie was a bit of a neat freak. Mickey approached the crib and peeked over the bumpered rail. The sight of the sleeping infant took her breath away. She didn't know why the wonder never dimmed, but it had been this way with her and babies as far back as she could remember.

She picked up the sleeping bundle and cradled her in front of her body so she could inspect every dainty feature. In just two weeks the baby had changed so much. The scrunchy, red-faced newborn had become a picture-book beauty. Their first girl, she would be spoiled rotten—like Mickey had been. She smiled at the affinity she shared with this little angel.

Emerald, they'd named her. Mickey liked it, but even before they'd brought the baby home from the hospital, Rick was shortening it to Emmy. Her flawless olive skin was touched with gold, and long dark lashes lay against her pudgy cheeks.

She squirmed and puckered her lips. She was perfect. So perfect, it moved Mickey to tears. But there was regret—and fear—mixed in those tears as well. Would she ever hold a child of her own? Would God ever grant her the one dream she'd clung to since she was a little girl?

God had been kind to allow many, many children in her life in the form of her precious nieces and nephews and with the daycare. Doug's children had become extra special to her over the past few weeks. She glanced up at the pink rosebud clock on the nursery wall. They were probably leaving for the bowling alley about now. She missed them. Felt like she was missing out.

She knew her friendship with Doug and his kids was a gift from God. But it wasn't the same. She longed to carry a baby inside her, feel it grow. Unlike some women, she'd never dreaded the prospect of childbirth. She wanted to feel the pain of pushing a child into the world. She wanted to nurse babies at her breasts and watch them change and grow from the day they were born. Maybe she was selfish for allowing nothing less in her dreams. But surely God hadn't created her to be a woman with such strong maternal desires, only to withhold the fulfillment of them from her.

Still, as her thirty-first birthday loomed only a few pages away on the calendar, she couldn't help feeling on the edge of a quiet panic.

Emmy wriggled and stretched, and Mickey snuggled her close. The feelings it triggered inside her, holding this new little life, had to be physical, hormonal. *Oh, please, God. I want to hold my own baby someday. Please . . .* Again, the tears flowed.

"Mick?"

Rick's voice startled her. She swiped at her damp cheek with one hand.

"Dinner's almost—Hey . . . why the tears?" He touched her arm. "You okay?"

She inhaled deeply and let out a shaky breath. "I'm fine." She could never hide anything from her big brother. "Your daughter is so beautiful . . . that's all."

He cocked his head, as if trying to decide if she was telling the truth. Apparently she fooled him because he turned his eyes on his daughter. "We made a pretty one, didn't we?"

"You did. But, um . . . I think Angie gets all the credit for the pretty part."

The baby stirred in her arms. Mickey hitched her up over her shoulder, and Emmy let out a very unladylike burp.

Mickey giggled. "*That,* she inherited from her dad."

Laughing, Rick puffed out his chest. He slung an arm around her and the baby. "Let's go check out that barbecue."

She followed him, grateful for the diversion.

✳ ✳ ✳

Kayeleigh slurped the last of her Diet Coke and slouched down in the ratty velvet seat in the dark theater. They finally got a Sunday without stupid Miss Valdez tagging along, and Dad had spent the entire day moping around like he'd lost his best friend or something.

Okay, she had to admit she was kind of sorry she and Landon had talked Dad into going to some lame kids' movie instead of going bowling like usual. She was getting pretty good at the sport if she did say so herself. And she'd read in Rudi's *Seventeen* magazine just yesterday that it was good exercise, too. She could already tell she'd lost a little weight. See if Lisa Breck called her "Chunkola" behind her back now.

Bowling would have been fun with only Dad. Maybe then he would have said two words to her instead of being all googly-eyes over Miss Valdez.

She'd worked up the courage to talk to Rudi about it last week, and her best friend had said something she hadn't thought about. "Your dad's probably awfully lonely, without . . . you know . . . your mom."

"What? Rudi, think about it. He's got five of us there almost all the time. How could he be lonely?"

Rudi had looked at her like she was crazy. "Are you ever lonely, Kayeleigh? Even with everybody else in the house?"

At first Rudi's question made her mad, but after she thought about it for a while, she could sort of see where she was coming from. The thing that got to her was: what if Mom could see them? She'd heard a lot of different stuff about heaven, and some of it made it sound like people in heaven could see down here on earth. She was pretty sure Mom wouldn't be happy about the way Dad looked at Miss Valdez. Or the way Miss Valdez touched him when she didn't think anyone was looking.

Rudi's dad had died when she was a baby, and her mom had married again. Howie wasn't like a stepfather to her because he was the only dad she remembered. So . . . maybe after you'd been in heaven awhile you didn't care so much if your wife or husband started liking somebody else.

It was all too confusing. She blew out a breath and tried to turn off her mind and concentrate on the movie. There were some funny parts, but it was pretty lame. From two seats away, Landon shot her a dirty look. He was getting to be a real pain . . . except when Miss Valdez was around. Then he suddenly turned into a perfect angel, and Miss Valdez treated him like he was God's gift to the world.

The surround-sound music swelled, and she focused on the movie screen. The cartoon characters were singing. It was a sad melody, and too late, she realized they were singing about trying to find their mother. She knew from the previews that the mother was dead. Dad had tried to talk them into a different movie, but she and Landon and the twins outvoted him. Now she was sorry. She snuck a glance at the twins. They wore identical gap-mouthed expressions. Kayeleigh looked at Dad, figuring he'd be watching the twins and Landon, worried the scene was too sad for them.

But his eyes were on the screen, too. Except he wasn't really watching. Her heart lurched. He was crying. The fancy dim lights on the walls of the theater reflected off the streaks running down his cheeks. He didn't know she was watching. She'd tried to forget that night, right after Mom died, when she'd come downstairs to find him rocking Harley and crying like a baby. Even though it had torn her apart to see that, she understood it. He'd lost Mom. Why wouldn't he cry—even if he was a grown man? But why was he crying now? Mom and Rachel had been gone for a long time now . . . months. Even she hardly cried about it anymore.

Truth was, sometimes when she tried to remember them, she couldn't. She couldn't remember how Rachel's voice sounded exactly, or Mom's. That scared her. What if *she* died? Would everybody forget about her, too?

Dad sniffed and swiped at his cheek with one hand. It was obvious he didn't know she was watching him. She felt her throat start to close. Tears pushed at her eyelids. *No. No. Think of something else. Don't cry.* Why did Dad have to go and make her feel like this? Why couldn't they just forget what had happened?

She forced herself to concentrate on the movie, but the story about a little boy who was searching for his mother defeated the purpose. She pried the lid off her Diet Coke and used the straw to scoop ice into her mouth. The cold felt good against the tightness in her throat. According to Rudi's *Seventeen* magazine, ice didn't have any calories at all. She could chew it until her teeth hurt, and maybe even burn up a few calories in the process.

She turned slightly in her seat so she couldn't see Dad from the corner of her eye. Working to get another portion of ice into her mouth, she let the movie's soundtrack fade into the background.

It had been a long
time since he'd been in
the world of singles.
Maybe he just didn't
recognize a brush-off when
it smacked him upside
the head.

Chapter Nineteen

I'm sorry I'm so late." Doug stood in the middle of Harriet's dining room, trying for a posture that demonstrated appropriate remorse.

But when he looked up, her dour expression hadn't changed. She took in a breath as if she were going to say something. Instead, she folded her arms over her chest and shook her head as if she could hardly believe he'd dared to be half an hour late.

"I . . . I don't think I'll need you to watch the kids again until later in the week. Maybe Friday night? Would that work?"

"Friday *night*?" Her eyes narrowed. "What's going on then?"

"Nothing much." He turned toward the living room, where the kids were watching some nature show on TV. "I thought I might . . . go out." His attempt to backpedal crashed, and he could see Harriet reading his mind.

"You're taking that Valdez girl out again."

He didn't deny it but merely nodded, working to keep his tone casual. "We thought we might go see a movie or something." The "we" part wasn't exactly true. He hadn't gotten up the nerve to call Mickey and ask her out yet. "I wanted to take her to dinner . . . as a thank-you for all the extra time she's spent with the kids."

He regretted the words before they passed his lips. Mickey hadn't given a tenth of the time to the kids that Kaye's mother had, and he was more likely to ask Harriet to *cook* dinner than to invite her out to a restaurant. He made a mental note to remedy that in the near future. But they were her grandkids, after all. And she claimed she wanted to spend time with them.

Besides, for as long as Kaye's dad had been gone—probably close to ten years now—he'd helped Harriet with repairs around the house. Mowed her lawn in the summertime, looked after her house while she was in Florida, and shoveled snow off her driveway any time she happened to be in Kansas during the winter. Not to mention he'd had the kids full-time while Kaye stayed with her mother for a week after Harriet's gall bladder surgery a few years ago. It seemed like it had been a fair exchange.

Until now, with Harriet staring him down.

She unfolded her arms and fiddled with the edge of the crocheted cloth on the dining room table. "I didn't want to say anything until now, Douglas, but I think it's time I tell you."

He waited, curious about what was coming.

"I'm moving to Florida. At the end of the month."

"Moving? *This* month? You don't mean for good?"

She gave a firm nod. "I'm listing my house and moving to Florida. Permanently."

He hadn't seen this coming. It took him a minute to find his voice. "But . . . the kids. What happened to all your talk about moving back *here* full-time? I thought you were at least planning on being here to watch them once school is out."

"I'll come visit the children. And maybe they can take turns coming out to Florida to spend a week or two with me."

Over my dead body. "This isn't a very good time to be selling a house. You know what the market's like right now. And the kids need their grandmother more than ever now, not to mention it's—"

"I've thought about this a good deal, Douglas. It's simply too difficult. There are too many things here I'd rather not be reminded of. I see what's happening with you and that Valdez girl." Her features softened and her voice became pensive. "I know you need to get on with your life. I'm not so narrow-minded that I can't understand that. But I thought you might at least wait a proper period of time before you started this . . . dating again."

"I'm not dating, Har—"

She held up a hand that closed his mouth. "Tell yourself that all you like, Douglas. Everybody in Clayburn has a different opinion."

Was it true? Had people really started seeing him and Mickey as a couple? But remembering how he'd danced with Mickey in front of half the town at Jack and Vienne's wedding, he realized he had nobody to blame but himself if rumors were flying.

A couple of times they'd run into people from Clayburn while they were in Salina with the kids, but surely this town wasn't so starved for news that folks ran home from a Doug-and-Mickey sighting and started phoning the prayer/gossip chains.

"It's obvious you don't really need me anymore." Harriet's strident voice interrupted his thoughts. "The kids will be fine."

"No. They won't. What will I do this summer? That's when the kids need you most, Harriet." It was when *he* needed her most. He and Kaye had breathed a sigh of relief each summer when Harriet watched the kids and they got a reprieve from the daycare bill for a couple of months.

"The daycare is open all summer. Let that Valdez girl take care of them if she's so fond of you."

"Would you stop calling her that?" He willed his voice down an octave. "Her name is Mickey."

Harriet bowed her head in what Doug took for an apology. But the set of her jaw told him she'd made up her mind. "Kayeleigh's almost a teenager. She'll be old enough to babysit come summer."

"I wouldn't saddle her with that kind of responsibility. Especially after what happened . . ."

"I'm not telling you what to do, Douglas. I have no doubt you'll figure something out. But I'm sorry. It's too hard." Her face softened, and she looked up at him with eyes brimming. "It's not just . . . Mickey. It's Kaye, Doug. It's too hard for me to be here with all the memories of her. I'll visit when I can, but I can't stay here." She moved toward the living room and beckoned the kids. "Kayeleigh, your dad's here. Come on, kids. Turn off the TV, and run and get your jackets."

Panic swelled Doug's throat. End of discussion? Harriet was leaving . . . leaving him in the lurch. And blaming it—in part anyway—on his friendship with Mickey. A purely platonic friendship. The thought stalled him, and he set it aside to deal with later. But platonic or not, Harriet had no right to decide his life for him. He'd been counting on her help with the kids when summer came.

He avoided her eyes and herded the kids out to the car. Pulling out of her driveway, he fought the childish temptation to lay rubber on the highway in front of Harriet's house.

"What's the matter, Daddy?" Sadie's worried face stared back at him in the rearview mirror.

"Nothing, sweetie. I'm . . . thinking about what to make for supper."

"Dairy Barn!" Landon yelled from the backseat.

"Not tonight. We've been doing that too much lately."

"You're not gonna try to cook, are you?" Sarah said.

Any other night he might have laughed at the quartet of scrunched-up faces reflected in the mirror. But with the prospect of a thousand nights of trying to come up with something for supper, he suddenly felt overwhelmed.

"It doesn't matter," Kayeleigh said. "I'm not eating anyway."

He couldn't ignore that. "You didn't eat last night, either. Do you feel okay?"

"I ate at Grandma's."

Doug looked over at her, a question in his gaze, but Kayeleigh avoided his eyes and turned to stare out the window.

"That was only a snack, Kayeleigh," Sadie challenged. "Besides, you didn't even eat yours." Her voice kicked into tattletale mode. "Grandma made chocolate chip cookies, and Kayeleigh gave hers to me and Sarah.

"So now you're telling on me for sharing? Nice, Sadie. Real nice."

An alarm went off in the back of Doug's mind. He'd written off Kayeleigh's eating habits to impending adolescence. But looking at her sitting beside him now, in spite of the fact that she was developing a womanly figure at an alarming rate, he thought her arms looked a little thin. Maybe it was just that he'd only seen her in thick sweatshirts all winter. Since she was a baby, Kayeleigh had been a little on the pudgy side. He'd worried about the teasing she might face, but Kaye always said she'd outgrow it when she hit puberty. Maybe watching what she ate now was part of that.

Puberty. Now there was a terrifying thought.

He shut off the warning bells and concentrated on the road. And on how he was going to turn a refrigerator full of moldy leftovers and half-empty cartons and bottles into something he could call supper. Dairy Barn was sounding pretty good. Maybe he'd drive through tonight, and then Sunday they could eat someplace nice. Except Sunday was Easter, and Mickey would probably go to her brother's house. All the more reason to ask her about going to a movie Friday night.

Of course, Harriet hadn't exactly agreed to babysit. But maybe she was right—maybe Kayeleigh was old enough to watch the kids for two or three hours if he was only twenty minutes away.

He hadn't talked to Mickey in over a week. He'd been in the field late almost every night, and either Harriet had picked up the kids from daycare or Mickey had gone home by the time he got there. She'd bowed out of last Sunday's trip to Salina. Said she was going to mass with her brothers and a family dinner afterward. But now he wondered. Was she giving him the brush-off and he didn't even recognize it?

Come to think of it, he'd tried to call her on Wednesday night and got no answer. As far as he knew, she didn't go to church on Wednesday nights. But everything had seemed fine when he'd talked to her on Monday.

They hadn't exactly discussed what had happened between them, but judging by their brief exchanges, something had changed in the way she responded to him. Something good, he thought. But maybe he only imagined that she was friendlier. A little flirty even.

But it had been a long time since he'd been in the world of singles. Maybe he just didn't recognize a brush-off when it smacked him upside the head.

Maybe she wasn't even aware that he'd actually planted a kiss in her hair that night on her deck. Still, remembering that night, he thought otherwise. And he *hadn't* imagined that she'd responded to him. Physically. He pushed away thoughts that took his mind places it didn't need to go.

Driving through downtown Clayburn, he noticed the lights were still on at Latte-dah. He whipped into an empty parking stall. "You guys stay right here. I'm going to get sandwiches for dinner."

"Plain mustard on mine!" Landon yelled.

"No mustard!" The twins took up an antimustard chant.

"I'm not taking special orders," Doug said, unbuckling his seatbelt. "You can put your own mustard on them when we get home. Or not." Before they could argue, he jumped out and shut the door.

Fifteen minutes and as many dollars later, he carried a soggy sack of smoked turkey and swiss sandwiches into the house. He followed the kids in and flipped on lights that spotlighted kitchen counters strewn with this morning's cereal boxes and yesterday's dinner dishes.

The dining-room table was worse. It would be a major undertaking just to clear off a space for supper. They'd just cleaned the place up a few weeks ago. How had things gotten to be such a wreck again?

He would organize another cleaning brigade Saturday morning. The kids wouldn't be happy about it, but that was tough. Kaye hadn't worried so much about whether they were happy or not. She was more concerned with whether they were learning important life lessons and growing into responsible young men and women. But then, Kaye hadn't faced the challenge of trying to be both mother and father.

He rushed the kids through dinner and helped them clean up the worst of the kitchen mess. When they were settled in with homework, he took the phone to his bedroom and dialed Mickey.

For the first time his palms were damp and his nerves a jittery mass, waiting for her to answer.

* ❋ *

I'm coming . . . I'm coming." Mickey set down the overflowing wheelbarrow and ran up the back steps to the deck. So much for getting the flowerbeds cleaned out before dark. Oh, well. It was only the third of April. A little early to put anything out anyway.

Brushing garden dirt from her hands, she slid the screen door open with one elbow. The evening air was balmy, and she'd left the French doors to the dining room open. She'd heard the phone at least twice before, and she'd let it ring until now. But this time her imagination started conjuring bad news scenarios involving her brothers and their sweet families, and she couldn't ignore it another minute.

She kicked off her Crocs outside the door and wiped bare, damp feet on the rug before stepping inside. She grabbed the handset, barely registering the *DeVore* on the Caller ID before she answered, "Hello?"

"Mickey? Hi, it's Doug."

"Oh, hi. Did you try calling earlier?"

"Um . . . yeah. A couple times."

"I'm sorry. I've been working out in the yard."

"Oh. Sorry. I can call back later if that's better for you."

"No, it's okay." She reached to close the door. The yard would still be here tomorrow evening. It was nice to hear his voice.

"So . . . how was your day?"

She hesitated. Did she imagine the trepidation in his voice? "It was okay." Somehow she didn't think he'd called just to chat. She gripped the phone tighter. She'd halfway expected this call. Expected he would call to cancel Sunday. And thinking about that possibility earlier this week, she'd felt mild relief. But now, with his voice soft in her ear, she knew that wasn't what she wanted at all. She missed him. *Please don't let me cry, Lord. At least not until I hang up.*

"I haven't talked to you for a while." He kept his voice low, but she could hear the kids chattering in the background. Or maybe it was the TV.

"Yes, it's been a while. How'd the bowling go Sunday?"

"Oh. We didn't go bowling."

"No?"

"No, we went to a movie instead." He hesitated. "That Disney show we were going to see a few weeks ago."

"Oh. Did you like it?"

He cleared his throat. "Since when did Disney movies get so stinking sad?"

She laughed softly. But remembering the movie, she realized he might not be kidding. "I told you that one was a tearjerker."

"You did. I should have listened to you."

"You should have."

He sighed. "I let the kids talk me into it. Next time I'll take you at your word. Maybe I can make up for it Sunday." She could hear his smile.

"Sunday?" She didn't like playing dumb, but she wasn't going to assume anything either.

"If you don't have . . . anything else going on, we'd—*I'd* like you to go bowling with us again. I think we all missed it last week."

She smiled into the phone. He didn't say they'd missed *her,* but she was pretty sure that's what he meant. "You missed the bowling, huh?"

He either didn't get her joke or he chose to ignore it. "But hey . . . Sunday's not really why I called." He cleared his throat. "Would you want to go out to dinner Friday night? Just me . . . no kids. Maybe we could catch a movie after—*not* a sad one," he added quickly.

She'd been all ready to take his rejection like an adult. Now he was asking her for a date. An official date. It didn't take her two seconds to decide. "I'd love to, Doug."

"Friday . . . or Sunday?"

"Both."

"Great!" She heard his grin over the phone lines. "Okay if I pick you up about six thirty?"

Why had she said yes so quickly? Things were great between them just the way they were. Did she really want to mess it up with a date? Not that she hadn't daydreamed a hundred times about those few minutes on her deck when he'd put his arm around her, and she'd leaned into his sweet warmth. She sighed.

"Everything okay?"

She gave a self-conscious laugh. She hadn't meant for him to hear her sigh. "Everything's fine. I'll see you Friday then?"

"I'm looking forward to it."

She felt herself blush and was glad he couldn't see her. She dropped the handset in its cradle and went to troll her closet for something suitable to wear on a "real" date.

Doug gave her a thumbs-up. It felt good to be in cahoots with him. Even if this wasn't exactly a covert sting operation.

Chapter Twenty

Robins chirped and chattered in the tops of the Bradford pears that bloomed up and down Clayburn's Main Street. April 6, but already the trees wore a cloak of new yellow-green leaves. Mickey tugged at the hem of her shirt, wishing she'd picked something more comfortable to wear.

"I hope you don't mind," Doug said again, maneuvering his pickup into a tight spot in front of Latte-dah. "I just didn't feel right leaving Kayeleigh with the kids too long."

"Not at all. This is nice. I've always liked the coffee shop." Well, that part was true. But she did mind a little that they were staying in Clayburn for their date. There was no way she and Doug wouldn't be the talk of the town after tonight. If they weren't already.

She put aside any hope of keeping her

friendship with Doug a secret from her brothers. They may not live in Clayburn's city limits, but rumors traveled faster than the pony express around here. And this would be a rumor of the highest caliber.

Doug put the truck in park and climbed out. "Hang tight," he said through the open window. "I'll get your door."

Feeling silly sitting there while he ran around the front of the vehicle, she pulled on the door handle. Nothing happened. Doug jerked on the handle from the outside. Nothing. The door didn't seem to be locked. She watched through the window as he fished his keys from his pocket and joggled them in the lock until the door finally unlatched. "Unfortunately, I wasn't just being thoughtful." He gave her a sheepish grin. "There's a trick to this door."

"And to think I was all impressed." She feigned a pout.

"Don't worry, if it had stayed stuck, I would have brought you something out to eat."

She laughed. "That's real big of you. Thanks."

He winked. "Wouldn't want you to starve to death." He put a hand on the small of her back and followed her inside.

She took a deep breath, savoring the heady aroma of strong espresso and cinnamon and vanilla. Immediately it brought back memories of the first night she'd gotten to know Doug at Jack and Vienne Linder's wedding. The place looked very different tonight. At a table near the window, a family with teenagers laughed together, oblivious to them. And an elderly couple sat side by side on the sofa in front of the fireplace, sipping coffee and reading hardcover books. Other than that, the place belonged to her and Doug.

She hoped it stayed that way. He'd made it clear this wouldn't be a late night, so maybe they could escape before their date became fodder for the *Courier.* She smiled to herself, imagining Doug himself stopping the presses to censor the gossip column.

Doug claimed a table on the other side of the fireplace. "This okay?"

"Sure." She took the chair he held for her.

"I'll go order for us. Do you know what you want or do you need to look at a menu?"

"No . . . I'll just have the soup and half a sandwich. Whatever the special is."

Vienne didn't seem to be working tonight, but the college-age girl behind the counter—Allison, Mickey thought her name was—smiled in her direction and took Doug's order.

He came back to the table with their drinks and they admired the art displayed on the wall over their table—some of it Jack Linders's—until the girl brought their food.

"So Kayeleigh's babysitting tonight, huh?"

"Yeah. First time. I hope I'm not sorry." He pulled his cell phone off his belt loop and checked the display.

"She'll do fine. I see her with the kids at the daycare. She's good with them. We probably ought to pay her for all the help she gives us on the days she's there after school." She didn't mention that Kayeleigh had been sporting an attitude lately. This wasn't the time or place, and besides, she'd chalked it up to the fact that the girl was on the brink of being a teenager. It was a tough age to be.

"I was hoping we could go to that new Mexican place in Salina."

"This is fine, Doug. Really. It's fine . . ."

The bells on the front door jangled, and he eyed the two couples coming in. A middle-aged couple she didn't recognize, and Trevor and Meg Ashlock, with their new baby in tow. Trevor raised a hand in greeting. She and Doug returned his wave in unison, but they didn't come over. For a minute Doug seemed to retreat to a faraway place, and Mickey wondered if there was something going on at work between them.

Doug motioned toward the foursome. "Those are Amy's parents," he whispered.

"Oh." That had to be a little awkward for Meg, though her smile and warmth toward the couple seemed genuine. She cringed at the image that formed of her and Doug having dinner with Harriet Thomas and wondered if he was thinking the same thing.

"Is your soup good?"

"Very." She took a sip as if to prove it, grateful for the change of subject.

"Save room for dessert. There are some big honkin' cream puffs in the dairy case calling our names."

"I don't dare. I'm still trying to lose the five pounds I gained over the holidays."

"Oh, come on. Live a little. You can bowl it off Sunday."

"Okay, okay. You twisted my arm." As if bowling a few lanes was going to work off a thousand calories.

Outside the wide front windows, the sun sank behind the storefronts. Unfortunately, that seemed to be the cue for Latte-dah to come to life. A group of high school kids drifted in and scooted two tables together for a rowdy pizza party—Vienne's latest offering. Two more tables filled up with retired couples. The soothing jazz that had been playing over the speakers was quickly drowned out, and she and Doug had to practically shout to hear each other.

Worse, it became obvious that they were being watched with great curiosity. When Clara Berger and her cronies parked at the table beside her and Doug—and a whisper-fest commenced—he touched her hand and cut his eyes to the gossips' table. "How about we take those cream puffs to go?"

She repressed a grin and nodded. "Good idea."

"I'll go get them."

She nodded toward the restrooms in back. "I'll be right back. Meet you outside?"

Doug gave her a thumbs-up. It felt good to be in cahoots with him. Even if this wasn't exactly a covert sting operation.

When she came out of the restroom, she avoided meeting any of the eyes she felt trained on her. Through the window, she could see Doug waiting for her, leaning on his truck. As soon as he saw her, he went around to get her door. Thankfully, it opened on the first try.

He jogged around to the driver's side and climbed in. He put the key in the ignition, but looking up through the windshield, he let out a snort of laughter. He tapped her arm and nodded back toward the coffee shop. "Don't look now, but we, um . . . we seem to be the main attraction."

Trying to be casual, she followed his line of vision to the front window of Latte-dah. Above the café curtains, no less than six pairs of eyes peeked back at them.

"Oh, good grief!" Mickey dissolved in giggles.

He clucked his tongue and lowered his voice. "I do believe they have us married off, on our honeymoon, and probably prematurely pregnant with our first child."

"Doug!" She was glad her face was already flushed from laughing. She could hardly believe he'd said that out loud.

"Well? Am I wrong?"

She rolled her eyes. "Sadly, no. It is Clayburn, after all. So how do you propose we deflect those nasty little rumo—"

Before she could spit out the last syllable, he leaned across the bench seat, wrapped his arms around her, and planted a kiss—a long, slow, I-mean-it sort of kiss—squarely on her mouth.

News of his shenanigans
would be all over town
by the time she got back
to work Monday
morning. Sooner than
that, no doubt. Only
nobody would know it
had been a joke. How
was she ever going to
face the rumors?

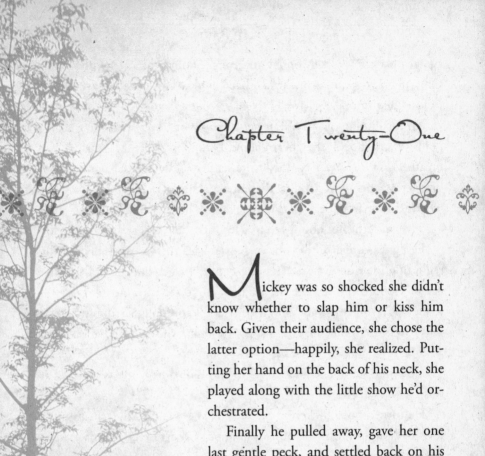

Chapter Twenty-One

Mickey was so shocked she didn't know whether to slap him or kiss him back. Given their audience, she chose the latter option—happily, she realized. Putting her hand on the back of his neck, she played along with the little show he'd orchestrated.

Finally he pulled away, gave her one last gentle peck, and settled back on his side of the truck. "There," he said, turning the key and revving the engine. "That'll give 'em something to chew on."

"I'll say," she muttered. "For a few weeks to come." Feeling a little breathless, she put her hands in her lap and tucked her chin.

Doug put the truck in reverse, stretched his arm across the back of the seat, and slowly backed onto Main Street.

Mickey sighed. News of his shenanigans would be all over town by the time she got back to work Monday morning. Sooner than that, no doubt. Only nobody would know it had been a joke. How was she ever going to face the rumors?

An involuntary gasp rose in her throat as she imagined the look on her brothers' faces if they heard about Doug's mischief. She pushed her breath down before it escaped. She hadn't said a word to any of her brothers or their wives about where she was spending her Sundays. Even when Rick or Tony or Alex teased her about her "old maid" status, she'd kept her mouth shut about Doug. Not that there was anything to tell.

Doug was quiet on his side of the vehicle. He was probably already regretting his rash actions. But she could not get that kiss out of her mind. Good thing he couldn't read her mind. She'd done her best not to let her daydreams wander to the possibility of Doug having such feelings toward her, but she couldn't control what she dreamed about him at night.

Now he'd gone and made one of those dreams come true—and it was all for a laugh.

He turned onto Pickering Street. "Okay if we take our cream puffs to your house? I'd invite you to mine, but I don't exactly want to split them eight ways."

"Eight?"

"Harriet might be there. She was going to check on the kids. And she does love a good cream puff."

Mickey laughed. "Sure. My house is fine. We can sit on the deck." If he could see right through her—know she was thinking of the last time they'd sat on her deck—he gave no hint.

He stared straight ahead until he slowed in front of her house and parked at the curb. But instead of getting out of the truck, he put the bag of cream puffs on the dashboard, turned in his seat, and reached for her.

There was nobody to show off for now. Nobody he was trying to fool. Except her? Trembling, she let him take her into his arms again, let his lips find hers. She drank in the sweet taste of him. Cream puffs had nothing on this man. She savored a kiss that was beyond anything her dreams were made of.

But what were his intentions? She slowly came to her senses and pushed away from him. "Doug . . . what is this? I don't—"

He reached for her tentatively. When she didn't respond, he put a hand over hers. "Mickey, I think—I think I might be falling in love with you."

"No, Doug." She started shaking her head. "No. I don't think . . . I don't think you can know that." *Oh, dear God. I'm not ready for this. Please . . . help me know what to say.*

His eyes challenged her. "Why can't I know that?"

She shook her head, overwhelmed. "It's too soon, Doug. You've only just lost . . . *Kaye.*" She whispered the name. The name of the only woman Doug had eyes for mere weeks ago. No matter how much she wished it were true, he couldn't possibly love her yet. Love didn't die that quickly—or grow that quickly, for that matter. *Did it?* Oh, but how desperately she wanted it to be true. She hadn't dared to hope until now. Or perhaps she had, but hadn't fully admitted it to herself. And now he'd gone and ruined everything.

She pulled her hand out from under his. "What was that all about . . . in front of the coffee shop? Is that your idea of a joke?"

He chewed at the corner of his lip. "I-I saw a chance to—to make my move." His mouth lurched in a lopsided smile. "I'm a little rusty, Mick. That was—clumsy. I'm sorry. But are you going to sit here and tell me you didn't feel something?"

She blew out a huff of air. "Of course I felt something, you idiot. That's not the point."

"What is the point, then?"

She shook her head. He'd said he *loved* her. "Doug, I never thought you could be interested in me—that way. It's so soon . . . after Kaye. I always thought the pressure was off with you."

He studied her for a moment, and what she saw in his eyes terrified her.

He reached as if to touch her arm, then drew it back, resting his hand on his knee. His hands fascinated her. The strong hands of a laborer. Yet so gentle when they caressed his children, or when they touched her.

"I meant what I said, Mickey." His voice was husky, and he reached for her hand, seeming confident this time. "Maybe I'm speaking out of turn, but I'm not going to pretend otherwise."

"Oh, Doug." Was it possible that she could feel the same way about him? So soon?

She'd known Doug DeVore for years. She remembered the twins as babies. Remembered when Harley was born, and Doug came in, passing out bubble gum cigars and bragging that he'd finally gotten that Harley he always wanted. She smiled at the memory. He still didn't own a motorcycle, but oh, was he devoted to that little girl.

She knew the kind of man Doug was, admired him as a father, and as a husband, but she'd never allowed herself to look at him the way she looked at him now. He'd been a married man most of the time she'd known him.

The weight of his hand smothered hers. "Mickey? What are you thinking?"

"I don't know, Doug. I . . . I'm confused." Maybe she had a right to love him now that Kaye was gone. But if he could forget Kaye so soon and fall in love with someone else—with her—what did that say about him? About *her*?

For the second time she pulled her hand away. "I can't think with you—touching me that way."

"I'm sorry." He didn't look sorry. But he rearranged his lanky frame back behind the steering wheel.

"It's just too soon, Doug."

He reached for her, then seemed to remember her rebuff and pulled his hand away. "Kaye's not coming back, Mickey. I loved her with every cell of my being, but she's not coming back. I believe God put you in my life for a reason."

"I . . . I don't know what to say."

"I won't rush you, Mickey. But I know what I want. And I intend to go after it." Tentatively, as if she were a wild animal he meant to tame, he reached across the seat and stroked her cheek with the back of his hand. "I love you."

"Doug . . ." Something inside her snapped, and her breath left her slowly. No man had ever treated her with the tenderness she felt beneath his gentle touch right now. Since college, in spite of the fact that her brothers' wives were always trying to set her up with somebody, she could count the dates she'd had on two hands. Clayburn wasn't exactly a mecca for eligible singles.

If Doug was ready for a relationship, why should there be any reason to hold back? He was a good man. A godly man. With him, she wouldn't need to worry for one minute that there were secrets in his past or things she didn't know about him.

She'd seen the kind of man he was, and if she hadn't, the entire town of Clayburn would have testified on his behalf. Everybody loved Douglas DeVore.

As if he'd read her mind, Doug took her face in his hands. "What's holding you back, Mickey?"

What *was* holding her back? Doug said he loved her. He knew what love felt like. She'd never been in love before, so maybe she was just slower to recognize it. She could trust him. Trust his love.

She placed her hands over his, trembling at the revelation. "I don't know what's holding me back, Doug. I . . . I think I might love you, too."

He enveloped her in his embrace and kissed her thoroughly. And she stayed there, willingly, feeling as if she were exactly where she'd always belonged.

Since he'd declared
his love for Mickey,
it seemed like Kaye
was all he could
think about.

Chapter Twenty-two

"ey, I hope it's not too late notice, but do you want to go to church with us?" Doug squeezed the phone between his ear and his shoulder and held his breath, waiting for Mickey's answer.

"This morning?"

"Yeah. We'd pick you up about eight forty-five. You don't have to dress up or anything."

"Well . . . um . . ."

He could almost hear her internal calculator tallying the minutes: how long it would take to shower, dry her hair, do her makeup, get the kids dressed—

The thought brought him up short. It wasn't Mickey's "calculator" he was hearing. It was Kaye's. If he didn't quit doing that—mixing them up in his mind, blending their two unique personalities into one—he was going to stick his big fat foot in his mouth one of these days and be in deep, deep trouble. He shook his head, as if doing so could reset his memory.

Mickey's short laugh broke his reverie. "I guess I could make it," she said. "But what do you mean I don't have to dress up? Can I wear what I wear to bowl?"

"Sure." She always looked like a million dollars. He wasn't worried about that.

"You're positive? I'm not going to get there and want to kill you because every other woman has a dress on, am I?"

"I promise. Anyway, you'd be the most beautiful woman there if you wore a gunny sack."

"Oh, aren't you racking up the brownie points?"

He smiled into the phone. "Yes, aren't I."

"Well, if I'm going, I don't have time to stand around chit-chatting."

"Okay, babe. See you in a little bit."

Babe. The endearment had rolled off his tongue so naturally, but he'd never used it with Mickey before. The dial tone rang in his ear. *Babe.* He wondered if Mickey had noticed, and more important, if she'd known that *babe* had been his pet name for Kaye.

Today would be a test of sorts. It had been over a week since they'd left the coffee shop and taken the cream puffs to Mickey's house—cream puffs they never had gotten around to eating. He smiled at the thought of those sweet kisses in his truck. Sweetness that had moved quickly to passion. He'd walked her to the door and left—before things heated up too much.

Since then they'd only seen each other briefly when Doug picked up the kids from daycare. But he'd called her almost every night after he got the kids in bed, and they talked for hours at a time. Their relationship had definitely gone to the next level.

He could talk to her so easily . . . and about anything. He was definitely in love with the woman. One thing ate at him, though: since he'd declared his love for Mickey, it seemed like Kaye was all he could think about. Last night he'd awakened in a sweat, from a dream about Kaye—and Rachel, too. He spent several minutes in a world where that terrible Thanksgiving Day had never happened. He'd floated on joy. And then, before he was awake enough to grasp that it was only a dream and his precious wife and daughter were gone, he relived Mickey's sweet kiss. And the guilt had overwhelmed him—as if he'd cheated on Kaye. Irrationally, a remnant of that guilt still clung to him now.

That was one thing he couldn't very well talk to Mickey about. He just prayed to God he didn't accidentally call her by Kaye's name one of these days. She might accept "babe," but if he ever called her "Kaye" . . . He shook off the thought. The more he worried about slipping up, the more likely it was that he would.

Mickey was waiting on the front porch when he pulled up to the curb a few minutes later. He jumped out and walked up the sidewalk, wondering how she would be with him today.

She had definitely spiffed up a little more than usual, with her hair down and brushing her shoulders, and her cheeks and lips rosy with makeup. She looked great. But a little nervous, maybe.

He and Mickey had talked about God a lot during their nightly phone calls. He'd been relieved to discover that she believed much the same as he did about the things that mattered: Jesus, salvation, taking the Bible as God's inspired Word, living a clean life. She'd told him she went to mass with her brothers and their families on the Sundays they had their big family dinners, but that was only once a month.

She'd confided how hard it had been growing up Catholic in Clayburn, where half the people belonged to Community Christian and the other half were split between First Baptist, the old Lutheran Church, and the New Covenant Church out on the highway.

It bothered him a little that church didn't seem more important to Mickey. But then, he didn't have much room to talk. If it hadn't been for Kaye's prodding, he probably wouldn't have gotten in the habit of church every week, either. He was glad she'd pushed him to go when they were newly married. Especially after what had happened. Since he'd lost Kaye and Rachel, Pastor Grady and their friends in the church had done their best to provide comfort and answers when he was struggling to make sense of things. It had made the difference between going crazy and going on. It was still hard to sit with his kids lined up on the pew and no Kaye at the end of the row to complete the "bookends"— and no Rachel in between. But Community Christian was the one place where he and the kids could be broken, yet still felt like they belonged.

"Good morning." Mickey gave an awkward little wave as they met on the sidewalk, and he realized she was as nervous as he was about how they should be with each other. Taking the bull by the horns, he went to her with arms outstretched.

She accepted his hug but turned her head when he tried to kiss her. He felt her looking over his shoulder.

"The kids, Doug . . ."

He drew back, chuckling. "I don't think it's going to mar them for life to see us kiss. In fact, they'd better get used to it, because I plan to be kissing on you all day."

"Douglas!" But her coy grin said she didn't exactly dread the possibility.

His spirits soared. Man, he'd missed her.

In the car she greeted each of the kids by name, and even Kayeleigh seemed to warm up to her a little.

But later, after church, when they went to Carlos O'Kelly's for lunch, Kayeleigh tried to orchestrate the seating so she was between him and Mickey.

"Huh-uh, sweetie, that's my chair," he said, taking her by the shoulders and steering her to the end of the table. "I'd like you to sit by Harley and help her with her dinner, please."

"No fair, Dad. I always have to babysit Harley." She dragged the chair out and plopped into it, slumping down with arms crossed over her chest.

Forcing his temper down, Doug glanced at Mickey to catch her reaction. "That's not true, Kayeleigh. Here, Landon"—he pulled a chair to the other side of Harley's chair—"you help Kayeleigh out. And put that video game down. I told you not to bring that in with you. We're eating."

Landon stretched his neck out and made a show of panning the table. "Where? I don't see any food."

"Don't get smart with me, buddy." He glared at Landon until he finally tucked the game in his pocket and assumed an identical posture to his big sister.

Great. This was really going to impress Mickey. She'd stood by silently, but he felt her watching—evaluating how he was handling the situation.

"Sorry," he mouthed to Mickey over their heads.

She shrugged, but by the little shake of her head and the look in those gorgeous violet eyes, he didn't think he was getting a very high score.

He pulled out her chair, took the one beside her, and casually slipped an arm around her shoulders. He pulled her close for a brief hug, testing the waters.

Trying for nonchalance, he glanced around the table. Landon's eyes bugged out, Kayeleigh slumped lower in her chair, and deepened her scowl, burying her nose in the book she'd brought. The twins looked at each other as if to say, "What in the world is Daddy *doing*?" Harley was the only one who'd missed his amorous attention toward Mickey, and only because she was leaning out of her highchair, trying to reach the basket of tortilla chips on the table.

Mickey must have felt the kids' stares, too, because she sat forward in her chair, shrinking from his touch, suddenly intent on unwrapping her silverware from the napkin.

Their server came, a sullen, high school-age girl who made Doug fear what Kayeleigh might be like at seventeen if he didn't nip her mood swings in the bud. He helped the kids order and got them settled with their drinks.

While they waited for their entrees, Mickey surprised him by reaching for his hand under the table. He pulled her hand onto his knee and knit his fingers with hers. Over the rim of her Diet Pepsi, she shot him another one of those demure, just-for-him smiles he was learning to love.

Their food came and the kids quit eyeing them. He and Mickey spent the rest of the meal playing footsie under the table and holding hands between bites. Mickey's smoky violet eyes said more than all the words she'd ever spoken to him put together. It was obvious her feelings were running as high as his, and he realized that today, for the first time since Thanksgiving, he felt truly happy.

Was it possible that
love had snuck up on
her just when she'd
almost given up on
ever finding the
right man?

Chapter Twenty-three

Doug parked the Suburban in front of her house, and Mickey reached for the door handle, reluctant to let the day end. "You guys want to come in for a little bit?"

The twins voted with a cheer and the click of their seatbelt releases.

"Just for a little while, guys," Doug warned. "You can play in the back while Mickey and I talk, okay?" He climbed out and went around to extricate Harley from her car seat.

Mickey herded Sarah and Sadie off the street into her yard. "Wait for Landon, girls. He can open the backyard gate for you."

Landon raced off across the yard with the twins trailing him.

From the backseat Kayeleigh challenged Mickey with narrowed eyes, then addressed her father. "I'm gonna stay in the car and wait."

Doug set Harley on the curb, keeping one hand on her pudgy arm. "No, I want you to watch Harley in the yard."

"Can't you take her with you? I watched her at the bowling alley."

"Kayeleigh, come on." Doug kept his voice low, as if not wanting to embarrass her, but Mickey could tell he was growing increasingly frustrated with her attitude.

Kayeleigh unfolded her long legs from under her and crawled out of the car, but as she passed by, she shot Mickey a look that said, "This is all your fault."

Over the top of the vehicle Doug rolled his eyes for Mickey's benefit. She forced a commiserating smile, but if Kayeleigh hadn't been twelve, she would have told Doug his daughter needed a good spanking. Yes, Doug was asking a lot of Kayeleigh, but she had been an insufferable brat all day. And now she was threatening to ruin the evening.

Mickey bit her tongue and waited for Kayeleigh to pick up Harley and carry her to the backyard. She led the way up the front walk. "You want something to drink?"

"Sure. I'd drink some iced tea if you have it."

"I can make it."

"Oh . . . no, don't do that."

She tossed a look over her shoulder. "I don't mind. I want some, too."

She went into the kitchen, filled the teakettle, and put it on the back burner to boil. She rummaged in the cupboards looking for tea bags. "So did you get your taxes done? Tomorrow's the day, you know."

She sensed him behind her, but he didn't answer. Instead, she felt his arms come around her from behind. He bent his head and nuzzled her neck.

She dropped the Lipton box onto the counter and turned to face him. "Hey, you . . . you didn't answer my ques—"

He cut her off with a kiss and locked her in the embrace she knew this entire day had been leading up to. When he let her up for air, she snuck a look over her shoulder and out the sliding doors that led through the dining room to the deck. The twins and Harley zipped back and forth across the yard, Landon close behind, growling like a bear. Their playful squeals floated into the kitchen through the screening. Good. They'd be happy out there for a while.

She turned her full attention to Doug, pulling his head down to match their mouths. Where had this man been all her life? Instantly she chided herself. *Don't answer that question, Valdez.* She didn't want to think about Kaye and Rachel—or even Doug's kids right now. For now it was only the two of them, together, with this incredible electricity zinging between them. Passion, maybe even . . . Was it possible that love had snuck up on her just when she'd almost given up on ever finding the right man?

Doug gave a little groan and pulled her closer, kissing her again and again.

Things were moving fast. Too fast. But she didn't care. She loved this man. She did. She'd waited thirty years for God to answer her prayers, and he'd answered them very, very well in Doug DeVore. "Thank you, Lord . . ."

"What's that?" Doug whispered close to her ear.

She hadn't realized she'd spoken the words aloud, but it didn't matter. He should know. "You're the answer to all my prayers, you know."

He pulled away and cocked his head. "I am, am I?"

"Yup. Now shut up and kiss me." She silently reveled in the fact that she could rattle off such a request to such a wonderful guy and be fairly certain he would comply.

As if to prove her thoughts, he laughed and kissed her again. But when he pulled back to look into her eyes, his jaw tensed. A sheen came to his eyes, and she knew the teasing moment had passed.

He ran a finger down the bridge of her nose. "Why don't you just marry me and get it over with?"

Oh. Maybe he *was* teasing. "Get it over with, huh?" She feigned a bashful grin, playing along. "Now, why would I want to go and do a fool thing like that?"

He stroked her cheek with the back of his hand. A delicious warmth surged through her veins.

"I'm serious, Mick. I love you. And if I'm not mistaken, you love me, too." He leveled a look that dared her to answer otherwise.

"I . . . Doug, I—"

He laid a finger to her lips, then bent to silence her with another kiss. "It's okay. I didn't mean to put you on the spot." His murmured words tickled her ear and thrilled her heart. "You just happen to be the best thing that's happened to me in a long, long time."

She sobered and drew back. He didn't say "the best thing that's *ever* happened to me." But maybe that was splitting hairs. This poor man had been through so much. It was a wonder he hadn't collapsed under the stress of his grief and trying to be a single dad to five kids.

She breathed his name out in a trembling whisper. "I . . . I think I do love you."

He lifted his chin and dared her with his gaze. "Then marry me."

"Doug . . ." He was going to break her heart if he didn't shut up. "Don't joke about this."

He pulled back and looked into her eyes again. "Mickey, I've never been so serious about anything in my life." His eyes said he meant it.

"Maybe it's too soon. Maybe you're asking me in—in the heat of"— she fanned herself with the flattened palm of her hand—"this thing that seems to happen whenever we touch each other."

The smile he gave her melted any doubts she had.

Behind them the teakettle started to hiss. She reached around him and turned down the heat. If only she knew how to turn the flame that burned between her and Doug down a notch.

He drew her close, rested his chin on top of her head. His voice broke. "I don't know how I would have made it through these last months without you. You—healed a place inside of me that I didn't think could ever be whole again."

"No." She shook her head. "God did that, Doug. All I did was love you. And that was easy." Her heart blossomed inside her. She felt blessed beyond words that this man wanted her in his life. He'd known one true love and lost it. To think that he'd chosen her—that he loved her enough to share his life with her—took the breath from her.

Doug pulled away, beaming from ear to ear. "Let's do it then. Let's get married."

She must have looked a little bewildered because he laughed and planted a kiss on the end of her nose.

"When? What exactly are you thinking about?"

He struck a swaggering John Wayne pose. "That would not be appropriate for me to say, ma'am."

She laughed at his pathetic impression, but quickly sobered. "This isn't something to joke about, Doug. Are you . . . are you seriously asking me to marry you?"

A shadow passed over his face. For one horrible minute she thought he was going to laugh at her for thinking he could have possibly been serious.

But he took both her hands in his, took a step back, and held her eyes with his. "I'm dead serious, Mickey. I've known true love, and I know that what I have with you couldn't be more true."

Could this really be happening? She'd dared to let herself dream about such a declaration from Doug, but she'd never thought it would come now—today. Joy inflated her until she thought she might float right out of Doug's reach. But his arms kept her tethered to earth, to the strong anchor of him.

One thought pricked at her, a slow leak that tempered her elation. "Are you sure, Doug? It hasn't been very long. Maybe you should . . . wait a while before you make such—declarations."

He squeezed her hands so tightly she almost winced. "Kaye's not coming back, Mickey. God put you in my life. I have no doubt of that. Why would I deny His gift?"

His words made her forget every rational reason that had been swimming in her head a moment ago. "I—can't think of a good reason." She tried to smile, but suddenly tears were too close. She pressed her lips together to keep from having a complete meltdown. *God, what are you doing here?* Doug was offering her the thing she'd prayed for all her life, and now she wasn't sure she was ready?

"Then marry me. Tomorrow."

"Tomorrow!" She yanked her hands from his grasp and pulled away. "That's not even funny, Doug."

He laughed. And catching her own reflection in the door of the microwave oven behind him, a look of horror still painting her face, she joined him. But it brought her to her senses. He might not be serious about "tomorrow," but he was serious about the "marry me" part, and if she said yes, her life was about to change in ways she probably couldn't even imagine. Wonderful ways, but change, nonetheless. And she'd never been great with change.

She backpedaled until she was leaning against the counter opposite him. "Could you please be serious for one minute?"

He took a step in her direction. "I am serious, Mickey. What do I have to do to convince you of that?"

"Stay away." She held up her hand to stop him. "I can't think straight with you so close."

"I rest my case," he said.

She trained her eyes on him. "Define tomorrow." She was starting to be frustrated with the perpetual twinkle in his eye.

"What do you mean?"

"You said, 'marry me tomorrow.' Define tomorrow."

As if to prove that he was making an effort to be serious now, he retreated to his corner of the boxing ring that her kitchen had become.

"Okay, you tell me. When's the first possible moment you could do this?"

"A . . . wedding you mean." He *was* serious. Yikes!

"Yes. A wedding. Doesn't have to be anything fancy."

She took a halting breath. She'd always dreamed of a big church wedding with all the trimmings. But that hardly seemed appropriate, considering Doug's circumstances. And really, besides her brothers and their families, and Brenda and the part-time girls at the daycare, who would she invite? Doug would probably have more guests than she would.

A small wedding wouldn't cost so much, either. She'd put most of her disposable income into her house and the garden. In fact, though she never touched her IRA, she'd almost drained her other little savings account paying to have five trees planted in the backyard last month. Still, that money would have been a drop in the bucket toward a big church wedding.

As if he could read her thoughts, Doug frowned. "How would you feel about a small wedding?"

She nodded slowly. "That would probably be best. But . . . define small."

He shot her another comical look and parroted her. "Define tomorrow. Define small. Do I look like a dictionary to you?" But he quickly held up a hand again. "Okay, okay . . . I'll be serious."

She kept a grin in check. "Thank you."

"I was thinking maybe just immediate family and a few other close friends."

"You do know I have three brothers and a ton of nieces and nephews. Do you count that as immediate family?"

"Of course." He thought for a minute. "So if we keep it that small, how soon do you think we could do this?"

She didn't have a clue how to calculate the answer to his question. She had a quick vision of years' worth of *Brides Magazine* checklists that all started with: *12 months before the wedding*. She didn't think that was what he had in mind. She clicked off calendar pages in her mind. It was April. An autumn wedding would give them six months. That would be cutting it close, but she could probably do it. Somewhere in her closet she had some files for wedding plans she'd made . . . before she'd given up hope.

"How about October?" As soon as she said it, she wanted to retract it.

He gave her an incredulous look. "October? Are you crazy?"

"What?" Maybe twelve months was how he defined "tomorrow."

"I'm not waiting that long, Mickey. I love you, the kids adore you. It makes no sense to wait."

This didn't seem like the time to bring up the fact that Kayeleigh didn't exactly adore her. Mickey ran a hand through her hair. "Then give me a date," she huffed. "I don't know what page you're on."

He crossed the kitchen in two strides and took her in his arms again. "I'm on the page that makes you my wife at the first possible moment. What could possibly take six months?"

She tilted her head to study him. "You didn't have much to do with making your wedding plans, did you?" She looked away and softened her voice. "With Kaye . . ."

He shrugged. "I plead the Fifth. She and her mom had things pretty well under control. My job was to stay out of the way."

"So when did you two get engaged?"

He studied her. "You really want to talk about this?"

They hadn't exactly avoided the subject of Kaye in the past. But certain aspects of it—the romantic part of their relationship—had sort of been the elephant in the room between them. But it was time to acknowledge it. "Yes, I really want to know."

He pulled a stool out from under the counter, but instead of sitting on it, he placed it between them, leaning on the counter and propping his feet on one of the rungs. "We picked out Kaye's ring at Christmas and—" A sheepish look came over him. "Oh, I suppose *you'd* like a ring? An engagement ring, I mean."

She raised a brow. "That would be a nice touch."

Doug straightened and reached behind him to slide open a long, narrow drawer that held boxes of aluminum foil and plastic wrap. Holding her gaze, he rummaged through the drawer and after a minute, triumph sparked in his eyes. "Ah-ha!" He pulled a plastic silver twist tie from the drawer and held it up.

"Come here." He took her hand and motioned her to sit on the stool. "Give me your hand."

She held out her left hand and sat motionless while he wrapped the twist tie around her ring finger. His mouth worked as he fashioned a diamondlike knot from the wired ends of the twist tie. Stifling a giggle, she looked up to meet dead-serious blue eyes. He held her hand tighter, until the wire from the twist tie pinched.

"Mickey Valdez, would you do me the honor of marrying me?"

"Oh, Doug."

He winked. "Saturday we'll go shopping . . . for the real thing."

"O . . . kay . . ."

"I haven't gotten an answer yet."

She grinned. "I'm thinking."

"And October is way too far away."

"When, then?"

He wasn't wasting any time. "We can talk more about dates Saturday . . . nail something down. But first I have to have an answer."

"Yes," she whispered.

He wrapped her in his arms, then, his touch sucking the breath from her, leaving her light-headed. Doug may not have worked as an EMT for a while, but he hadn't lost his skills, and he quickly resuscitated her with mouth-to-mouth.

He'd set
something in motion
with Mickey tonight
that would change his
life forever. And not
just his, but his kids'.
And Mickey's.

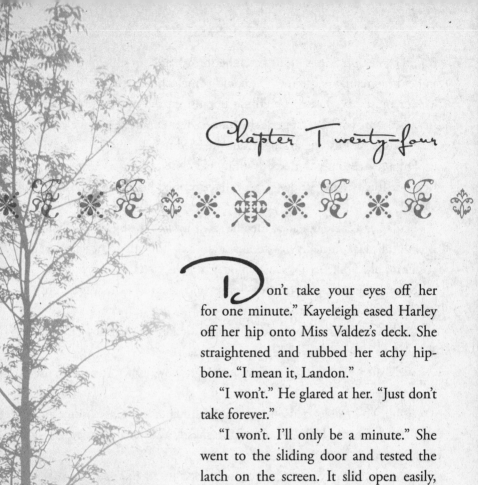

Chapter Twenty-four

"Don't take your eyes off her for one minute." Kayeleigh eased Harley off her hip onto Miss Valdez's deck. She straightened and rubbed her achy hipbone. "I mean it, Landon."

"I won't." He glared at her. "Just don't take forever."

"I won't. I'll only be a minute." She went to the sliding door and tested the latch on the screen. It slid open easily, and she stepped into the kitchen. It took a minute for her eyes to adjust from the bright sunlight, but when she became accustomed to the dim light, she froze right where she was standing.

Dad and Miss Valdez stood at the stove, tangled in each other's arms, breathing hard and making out like a couple of characters in the stupid soap operas Grandma watched.

She tried to clear her throat, but no

sound came out. She couldn't catch her breath and, in spite of the voice in her head telling her to run, she couldn't make her feet move. But Miss Valdez must have heard something because in the middle of messing up Dad's hair with her fingers, she looked over at Kayeleigh and gave a strangled gasp. Pushing against Dad, she tried to get loose.

For a few seconds Dad kept pulling her closer, trying to keep kissing her, but finally Miss Valdez practically screamed his name. "Doug . . . Doug!"

Dad's head came up, and when he saw Kayeleigh, he blew out a heavy breath. His face turned forty-six shades of red. The only time she'd ever seen him blush like that was when he was mad.

Miss Valdez straightened her clothes and acted like she was all busy pouring hot water into teacups.

Dad moved to the opposite side of the kitchen. "What do you need, Kayeleigh?" He sounded like he was mad at her.

Well, she wasn't too happy with him right now, either. "I need to use the bathroom."

"Oh!" Miss Valdez put on her bright-and-cheery teacher's voice and pointed down the hallway. "Go right ahead. You remember where it is . . . last door on the right."

Kayeleigh finally got her feet to work and all but ran down the hall.

"The light switch is right over the sink, honey," Miss Valdez called after her.

Kayeleigh shut the door on the fakey, chipper voice. "Don't call me honey." She hissed the words between clenched teeth, wishing they'd hear her, but knowing they couldn't. She stood in the dark, trying to think what to do. Her own cheeks grew warm, then hot.

She groped for the sink, turned on the cold water, and splashed her face. What did *she* have to be embarrassed about? She hadn't done anything wrong. They were the ones who should feel guilty.

Through the door she could hear them talking, their voices low and hurried. Like they were trying to figure out how they were going to explain everything when she came out of the bathroom.

She was no dummy. She knew what they'd been doing, and it made her want to puke. Maybe she'd just stay in here forever. It was pitch dark in the bathroom, but she held her hands out in front of her. She couldn't see her fingers, but she could feel them trembling.

She fumbled around on the wall, looking for the light switch. What was Dad *doing*? Why was he acting like this with that dumb woman? She was so mad at him she thought she might explode. Had he forgotten about Mom already?

She wanted to hit something. Instead, she finally located the light switch and used the toilet. She washed her hands twice and dried them on the fancy towel that wasn't much bigger than a washcloth. She turned off the light again and stood by the door trying to listen for Dad and Miss Valdez. They were quiet now. Maybe they'd gone outside.

She opened the door a crack and looked down the hallway, listening again. Silence. She crept down the hall and peeked into the kitchen. Empty. The curtains covering the sliding doors had been pushed all the way open, and she could see Dad and Miss Valdez sitting on the deck with their tea, acting like nothing had happened.

She wasn't about to go out there. Harley was playing on the steps to the deck, singing and talking to herself. Miss Valdez was keeping an eye on her, and Dad was right there. Kayeleigh tiptoed away from the doors and walked through Miss Valdez's house to the front door. She let herself out and walked to the Suburban parked at the curb. She climbed into the backseat and sat there, her back stiff against the dingy upholstery, her thoughts totally messed up.

She heard a noise across the street and saw some kids come out of the house across from Miss Valdez's. She slunk down in the seat, praying they hadn't seen her.

When her muscles ached from the awkward slumped position, she slowly eased her legs up onto the bench seat and curled into a fetal position. She closed her eyes and forced herself to think about other things—allowed herself to daydream about Seth Berger kissing her the way Dad had kissed Miss Valdez.

She wondered if Seth ever thought about that night they'd danced together at Vienne Kenney's wedding. Did he think about it as much as she did . . . which was pretty much all the time? He'd been flirting with her at school. At least Rudi called it flirting when Seth starting acting crazy any time she was around, making jokes and even getting in trouble with the teachers because he was trying to make her laugh in the middle of class.

She got in trouble with the teacher once when he was goofing off, making her laugh. She couldn't help it. The guy was funny. Seth had been really nice to her after class that day, like he was trying to let her know he was sorry for getting her in trouble. She didn't care about that. Mrs. Lawson was stupid anyway.

She wished Mom were here to talk to. That thought brought back the image of Dad kissing Miss Valdez, and her stomach went all queasy.

A tree branch brushed the roof of the Suburban. Back and forth, back and forth. She felt herself drifting toward sleep in the quiet warmth of the vehicle. A part of her wished she could just go to sleep and never wake up.

※ ※ ※

Doug pulled into the garage and turned off the engine. Barking orders to the kids, he opened his door and got out, then slammed it, hoping it would wake up Kayeleigh. She'd scared him half to death disappearing like that. He and Mickey had searched for her for ten minutes before he'd thought to look in the Suburban. He hadn't chewed her out because he knew why she'd gone into hiding.

She crawled out of the backseat now, shooting him a look of contempt as she swept past. He sighed. He'd have to talk to her about what happened . . . what she'd seen. Well, of course. He'd have to talk to all the kids. He was engaged. They needed to know that. And the sooner the better since he'd pretty much given Mickey permission to tell the world. Oh brother . . . that meant he'd have to call Harriet, too. Well, fine. Now she had a legitimate reason for running off to Florida.

Engaged. It had sounded like such a good idea when Mickey was in his arms and they were making plans. But now, in the dim light of the messy garage, with Kayeleigh glaring at him, it didn't fit quite so comfortably.

A sinking feeling gathered in his gut, and he yanked Harley's seatbelt harder than necessary. She jammed a thumb in her mouth and looked at him from beneath a rutted brow.

"Come on, punkin, let's get you to bed." He tried to make amends with his voice. It wasn't Harley's fault he was out of sorts.

Forty-five minutes later, with all the kids in bed, he sank down on the sofa. He kicked off his boots and, with one stockinged toe, nudged a stack of dirty dishes to one corner of the coffee table before propping his feet on its sticky surface. He needed to regroup. He'd set something in motion with Mickey tonight that would change his life forever. And not only his, but his kids'. And Mickey's.

There were a million questions to be answered. Would she come here to live? Her house wasn't big enough for all of them, but he couldn't imagine her giving up the garden she'd worked so hard to create. Looking around their house . . . *his* house. He had to quit thinking in terms of *they* and *we,* meaning him and Kaye.

Trying to see this house through Mickey's eyes, he cringed inwardly. The place was in shambles. Kaye never would have earned any "world's tidiest housekeeper" awards. With six kids and a part-time job, he'd never expected her to. But without her to do even a modicum of housekeeping, things had gone beyond "cluttered" and straight to "filthy." With the crazy schedule he was keeping between the farmwork and the pressroom, he'd let things go.

He would have to do something drastic—and soon—if he didn't want Mickey to run screaming from the house next time she was here. She'd only been to the house that one time she brought the kids home. Looking back, he thought that was the night he'd first started thinking of her *that way*. She'd made him realize how desperately he'd missed a feminine voice in the house, in his world, at the end of a long workday.

Was he disloyal to have felt that way so soon after Kaye's death? But it was his very belief in God, in an eternity in heaven, that never allowed him to entertain thoughts Kaye could come back—or would even want to. Wasn't that a healthy attitude? Wasn't he just being realistic?

And he had his kids to think of. Except for Kayeleigh, they'd had a special place in their hearts for Mickey—Miss Mickey—for half their lives. And he had no doubt Mickey would win Kayeleigh over eventually. They needed a mother—Kayeleigh especially—and Mickey was already as close to being "Mommy" as anyone besides Kaye could ever be. The other details—the wedding plans, their housing situation, Kayeleigh's attitude—those would all work themselves out with time.

Like an idiot, he'd promised Mickey they'd go ring shopping Saturday. She didn't strike him as a woman with expensive taste, but even if she picked out the cheapest diamond chip in the store, how was he going to pay for it? He'd have to call tomorrow and see how much available credit he had on his MasterCard. He'd paid it off when Kaye's life insurance check came. But since then he'd struggled to pay it off every month. If he maxed it out paying for a ring, then he had nothing for emergencies. Or the wedding. Who knew what that would set him back? Mickey's parents were gone, and he didn't get the impression she had a lot of money. And what if—?

No. He snatched the TV remote from the cluttered coffee table, clicked the power button hard. The drone of a sitcom laugh track shut off the gush of thoughts, and he settled back on the lumpy cushion.

She was as down-
to-earth as they came.
He liked that about
her. She was the best
of all worlds.

Chapter Twenty-five

"Ooh, what about this one?" Mickey bent over the jewelry case and tapped a pink fingernail on the glass. She'd confessed that she paid thirty dollars for a manicure just for the occasion.

Doug shrugged. "It's nice."

She looked up at him over one shoulder. "But you don't like it?"

"It's whatever you want, Mick. You're the one who's going to be wearing it."

"For the rest of my life."

Why did those words unsettle him?

Because the rest of Kaye's life was so short.

He put a possessive hand on the small of Mickey's back, reminding himself who he was with. Mickey looked beautiful today, her hair long and shiny around her shoulders. He was proud to have her on his arm. If she'd had any idea how beautiful she was, she would surely have thought herself out of his league. Instead she was as down-to-earth as they came. He liked that about her. She was the best of all worlds. And he was blessed to be here shopping for a ring to place on her finger.

"Have you found anything you'd like to try on?" The sales associate who'd first waited on them was back after helping another customer.

Mickey dismissed her sweetly. "Not yet, thanks."

The young woman spoke to Doug over Mickey's head. "Let me know if you have any questions."

"Thanks, we will."

When she went to greet another customer, Mickey elbowed Doug. "They're all so expensive," she whispered.

He'd been thinking the same thing, but told her what he thought she'd want to hear. "You're worth it. You pick out what you like. Within reason . . ."

"I don't think anything in this case is within reason, Doug."

"Well, you've got to have a ring. We need rings." He never had put his wedding band—the one Kaye had placed on his finger thirteen years ago—back on since that day he'd taken it off at the bowling alley. He'd tucked it away in his dresser drawer with some other keepsakes. But his finger still bore an indention from the ring. He rubbed at the band of white skin encircling his tanned, leathery hands. He wasn't sure if he should tell Mickey that the money for their rings would probably come from what was left of Kaye's and Rachel's life insurance, after the funeral costs, of course.

He brushed off the morbid thoughts. "You need a wedding ring," he said again.

Mickey held out her left hand. "It doesn't have to be a diamond though, Doug. What if I lost it out in the garden?"

"You'd wear it to garden in?" He wondered where she thought she was going to garden. But they hadn't had the where-will-we-live conversation yet.

"Probably not, but what if I forgot? What if it slipped off in a bag of manure and got buried with a barberry bush or something?"

He laughed. "You sound like you've already got it all planned out."

"No, but if we spent two thousand dollars on a ring"—she nodded toward the jewelry case where that was one of the lower price tags—"I'd be scared to ever wear it."

"Well . . . what, then?"

"We could just get wedding bands. Thin silver bands."

The tightness in his chest eased a little. He wasn't sure where two thousand bucks would come from. "Is that what you want?"

She bent and perused the jewelry case again. "I thought I wanted a diamond, but"—she tossed her head in the direction of the jewelry store—"that's a lot of money. I can think of other things I'd rather spend it on."

"Like what?"

She shrugged, looking sheepish. "Well, it's not exactly my money to spend."

He put an arm around her waist and steered her toward the front door. "Let's go get a cup of coffee and talk some things through."

She raised a questioning brow at him and trailed him out to the sidewalk. A Saturday's worth of vehicles lined Santa Fe in front of the jewelry store. He shaded his eyes and looked across the street. "Isn't there a coffee shop in the next block?"

She nodded and led the way south. A few minutes later they had pretzels on order, and she was sipping some fancy coffee drink while he nursed a mug of black brew that didn't taste nearly as good as the Folgers he usually drank. Not to mention he could have bought three pounds of coffee beans for what he'd paid for their drinks.

Mickey rearranged her napkin under her coffee and angled her body toward him.

Pulling out the small notebook he kept in his back pocket, he repositioned his chair and leaned against the wall. "Let's work out some details, okay?"

Her eyes lit and she nodded like an eager puppy.

He slipped a ballpoint pen from his front pocket and jotted the words "wedding date" across the top of the narrow page.

She leaned across the table to read them.

"And the sooner the better." He touched her nose.

"Well . . . first we need to talk about where, and how many people, and what all we have to do before we can even have a wedding."

"Okay, where?" He made a row of *W*s down the side of the paper, turning the first one into *Where?*

"St. Mary's?" She hunched up her shoulders as if she expected him to challenge that.

He rubbed his chin. "I wouldn't have to . . . convert, would I? If we got married in your church?"

She shook her head. "I'm not sure. I guess we could ask Rick."

"Yeah, about that . . ." They'd planned to stop off at her brother's after they bought the rings to announce their engagement and reintroduce Doug to the brothers—Rick and Tony, anyway. Alex had called her cell phone on the way to Salina to say he couldn't make it. From her end of the conversation Doug could tell that Alex Valdez knew something was up, and he was trying to get it out of her. She just kept saying, "Rick and Tony can tell you all about it."

Doug had grown up knowing who the Valdez brothers were. Who didn't know the stars of the basketball and baseball teams? Rick still held some records at Clayburn High, Doug thought. But he doubted the brothers remembered him. Rick and Tony were out of high school by the time he got there, and Alex had been a senior when Doug was a freshman.

Still, he was more than a little nervous to meet Mickey's older brothers again under these circumstances. Mickey had told him she thought her brothers suspected the reason they were coming, but she wanted to keep them guessing.

"You don't think they're planning to kill me or anything, do you?"

She gave him a playful slug. "Quit worrying. They're going to love you as much as I do."

But he thought Mickey looked a little worried herself.

"Yeah, well, I guess we'll find out," he said.

She ignored him and went back to the topic of his conversion. "Maybe we can ask Angie about St. Mary's. She grew up there. She'd know. And she's a good Catholic."

He broached a subject they should have talked about long ago. "I don't think I could convert, Mick. And not the kids, for sure. Don't you guys have to promise to raise your kids in the church?"

"It's not really my church . . . not anymore. And I wouldn't ask you to, Doug. Convert, I mean. *Any* of you. I-I guess I'm not a very good Catholic."

He cocked his head. "What's with the 'good Catholic' stuff all of a sudden?" Mickey had seemed to like the worship service when she'd gone to church with him and the kids. She'd always talked about God like she knew Him, had a relationship with Him. That was all that mattered to Doug. He didn't care much about denominations. That was why he and Kaye had started going to Community Christian. It hadn't made Harriet too happy, but Kaye put her foot down, and Harriet eventually quit trying to get them back to the First Baptist church Kaye grew up in.

Mickey took a sip of her coffee, obviously a diversion tactic. "I didn't mean anything by it. I'm just thinking my brothers might not be too happy if I don't get married in the Church."

"They might not be too happy you're marrying a widower with five kids, either."

Her slow nod told him she agreed.

The waitress brought their pretzels and Doug squeezed mustard into the paper basket and took a bite before looking at the list again. "Okay, let's move to something else for now." He scooted the basket to one side and filled in the other *W*s on the paper. *Who, What, When.* "Hey, here's something we can fill in." Beside *Who*, he wrote Doug DeVore and Mickey Valdez. "And this . . ." He wrote the word *wedding* beside *What*.

"Yay! We're making progress!" She clapped loud enough to make the elderly women at the booth across the coffee shop turn to stare.

Laughing, he folded his hands over hers and eased them to the table. "Shhh!"

She looked embarrassed, but the twinkle remained in her eyes.

He dipped a hunk of pretzel in mustard and popped it in his mouth. "Okay, here's one." He hated to ruin the mood, but if he wanted to marry this woman, they had to get some things ironed out. "Where are we going to live?"

"Your house." She pointed to his list. "Write it down."

He let the ballpoint hover over the paper. "You're sure about that? You've been there, Mickey. You know what you'd be getting into."

"Well, sorry, but you guys aren't going to fit in my house. Unless you want to sleep in the garage."

"Be serious."

Her eyebrows went up. "Maybe I am."

He scooted his chair back from the table and leveled a stern look at her. "Mickey, I don't want you to regret this."

Her expression turned serious. "Okay. I'll admit I'd like . . . I wish we could find a house in town together. But we don't have to do that right now, do we? We can live at your place for a while . . . while we look."

"Fair enough." She'd said in town. Did he dare tell her he and Kaye had scrimped and saved to buy the farm he'd grown up on? He couldn't imagine ever leaving there. But now wasn't the time to bring that up.

She jabbed at the list. "Write it down."

He jotted *my house* at the bottom of the list and clicked the pen off.

But she nabbed it out of his hand, clicked it back on, and crossed out *my*. In its place she wrote *OUR* in big capital letters.

His chest swelled with warmth, and he reached across the table and ran a finger down the smooth plane of her cheek. "I love you."

Smiling, she reached to dab at the corner of his mouth with her napkin. "Mustard," she explained, kissing her fingers and transferring her kiss to the spot she'd just wiped.

"What would I do without you?" He made his voice light, but her simple action moved him more than he let on. In the same way Kaye had completed him, Mickey was the missing piece of his life. He'd always been a leader, a man's man. But in so many ways, he needed somebody to take care of him. Someone to baby him a little. Mickey did that. And he loved her for it. He longed for the day they were married.

"Okay, what's next?" Mickey poised the pen over their list again. "I know." She added another *W* to the list and turned it into *Why*.

"Why?"

She nodded, then scratched something on the list. When she was finished, she rotated the paper and pushed it over to his side of the table.

Because I love you, it said.

That did it. "Let's get married."

She eyed him suspiciously. "I thought that was the plan."

"No. I mean now. Right now. Let's go find a justice of the peace . . . or whatever it takes." He stabbed at the list. "None of this stuff matters, Mickey. If we try to solve all these questions, we'll still be trying to work out details a year from now. Let's just do it."

"Doug . . ." A deer-in-the-headlights look glazed her eyes. "You can't just get married on a . . . a whim."

"It's not on a whim. We've talked it out. We'd just be skipping all the stupid stuff. The expensive stuff—" He held up a hand. "And don't worry, I don't mean the ring. I want you to have a ring. We'll go back and get it today." He took her hand and caressed her fingers. "But do we really need a big, fancy wedding? Especially if it's going to cause trouble with your brothers and the Church . . . ?"

He waited for her to respond, trying to read her thoughts in her expression.

"I don't know, Doug." She still looked a little shell-shocked. "You don't mean 'today' literally, I hope."

He did, but maybe that was expecting too much. "Not today, but soon. Next weekend if we can. I'll call the courthouse and see what we need to do. Can you get a couple days off of work?"

She nodded. "But what about the kids?"

"What about them?"

"Would they—come with us?"

"Oh. No. Of course not. I'll figure something out. Maybe Wren can watch them for a couple days. We couldn't go to Hawaii or anything, but maybe we can plan a little getaway in Kansas City. Then next summer we'll do a real honeymoon. I promise."

She reached up and put a gentle finger over his lips. "Shhh. Don't make promises you might not be able to keep. We'll just take things as they come, okay?"

He nodded. She might really go for this. He was torn between relief and panic. If she was willing, they might be man and wife this time next week.

"I . . . I'd need to rent my house out . . . or"—she swallowed hard—"sell it."

"You could rent it out for now. We can decide what to do later. There's no need to rush into anything."

The outline of her tongue puffed out her cheek. "Um . . . excuse me, but isn't that exactly what you're talking about? Rushing into things?"

"You know what I mean. The piddly stuff. We can figure that out later. For now let's go pick out a ring. With what we'll be saving in wedding expenses, you can choose the biggest honkin' ring in the store."

"Oh, Doug." Her eyes lit up and she shivered with excitement.

He pushed back his chair and grabbed her hand. "Come on, babe, let's do this."

He planned to tell
the kids tonight.
But the prospect sent
a shudder of panic
through him.

Chapter Twenty-six

Doug pushed open the door to Wren's Nest and let it slam hard enough to jangle the bells, announcing his arrival. Wren's giant striped tabby cat sauntered around from behind the counter, but no Wren.

He inhaled the inn's distinctive scent of apples and cinnamon and fresh-brewed coffee, and his stomach grumbled. After a minute he cleared his throat and called Wren's name. He thought he heard a clothes dryer running and started around the counter to see if she was in the back.

The cat chose that moment to wrap its furry self around his leg. If it hadn't been for the counter catching his fall, Doug would have been flat on the floor, the stupid cat squashed beneath his weight. He gave the critter a gentle shove with the toe of his boot.

At that moment Wren Johannsen came

bustling out from the laundry room, a stack of folded, fluffy white towels cradled in her arms. "Douglas, I didn't know you were here. Goodness . . . have you been waiting long?" The cat transferred its affections to Wren, and she nudged it with a tiny foot. "Get out of the way, Jasper, you silly old cat."

"Just got here."

"Well, come on in the dining room. I've got a couple slices of Peaches and Cream Cheesecake in the refrigerator." She deposited the towels on the counter and led the way into the sunny dining room. "How are you?"

The note of sympathy that always accompanied that question was thick in Wren's voice, but somehow he didn't mind it so much coming from her. Wren had loved Kaye—and by proxy, him—like her own. In fact, she'd played matchmaker for them when they were barely out of high school and Kaye was helping Wren out at the inn.

"I'm doing good. How about you?" He folded himself into a chair underneath a too-small table, watching while she poured coffee and served up slices of her famous cheesecake.

When she joined him at the table, she made it easy for him. "Let me guess: you're needing somebody to watch those precious kiddos of yours?"

"As a matter of fact, I am."

Her eyes sparked with mischief. "It wouldn't have anything to do with a certain pretty Valdez girl, would it?"

He laughed. "I see the rumor mill is alive and well in Clayburn, USA."

Her expression turned serious. "Is it only a rumor?"

His smile apparently betrayed him.

"It's true then, Doug? You're . . . seeing Mickey Valdez?"

"I'm not just seeing her." He leaned across the table and lowered his voice. "We're getting married, Wren."

A plump hand flew to her bosom. "Married? You're joking."

"Not one bit. Friday, in fact. That's why I'm here, actually. I wanted to ask if you'd mind watching the kids while we take a couple days off for a honeymoon?"

"Doug . . . ? Friday? *This* Friday?"

Try as he would, he couldn't temper his smile. "We just decided to go for it."

She tilted her head and eyed him, no trace of the joy he'd expected from her at the news. "This Friday?" she said again.

It struck him then that maybe she was hurt not to be invited to the wedding. "We're being married by a justice of the peace," he said quickly. "In Salina. Just the two of us."

It had been an amazingly simple matter to obtain a marriage license this morning. The ceremony was set for Friday afternoon at two o'clock with Judge Miriam Rickard. The clerk who'd helped him with the license said they didn't even need to bring witnesses if they didn't want to. "We can get someone from the offices to stand in as witnesses for you," she'd said.

"We didn't want a big wedding," he told Wren now. "I'm sure you understand."

"Oh, Doug." She shook her silvery head slowly. "It's . . . so soon. So soon after Kaye and Rachel. Are you sure about this? Why, it's barely been . . ."

He could see her ticking off the months in her head, and saved her the trouble. "It'll be five months." Why was she doing this? Why did she feel the need to spoil his happiness?

"Not even five months? Oh, Douglas, don't rush into something, honey."

"I'm not, Wren," he assured her. "We're not. We've talked this through."

She seemed not to hear him but went on, her voice almost pleading. "You've been through so much. Give yourself time. It takes time to get over something like this. To fall in love again. It's too soon. It's just too soon."

He nodded, intending no commitment. He didn't want to hear what she had to say. He forked another bite of cheesecake. "This is good stuff."

Wren reached up to pat his cheek—a gesture oddly reminiscent of Kaye. "I'm not saying Mickey doesn't love you, honey. Who wouldn't? But you need time to . . . process all this. And what about the kids? They—"

"Oh, the kids love Mickey." He grasped at the thin strand of reason she offered him. "And she loves them."

"I'm sure she does. But this will be quite an adjustment . . . for all of you." She picked at a crumb on the embroidered tablecloth. "Where will you live?"

He was winning her over, he could tell. "We'll live on my place. She's going to rent out her house. Say . . . you don't know anyone looking for a place to rent long-term, do you? Maybe with the option to buy?"

"Mickey's beautiful garden . . . she's going to let that go?"

He shrugged. "We're not sure. She might hang on to that. It'll depend on what the renters want."

He'd found out last night that it was killing Mickey to think of leaving her garden. She seemed to think she'd have time to keep it up after she moved out to his house. "I could just go there for a little while after work each evening," she'd told him. "So it doesn't go to pot."

Why she'd want to keep a garden for strangers, he didn't know. He'd suggested starting one at his place, but she hadn't seemed too enthusiastic about that. But they'd work it out. He had a feeling these things wouldn't even be important once they were married.

He scraped up the last of his cheesecake with one tine of his fork, and looked pointedly at the clock. "I need to get going. If you don't think it'll work for you and Bart to keep the kids, I can find someone else." He had no idea who that might be, especially with Harriet in the midst of packing up for her move, but he'd do what he had to do.

She pshawed and waved him off. "Of course we'll keep them. If you're sure this is what you want to do. But please, do think about it,

Doug. I-I feel a little responsible, since I was the one who got you two started."

"The Linders' wedding reception, you mean?" He'd almost forgotten it had been Wren who suggested he dance with Mickey that night. That really had been the start of all this.

Wren nodded. "Maybe I was a little too . . . eager to pair you two up."

"You played matchmaker for me and Kaye, too, as I recall. And look how that turned out." He forced a smile.

"Just promise me you'll pray about it, Doug. Maybe you should talk to Trevor. He's been where you are. He'll have some good advice. I'd hate to think I rushed you into something that wasn't God's design for you."

He gave a noncommittal grunt. It really wasn't any of her business.

Wren seemed not to notice and continued her lecture. "You know, if you decide to put it off, you can always get married later on. It's not quite so easy to get out of the opposite decision. Just promise me you'll pray about it," she said again. She gave him a smile that said *she* would be praying.

"Do you want them here, or would it be easier to come out to my place—*our* place?" Good grief. He'd finally trained himself to think in singular term, and now he'd need to get used to thinking of his home and possessions in plural terms again. *Theirs.* His and Mickey's.

"Whatever's easier for you. Maybe they'd like to come here. I only have one room filled for the weekend so far, so Kayeleigh could have a room to herself."

He grinned his appreciation and put Wren back in his good graces. Kayeleigh would be thrilled to stay at the inn. Maybe it would help temper her reaction to the news that he was marrying Mickey. He planned to tell the kids tonight. But the prospect sent a shudder of panic through him.

First he had to tell Mickey that they were on for Friday. The snowball was headed downhill and picking up speed fast. He rose and put a hand on Wren's shoulder. "Thank you, Wren. I owe you big-time."

"You don't owe me a thing, Douglas. I just want you to be happy. That's all anybody wants."

He chewed on that thought driving into town to work. To be happy. Wren had hit the nail on the head. That's all he really wanted. He'd lost so much. But when he was with Mickey he felt alive again. Regardless of the doubts Wren Johannsen had planted in his mind this morning, he surely deserved to know love again, to be happy again after all God had required of him.

And if *he* didn't, no one could argue that his children didn't deserve the love Mickey offered them.

✳ ✳ ✳

Kayleigh was just getting interested in the new reality show when Dad grabbed the remote out of Landon's hands and switched the TV off. "Listen, guys, everybody come in here. I've got something to tell you. On the couch. Come on, everybody. You can watch TV later."

"Harley, too, Daddy?" Sarah asked.

"Harley, too."

At that Harley squealed and toddled off to the kitchen.

"I'll get her." Kayleigh chased the baby down and carried her back to the living room where the twins and Landon sat in a row up on the sofa, as if they were sitting in church.

She propped the baby between Sarah and Sadie, then perched on the arm of the sofa. Dad sat on the coffee table facing them, one leg propped on the opposite knee. But one look at his face, and Kayleigh's heart stopped. He had the same serious expression he'd worn Thanksgiving Day . . . when he'd sat them down like this at Grandma's to tell them Mom and Rachel had died.

Kayeleigh wrapped her arms around herself and tried to keep her knees from trembling.

But everybody she loved was here. She sucked in a breath. Had something happened to Grandma Thomas? Or Seth? Had something happened to Seth Berger? But no, Dad didn't even know about her and Seth, and even if he had, he wouldn't call the other kids together for something like that.

Dad scooted back on the coffee table and cocked his head, his serious expression changing into a smile. Kayeleigh breathed a little easier at that. He almost looked embarrassed . . . like that time when Mom caught him eating the cookies she'd baked for Vacation Bible School. They'd gotten in a big fight about it. She overheard and came into the kitchen where Mom was chewing Dad out and he was trying to apologize, but she wasn't forgiving him. It had taken all of Kayeleigh's courage, but she finally shouted to get their attention. "You guys! Does it make a whole lot of sense to be fighting about *Bible* school?"

For some reason, that had cracked them both up, and the next thing she knew, they were doubled over laughing, and then in each other's arms hugging and kissing like the fight had never happened. And like they'd forgotten she was even in the room.

The memory made her feel warm inside.

"I've got some news to tell you guys," Dad said, snapping her back to the present. "Good news."

She straightened and leaned forward. Maybe Bindy was going to have puppies again! But no, that couldn't be it. Dad had taken her to the vet after the last batch, because Mom said they could barely afford to feed their kids, without having puppies to buy food for, too.

"Miss Valdez—" Dad cleared his throat. "Miss Mickey and I are engaged."

The clock on the wall ticked into the silence as the kids looked at each other.

Finally Sadie turned to Dad, her forehead wrinkled. "You mean engaged . . . like you're gonna get married?"

Landon poked her with an elbow. "What'd you think, dummy?"

Dad didn't even yell at Landon for calling his sister a dummy. Instead he smiled really big. "That's right. We're getting married."

Kayeleigh's breath caught. She could barely wrap her brain around *engaged.* But *married*?

"In fact," Dad said, sounding all happy, "we're getting married this Friday. Mickey's going to come and live here and be . . ."

No way! He couldn't be serious.

Dad looked at her, then, and she somehow knew that he'd been about to say, "and be your mom." But he let his words trail off. It was a good thing, too, or she would have slapped him. Hard. Right across the face.

Sarah and Sadie started bouncing up and down on the sofa cushions, and Harley laughed and clapped her hands together. The baby couldn't understand what Dad had said. And the twins were just excited because they liked Miss Valdez. They didn't understand what it meant. That their teacher would be with Dad . . . the way Mom was.

She hugged herself tighter, her stomach churning. Her breath wouldn't come, and she clutched the upholstery of the sofa arm, praying for courage. "You're not . . . serious?" she finally managed to squeak out.

"Of course I am, Kaye."

"Don't call me that!"

Dad looked like he didn't even realize he'd called her by Mom's name. He did it all the time lately.

"What about Mom?"

"Kayeleigh . . ." He reached to touch her knee.

She recoiled and shoved his hand away. "You don't even care!"

"What are you talking about?" He crossed his arms over his chest like he did when she was in trouble. But his voice was soft. "Of course I care, Kayeleigh. I wouldn't be talking to you about this if I didn't care."

She didn't know what that had to do with anything.

Beside her, Sadie jumped off the couch, still grinning like an idiot. "Is Miss Valdez gonna have a wedding dress like Mama's?"

Kayeleigh pushed her down to the sofa. The chain reaction caused Harley to flop over onto Sarah's lap.

"Hey . . . !"

"Shut up, Sadie." Kayeleigh tried hard to keep the tears from her voice. "Don't you get it? Dad's betraying her!"

"Kayeleigh. Why would you say something like that?" Dad got a hurt look in his eyes.

She looked away.

"Kayeleigh? Honey, look at me."

She glanced up, just enough to keep from getting in trouble, then planted her eyes in her lap.

Dad patted her knee gently and spoke in a whisper. "I loved your mother more than you will know. She was—" His voice broke.

Kayeleigh's heart broke with it.

Dad put a finger under her chin and lifted it until she couldn't avoid his eyes. "Honey, there will never be anyone like your mom. No one can ever, ever take her place. But . . . she's gone. And we have to go on with our lives."

Kayeleigh tried to swallow, but it felt like there was a butcher knife lodged in her throat. "You're betraying Mom." Her voice came out in a monotone. "You're betraying all of us."

"What's that? Be-train?" Sarah juggled Harley into her lap.

"Nobody is betraying anybody." Dad's voice turned hard now, and his glare pinned her to the spot. "And I don't want to hear any more talk like that."

She slid off the arm of the sofa and swept past him, jaw clenched as she scrambled up the stairs to her room. She didn't care *what* the Bible said. She would never forgive him as long as she lived. Never.

On his wedding
night he wept for
all he'd lost.

Chapter Twenty-seven

"I, Michaela, take you, Douglas, to be my husband." Mickey looked up into Doug's eyes, her voice echoing in the dim courtroom. "To have and to hold, in sickness and in health, for richer, or for poorer—"

Doug winked at her on the word *poorer,* and she almost snickered. Avoiding his eyes, she stared into the empty gallery over his shoulder and finished making the same promise to him that he'd made to her. "In all that life brings our way, before God and man, I promise to love only you as long as we both shall live."

As of this day, she had an anniversary to celebrate. *April 27.* It would be a day marked in red on her calendar—*their* calendar—for the rest of her life.

The judge, who could've easily passed herself off as a college coed, turned to Doug. "You have rings to exchange?" She

215

asked it the way she might have asked if he had change for a dollar.

He nodded and fished in the pocket of his suit coat for Mickey's wedding band. They'd had the rings sized and had only picked them up on the way to the courthouse this afternoon. Mickey ran her finger over the diamond engagement ring she'd been wearing for all of an hour.

Doug came up with both wedding bands and pressed his ring into Mickey's palm.

"You first." The judge nodded at Doug. "You may place the ring on her finger."

Mickey tried to keep her hand from shaking while Doug worked the plain wedding band over her knuckles. She'd treated herself to a manicure yesterday. But no amount of nail polish or hand cream could camouflage hands that were work-worn from constant washing at the daycare, not to mention the garden dirt she was sure had worked itself into her very pores.

Doug didn't seem to notice. She could feel his emotion as the thin silver band slipped over her knuckles and into place. She fiddled with her engagement ring, residing for now on her right ring finger.

Doug wrapped his hands around hers. She swallowed hard and took the plain matching band of silver they'd picked out for him on Saturday. She slid it onto his left ring finger, letting her hand rest on his for a long moment.

Doug clasped her hands again, and they stood there, waiting for Judge Rickard to read the little blurb they'd found online about the rings.

The judge cleared her throat and slipped the sheet of paper from the thin manual she held. "The wedding ring is an outward, visible symbol of the unbroken circle of love." She read the words with all the emotion she might use for a legal brief. "It signifies to the world that this man and this woman have pledged their loyalty to one another before God. Wear these rings in remembrance of one another and in respect for the covenant of marriage."

The young woman turned a page in the manual and froze. She leafed back through the booklet, confusion shadowing her face. After more page turning, she shrugged and gave them a sheepish smile. "Oops. Looks like the vows were supposed to come before the rings. No big deal. I think we're still legal."

Doug looked at Mickey, a silent apology written on his face.

But the judge's voice warmed, and she found a smile for them before asking the age-old question of each. "Do you take this man (this woman)? To be your husband (to be your wife)?"

"I do," Mickey said.

"I do," Doug echoed, his eyes swimming.

And for that one moment, everything about this day felt right.

✳ ✳ ✳

Their hotel was at the edge of town, with traffic from I-70 zooming by the overpass above. The room Doug had reserved was at the end of the narrow hallway. When he unlocked the door for Mickey, the stench of stale cigarette smoke and dirty socks hit her in the face. She breathed through her mouth and went to try to open a window while Doug double-locked the doors.

She was fumbling with the controls on the heating and cooling unit when she felt his arms on her shoulders. "Hey, Mrs. DeVore . . ."

Ever since they'd picked out the rings last Saturday, she'd practiced writing her new name—*Michaela DeVore*—in a fancy, flowing script. But somehow, hearing him call her that now startled her. She was a *Mrs.* now. *Mrs. Douglas DeVore. Mickey DeVore.* In her thoughts the name fit awkwardly, like a jacket she'd borrowed from someone else.

"Come here, you." Doug pulled her toward him, his voice husky. "I love you. You know that?"

She straightened and turned into him, nodding against his chest. She hadn't expected to be so nervous about this night. She was thirty years old. She'd read plenty of books and magazine articles, talked with her married girlfriends about this part of marriage. Since that first passionate kiss, Doug made no secret about his desire for her. But he'd respected her desire to save herself. For him.

But now that the moment was here, she felt shy and unsure of herself.

He seemed to sense her tension and rubbed slow circles on her back, through the fabric of her silk shirt. He kissed her hair, murmured in her ear. She could feel the desire, the urgency in his caresses. What if she was a disappointment to him? What if . . . things didn't work the way they were supposed to?

She thought of the brief ceremony this afternoon and how different it had been from what she'd dreamed of. Since she was a little girl, she'd wanted to wear a big white dress and have five bridesmaids and a church full of people. Instead, she'd worn an ordinary black skirt and this cream-colored silk shirt. She'd only worn it for a few hours . . . and now Doug was fumbling with the top button.

She pulled away. "I—let me go wash up." She reached for her overnight bag. "I'll be right back."

He smiled and slid his hands down her arms. "I'll be here."

In the bathroom she inspected her face in the mirror. Her makeup had faded, and dark circles smudged the crescents under her eyes. Her hair had turned into a frizzled mop. She would make him turn the lights off before—

She unzipped her makeup case, retrieved her toothbrush, and turned on the faucet. The water ran hot, steaming up the mirror. She brushed her teeth until she was afraid her gums would bleed. Finally she couldn't stall any longer.

Stepping out of her clothes, she averted her eyes from the mirror and hurriedly slipped into the honeymoon negligee she'd bought at Walmart last week. Risking one quick glimpse at her image through the haze of steam, she turned off the bathroom light, took a shallow breath, and opened the door.

The room was dark, lit only by the dim glow of the lamp by the door. Doug was sitting on the edge of the bed, forearms resting on his knees. He took one look at her and crossed the room to take her in his arms. "Are you okay?"

She took a wavering breath and buried her face in his shoulder. "I . . . I'm scared to death." The tears came and she couldn't seem to hold them back. "You . . . this isn't new for you."

"No. Not in one way." He tightened his arms around her. "But it's new with you."

"What if I don't know . . . what to do?"

"You'll know." She heard the tender smile in his voice.

But he'd been with a woman who'd had years to learn how to make him happy. How could he help but compare her to Kaye? And how could she not come up short? Kaye had been so vivacious, had always seemed so self-confident.

He put a hand on top of her head and tipped it back, seeking her eyes.

She locked her gaze with his, holding on for dear life.

He captured her hand in his. Asking permission with his eyes, he led her to the other side of the bed. She sat on the edge of the mattress, and he knelt in front of her.

"It's okay, babe," he whispered. "We'll go slow. I promise. We'll take as much time as you need. We have a lifetime to figure it out. Together."

※ ※ ※

Sunlight seeped through the crevice between the halves of the heavy hotel draperies. Doug threw his arm over the womanly form breathing softly beside him. He pulled her close and pressed his forehead against her back. Only half awake, he grasped at the memories playing through his mind like a jerky movie trailer. There was Kaye, smiling her million-dollar smile, trying to tell him something. But her laughter was drowned out by the dispassionate voice of a female judge. "By the authority vested in me in the State of Kansas, I pronounce that you are man and wife."

He started and rolled over, then sat up in bed, squinting through the darkness to read the numbers on the digital clock on the hotel nightstand. Seven fifty-four. Beside him in the bed Mickey's dark hair floated over the white pillowcase in waves. He shook his head, trying to clear the disturbing dream.

He was married. Again. He'd been given a new chance at happiness. But last night had been a shaky start to his life with Mickey Valdez. She'd been like a frightened child. Her apprehension, and the gift she offered him, touched him deeply, and he'd found it easy to be patient with her. She warmed to his kisses, and the love they made was sweet and gentle. Like his first time with Kaye.

When they finished, with Mickey sleeping in his arms, unexpected tears had come. Tears for Kaye. He missed her so desperately in that moment. And he could never share with Mickey how he'd longed for his wife—for Kaye—even while holding his new bride in his arms.

On his wedding night, he wept for all he'd lost. For Rachel, and for the life that had been stolen from him.

He wept because, no matter how hard he wished it so, Mickey was not—and never would be—Kaye.

God had given her
exactly what she'd
always dreamed of.
So why did she feel
so ambivalent?

Chapter Twenty-eight

Mickey pressed the doorbell again, then clasped her hands together, trying to rehearse a speech she hadn't yet written in her mind.

"You're nervous." Behind her, Doug put his hands on her shoulders and massaged her taut muscles. Any other time she would have appreciated it, but right now she had to fight the urge to shake him off.

"A little bit."

Grinning, he put a hand on the back of her neck and kissed her temple. "You were nervous Friday night, too, and look how that turned out."

She felt the heat creep up her neck, but secretly she was glad he'd teased her about that night. He'd seemed quiet, preoccupied since they'd first . . . made love. She'd almost worried that he was disappointed. It was good to hear him imply that things had turned out okay.

But right now her fears about her brother took center stage, and she wouldn't allow Doug to change the subject. "I just don't know how Rick is going to take this."

"You promised they wouldn't kill me, remember?"

"Would you stop it, Doug!" She hadn't meant to snap at him and patted his arm in apology. "I'm sorry . . . but that's not helping."

She and Doug had stopped by her brother's house last weekend after they'd picked out the rings. But no one was home, and she'd decided later it might have been a case of divine intervention. She'd talked about Doug and the kids to her brothers, and a little more to Angie, but she'd never let on how close she and Doug had become. For all they knew, he was just a good friend she'd had a few dates with. After they'd decided to get married so quickly, she'd talked Doug into waiting to tell her brothers until after they were married. Now she regretted the decision.

She reached for the doorbell again, but the door flew open and Angie stood there smiling. "Mickey! Come on in." She looked past her and gave Doug a polite smile.

"Angie, this is Doug DeVore."

"Welcome, Doug. We've heard so much about you. It's about time Mickey brought you around so we could meet you. Come on in."

She led them inside. "Alex and Tony won't be here until after dinner. They had to change some plans since this isn't our regular weekend to get together." She turned and shouted up the stairway. "Rick! Mickey's here. He's getting Emmy up from her nap," she explained.

"Oh, good. I was hoping she'd be awake." She turned to Doug. "Wait till you see this baby." Emmy would give them something to talk about. And maybe serve as a buffer.

An infant's coos floated down to them, and Rick appeared at the top of the stairs with Emmy in his arms.

"Hey, baby sister. There you are. We were starting to think you weren't going to show up." He descended the stairs to plant a kiss on her cheek, handing the baby over to her. Like Angie had, he threw a polite nod Doug's way and stood there waiting for Mickey to introduce them.

She gave Emmy a squeeze and breathed in the heady baby scent. "Rick, Angie, this is Doug." She took another deep breath and affected an enigmatic smile. "This is . . . my husband." She'd intended to wait and tell all her brothers at once, but there the words were.

Her brother and his wife exchanged looks that said "Did I miss something?"

"Doug and I . . . got married Friday." Mickey tried to inject a cheer she didn't feel into her voice. "We're on our way home from our honeymoon, actually. That's why we asked if you could change the date."

"What?" Rick's gray-frosted eyebrows knit in a frown. "You're not serious, Michaela." It was a statement, not a question. And she was in trouble when he called her by her given name. He was taking it about like she'd expected, though.

Doug stepped forward and offered his hand. "It's true. I'm the lucky man. It's good to meet you . . . well, to see you again. You won't remember me, I'm sure," he explained, "but I was an admiring fan back when you played basketball at CHS. Saw a couple of Marymount games when you were playing for them, too."

Mickey could have kissed him right there. If there was any way to worm his way into Rick's good graces, talking about his old basketball days was a good start.

Rick shook Doug's hand, and Mickey saw the fury that had been boiling beneath his dark complexion subside a little. Still, he didn't acknowledge Doug beyond the handshake and turned to Mickey instead. "Is it true? Are you really *married?*"

"We are, Rick."

"Um . . . I don't recall getting an invitation." He wasn't smiling.

"We didn't want a big wedding, Rick. It was . . . just the two of us."

"You didn't get married in the Church, I take it."

A terrifying thought occurred to her. Would her brother try to get them to annul the marriage because the ceremony had been performed outside the Church? She hurried to explain. "We were married by a judge, Rick. I told you guys about Doug's situation." She turned to include Angie. "We wanted to keep things as simple as possible. We . . . we love each other, and I love Doug's children. We feel like this is what God wanted for us."

A row of ridges furrowed Rick's brow. "I'm not sure I would presume to know what God wanted."

Mickey prayed for Doug to jump in and take up their defense, but he stood there, scrubbing at the carpet with the toe of his boot.

Rick's dark eyes narrowed. "It would have been nice to have been invited. Who walked you down the aisle?" His voice held deep hurt.

Mickey realized then that her brother had always, rightfully, presumed it would be him who would perform that duty.

"There . . . wasn't exactly an aisle. We got married in the courthouse. On Friday." She shifted Emmy to her other hip. "Rick, I'm happy. Can't you just be happy for me?"

The baby squirmed in her arms, and Mickey clicked her tongue and cooed, trying to keep her content, praying Rick would come around.

Angie put a hand on her husband's arm. "Rick, please . . ." She turned to Doug and Mickey. "We are very happy for you, both of you." Her expression begged them to excuse Rick's rudeness.

But he shrugged Angie off with a scowl, not acknowledging her congratulations.

"Why don't we go into the kitchen? Dinner is almost ready. Mickey, you can keep me company while I get things on the table." Angie left them no choice but to follow her through the great room into the large sunny kitchen.

Rick and Angie's two youngest boys came up from the basement playroom as they settled around the kitchen table. "Aunt Mickey!"

"Hi, guys. How's it going?"

Ricky ran to give her a hug, but the six-year-old stopped short when he saw Doug sitting beside her.

"Guys, this is my husband, Doug. He's your Uncle Doug now."

"You guys go back downstairs," Rick barked. "We'll call you up when lunch is ready."

The boys flinched as if they were being punished, but they held Doug with curious stares as they slinked backward toward the stairs.

Lunch was an awkward affair with the children misbehaving and the adults tiptoeing around the one thing they were obviously all thinking about. Doug tried to make conversation, but after Rick rebuffed him several times, he finally gave up and concentrated on the huge plate of food Angie had set in front of him.

By the time Tony and Alex showed up, Mickey was ready to throttle her brother. Fortunately, eight kids and a fussy baby created enough distraction that they managed to dodge any discussion of her brothers' opinions about her marriage.

They ate homemade ice cream in the backyard, but as soon as Doug's bowl was empty, Mickey made excuses to leave.

"You call me," Rick said pointedly as they walked to the car. "We'll talk." He gave Doug a nod that Mickey knew well enough to interpret as "I have a few things to say to you, too, buddy."

She could well imagine the conversation that ensued between her brothers and their wives once she and Doug pulled out of the driveway in his pickup.

The drive home—to their first night together in Doug's house—was spent in silence. She guessed he was trying to imagine the next family dinner at the Valdez zoo, with his five kids added to the mix. Of course, given the way Rick was handling things, they might not be invited.

She swallowed back tears at the thought. Surely Rick would eventually get used to the idea that she was married. Angie could usually talk some sense into him. But what if she had, by marrying Doug, sacrificed, even for a little while, one of the most precious parts of her life? She couldn't imagine not going to those family get-togethers with her brothers' families every month. At the same time she had trouble envisioning Doug and his brood fitting in.

She'd dreamed about the day she'd bring a man home to meet her family—of seeing warm approval in her brothers' eyes. But that dream had included a long courtship and a fiancé growing to know her family. And it certainly hadn't included five ready-made children.

She was glad they'd arranged for the kids to stay with Wren again tonight. Even though she missed Doug's kids, tonight she was in no mood to deal with all the adjustments they faced.

Tomorrow she and Doug would move her things into his house, try to get organized before they went to pick up the kids at Wren's. Then come Tuesday morning, she would wake up in her new life—in a new place, beside her new husband. She would drive the twins and Harley to daycare. Kayeleigh and Landon would walk over to the daycare after school like always. And come five thirty, she would bring the kids home. She would make supper, help the kids with their homework maybe. Start a load of laundry . . . or two. It would be the start of a brand-new life—their "new reality," as Doug had taken to calling it.

God had given her exactly what she'd always dreamed of. So why did she feel so ambivalent? Something wasn't fitting. Deep inside her. What had only been a faint whisper for the past couple of days grew in intensity. She wasn't ready.

God had given her the desire of her heart. What she'd *begged* Him for. And she did want this—all of it. She just hadn't been prepared to get it all at once.

Right now all she wanted was to go back to her own house—alone. Crawl into her comfy bed in her quiet room and have a good cry.

Darkness came far too quickly, and at ten o'clock Mickey heard Doug turn off the TV and lock the front door. He came up behind her, where she was washing dishes at the sink, and kissed her cheek. "I'm gonna hit the hay. Turn the lights out before you come to bed, would you?"

Without waiting for a reply, he headed back to the bedroom. She heard the water running as he brushed his teeth and got ready for bed.

She wasn't really sleepy. Most nights it was eleven before she turned out the lights. But it seemed like Doug expected her to come to bed with him, so she finished the dishes, turned out the lights, and went back to the bedroom.

Doug came out of the bathroom and climbed into bed—the side of the bed she usually slept on. He held up a corner of the quilt. "Do you think you'll need extra blankets? We turn the furnace way down at night."

Mickey wondered who he meant by "we." She felt like a guest in his home, only she wasn't sleeping in the guest room. "I'll be fine," she said.

She took her nightgown into the bathroom to change. She hung her clothes on the hook on the back of the door. In spite of the fact that all of Kaye's clothes were gone from the closet, and her toiletries had been cleaned out of the medicine cabinet, her presence seemed to permeate the room. The house.

Mickey climbed into bed beside Doug. They exchanged nervous smiles, and he patted her hand. She usually read a little before falling asleep, but he turned off the lamp on his nightstand, so she did likewise, tensing when he reached to touch her.

The familiar pangs of longing that he always aroused in her came over her, but she wasn't sure she could love him that way in this room where Kaye seemed to dwell in every corner, in the very walls. Her touch was in the arrangement of books on the nightstand, in the basket of dusty silk flowers that adorned the dresser. More than that . . . *worse* than that, Kaye was in every breath Doug took, in his heart, in his kisses.

She rolled away from him and pulled the quilt up around her chin. Even the quilt held the faint scent of Kaye's perfume.

Doug didn't pursue her, but rolled to his own side of the bed.

She lay there, afraid to breathe, afraid to move, lest he reach for her in the darkness.

Finally, her husband's breathing took on an even cadence, and she let some of the tension seep from her muscles.

Oh, dear God, what have I done? What have we done?

She was a newlywed. She shouldn't feel sad.

Chapter Twenty-nine

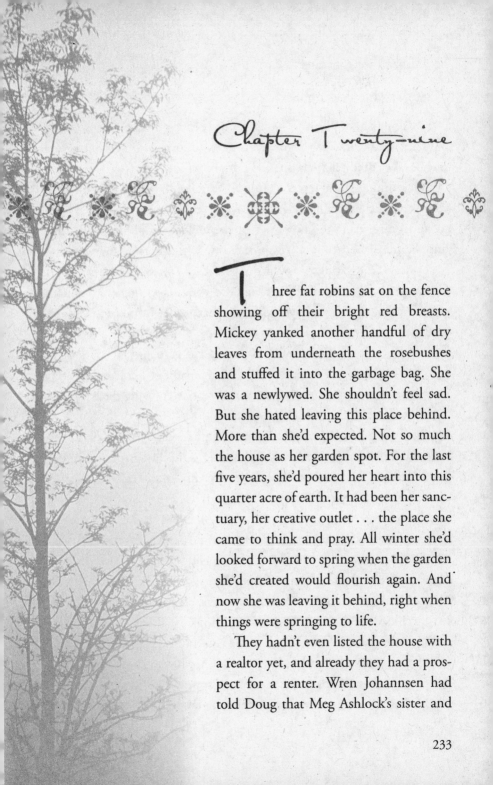

Three fat robins sat on the fence showing off their bright red breasts. Mickey yanked another handful of dry leaves from underneath the rosebushes and stuffed it into the garbage bag. She was a newlywed. She shouldn't feel sad. But she hated leaving this place behind. More than she'd expected. Not so much the house as her garden spot. For the last five years, she'd poured her heart into this quarter acre of earth. It had been her sanctuary, her creative outlet . . . the place she came to think and pray. All winter she'd looked forward to spring when the garden she'd created would flourish again. And now she was leaving it behind, right when things were springing to life.

They hadn't even listed the house with a realtor yet, and already they had a prospect for a renter. Wren Johannsen had told Doug that Meg Ashlock's sister and her husband were moving to Clayburn and needed a place to live. Even though it didn't make good financial sense, Mickey liked the rental option much better.

All along she'd talked to Doug about keeping up the garden, coming here after work each night. He'd never argued with her, but by his silence, she could tell he wasn't too hot on the idea.

But working out here, imagining what it would be like to come here with someone else living in the house, she realized why Doug had been so noncommittal. She saw now that it probably wouldn't work—not only because she'd have to bring the kids with her, but she wouldn't have access to the sinks or even the garage, and it would be awkward for everyone. Who wanted their landlord working in their yard almost every evening spring through fall? And that's what it took to keep the garden looking its best.

Besides, half the pleasure of working in the garden was sitting there for a few minutes every evening enjoying the fruits of her handiwork. If the house were rented, it would be someone else enjoying the beauty of the garden, while she did all the work.

She stuffed another handful of leaves and debris into the bag. Doug thought she was over here packing her things, deciding what furniture and decorative items she wanted to move to his house. Instead, she was out here mourning over the fact that gardens weren't moveable. She tried to take comfort in Doug's promise that she could have all the garden space she wanted at his place. "Bring your flowerpots," he'd said. "You can fill the front porch with flowers." Somehow it was hard to imagine her elegant pots on the farmhouse porch that was always cluttered with bicycles and skates, and overrun by a trio of dogs and a quartet of cats that, unlike well-mannered Sasha, would be all too happy to eat the tops off her flowers the minute they bloomed, and turn her potting soil into kitty litter. Besides, if they decided to sell her house instead of rent it, the pots would help make her house look appealing.

She heard the phone ringing inside. That would be Doug, wondering if she was ready for him to come and take a load to his place—*their* place. It was tempting not to answer.

She *wasn't* ready. For a desperate moment she was tempted to tell him she'd decided to keep her house. That way she—they—would have a quiet sanctuary to come to when things at his house got too wild.

But that made no financial sense. The daycare paid her barely enough to make her mortgage payment, pay the utility bills, and keep the pantry stocked. Combining her income with Doug's would allow them to do some work on his house. And boy, did it need some work.

Until she'd slept there last night, showered and dressed in the tiny master bathroom this morning, she hadn't realized how rundown the place was. She was eager to roll up her sleeves and get things organized, put her own touches on the house. But first the place needed a good cleaning.

The phone kept ringing. Sighing, she dragged the trash bag behind her, depositing it by the garage before she went inside.

She wiped her hands on her jeans and picked up the phone. "Hello?"

"Hey, babe. How's it going?"

"Slow. I . . . kind of got sidetracked in the garden."

"Oh. Well, are you ready for me to come over there yet? I don't want to leave the kids too late at Wren's."

She heard the impatience in his voice and felt guilty that she was delaying him. He'd taken another day off of work to help her move some things out of her house. "You can go ahead and come now. I've got a few things ready to go. I can get the rest some other night this week—or next weekend."

"I don't want to make twenty trips. If you're not ready, just say so." Now it sounded as if he were speaking through a clenched jaw.

"I'm ready." It was an effort to keep the defensive tone out of her voice. "It won't take long to load stuff up."

"Okay. I'll be there in a few minutes then."

She hung up and looked around her tidy little house, mentally making a list of things she wanted to take to Doug's. She hurried back to the bedroom and opened the dresser drawers, and threw some clothes into a suitcase.

Sasha sauntered into the room with a plaintive meow. She obviously sensed something unusual was going on—or she was unhappy with being left over the weekend. Mickey ran a hand over Sasha's silky calico coat and cooed reassurance. The cat arched her back to match Mickey's strokes.

"It'll be okay, kitty. We're going on an adventure." She zipped up her bags and put them on the floor. At Doug's house last night, she'd unpacked her bags from their "honeymoon," so her makeup and toiletries were already there.

When she started dumping the contents of the vanity drawers into a box, Sasha slithered underneath the bed skirt. Mickey worried about how her cat would adjust to life in a new home. At least all the DeVore animals were of the outdoor variety.

Tonight they'd pick up the kids from Wren's. Mickey had missed them more than she expected to. At the same time she was nervous about what her role would be once they were all living under the same roof. Except for Kayleigh, the kids seemed to adore her, and they'd always minded her just as if they were at the daycare.

Kayleigh was another story. Since she and Doug had announced their plans to marry last week, Kayleigh had gone from studied indifference toward Mickey to outright hostility. Doug kept it tempered, but what would it be like when he wasn't there?

She hauled the two suitcases to the front door so they'd be ready for Doug to load, then went to the kitchen and tossed food from the pantry and the refrigerator into boxes. It wouldn't go to waste at Doug's house. In fact, the thought of grocery shopping for a family of seven was enough to make her quake in her shoes.

She heard Doug's truck pull in to the driveway and ran back to the bathroom to check her hair. She didn't want to be one of those wives who let herself go once the ring was on her finger.

That thought reminded her that she'd taken her rings off to work in the garden. She went to retrieve them from the little dish by the kitchen sink. Doug knocked before letting himself in the unlocked front door.

He planted a perfunctory kiss on her cheek. "This stuff ready to go?"

"Yes, but don't you want to put the big stuff in first?"

"What big stuff?"

"Well, I thought I'd bring a couple of chairs and maybe that end table." She pointed in the direction of the living room.

He appeared not to hear her. He hefted a bag in each hand and carted them out to the pickup.

"Well, nice to see you, too," she said to the empty room. She lugged the end table from beside the sofa to the door. It would make a good nightstand in the master bedroom at Doug's. She racked her brain to remember what else she'd thought of bringing when she walked through the farmhouse this morning. Drawing a blank, she rolled up two throw rugs to hide the worn spots in the living room carpet at the farmhouse. That done, she collected some of her favorite decorative items off the top of the bookcase, just so Doug wouldn't think he'd wasted a trip.

He came back in, and she pointed to the hodgepodge pile she'd assembled by the front door.

"This is what you want to take?"

She nodded, growing irritated with his tone.

He propped his fists on his hips. "Mickey, where are we going to put this stuff? You think we can fit all this in my house?"

What was this? A few minutes ago he'd been harping because he wanted to be sure to have enough stuff to fill the pickup. She pasted on a smile and tried to keep her voice light. "*Your* house?"

Again he ignored her comment, as if he hadn't heard her.

Her temper simmered on its way to a boil. She forced herself to count to ten. "We can always bring stuff back if we don't need it."

He shrugged and bent to collect an armful. "What's this?" He held up the pet carrier.

"It's for Sasha. For in the car."

"You're bringing her tonight?"

"Well, I don't want to leave her here alone again."

He set the carrier back on the floor. "Don't you think we're going to have enough adjustments without throwing a cat into the mix?"

"But she was alone all weekend."

"Exactly. And she was fine. What's one more night? She's got food and water. You can stop by in the morning and check on her if you think you need to."

"It's just . . . she's not used to being left alone for so long."

He gave a dismissing wave. "Suit yourself. Seems like it would be better to wait until we get used to a routine before we try to fit a cat into the chaos."

"Doug, she won't be any trouble. She'll probably go hide under the bed for a couple of days anyway and—"

"You mean under the porch?"

"Doug, we already talked about that." He'd been hinting that he didn't want Sasha in the house, but that was one thing she was going to put her foot down about. Sasha wouldn't survive a night against those tough farm cats.

Without a reply he nudged the carrier out of the way with the toe of his boot and gripped the end table with both hands. Propping it against one thigh, he shoved the door open with his hip.

Mickey went to hold the door for him. He brushed past with his back to her and carried the table out to the pickup.

Before he came back for the next load, she unplugged two lamps and added them to the pile, just for spite. This was not a good way to start a marriage, but he was being a jerk, and right now she wasn't in the mood to concede anything.

She had to keep reminding herself that this would be an adjustment for all of them.

Chapter Thirty

Yeeooowwrrlll!" Sasha shot off the sofa and lit down the hall in a streak of calico.

"Sorry, Mickey! Sorry! I didn't mean to . . ." Landon spoke through hands clapped over his mouth and eyes as round as marble shooters.

"What happened?"

"I sorta accidentally sat on her."

Mickey felt her adrenaline spike, but she forced herself to remain calm. "It's okay, buddy. It was an accident." She was glad Doug was outside so she didn't have to listen to his I-told-you-so.

But just then the back door slammed, and Doug yelled a word Mickey was pretty sure the kids weren't allowed to use. She jumped up and went running. "What happened?"

"That"—he gritted his teeth—"*cat.*"

Mickey could see he was working hard to rein in his temper. "What happened?"

"She just about broke my neck, that's what. I opened the door, and she ran out and I tripped over her."

Mickey gasped. "She got out?" She looked past Doug to the yard. The sun was settling onto the horizon, and it would be dark in a few minutes. "You mean she's still out there? Why didn't you get her?"

He shot her a look of disdain. "You mean besides the fact that I was trying to keep from breaking my neck?"

Mickey let out a growl of her own and flew out the door, calling for Sasha. "Here kitty, kitty . . ."

Doug followed and came up behind her, putting his hands on her shoulders. "She'll be fine, Mick. Just leave her be. She'll come back when she gets hungry."

She shrugged out from under his touch and answered between clenched teeth. "She doesn't have claws, Doug. She can't defend herself out here. She can't even climb a tree to get away from the dogs."

"The dogs are penned up. Come on in. She'll come back. You're not going to find her in the dark."

Mickey swallowed back tears. She should have listened to Doug and left Sasha at home, where she was safe. If the dogs didn't get her—or coyotes—Sasha would be lucky to survive two days at this madhouse with Landon sitting on her and Harley yanking her tail.

She waved Doug away. "Go on in. I'm going to try to find her."

"Fine." Behind her the back screen door slammed.

For the next twenty minutes she circled Doug's acreage and walked around the barn calling for Sasha. She'd heard Doug warn the kids not to go in the old barn, saying it was unstable. That was probably exactly where Sasha was hiding, but she didn't respond to Mickey's voice. By the time she got back to the farmhouse, the DeVores' four outdoor cats were trailing her like rats after the Pied Piper, but still no sign of Sasha.

Peering into the dusk, she scanned the horizon one more time, then looked up into the night sky. "God, please help me find her. Don't let anything happen to her." Doug would think she was silly praying for a cat, but she didn't care.

She went back into the house with her head down, leaving the door ajar so she could hear Sasha through the screen if she came back.

Doug had turned off the TV and was trying to get the kids organized for what Kayeleigh said her mom called a "cleaning spree." Kayeleigh seemed determined to bring up "how Mom did it" at every opportunity. And so far Mickey hadn't done anything "how Mom did it" . . . in other words, Mickey couldn't do anything right.

She was trying not to be too fussy, but Doug and the kids had supposedly cleaned the house before she moved in. If that were true, she was glad she hadn't seen the "before" photos. She hated to start out their marriage nagging, but she couldn't live this way. She'd mustered up as much tact as she could find and asked Doug if they could take this evening, as a family, to do some deep cleaning. The kids had griped when he announced the plan, but then they wouldn't be normal kids if they got excited about housework. And Doug seemed agreeable.

She'd tried to make an event of it. Doug had grilled burgers for dinner, and together they made homemade ice cream for later, when they were finished. Earlier, when Mickey put potatoes, wrapped in foil, in the oven to bake, Kayeleigh informed her that "Mom always just butters the potatoes and puts them right on the rack to bake."

The filthy, crusted-over oven hinted that Kaye might have baked a lot of things that way. Mickey bit her tongue and added *clean the oven* to her project list for Saturday. At least Kayeleigh was speaking to her. After the reception she'd received when Doug announced they were getting married, she'd expected to be ignored—or worse.

She had to keep reminding herself that this would be an adjustment for all of them. And Doug and his kids had already made the most horrible of adjustments. She tried to take that into account, too.

"What do you want me to do?" she asked Doug now, keeping one ear tuned to the door for Sasha.

"Do you want to take kitchen duty?" He put an arm around her, testing, she knew. "I'm going to go out and cut a slat to fit that bed frame, then I'll help Kayeleigh and Landon do the living room and bedrooms. We'll keep an eye on Harley. Sound okay?"

"Um . . . how about if I get Sarah and Sadie on my team?" It didn't exactly seem fair for the six of them to go off together while she slaved by herself in the kitchen.

The twins cheered and ran to claim her hands.

"Oh, sure." Doug looked sheepish. "Didn't mean to make the teams so lopsided."

"I didn't know this was a team sport." She forced a smile and raised an eyebrow, trying to add levity to a topic that didn't exactly feel light.

But he laughed and reached over the girls' heads to kiss her.

"Ewww." Landon screwed up his nose. "Could you guys not do that in here?"

"I like it when they kiss," Sadie said. "Kiss Miss Mickey again."

"Yeah!" Sarah echoed her twin.

"Kiss Miss Mickey! Kiss Miss Mickey!" Harley joined in the chant.

"Just don't look, Landon."

Grinning at Mickey, Doug moved the twins and Harley out of the way, grabbed her in a bear hug, then dipped her for a Scarlett and Rhett clench. "Close your eyes, buddy. Hurry, close your eyes. Here it comes . . . ewww gross . . ." Doug mimicked Landon and plastered another kiss on Mickey, milking it for laughs.

The three little girls cheered and Mickey giggled, extricating herself from his arms reluctantly, her spirits worlds lighter—until she caught sight of Kayeleigh leaning against the doorjamb. Arms folded over her chest, the look on the girl's face made Mickey suspect she was remembering, with pain, a time when it had been her mother giggling in Doug's embrace.

Sobered, and aching for Kayeleigh, but knowing she was not the one to comfort her, she gathered the twins, one under each arm, and pointed them in the direction of the kitchen. "Come on, you two. We've got our work cut out for us."

It never crossed her mind that they might make a baby together.

Chapter Thirty-one

Kayeleigh's legs felt like lead as she trudged back to the master bedroom. She could hear Sarah and Sadie laughing with Miss Valdez in the kitchen. They got the easy job and she got stuck cleaning Mom and Dad's room—Dad and *her* room, she corrected herself.

She paused in the hallway outside the half-closed door, sucking in a shallow breath. She could hardly stand to look at the bed and think about Dad sharing it with her. Until last night, the queen-size bed hadn't been made since that terrible Thanksgiving morning. Now it was neatly made up, the pillows stacked just so against the headboard.

Apparently Miss Valdez wasn't only a neat freak at the daycare. Dad had made them clean the whole house before they went to Wren's—before he ran off and got married without even asking what they thought about it.

But apparently that wasn't good enough for *her*.

Miss Valdez must have made a big deal over what a mess the house was, and Dad cracked down on all of them. He'd been a big crab since the minute they got home. Not that she actually heard Miss Valdez say anything, but Kayeleigh wasn't blind. Kayeleigh had seen the look on *her* face when she'd stepped through the door with all the junk from her house in town. Home from the honeymoon and making herself right at home in their house. *Mom's* house. It made Kayeleigh want to throw up.

Ever since she'd walked through that door as Dad's new wife, they couldn't leave so much as a Kleenex lying around without Dad climbing all over their case. Just this morning he'd chewed their butts again about not doing a good enough job of cleaning last time. So now they had to spend the whole night on another stupid cleaning spree.

Dragging a giant black trash bag behind her, she pushed the door open and crept into the room as if there might be a boogeyman waiting there for her.

She *was* a little embarrassed at how messy the house had gotten since Mom die—She stopped the word from forming in her mind. Since Thanksgiving. She really had tried to keep things straightened up, just in case Mom could see them from heaven. But no matter how she tried, it never lasted for long.

Since Grandma had moved back to Florida, Wren had come out a couple of times to help, but with Harley running around messing stuff up as fast as they could clean it, it wasn't easy. Not to mention Landon the Slob.

Gathering up the trash throughout the house had always been her chore. No big deal usually, but today it felt like climbing that mountain they'd studied about in geography last week—Mount Everest. It felt as if she were carrying a thousand pounds on her back as she walked through the bedroom to the master bath.

Mom's little basket of makeup and perfume was gone from the counter, and Mickey's things sat in its place.

For a long time after Mom died, this room had smelled like her—a sweet vanilla and baby powder scent. It smelled different now. Like *her*. Mom's dingy pink bathrobe that used to hang on the back of the door had been replaced with Mickey's fancy lavender robe. After Mom died, Kayeleigh used to sneak in here and bury her face in the folds of that pink robe, wrap the sleeves around her shoulders and pretend Mom was giving her a hug.

She reached out and fingered the sleeve of Mickey's robe, feeling like she was doing something forbidden—and wishing she could wad the robe up and stuff it down the toilet.

She took a ragged breath and looked past Mickey's bottles and sprays lined up on the long countertop. Mom had always said that when Kayeleigh and Rachel were both teenagers, the four girls could move into this room with its separate bath and twin sinks. She'd dreamed about that day—she and Rachel had looked through the JCPenney catalog one autumn day, picking out the bedspreads and rugs they would have ordered if they were teenagers. Her throat closed up, and she put a hand on her chest and sucked in a breath. She hadn't thought of that memory with Rachel since that day.

She would never share this bedroom with Rachel. She didn't think she ever wanted this room now, even if Dad would let her. It would just be too weird.

She emptied the overflowing wastebasket from under Dad's sink into the trash bag. She opened the cabinet under Mom's sink. The little wicker trash basket was almost empty since she'd cleaned in here last week. It held a few tissues and a contact lens package that must have been Mickey's. Thanks to Mickey, Dad had ordered her to empty out all the cupboards and scrub everything top to bottom. It was his stupid bedroom. Why didn't he do it if it was so important that it be spotless for *her*?

. She yanked the trash basket out and piled the stack of clean towels beside it—the ones Mom only got out when they had company staying overnight.

She dropped to her knees and stooped to look into the cupboard. A handful of trash had apparently missed the basket and collected in the corner. She wrinkled her nose and scooped everything to the front of the cupboard. A lipstick-stained Kleenex floated to the floor. That pretty peach color Mom always wore. Gingerly, Kayeleigh smoothed the tissue out on her knee and stared at the perfect, pouty lip prints, trying to remember Mom's smile, the twinkle her blue eyes always held when she laughed.

The image wouldn't come.

Mom had only been gone a few months, and Kayeleigh had already forgotten what she looked like. Dad had taken down all the pictures of Mom and put away the photo albums before he ran off and got married. Now Kayeleigh didn't know where they were. Maybe she would search for them. She had a right to a picture of her own mother.

But it bothered her that she couldn't remember. By heart. And if she couldn't remember now, what would she remember a year from now? Or two? Or on her own wedding day?

She put her face in her hands. Why did it still hurt so bad to think about Mom? Grandma said that as time passed, memories of Mom would make her smile again. But that hadn't happened yet. Mostly she wanted to not think about any of it—Mom, Dad and Miss Valdez . . . It all just hurt too much.

She folded the tissue into a tight square and tucked it in her pocket, careful not to tear it. With a square of paper towel, she swept the rest of the trash into the wastebasket. She tipped it upside down over the open garbage bag, but the bag shifted and trash scattered every which way. Something clattered onto the tile floor and a flash of purple plastic caught her eye as it slid across the tile, then came to rest against the baseboard. She scrambled to retrieve it.

Picking it up with two fingers, she inspected the odd object. It looked like a thermometer. But they didn't have a thermometer like this. At least Kayeleigh had never seen one. Mom always used one of those strips you put on your forehead.

Besides, if this was a thermometer, why would Mom have thrown it away? She looked closer and her stomach knotted. It *wasn't* a thermometer. It was—She turned the thing over. The initials *e.p.t.* were printed in blue on the plastic case.

Wait a minute . . . She'd seen TV commercials for this thing. Mom hardly ever let them watch TV, but they watched it all the time now. Usually Dad made them change the channel when commercials for "lady stuff," as he called it, came on. But she'd seen enough of them to know some stuff.

She turned the plastic thing over again and studied it. There was a little window on one end with a blue plus sign showing in the opening. She knew what that meant. It meant positive. It meant a woman was pregnant. The couple on TV always kissed and smiled, all happylike, when they saw that plus sign.

But why was there one of these pregnancy test things in the trash can? Her breath caught. *Miss Valdez.* She'd used this bathroom last night, taken a shower and dressed in here this morning. Kayeleigh looked at the blue plus sign again and caught her breath. Was Miss Valdez *pregnant*? That's what a plus sign meant. At least that's what the commercials said.

She glanced back toward the bedroom. Dad had packed up the crib and moved Harley into Kayeleigh's bedroom the first night Miss Valdez had moved in. Kayeleigh liked having Harley in her room, but tried hard not to think about *why* they'd wanted the crib out of their room. About Dad and Miss Valdez together in that bed doing—whatever . . . It never crossed her mind that they might make a baby together.

A sick feeling rolled around in her stomach. She flung the plastic stick at the trash bag and slumped against the wall, holding a hand over her mouth. Dad and Miss Valdez had only been married a few days, and she was already going to have a baby? Could it happen that fast?

Her stomach flip-flopped again as a terrible thought settled in her brain. What if that was why they got married? What if Dad and Miss Valdez—sick!

She wondered if Dad even knew. Maybe Miss Valdez was keeping it a secret from him. Maybe she tricked him into marrying her, and that was why she'd hidden that thing clear back in the corner of the cupboard.

She stared at the purple stick half-hidden in the folds of the trash bag. Maybe she would leave it lying on the counter. If Dad didn't know, he should. And if he did know, then leaving it out in the open would let them both know that she knew their terrible secret.

Still feeling queasy, she grabbed the side of the bathtub and pulled herself up. She stood perfectly still, listening for the hum of Dad's jigsaw. From the garage the muted, high-pitched buzz droned, then stopped abruptly.

A minute later the kitchen door opened and Dad's voice boomed, "Kayeleigh! Come here."

Blood racing, she grabbed the plastic stick and stuffed it in the front pocket of her jeans with Mom's lipstick tissue. Tugging at her T-shirt, she tried to hide the telltale outline in her pocket. She gathered the rest of the trash off the floor, replaced the wicker basket under Mom's sink, and hurried out to the hallway.

Dad was standing in the kitchen at the end of the hall, a pair of pliers in hand. "Oh, there you are. Good. How's it going in the bathroom?"

She held up the bag in reply, acutely aware of the bulge in her pocket, hoping her face didn't give away her discovery.

Dad seemed not to notice. She swept past him and carried the trash bag out to the garage, where she tossed it in the bin.

He followed her. "Where's Landon? Did he finish dusting the living room?"

"How am I supposed to know?"

He took a step toward her, his jaw set. "Kayeleigh. Do not use that tone with me."

She narrowed her eyes at him. "I don't know where he is. Probably sitting on his butt watching TV." She muttered that last part under her breath, but just loud enough that Dad would hear.

The muscles in his cheek stretched over his jaw and he leaned forward.

For a minute she thought he was going to let her have it, but he just gave her the evil eye for a long minute.

"I'm finishing up the garage"—his voice softened a little—"and then I'll be back to help you in here."

She followed him out to the kitchen and filled a scrub bucket with warm, soapy water. When she heard the whine of the jigsaw from the garage again, she carried the bucket back to finish cleaning the bathroom.

Running her fingers over the outline in her pocket, she tried to think what it meant, and who she should tell about what she'd found.

This couldn't be
good — to have your
wife mad at you before
you even got to
celebrate your one-week
anniversary.

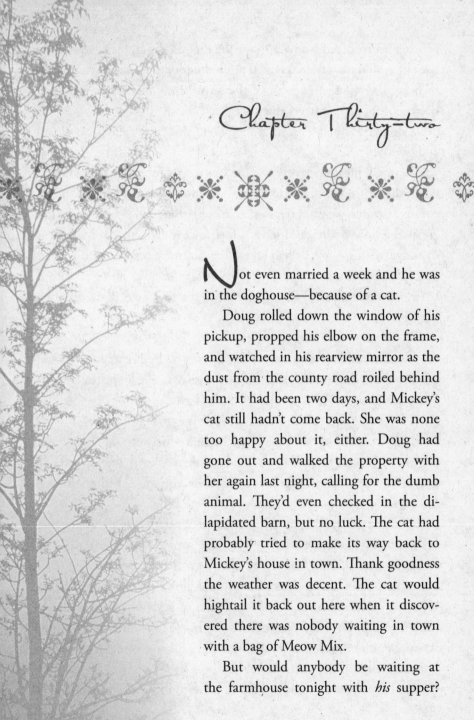

Chapter Thirty-two

Not even married a week and he was in the doghouse—because of a cat.

Doug rolled down the window of his pickup, propped his elbow on the frame, and watched in his rearview mirror as the dust from the county road roiled behind him. It had been two days, and Mickey's cat still hadn't come back. She was none too happy about it, either. Doug had gone out and walked the property with her again last night, calling for the dumb animal. They'd even checked in the dilapidated barn, but no luck. The cat had probably tried to make its way back to Mickey's house in town. Thank goodness the weather was decent. The cat would hightail it back out here when it discovered there was nobody waiting in town with a bag of Meow Mix.

But would anybody be waiting at the farmhouse tonight with *his* supper?

Mickey hadn't dared blame him for the cat's disappearance—and if she had, he would have been quick to remind her that he hadn't wanted her to bring the stupid thing out to the farm in the first place. But she'd been cool toward him ever since—

Well, to be honest, ever since they'd returned from Salina as husband and wife.

He shook his head slowly and blew out a stream of air. This couldn't be good—to have your wife mad at you before you even got to celebrate your one-week anniversary. He made a mental note to call Maizie at the flower shop and have some flowers delivered to Mickey at the daycare tomorrow. It had taken him almost ten years to learn that a simple vase of flowers was worth its weight in gold, and guaranteed to knock three days off an argument. That had always done the trick with Kaye.

He had a sudden image of her meeting him at the back door one day last fall, holding the vase of pink carnations he'd sent, and wearing a smile that told him not only was he forgiven, but he just might get lucky tonight.

He shook his head, trying to shake the image loose. A month ago he'd worried that he was forgetting her—her face, her voice, her touch . . . Now it seemed she visited his memories at the most inopportune times. He was beginning to feel like he was cheating on both his wives.

He slowed the pickup and turned down a rutted lane that went past his South 80—the one parcel of land he owned that wasn't adjacent to the farmstead. He'd had several chances to lease it when money was tight, but he wouldn't let it go. Kaye might have been able to stay home if he'd have taken a risk. If he hadn't been so stubborn. Until Landon started school, Kaye had been able to stay home full-time with the kids. It was a point of pride for Doug. No wife of his was going to take a job outside their home if he could help it.

But in the end he couldn't help it. Kaye took a job as a secretary at the high school, and they'd squeaked by. She always said she didn't mind working, but he knew she'd only said it for his sake. *No wife of his . . . No wife . . .*

His thoughts brought him up short. What about Mickey?

He scrubbed his face with one hand and forced his thoughts to practical things. There was rain in the forecast, and if he didn't get into the field with the disk tonight, he might miss his only chance for a while.

The clock on the dashboard radio turned to 7:52. He punched the accelerator. If he was late for work again, he'd have all the time in the world to work his ground because he'd leave Trevor no choice but to let him go.

※ ❈ ※

Mickey was in the middle of reading *Jesse Bear, What Will You Wear?* to the three- and four-year-olds at the daycare when Brenda came to stand behind the reading corner, waving to catch her attention. She hurried through the rest of the book and turned the kids over to Holly Miller, the high school girl who'd been helping out after school.

"Is everything okay?"

Worry etched Brenda's face. "The middle-school kids just got here, and Kayeleigh's not with them. Landon said he saw her walking with Seth Berger."

"Oh, brother . . ." Mickey rubbed her temples, then glanced up at Brenda. "I'm going to give her five or ten minutes. If she doesn't show up, I'll give Doug a call."

"Are she and Seth an item?"

Mickey shook her head. "Not that I know of. But then, Kayeleigh doesn't exactly pour her heart out to me."

"She's not taking it so well, huh? You and Doug getting married?"

"No. And this is probably a test . . . a bucking-my-authority sort of thing."

"No doubt." Brenda patted her shoulder. "Welcome to life with a teenager."

"Gee, thanks."

"How's it going with the rest of the kids?"

She forced a smile and blinked back unexpected tears. How could she tell Brenda that married life was nothing like she'd imagined? She loved them to pieces, but the kids took up every spare minute—and she had the twins and Harley at daycare all day, too.

Tomorrow was the one-week anniversary of her so-called wedding, and so far she and Doug had made love exactly twice since they'd gotten home. Oh, but they'd managed to find time for three arguments. The ratio did not bode well for the future.

Doug had come home from work every night this week to hop on the tractor and go straight to the field, leaving her to feed the kids and help with homework. Since Tuesday there hadn't been a spare minute to go by and check on her house and garden. And on top of everything Sasha was still missing, and Doug didn't seem to give a hoot.

She cleared her throat and twisted the thin silver band on her left hand, avoiding Brenda's eyes. "It's been a little hectic, but we're working things out." She checked her watch. The middle school let out at 3:30. Kayeleigh usually made it to the daycare by 3:45, and it was already a little after four.

She slid her chair back and grabbed her jacket off the hook behind her desk. "Listen, I'll be back in a few minutes. I'm going to go look for Kayeleigh. I have a feeling they're just taking their sweet time."

"You go on," Brenda said. "I'll hold down the fort."

It felt good to get outside. The temperature on the bank marquee said 62, but the sun made it feel even warmer. Mickey headed north, then west on Maple, following the route she knew the middle-school kids usually took.

About two blocks from the school, she saw Kayeleigh's friend Rudi walking with another girl she didn't know. She quickened her pace and called the girl's name.

A cautious smile grew on Rudi's round face.

"I don't know if you remember, but I'm Mickey Valdez—DeVore," she corrected herself. "I'm Kayeleigh's . . . I married her dad."

"Yeah, I know. Plus I remember from when I used to come to day-care when I was little."

She'd forgotten. "Have you seen Kayeleigh? She hasn't shown up at daycare."

"She was walking . . . to daycare," Rudi added quickly, shifting from one foot to another. "But I think she was with Seth."

"Were they going anywhere else?"

"Oh. I'm not sure, but . . . they might have stopped by Latte-dah first . . . for a smoothie or something."

It was obvious Rudi knew more than she was letting on.

"Thanks, Rudi. And I won't mention that I talked to you."

The girl looked relieved.

Mickey turned and headed back toward Main Street. When she got within view of the coffee shop, Kayeleigh and Seth Berger were coming out of Latte-dah, drinks in hand. He had his arm around her, and they were head to head. She couldn't hear what they were saying, but Kayeleigh's flirty laughter floated across the street.

Mickey cut through the alley to avoid being seen. She'd see what Kayeleigh had to say for herself when she got to the daycare.

Back at work she shrugged out of her jacket and hurriedly hung it up, explaining the situation to Brenda, who promptly disappeared into the playroom.

Two minutes later the door opened and Kayeleigh walked in, back-pack slung over one arm, Latte-dah cup nowhere in sight.

"Kayeleigh, where were you? We were worried."

"I was just walking home from school."

Mickey looked pointedly at the clock on the wall near the door. "School got out almost forty minutes ago. We've been worried about you," she said again.

"Sorry. I guess . . . I guess I walked slow today. I'm fine."

Mickey took a deep breath. Did she dare confront Kayeleigh? Or should she wait and let Doug handle it? She didn't feel she'd earned the right to play Mother yet. But she had a responsibility to deal with this as Kayeleigh's daycare provider regardless. She asked herself how she would have dealt with this if it had happened six months ago, and had her answer.

"Come here, please."

Kayeleigh took a half-step toward Mickey's desk.

"I'd like you to come and sit down for a minute." Mickey pointed to the chair in front of her desk. "We need to talk."

Kayeleigh slumped into the chair, hugging her backpack and fiddling with the zipper pull.

"You walked straight home after school?" Mickey felt a little guilty baiting her, but she wanted to see how she'd respond.

Kayeleigh mumbled something that sounded like "yes."

"Kayeleigh, look at me. You didn't stop anywhere between here and school?"

"Why are you interrogating me?"

"I'm not interrogating you. I'm just making sure you're following the rules—"

"My dad makes the rules, and if he—"

"I'm not talking about the rules at home. I'm talking about the daycare rules. I'm the director here, and the rule is that if you come from school, you come directly here, the shortest route possible, no stopping along the way. I think you know that."

"Well, I did."

"Did what? Kayeleigh. I'm going to ask you again. Did you come straight here from school?"

"Yes!"

"Then why did I see you coming out of the coffee shop?"

The blood drained from Kayeleigh's face. She'd been caught red-handed. "I don't want to talk about it."

"Would you rather talk to your dad about it?"

"Fine. Anything so I don't have to talk to you." She hoisted her backpack and stormed out the front door.

By the time Mickey collected herself and went after her, Kayeleigh was half a block down the street, running back in the direction of Latte-dah.

He composed his
words carefully before
he spit them at her.

Chapter Thirty-three

What was I supposed to do, Doug?"

Doug had never seen Mickey so worked up.

She threw a dish towel onto the counter. "I treated her like I would have any other child who behaved the way she did while in my care."

"Why didn't you call me?" He felt like he was playing mediator for a couple of six-year-olds. He'd sent Kayleigh to her room and was trying to get to the bottom of what had happened between her and Mickey. All he knew was that when he got home from work tonight, happy because he'd finished the farmwork early and could actually spend an evening at home, he'd been met by this firestorm—Kayleigh in tears because Mickey had grounded her, and Mickey up in arms because he questioned her actions and didn't immediately back her up.

Hands on hips, she stood in the middle of the kitchen and spat the words. "I didn't call you because I know how busy you are at work. I didn't want to bother you with something I thought I could handle myself."

"Well, it goes without saying: you apparently *couldn't* handle it yourself."

Her eyes narrowed and the tendons in her jaw pulled into a taut line. "What is that supposed to mean?"

He composed his words carefully before he spit them at her. "I don't think it was your place to ground Kayeleigh."

"What did you expect me to do? Just let it go?"

"No, but you could have waited until I got home, so we could talk about it. Decide together."

"We should talk about it, Doug. I'm not saying 'subject closed.' But it's not like there was any question whether she'd lied to me or not. I couldn't let that go."

"So you saw her with Seth?"

"Yes, I did. They were coming out of the coffee shop with smoothies, and she—"

"You know it was smoothies they were drinking? What are you, a detective?"

She gave a frustrated growl. "That's not the point."

He held up a hand and forced his voice down. "I'm sorry." How did every conversation manage to turn into an argument?

Mickey took his cue and softened her voice. "The point is, when she got back to the daycare—almost half an hour late, by the way—I asked her specifically if she came straight there. She looked me in the eye and told me she did."

Doug nodded. "Okay. I just wish you would've let me handle it."

"Well, believe me, next time I will. I should have called you out of work to come and get her."

"What would that have accomplished?"

"Doug—" Mickey looked toward the stairway, as if she were afraid the kids might be listening. But they'd been in bed for an hour—after a dinner eaten in silence. "If I'm going to be in charge of Kayeleigh, I've got to have some clout. When you defended her in front of me like that, you stripped me of any authority over her—over all the kids."

He exhaled and bowed his head briefly, trying to look appropriately contrite. "You're right. I'm sorry. I probably shouldn't have done that. But come on . . . give the kid a break. She hasn't exactly had it easy these last few months. She . . . she's still grieving."

His own words took him by surprise. He hadn't thought of it that way exactly, but it was true. "You're taking everything so personally, Mickey, but I don't think this has anything to do with you. The kids are still grieving. *We're* grieving. All of us. It . . . it hasn't been that long."

"You make it sound like you're all in this together. Where does that leave me, Doug?"

"There you go again, making it all about you."

"No. That's not what I mean. It's just . . . I can't compete with that, Doug."

"Nobody's asking you to compete. This isn't a competition."

"Well, it sure feels like one." She wheeled and strode down the hall.

He started after her, then shook his head. Let her fume a little. She was being ridiculous.

But it was Doug who fumed all night. He went out to the garage, feeling as if he'd been banished from his own home. At least he got some shelves cleaned off that he'd been meaning to sort through. When he got up the courage to go into the house around ten, Mickey had turned out all the lights and locked the front door.

She was in bed, asleep, curled up so close to her edge of the mattress that he was afraid she'd fall out. Well, let her. Maybe that'd knock some sense into her.

He got ready for bed and assumed a similar position on his side of the mattress.

The next thing he knew, a sliver of morning light was coming in through the curtains. He hadn't heard Mickey's alarm clock, but the shower was running and her side of the bed was empty.

He eased out of bed and went down the hall to make coffee. When he came back to the bedroom, Mickey was making the bed, dressed in a fluffy robe, her hair wrapped in a towel.

He tested the waters. "Good morning."

"Morning." Not meeting his eyes, she yanked at the bedspread and punched a pillow into place on the headboard.

Okay. Still a bit chilly. Fine. He liked quiet in the morning anyway.

He showered and dressed quickly and went to the kitchen. The fresh scent of laundry soap and dryer sheets permeated the air, and he found Mickey in the laundry room folding clothes. She didn't look up when he walked through the room and went out to retrieve the morning newspaper.

He pulled the paper from its niche below the mailbox and tucked it under his arm. When he straightened, a flash of white caught his eye.

He looked up to see Mickey's cat sitting at the edge of the driveway. Smiling to himself, he squatted on his haunches and held out a hand, calling the cat quietly. He couldn't have bought a better peace offering at any price.

The cat took two steps toward him and retreated one step back, until finally it was close enough to sniff his fingers. He laid the newspaper down and nabbed the cat. It let out a yowl when he scooped it up, but quickly settled into his arms. Leaving the paper on the ground, he carried the cat through the garage and into the laundry room.

Mickey was bent over the dryer, scooping out a load of white T-shirts and underwear.

He cleared his throat loudly. "Look what I found."

Arms loaded with the clean laundry, she straightened. She took one look and a smile filled her eyes. "Sasha!" She dropped the laundry in front of the dryer and stormed Doug, nearly crushing the cat between them. "Where was she?" She looked into his eyes for the first time since last night.

"Just waiting out on the driveway. See, I told you she'd come back."

Mickey didn't respond but nuzzled the cat and whispered sweet nothings to it, while it purred like there was no tomorrow.

Doug stood with his arms folded over his chest, watching the happy reunion. She looked up from stroking the cat, and without a word, her eyes told him his peace offering had done the trick.

"You know, a lesser man couldn't help but be a tad jealous right now."

To his surprise, her eyes welled with tears. "Thank you, Doug."

He wanted to close the distance between them, take her in his arms, take her back to bed. But there was that blasted cat between them. And Mickey didn't seem inclined to remove it. And besides, he heard the kids stirring upstairs.

She vacillated
between wanting
to weep and wanting
to give him a piece
of her mind.

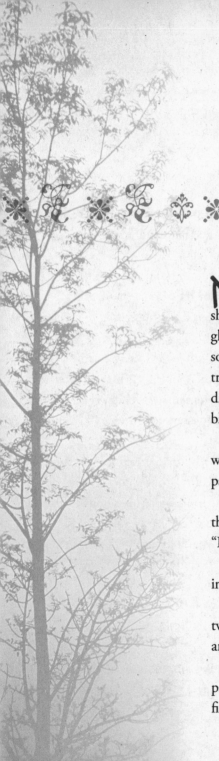

Chapter Thirty-four

Mickey flung the smelly tennis shoe off the sofa, just missing a nearly full glass of milk somebody had left there to sour. She didn't want to cause any more trouble with Doug, but if something didn't give around here, she was going to blow a gasket big-time.

She kicked the other shoe out of the way, searching again for today's newspaper.

When the second shoe clunked against the wall, Doug hollered in from the kitchen. "Landon? What's going on in there?"

"It's me, Doug. Landon's outside. Playing." She hoped to hammer home a point.

Doug appeared in the doorway between the kitchen and living room. "What are you doing?"

"I'm trying to find this morning's paper, but I don't know how anyone can find a blessed thing in this place. Look at

269

this, Doug. Just look . . ." She stretched out her arms to encompass a living room cluttered with toys and dirty clothes and dishes with crusted-on food. Who knew what else lay underneath the first grimy layer.

"Well, call the kids in. Make them clean up their stuff. You shouldn't have to do it."

"I told them to clean up before dinner."

"And did they?"

"Excuse me?" Incredulous, she stepped to one side in case he'd missed the view before. "Are you looking at the same room I'm looking at?"

He shrugged. "Let's see, I'm going to guess . . . no, they didn't."

She wasn't in the mood for his sarcasm. "I cannot stand this mess another minute, Douglas! I can't even imagine what it's going to be like next week when they're all out of school!"

"Mickey, six kids live in this house. It's not *going* to stay clean."

Doug didn't seem to notice that he'd misspoken. Or maybe he was referring to himself as the sixth child. She immediately felt cruel for having such a thought. She'd heard him slip up before. The idea of being dad to six kids was so ingrained in him.

Although there wasn't a day that went by that she didn't confront Kaye's memory in this house, it had been a long time since anyone had spoken Rachel's name. But Mickey understood why. It brought a lump to her throat just to think of the sweet little girl.

Doug went on, obviously unaware of what he'd said. "Mickey, this is what life with kids is like. Surely you knew that when you married me. You've worked with kids long enough to know—"

"But I never realized how much it would take out of me to have them all day long at daycare and then come home and have them all night, too." She glared at him.

"Well, welcome to my world." He spoke through gritted teeth. "It's not like I'm out playing golf or down at the bar having a beer with the guys when I get off work, you know."

She'd never heard such venom in his voice. She vacillated between wanting to weep and wanting to give him a piece of her mind. The latter seemed the easier choice. "Maybe not, but when you do finally get home, at least you have a nice meal ready for you and a few minutes to sit in front of the TV." She matched his caustic tone. "I don't even get that. I'm on duty from the minute I wake up until the minute *you* go to bed."

"And who got up with Harley last night?"

"What do you mean? I—I didn't know she woke up."

"That's right, because when you go to sleep, you can turn it all off. I can't even sleep without one ear to the door in case something goes wrong with the house, or one of the kids gets sick."

Admittedly, she hadn't heard Harley wake up last night. And yes, she did put all her responsibilities out of her mind once she crawled under the covers. "If I didn't, I'd be a mental and physical wreck. As it is, I'm doing good to get six hours of sleep a night. Between the house and the laundry and groceries and making sure the kids have lunches packed, it's almost always after midnight before I finally get to bed."

"You bring that on yourself, Mick. Nobody is asking you to keep this house looking like a showroom."

"Believe me, this is a far cry from a showroom. I don't see how you can function like this!" She kicked at a book bag one of the girls had dropped in front of the sofa after school. "How anybody ever finds anything in this pigsty is beyond me. And you know . . ." She was gathering steam now. Might as well get it all out in the open while they were at it. He couldn't get much angrier than he already was. "Would it kill you to ask the kids to help me out once in a while?"

"*You* ask them." He threw up a hand as if he were tossing all reason to the wind. "If you want help, Mickey, ask for it. There's no reason those kids can't help you out."

"I don't think I should always have to be the bad guy."

"Well, I'm sorry, but I'm not here to see what it is you need them to do. You're going to have to be a big girl for a change and handle it yourself."

"What is that supposed to mean?"

"Mickey—" He waited a beat too long, and the look on his face said he'd been holding back a blow that he was about to deliver with pleasure.

He pawed at the floor like a tormented bull. "You're acting like a child! You're acting like a spoiled princess with three doting brothers, who's always gotten everything her way and who's never had to make a sacrifice for somebody else."

"And you're acting like a tyrant who's never had anybody dare to challenge his authority before." Hackles flaring, she furrowed her brow and lowered her voice in a fair imitation of him. "Get that done right away. No questions asked. When I say 'jump,' the proper response is 'how high?' "

It was clear she'd pushed too far with that one. Doug's jaw tensed and his face went red. "Are you talking about you or the kids?"

That threw her. "What do you mean?"

He jabbed at the air with a finger. "Is that how you think I treat you? Is it?"

"No." She took a step backward, wishing she could take back her words as easily. Doug *wasn't* that way with her. And he was never harsher with the kids than he needed to be. "Never mind. I shouldn't have said that."

"No. You said it. It didn't just come out of nowhere. You must have meant something by it."

She looked at the floor, on the verge of tears. "This . . . this isn't like I thought it would be." Her voice wavered and she shook her head, not wanting to cry but powerless to stop the tears. "Nothing is like I thought it would be . . . for you and me. We never see each other, Doug. Kayeleigh hates the very sight of me."

"She doesn't hate you, Mick. She's twelve. Give her a break. Weren't you ever twelve?"

She waved him away. "Just forget it. You don't understand what I'm saying."

"I'm trying." But the hard edge to his voice wasn't convincing.

She was broken. She only wanted him to take her in his arms now, tell her that things would get better. That they'd work it out, that they'd find the sweetness they'd had with each other before.

But he didn't do that. Instead, he stood there, tapping his foot, as if he couldn't wait for her rant to be over so he could get to something more important.

She sighed. "Can we just forget all this? I shouldn't have said anything."

"But you did." Now it was his turn to look at the floor. "Mickey, I'm sorry if things aren't like you thought they'd be. I don't know what to do about that. I can't exactly send the kids away."

"I'm not asking you to do that, Doug. Don't be ridiculous."

"Well, what you're asking isn't realistic."

"The kids take care of their stuff at daycare. I don't see why they can't do the same here." An idea started taking shape in her mind. "What if . . . would you be willing to let me do some organizing around here? Maybe if the kids had a place to put things, they'd be more responsible."

"What exactly do you have in mind?"

"For one thing, I could bring some of the bookshelves from my house. We need to get stuff out of there anyway if we're going to rent the place out. And maybe the kids could start using the back door, so we could at least keep the living room clean. Aren't you embarrassed to have people see the place like this?"

He shrugged, but she could see that he'd lost a little steam and he was opening up to her idea. "When would we do this great transformation?"

"I don't know. Maybe over the weekend? We could make the first day of summer a fresh start that way."

He shook his head. "Don't you remember, I've got that EMT training thing in Salina. I've got to leave here by seven Friday morning, and I won't be back until late Saturday night."

"What if I do it while you're gone?" She looked around the room, and the adrenaline started flowing as fast as the ideas. "What if I take a couple days off? I've got days coming, and I need to take them before school's out anyway."

"What about the kids? And how are you going to move bookcases by yourself?"

She glanced at the clock. "I know it's late, but . . . would you consider helping me move the heavy stuff tonight?"

He opened his mouth and she waited for his protest, but then he blew out a breath and shrugged. "Okay. Let's do it. Can we do it in a couple of trips?"

"Easily."

"But what about the kids?"

She didn't want to push her luck, but she dared to anyway. "Do you think Wren and Bart would consider having them for the weekend . . . again?" The Johannsens had kept the kids for three nights while they were on their honeymoon, but they'd seemed to genuinely enjoy it. "We won't make a habit of it, I promise. It'd just be after school tomorrow and Friday and all day Saturday . . ."

"It's awfully short notice." Doug looked skeptical, but he nodded. "I guess we can ask."

"Thank you." She couldn't believe how their fight had suddenly evolved into a project—one that felt like it might solve a lot of their problems.

"I'll go tell the kids," Doug said, actually sounding enthused. "Meet you out in the truck in five."

As she moved her treasures from her house to Doug's, she started to feel something shift in her heart.

Chapter Thirty-five

Mickey crawled out of bed and walked down the hall in her nightgown. Seven o'clock on Saturday morning and the house was blissfully quiet with the kids still at Wren and Bart's. The sun gleamed through windows that sparkled with her efforts.

As she wandered through the downstairs rooms, every muscle screamed for relief, yet she felt like turning cartwheels. She had never worked so hard in her life as she had these past two days. She'd gotten up with the sun and worked steadily until after midnight two nights in a row. Without the kids to demand her attention, she'd been able to accomplish far more than she'd dreamed.

She still had a day's worth of finishing touches she wanted to put on her project, but almost overnight the house had been completely transformed. She could hardly wait for Doug and the kids to see how it had turned out. As much as she'd enjoyed the solitude of these last two days, she was beginning to miss them. A fact that caused her to breathe a sigh of relief. It had worried her a little that she felt so . . . unencumbered without them.

Not only had she organized the entire downstairs so that everything had a place, but she'd also discovered cans of leftover paint in the garage and had touched up the walls where the kids had banged into them and repaired nail holes where she'd taken pictures off the walls and replaced them with paintings she'd brought from her house.

She'd taken down the dusty draperies and curtains throughout the house, too. Some she'd washed and rehung, others she'd tossed and replaced with curtains from her house. The entire downstairs looked fresh and clean and organized.

With her careful placement of shelves and baskets, she thought the kids could keep the place tidy with just a little effort. No more than they were used to when they were at daycare.

She'd made half a dozen trips back and forth to her house, collecting books and decorative items she'd missed. As she moved her treasures from her house to Doug's, she started to feel something shift in her heart.

For the first time since moving in with Doug and the kids, she didn't feel as if she were living in another woman's house. The farmhouse had her touch on it now, and with that she finally felt like she belonged here.

The house had good bones. They'd just been hidden behind poor furniture arrangement—and a lot of clutter. Moving the furniture had given her a chance to do some deep cleaning, and the weather had allowed her to open up the house and circulate some fresh air. She inhaled and smelled only the clean scent of fresh paint and lemon polish and Windex.

Humming, she went through to the kitchen to start a pot of coffee. The empty countertops gleamed, and when she opened the cupboard doors, organized shelves greeted her. She'd packed away much of Doug's kitchen equipment—Kaye's, actually—and replaced it with the dishes and decorative items she hadn't had room for until now.

Before they could rent her place out, they'd have to deal with the two dozen boxes of stuff from the farmhouse that she'd stored in her garage, but at least they were out of here now. Maybe they could have a garage sale in town later this summer. That would be something the kids could all help with.

She planned to tackle their bedrooms and the bathroom upstairs next, but she didn't dare do that without them there to help.

Looking through to the laundry room, she admired the rows of bookshelves under the windows. With stickers and art supplies she'd collected from garage sales, she'd made clever labels for each child. Now she had a place to stack their clean laundry until they could put it away in their rooms, and they had a place to store their book bags, jackets, and toys at the end of the day.

She'd taken down the cherry-print curtains from the dining room and hung them at the laundry room windows. They fit this room much better.

Continuing her tour through the house, she moved to the dining room. The space looked positively elegant with the sideboard cleared of clutter, and the lustrous brown draperies from her living room in town puddling on the wood floor.

The stained, worn braided rugs had been relegated to the trash bin, and she'd polished the floors till they gleamed. Never mind that the scuffs from roller skates and Tonka trucks still shone through the wax. Doug would probably think that particular patina worth preserving anyway.

She showered and dressed, then made a quick trip into town to load up some of her houseplants that she'd been storing at the daycare since she moved out. The center was dim and quiet, and seeing the twins' and Harley's names on the cubbies in the entryway made her miss the kids terribly. It would be fun to pick them up from Wren's tonight. Right after she gave Doug a proper welcome home.

Smiling at the thought, she hauled two large leafy ficus trees and a collection of smaller philodendrons and ferns out to the car. She could hardly wait to get back to the house and arrange them in the sunny corner of the living room where she'd cleared a space for them. They would be an oasis and an anchor in the room. It had about killed her moving the heavy bookcases in that room to the opposite wall, but the arrangement worked much better and kept the television from being the focal point of the room.

She was dragging the second plant inside the house when the phone rang. She brushed the dirt off her hands into the pot, left it sitting in the middle of the living room, and ran to grab the phone.

"Hey, babe, it's me."

"Hi, Doug. How's it going?"

"Good. Everything going okay there?"

"Better than okay." She smiled, looking around the tidy room. "You won't believe how much I've already accomplished. I got the—"

"Listen, babe, sorry to cut you off, but we're on a break, and I need to make this quick. Wren left a message on my cell phone last night."

"Oh?" Mickey's mind raced straight to the worst-case scenario. "Is everything okay with the kids?"

"This isn't about the kids. But she said she'd tried to get hold of you and got no answer."

Mickey stretched to look at the answering machine. The light was blinking. "I'm sorry. I've been in and out, and I haven't checked for messages."

He clucked his disapproval. She could almost see his frown and his head wagging. "You really need to check it. What if it was one of the kids?"

She swallowed back the angry words that pushed into her throat at his accusation. "You said the kids are okay. What did Wren want?"

"Meg Ashlock talked to her, and I guess her sister wants your house."

"Really?" For some reason that news made a knot twist in Mickey's belly. But then she looked out over Doug's house—*their* house—and remembered how empty her house in town was now that she'd moved most of her belongings here. The knot fell loose. "That's great."

"Except . . . there's a catch."

"Oh?"

"They want to move in next week."

Her hand flew to her throat. "No way. There's no way I could have it ready that soon. It'd take a week just to get the rest of my furniture moved out." After all the work she'd done these last two days, her strength flagged at the mere thought.

"According to Wren, they need to get into something right away. Wren said they might even want a furnished place."

She hesitated. "I'm not sure I want renters tearing my stuff up."

"They might find something else if we hedge. We could really use the money, babe. I'll help you get stuff moved out. I promise. And don't forget Monday's Memorial Day. You don't have to work, right?"

"No . . ."

"We can rent a storage unit for anything you don't want to leave in the house." She heard voices in the background. "Listen, Mick, I've got to run. The next session's starting. We can talk when I get home, okay?"

"Yes . . . okay." She hung up, feeling slightly numb. And wishing she had another two days to herself. Instead, Doug would come home tonight, they'd go get the kids, tomorrow would be taken up with church and getting everything back to normal—hopefully a new normal with an organized house—and then the kids would be out of school, and every spare minute of the next few days would be spent trying to get her house ready for renters.

She flopped into a chair at the kitchen table. So much for the breather.

The phone rang again. She let out a growl and reached for the handset, working to modulate her tone. "Hello?"

"Mickey?" Wren's tremulous voice came over the line.

Mickey tried to organize her thoughts, thinking what answer she'd give Wren about renting her house to Meg's sister. She needed more time to think things through.

"Oh, Mickey. Have you—?" Wren's voice broke. "You haven't heard from Kayeleigh, have you?"

"Kayeleigh?" Mickey sprang to her feet, every sense on alert. "No. She's there with you, right?"

"No, Mickey, she's not. The girls and Landon were in the lobby playing Monopoly. I went to change Harley's diaper, and when I came back, Kayeleigh was gone."

There was something
akin to fear behind
the defiance in her
blue eyes.

Chapter Thirty-six

Mickey held the telephone tighter to her ear, trying to make sense of Wren's words.

"I thought Kayeleigh was with the other kids," Wren said through tears. "But Landon says she left. With that Berger boy . . . Seth. She didn't tell anyone. She just left, and she didn't say when she'd be back."

"Oh, dear." Mickey pressed the cordless phone to her ear, pacing from one end of the kitchen to the other.

"I'm so sorry," Wren said again. "I truly had no idea she was gone. I sent Bart looking for her, but he came back a few minutes ago. He'd walked all over town and didn't see hide nor hair of her. He just now left in the car to look for her."

"Have you called anybody? Seth's parents? Doug?" She didn't know whether to pray Wren hadn't called Doug, or wish she had. The last thing she and Doug needed between them was more trouble over Kayeleigh.

"I rang the Bergers'," Wren said, "but no one was home. I called Clara—she's Seth's grandmother, you know—and she said Paul and Cindy are out of town for the weekend. Seth's older brother was supposed to be holding down the fort. Do you want me to call Douglas?"

"No," Mickey said a little too quickly. "I—I'll call him. But he's in meetings all day. I don't want to bother him if we don't have to." She grabbed her purse and probed the side pocket for her car keys. "I'm coming in to town. Neither one of those kids can drive yet, so they can't have gone too far."

"I feel just terrible."

Mickey could almost see the sweet woman wringing her hands. "It's not your fault, Wren. If you'll stay with the other kids, I'll track her down. We've . . . well, this isn't the first time Kayeleigh's not been where she's supposed to be. I'm sure she's fine." She wished she felt as confident as her voice sounded. "I'll let you know as soon as I have any news."

She hung up the phone and scrambled to think what she should do. She did not want to have to call Doug out of his meeting, but remembering the last time Kayeleigh had pulled a stunt like this, she didn't dare wait too long to call him.

Entering Clayburn's city limits a few minutes later, Mickey realized she didn't have a clue where to look. She'd start at the coffee shop, since that was where Seth and Kayeleigh had gone on their little after-school tryst. If they weren't there, she'd look up the Bergers' address in the phonebook. She thought they lived over on the east side of town, but she wasn't sure.

Cars lined Main Street in front of the coffee shop. Everybody was out for Saturday morning donuts and coffee. She pulled into an empty space at the end of the block and jogged to the front door.

The rich aroma of espresso hit her the minute she opened the door, but a quick glance around the coffee shop told her Kayeleigh wasn't here. Jack was behind the counter taking orders, and Vienne was tamping down shots at the shiny espresso maker.

Two people stood in line waiting to order, and Mickey slipped to the other end of the counter near the cash register. When Jack had relayed the last order to his wife, he turned to Mickey. "I'm filling in this morning, so if you have a 'usual,' you'll have to help me out."

"Oh, no. I don't care for anything. I'm looking for my—for Kayeleigh DeVore."

"One of Doug's girls?" A slow smile came to his face. "Hey, did I hear right that you and Doug tied the knot?"

She nodded, forcing a smile. "Yep. Last month." It startled her to realize that their one-month anniversary was the day after tomorrow. It seemed like yesterday—and it seemed like a lifetime ago—that they'd stood before the judge and promised forever.

"Well, congratulations!" Jack's grin pulled her back.

Behind him Vienne threw her a radiant smile and added her best wishes over the noise of the steamer.

"Welcome to the ranks of newlyweds," Jack said. "You're looking for Katy, you said? I'm not sure which one she is."

"Kayeleigh," she corrected. "The oldest. She's twelve, long blond hair. She might have been with Seth Berger?"

"There were a bunch of teenagers in here earlier, but I don't remember seeing one of Doug's kids." Jack scratched his chin and turned to his wife. "Do you know if she was in here, babe?"

A needle of envy pricked Mickey, seeing the love that oozed between them.

Vienne shook her head. "Sorry, I don't remember seeing her. Rudi Schmidt was in here with her mom. She and Kayeleigh run around together, don't they? But Kayeleigh wasn't with them."

Mickey thanked her and started to ask if they knew where Seth lived, then decided she didn't need to start any rumors. She'd look it up herself. "Can I borrow a phonebook?"

"Sure." Jack reached under the counter and laid the thin book in front of her.

She made a mental note of the address and, a few minutes later, drove slowly along the route to where Seth lived, her eyes darting from the sidewalk on one side of the street to the other. When she located the Bergers' house, she pulled into the driveway and walked slowly to the front door, trying to decide where she would look next if Kayeleigh wasn't here, or worse, how she would handle it if she was.

She rang the doorbell twice and was about to go back to the car when the door opened and a sleepy-looking, wild-haired teenage boy stood squinting at her. "Yeah?"

"Hi. Sorry if I woke you up. Um . . . is Seth here?"

He grunted. "I think so. Hang on." He opened the door wider and yelled behind him at the top of his lungs, "Seth!"

Mickey heard a television blaring in the background, and she saw movement behind the older boy. A second later Seth appeared at his brother's side. By the look on his face, she didn't think he recognized her.

"Hi. I'm Mickey DeVore. I'm trying to find Kayeleigh. Have you seen her?"

Without acknowledging her question, he echoed his brother, yelling over his shoulder for Kayeleigh.

So she *was* here. Her relief was replaced by fury that boiled up in her like lava. How should she handle this? She'd learned her lesson last time. She'd wait for Doug to dole out the punishment, but somehow she still had to get Kayeleigh home.

She craned her neck for a view of the stairway between the brothers and saw Kayeleigh's blond head bobbing up the dark stairwell. Her face was flushed, and she wore a sheepish half grin.

Mickey waited for an explanation, but Kayeleigh just stared at her.

"We've been looking all over for you. What is going on?"

Seth put a possessive arm around Kayeleigh, but she backed away from him and propped her hands on her hips. Her eyes blazed with defiance, and her grin turned to a smirk. "I told Landon where I was."

"But you didn't ask us if you could leave Wren's. Wren and Bart are worried sick."

"Well, they didn't need to be. I'm fine. I told Landon," she said again.

Mickey took a deep breath. "But you didn't ask Wren—or me."

Kayeleigh ignored that. "Where's Dad?"

"He's still at his meetings in Salina. He'll be back this evening. You need to come with me."

"Dad won't care if I'm here."

"That's not the point. You didn't ask permission. Wren was the one in charge of you and—" She eyed the Berger boys. "We'll discuss this later . . . with your dad. For now you need to come home with me."

Kayeleigh moved back toward Seth, and he wrapped long, muscular arms around her from behind. A frisson of alarm went through Mickey. Their way with each other was far too cozy for two young teens. She turned to the older brother. "Are your parents here?"

His Adam's apple pumped in his throat. "Nope. They're in Cancun."

"You guys are home alone?"

"Yup." His stance said, *And what are you gonna do about it?*

"Come on, Kayeleigh. We need to go." She turned and put a hand on the screen door handle.

"I'll walk back to Wren's," Kayeleigh said behind her.

Mickey turned and straightened, stretching to her full height, but even so, she was only a fraction of an inch taller than Kayeleigh. "No. You're coming with me."

"No. I'm not." There was something akin to fear behind the defiance in her blue eyes.

But Mickey sensed that Kayeleigh was emboldened by her audience. Seth tightened his hold on her.

Mickey reached for the door again. "Fine. But you need to know I'm calling your dad."

"Fine." Kayeleigh mimicked her. "He won't care."

Mickey tensed. *He'd better care.*

She let the screen door slam behind her and tried to ignore the rude comments the older brother made behind her back . . . something about not letting the door hit her on the way out.

By the time she got to the car, Mickey's hands were trembling. What was wrong with her that she'd let a sassy twelve-year-old intimidate her? But she'd told Doug that day Kayeleigh had lied to her about being with Seth that she'd let him handle it next time. Well, here they were at next time. So let him. This was not her problem.

Except she knew that *she* was the one who would somehow bear the consequences.

What sort of trouble had brewed between the two of them in the space of the short trip home from town?

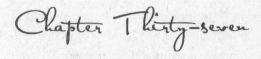

Chapter Thirty-seven

Doug pulled into the driveway just before dark, worn out from the training seminar and looking forward to having a few hours of the weekend left to relax.

He hoped Mickey wasn't too exhausted from the big organizational spree she'd been on. When he'd last talked to her, she sounded a little out of sorts. He knew from experience that a project like this sometimes took on a life of its own. She'd probably have the house so torn up it would take a week to put things back together.

He'd called and offered to go on into town and pick up the kids at Bart and Wren's, but Mickey said she needed to pick up a few groceries anyway and she'd get them. The Suburban wasn't in the driveway, but maybe she'd cleaned out the garage and made room to park in there. That was another thing she'd been complaining about. He halfway hoped they weren't home yet, so he could have a few minutes to unwind. As much as he loved his kids, they weren't exactly conducive to a relaxing evening.

But no sooner than the thought was out, he heard the roar of an engine behind him, and Mickey pulled into the drive and parked behind him. He got out and started for the driver's side of the vehicle.

The twins jumped out of the back and raced to embrace his knees. "Daddy! Daddy!" Their gleeful squeals made him smile. He'd missed them. All of them.

He rubbed their heads and lifted each one in turn into the air for a quick hug and an Eskimo kiss.

Landon met him with a high five. Even Harley toddled toward him as fast as her pudgy legs would carry her. Halfway there, she fell on the driveway, but got right back up, still grinning from ear to ear. He hurried to scoop her up and blew raspberries on her neck.

Mickey and Kayeleigh got out of opposite sides of the Suburban and slammed their doors in unison. Kayeleigh wore the scowl that was becoming her trademark, and Mickey's expression mirrored Kayeleigh's. They hadn't been together all weekend. What sort of trouble had brewed between the two of them in the space of the short trip home from town?

He shooed the little girls up onto the porch, placed a quick kiss on the top of Kayeleigh's head, and went to give Mickey a hug. "Hi, babe."

"Hi." The V-crease between her eyebrows deepened a little. "How'd your meetings go?"

"They were okay. Everything okay here?"

She gave a furtive glance toward Kayeleigh. "We'll talk about it later," she mouthed. "I got a lot done on the house," she said, loud enough for the kids to hear.

"Oh. And hey, did you talk to Wren about *your* house? Does that couple still want it?"

"I didn't get a chance to talk to Wren—about that." Again, she gave a pointed nod in Kayeleigh's direction.

He was in no mood to referee one of Mickey and Kayeleigh's disagreements right now. Trying to steer clear of the topic, he grabbed his overnight bag from the car and climbed the steps to the porch.

Kayeleigh dashed ahead of him and opened the front door. The minute she stepped inside, she started yelling. "What did you do? Why did you do this?"

Doug shot Mickey a look. She only turned and ran up the steps.

He raced up the porch behind her. "Kayeleigh? What's wrong?"

Kayeleigh stood in the doorway with an expression of horror mixed with accusation. He followed her gaze to a living room he barely recognized. He moved through the room and quickly realized that the transformation applied to the entire downstairs.

Not only had the furniture been rearranged and new rugs laid on the floors, but every table and countertop had been cleared of clutter, leaving only the sparest of decorations in their place. His house looked a lot like Mickey's house in town, and the thought brought the realization that she'd moved a lot of her stuff in. So then, where was *his* stuff?

"Dad? Do something!" Kayeleigh stood there with her arms outstretched and with that horror-struck expression now cemented on her face.

He turned to Mickey, making great effort to keep his voice even. "*This* is what you did while I was gone?"

She nodded, obviously pleased with herself, and waiting for his praise.

Well, he couldn't give it to her. Speechless, he walked slowly through the rooms. Kayeleigh trailed him, repeating, "Dad? Dad?" as if a tornado had struck and she thought he could somehow undo the damage.

"Where's the wing chair?" He pointed to an empty corner of the dining room.

"I moved it into our bedroom . . . for now. It could use reupholstering eventually. What do you think?" She looked at him with wide eyes, an eager puppy waiting for a bone.

He strode through an equally naked kitchen to the laundry room.

"Here are the shelves I was telling you about." Mickey stood in front of the curtains—curtains Kaye had spent hours sewing for the dining room, curtains that were perfectly suited to the dining room. With a Vanna White flourish, Mickey indicated the labeled shelves beneath the curtains.

By now the other kids had traipsed in behind them. "Hey! How come Mom's curtains are in here?" Landon had a befuddled look in his eyes, and the little girls were wandering around, looking lost in their own house.

"Dad?" Kayeleigh said again.

"Hang on, Kaye."

"Don't call me that, Dad!"

He shook his head, confused by her remark, but when his own words replayed in his mind, he realized he'd shortened her name to Kaye's. He put a hand at the nape of her neck and gently massaged. "Sorry, honey."

"What do you think?" Seeming oblivious to Kayeleigh's pain, Mickey waited, looking ever more like a needy puppy.

He shrugged, angling for an answer that wouldn't hurt her.

Mickey straightened a pile of books and junk mail on the shelf marked with his name. "If everybody could start using the back door," she chirped, "then you can each pile your stuff on your own shelf as soon as you walk in the door. That way the clutter won't make it into the rest of the house in the first place."

Doug spun around, taking in the rest of the room. The tops of the washer and dryer were spotless, and the usual piles of clean and dirty laundry had been put away, and the area around them swept and scrubbed clean. His easel was in the corner where it always stood, an empty stool in front. "Where are my paints?"

Almost strutting, Mickey crossed the room and pulled a shoebox off a low shelf adjacent to the washer. She lifted the lid to reveal his oil paints neatly lined up. Not exactly convenient, but it wasn't like he used them every week. And it did get them out of harm's way. He stuck his hands in his pocket and went back through the kitchen to the main living area.

Mickey followed him. "So what do you think?"

"It . . . it looks like you worked your tail off."

He hadn't meant it as a compliment exactly, but she preened like a proud peacock. The kids trailed into the living room one by one.

"Do you like it?" Mickey pressed.

"Mickey, I'm not sure we can keep everything the way it is."

Her face fell. "What do you mean?"

Kayeleigh took up her battle cry again. "Dad? Do something!"

"You stay out of this, Kayeleigh."

His daughter looked as though he'd struck her, and he was immediately sorry for snapping at her. He understood how she was feeling, but the last thing he needed was to take sides with her against Mickey.

Mickey tilted her head. "Stay out of what? Did I miss something here?"

Doug tried to change the subject. "Have you guys eaten?"

"Wren fed the kids. I'm not hungry." Mickey glanced from Kayeleigh to Doug and back again, looking confused. "What's wrong, Doug?"

"We'll talk later."

He looked at Kayeleigh, who suddenly seemed overly interested in the rug they were standing on. Her face was flushed, and she was biting at the corner of her lip, looking like she'd just robbed a bank. Okay, maybe *he* was the one who'd missed something here. "What's going on?"

"Kayeleigh?" Mickey turned to her, waiting.

No response.

"I'm giving you a chance to tell your dad your side of the story," Mickey coaxed, "but if you don't, then I'll tell him mine."

Doug tensed. "What story? What's going on?"

When Kayeleigh finally looked up, there was venom in her eyes. "I'll tell you what's going on!" She pointed at Mickey, practically hissing. "She comes in here and takes over *our* house! Look at it, Dad." She opened her arms. "It doesn't even look like our house anymore. It looks like *her* dumb house. Did you tell her she could take all Mom's stuff down?" Her poison was aimed at Doug now.

"Kayeleigh—stop it right now." He struggled to find a defense for Mickey. She *had* taken over their house. She'd led him to believe she was going to do some cleaning and some simple organization. If he'd known she had this . . . *makeover* . . . in mind, he never would have allowed it.

But he wasn't about to discuss it with her in front of the kids. He took a deep breath and turned to Kayeleigh. "Listen, I want you to supervise the kids . . . get everybody ready for bed. Mickey and I are going to take a walk, and when we get back, we'll sort things out." He wasn't even sure what all needed sorting out, but Mickey could fill him in, and together they'd talk to Kayeleigh about whatever it was that was going on between them.

But first he needed to have a word with Mickey. Before she obliterated every scrap, every memory of Kaye from his house.

Oh, if only they could go back. If only they could undo this colossal mistake.

Chapter Thirty-eight

The sound of their tennis shoes crunching along the gravel road couldn't drown out the anger simmering between them. Mickey walked faster, pretending she couldn't sense that Doug was trying to slow her down.

He reached to touch her, and his hand felt hot on her bare arm. "Do you see what I'm saying, Mick?"

She pulled away, and he sidestepped, placing more distance between them. They walked in silence for a full minute before she finally found her voice. "Doug, I was only trying to help. To make things easier for you and the kids—and for me. I'm the one who has to deal with all the messes. I'm the one who suffers most because of the clutter." She shook off the voice inside that took her to task for daring to call what she'd experienced "suffering" in light of all Doug had been through.

"I already told you," he said, "it's not the clutter. The shelves in the laundry room are great. That was a good idea. But you redecorated the whole house. You didn't ask anybody, you just started rearranging our furniture, taking down our things—*her* things. . . ." His voice trailed off, and she sensed the emotion behind it.

But she was tired of tiptoeing around his emotion. It was high time they talked about it. And this was as good a night as any. She took a deep breath. "Doug, is it fair that I have to live in a mausoleum of memories of Kaye? It's my house, too. I gave up everything for you, for your kids. It seems only fair that I could have a little say in how the house is decorated. That I could fix things up so they're not so hard to clean, and so we don't have to be ashamed to have company over."

He stared over at her, his legs pumping faster. "I think you care a little too much about what people think."

"And maybe you don't care enough." She quickened her pace to catch up.

"It never bothered Kaye if the house didn't look like a page out of a magazine. She was too busy caring about *people* to worry whether she was making a good impression or not. She knew how to make people feel at home in our little *hovel.*"

Sarcasm did not become him, and she shot him a look that said as much.

He ignored it. "I happen to like the way Kaye had the house fixed up, and I don't appreciate you ripping into it. The least you could have done is ask me first."

She couldn't believe what she was hearing. "I thought that's what this weekend was all about. I told you what I wanted to do."

"You told me you wanted to get things organized. I came home to a house I didn't recognize. Did you think for one minute about the kids, Mickey? As if they haven't lost enough, as if they haven't had enough upheaval in their lives, you go and change everything about their home. Everything that would remind them of their mother."

If he was trying to make her feel like an insensitive moron, it was working. "I didn't touch their rooms, Doug. Or your room."

He narrowed his eyes. "*My* room?"

She ignored that and started walking again. He tramped beside her.

"Doug, I was just—trying to create some space that was *ours*. I didn't even really intend to redecorate. But once I started moving things to clean, I saw how some of my furniture fit the spaces better." They were walking fast enough now that her breath came in short huffs. "One thing led to another, and it sort of snowballed."

He gave her a look that said that was a gross understatement.

"I don't think it's asking too much to put a few of my own touches on the house. And it's an insult that you couldn't even tell me it looked nice."

"And it's an insult to my wife that you felt the need to redecorate a house that was perfectly fine the way it was."

She stopped dead in the middle of the road, hand on hips, breathing hard. "Excuse me. Your wife? I thought *I* was your wife."

A red line crawled up his neck until his cheeks were flushed. He stared at the road. "I'm sorry. I didn't mean it that way."

She worked to keep the pain from her voice. "How *did* you mean it, then?"

He acted like he was about to say something, then closed his mouth, shook his head. His silence hurt her more than she could have imagined.

"Doug?"

He looked anywhere but at her. "Mickey, I just— Everything's happened so fast. For you and me. For . . . us. I take full responsibility for that. I'm not trying to shift the blame onto you for what we've—"

She held up a hand, her eyes stinging, not wanting to hear whatever it was that he was going to say next.

His contrition seemed sincere enough, but the weight of his blunder anchored her to the country road. His words had revealed the truth: he still saw Kaye as his wife. Not her.

The fact that he didn't reach for her in that moment, that he didn't repeat his apology, sealed her perception. A wave of nausea swept over her. Like an animal caught in a trap, she struggled against the truth, not wanting to believe what she knew in her heart.

Doug didn't love her. He never had. He'd always—and still—loved a woman she could never compete with. Never measure up to. And she could see no way out of her trap.

It was foolish to try to convince him of her right to change the house. There was nothing to be accomplished arguing. For whether he realized it or not, it wasn't her changing the house he was angry about. It was her—and the fact that she wasn't, and never could be, the woman he went on loving.

This wouldn't be solved. Only dealt with. She swallowed hard. "I'll put things back the way they were—in the house. As much as I can."

"No—leave it. Leave it. There's no reason."

He shook his head, and she didn't think she'd ever seen such profound sadness in a man's eyes. In that instant she wanted to reach out, take him in her arms, and comfort him, kiss away his sorrow. But he'd made it clear her kisses had lost their value with him—if they ever had any.

She couldn't cure a wound she was partly responsible for. And they still had the more immediate problem of Kayeleigh to worry about first. They were coming to the end of the road, where they usually turned around to head back. But Doug kept walking. Fine. That would give her time to open another wound, too.

"Doug, we need to talk about Kayeleigh."

He bristled and slowed his pace. "What about Kayeleigh? What was all that about?" He gestured back toward the house.

"She ran off from Wren's."

"What do you mean, 'ran off'?"

"She snuck out this morning . . . with Seth Berger. Wren called, frantic. I guess Bart walked all over town looking for them."

"What? You didn't call me?"

"You can't be serious? After what you told me the last time I called you?"

He opened his mouth to speak, and she could almost see him recalling his own words—*you should have let me handle it*—from the last incident with Kayeleigh. He closed his mouth and said nothing.

She let it go. For Kayeleigh's sake, they had to talk this out. "I went into town and found Kayeleigh at the Bergers' house. The parents are on vacation, and the boys were there alone. Kayeleigh was there with them."

"What are you talking about?" His tone said he didn't believe her.

She nodded, prepared to be the bad guy. "When I told her to come out to the car with me, she refused. I left her there. By the time I got—"

"You left her there? Why would you do that?"

The dagger didn't hurt any less because she was expecting it. "What was I supposed to do—drag her out by her hair? As I was backing out of the driveway, I saw her running out of the house. I let her walk back to Wren's. She didn't argue when we loaded the car to come home."

"You're sure she didn't tell Wren she was leaving? How did you know where to find her?"

"She told Landon. But she never got anyone's permission. Wren and Bart were worried sick. And so was I."

"Maybe she didn't realize—"

"Doug." He didn't want to believe his little girl could have become the lying, disrespectful adolescent Mickey had seen her become. But as much as possible, she was staying out of it. It only put a thicker wedge between them as a couple. She put up her hands in surrender. "I'm leaving it for you to deal with, but I wanted you to know the truth about what happened."

"I'm not sure you know the truth."

"Fine. Believe whatever you want." Feeling as if her knees might buckle, she turned to head back to the house. "I'm tired. Can we just . . . go back?"

He waved her off and kept on walking.

Oh, if only they *could* go back. If only they could undo this colossal mistake. She couldn't stand the pain of leaving herself exposed, vulnerable to Doug. She imagined stepping into a suit of armor. But before she locked herself into the protective fortress, she allowed her love story with Doug to parade before her one last time, like a person's life flashing before them in the throes of death.

She seemed to view with clarity every tender moment she'd shared with him in their short time together. Holding hands under the table, stolen kisses when the children were otherwise occupied. The silver twist-tie ring Doug had fashioned for her the night he'd asked her to marry him. His tender way with her on their wedding night, as she'd offered herself to him, willing and pure.

Why she tortured herself with the memories, she didn't know. They were all a sham. She would not parade them out again. It was done.

There was no annulment in the world that could undo what had happened to her heart.

Something about the
sweet way he'd
spoken the apology
put a lump in her
throat. At least

somebody here
loved her.

Chapter Thirty-nine

The sun was low in the sky as Mickey drove home from Salina on Highway 40. June was half over and almost overnight, the wheat fields had turned to gold. Doug predicted they'd be harvesting in a week and finished by the Fourth of July. She discovered that he always took his vacation time from his job in town at harvest time . . . which meant he rarely got a real vacation. Which meant she probably wouldn't, either.

Pulling into the driveway a few minutes later, she tooted the horn for help unloading the car. She'd taken advantage of Doug's rare evening home to make a grocery run.

Landon was the first one out the kitchen door. He flung open the back door and started rummaging through grocery bags. "Did you get anything good?"

"Hey, buddy, let's get them in the house before we start eating them, okay?"

Landon shot her a sly grin. "Sorry." He threaded his skinny arms through the handles of four bags and lugged them into the house. Something about the sweet way he'd spoken the apology put a lump in her throat. At least somebody here loved her.

The twins showed up behind Landon, and Mickey came around the car to load them up with bags.

She was gathering up the last of the groceries when Doug appeared beside her. "You got everything."

They'd gotten good at avoiding each other's eyes. "Yeah, I've got it."

"Sorry. I was getting Harley to bed."

"It's okay. I've got it. The kids helped."

"Good. Everything go okay?"

She nodded and risked a glance at him. He was in need of a haircut, and his face was sunburned. He looked tired.

She worried about how hard he worked. Between the farm and his job in town, he often put in twelve-hour days or longer. But he'd promised the kids that they'd all go to Wilson Lake for a long weekend as soon as the wheat was cut.

She was just grateful they'd been able to get her house ready for the renters before harvest hit. While Kayeleigh babysat, she and Doug had worked for a week of evenings, getting the rest of her things into storage, cleaning the house, and getting the yard in shape. The gardening wasn't nearly as satisfying, knowing she wouldn't be there to enjoy it, but it had served as therapy for the ongoing pain of her discovery about Doug's feelings—or lack thereof—for her.

They hadn't talked about it since that night he'd taken her to task for redecorating his house—*Kaye's* house. But the weight of it hung between them, held inert by the constant busyness of their lives.

The crisis with Kayeleigh had trumped her redecorating fiasco, and Doug hadn't broached the subject again. In a halfhearted effort to compromise, she had moved a few of Kaye's knickknacks back to where they'd been, but other than that things stayed where she'd put them, and Doug hadn't commented about, either. But his initial reaction had taken all the joy out of her efforts.

Since that night they'd slept in the same bed . . . but without touching. Each night she'd waited until he was asleep before creeping into their room. Doug rose an hour before her alarm clock went off and was usually gone to work before she emerged from the shower.

In between they were polite strangers. *Please pass the salt. How was your day? Did Harley take a nap?* Without discussing it, they'd agreed not to argue. To coexist for the kids' sake.

"I think I'm going to work out here for a while." Doug angled his head at the makeshift workshop on the opposite side of the garage. "Unless you need help putting the groceries away?"

"The kids can help me."

He nodded and turned away. She went into the house and started putting groceries away, enlisting the twins' help.

The renters had moved in to her house two weeks ago, and she'd let go of it in her mind. But she felt oddly displaced. Doug's disapproval of the decorating she'd done in this house had siphoned away any pleasure she'd felt in the accomplishment. Now she was a stranger living in someone else's home.

At least she was getting along with the kids. Doug had apparently talked to Kayeleigh. The girl's outright antagonism had changed to smoldering indifference. Mickey tried to stay out of her way as much as possible.

She opened the refrigerator and rearranged things to make room for the two gallons of milk this family went through every couple of days.

The younger kids seemed not to notice the change that had occurred between her and Doug. If anything, they'd grown more attached to her, seeking her out where they'd looked to their father before. She'd always had a special place in her heart for the DeVore kids, but as she withdrew from Doug, she seemed to draw closer to his children. That fact sent a chill through her on the rare occasions she stopped to ponder where her relationship with Doug might end up.

Except for their honeymoon and the first few weeks after they'd come home, they'd had a marriage in name only. She didn't know what Doug had imagined their life together to be, but for her, nothing was like she'd dreamed.

She'd wasted so much time longing for what she didn't have, when what she did have seemed like a pleasant dream now—a tidy, attractive house with no one to mess it up, the freedom to come and go as she pleased. The privilege of coming home from work and relaxing or working in her garden.

"Mickey?" Landon stood at the door holding the phone. "It's for you."

She took it from him. "Hello?"

"Mickey, it's Angie. I . . . we wondered if you—and Doug and the kids, of course—were coming Sunday."

A thread of sorrow ran through her as she realized how long it had been since she'd been with the Valdez clan, with her nieces and nephews and precious little Emmy. The last time she'd seen her brothers—their introduction to Doug—had been disastrous. Rick never had called her like he said he would. She'd phoned Angie and begged off of the June get-together, claiming they were still getting settled. She was surprised to realize that July's gathering loomed less than two weeks away. "I-I'm not sure yet, Angie. We've been so busy we haven't even talked about it. Let me talk to Doug, and I'll get back to you."

"Sure. Is everything going okay?"

"We're busy," she repeated. "Harvest will probably be next week, and Doug's trying to get everything ready for that . . . on top of work. But thank you for calling. I'd like to come."

There was a long pause before Angie's voice came softly. "I really hope you'll come, Mickey. Rick's just being an overprotective big brother. He didn't mean the things he said."

"I think he did mean them, Angie. But I . . . I understand."

"Give him time, honey. He'll come around."

"Thanks, Ang. I'll get back to you tomorrow, okay?"

"Whenever you can. We'd love to have you—*all* of you."

Hanging up the phone, she screwed up her courage and went out to the garage to broach the subject with Doug.

He stood at the workbench, wearing protective glasses and earplugs. When she touched his arm, he jumped as if she were a snake.

Two months ago they would have cracked up and ended up laughing in each other's arms. Tonight that seemed beyond impossible, and Doug's stern face proved it. "What's wrong?"

She nodded back toward the house. "That was Angie on the phone. Our family get-together is next Sunday. They wonder if we're coming."

He chewed his lower lip. "You go if you want to. I don't think I'm exactly welcome there."

"Doug. Please. Angie said that Rick . . ." She let her voice trail off, because she wasn't sure Angie was right about Rick's feelings on the subject. "Would you please come? You'll never get to know my family, and they'll never get to know you, if we don't spend some time with them."

He shook his head and blew out a breath that sent sawdust scattering. "I don't think I can do it."

"Do what?"

His lips melded into a tight line. "I'm sorry. You go if you like."

Her heart fell. Not because he wouldn't go, but because she'd heard what he'd failed to say: *You go if you like. I can't pretend we have a marriage in front of people who never thought we should marry in the first place.*

Like nearly everything
he did these days, his
actions riddled him
with guilt.

Chapter Forty

Doug hid out in the garage until he was sure Mickey had gone to bed. Like nearly everything he did these days, his actions riddled him with guilt. He knew how much Mickey adored her brothers, and how much she longed to keep her relationship with them, but with everything else pressing on him, the last thing he needed was more of the treatment he'd received from them the day Mickey introduced him. He got plenty of disrespect in his own home these days, thank you very much.

The house was quiet, and he took off his shoes before walking through to turn off the lights Mickey had missed. When she'd revamped the downstairs rooms, she'd brought several small lamps from her house and scattered them about the house. He usually went to bed before she did, and more mornings than not, he awoke to find the bulbs had been left burning all night. Maybe when she saw the electric bill next month, she'd see why he constantly reminded her to turn them off before she retired for the night. Not to mention that fool cat of hers was likely to knock one of them over and start the house on fire.

Mickey was asleep when he entered the room, hugging her side of the bed, her breath coming evenly. Another wave of guilt crashed against him. He leaned against the door and watched her sleeping. She was so beautiful. And kind and generous. Despite their differences, Mickey was the kind of woman he might have loved under different circumstances.

The whirlwind days of their courtship twirled through his mind. He'd been wrong to talk her into marrying him so quickly. He knew that now. He'd followed his emotions—and his hormones—just wanting something to stop the pain.

He went into the bathroom and quietly closed the door behind him. He stood looking at his reflection in the mirror. There wasn't a thing he could do about their decision now. Marriage was till death parted them. He'd never believed anything else. And for the second time in his life, he'd pledged to love and honor "for better or worse."

He was determined to honor his vows to the best of his ability. He only wished he loved this woman the way he'd loved the first. For Mickey's sake as much as his own. This wasn't fair to her. He felt like a jerk, and she deserved better.

He got ready for bed and carefully turned the covers down, not wanting to disturb her. He crawled under the sheets and turned his back to her, pushing away the desire that came over him, because it wasn't her he wanted. And it wouldn't be fair to pretend otherwise.

As he lay there in the dark, memories of the love he'd shared with Kaye in this very bed returned in vivid detail. He squeezed his eyes shut, trying his best not to remember. But how could he forget thirteen years of loving someone like Kaye, someone he'd given himself to so completely?

And how could he ever have given himself to someone else . . . when he was still in love with Kaye?

❊ ❊ ❊

The ceiling fan whirled above the bed, breaking the moonlight into slices. Kayeleigh pulled the blankets up over Harley's shoulders and snuggled next to her baby sister, sniffing the sweet, fresh scent of her hair. It was good to have somebody sharing her bed again. Except when Harley was a wiggle worm and ended up sideways in the bed, kicking in her sleep. Or when her diaper leaked. That wasn't so much fun. But she was thankful to have her baby sister in bed with her every night. Rachel's spot didn't seem quite so empty now, and Kayeleigh was glad Mickey had talked Dad into putting the crib away for good.

Something had happened between Dad and Mickey. Kayeleigh didn't know what it was, but she had a terrible feeling it was her fault. She never should have treated Mickey the way she did. Never should have gone to Seth's house that day in the first place. It was stupid. She knew better.

But he would have made fun of her, maybe never talked to her again, if she'd told him no. And the truth was, she wanted to go with him. She liked the way she felt when she was with him.

But she didn't like the way things were between Dad and Mickey. He'd gotten to be a big fat crab. He'd chewed her up one side and down the other for going to Seth's that day.

Mickey, who always used to be so happy, now looked sad all the time. Kayeleigh never caught her and Dad kissing or even talking much anymore. It seemed like they were both mad at each other all the time—except they never fought. Not anymore, anyway.

Sometimes she thought she'd prefer that. If they'd just yell at each other, say what they were thinking. Instead, they tiptoed around each other like she'd tiptoed around Mickey when Mickey had first started loving Dad.

Her own thought startled her. Mickey did love Dad. She could tell. Even when Dad was sort of mean to her, she watched him with a sad, faraway look in her eyes—like she wanted him to treat her the way he used to.

She didn't know what Mickey had done to make Dad change his mind. Not that long ago, he'd liked her plenty. Her face grew hot, thinking about the times she'd caught them making out.

She should have been glad about this turn of events. Hadn't she just told Rudi a few weeks ago that she wished Dad would get a divorce?

"No, you don't want that, Kayeleigh," Rudi had said. "Let your dad be happy. Why shouldn't he be?"

"Because it's not fair to Mom."

Rudi had planted her hands on her hips, looking like Miss Gorman did when they were goofing off in choir. "No offense," she said, "but think about what you're saying, Kayeleigh. Don't you think your mom would want your dad to be happy?"

"Sure . . . but not with Miss Valdez." Now she wondered. Mom sure wouldn't like the way Dad was lately. She would tell him to snap out of it. Or she'd tell him something funny Harley or Landon did, and she'd keep telling him stories until she finally got him to laugh. It wouldn't have taken long, either. Mom and Dad had laughed a lot.

Dad laughed with Miss Valdez—*Mickey*—too. At least he used to. But it seemed like it all changed that night she'd left Wren's to go to Seth's house. She thought back to that day. It gave her a strange feeling low in her tummy to remember how Seth had put his arms around her, kissed her. Touched her in a way no boy had ever touched her before.

She'd liked the way it felt. But it scared her, too. Truth was, she'd been glad Mickey showed up when she did. Seth's brother, Ben, made her feel a little creepy the way he looked at her. And she didn't like the way Seth acted when his brother was around. He got all cocky and turned into a big show-off.

Why couldn't she just have gone with Mickey? Why did she have to be such a jerk and mouth off to her like that? Mom would have killed her if she'd done that to her. No. Mom never would have *had* to come and get her, because she never would have done such a stupid thing when Mom was alive.

Everything had changed on that terrible Thanksgiving Day. The unbearable, almost physical, pain she'd felt in the beginning had eased a little bit, but if she thought about it too much, even that very fact made the pain come back again. It hadn't been a year yet. Maybe something was wrong with her that she wasn't still crying herself to sleep every night like she had at first, aching for Mom till she couldn't think about anything else, feeling like she was going crazy.

Sometimes she wondered if she'd ever again experience that pure joy she remembered from when they were all a family—Mom and Dad and her and Rachel and Landon and Sarah and Sadie and Harley. Laughing in the car on the way to church because Harley said something funny. Or praying together, holding hands around the kitchen table.

She remembered that first night Mickey had come to their house and eaten Dairy Barn burgers with them. Their house had seemed happy again that night. She'd liked having Mickey smiling at the table, sneaking most of her hamburger to Harley and winking at her, like they shared a secret together. She'd even liked hearing Dad and Mickey laughing together in the kitchen doing dishes later.

Of course, she hadn't known then that Mickey would make Dad fall in love with her and forget all about Mom. A thought struck her, hit her so hard it felt like her brother had landed one of his famous belly punches: maybe it wouldn't be such a terrible thing for Dad to forget about Mom. Maybe that's why he liked Mickey—because she made him forget.

Moonlight outlined the desk in the corner, and she thought about the e.p.t. test thing she'd hidden there—the one she'd found under the sink in Mom and Dad's bathroom—*Mickey* and Dad's bathroom. She'd been watching Mickey closely ever since that day, trying to tell if her stomach was getting pudgy the way Mom's had when she was first pregnant with Harley.

They'd all been so happy that day when Mom told them she was having another baby. Kayleigh was only nine years old, but she remembered like it was yesterday. The twins were little then, and Daddy had picked them up and put one on each shoulder and marched around the living room sing-songing, "We're gonna have a baby . . . we're gonna have a baby . . ." She and Rachel and Landon clapped and cheered along, and Mom just laughed and put her hand flat on her tummy where the baby was growing.

She smiled into the darkness. It was good to have a memory of Mom that could make her smile. Maybe there were more wherever that one had come from.

"Please, God," she whispered. Too loud, apparently, because Harley stirred beside her and popped her thumb into her mouth, sucking noisily. Kayleigh put a gentle hand on Harley's back and rubbed softly.

What if Mickey really was going to have a baby? The e.p.t. thing had a plus sign. Positive meant pregnant. She was sure of that. But she didn't know how long it took for a woman to start looking like she was pregnant.

Still patting Harley, she squinted at the alarm clock on the nightstand. It was almost midnight.

When she was sure Harley was asleep again, she crept out of bed and got the e.p.t. out of its hiding place in the back of her desk drawer. She took it down the hall into the bathroom, closed the door, and turned on the light. The plus sign was still showing. Tucking the stick into the pocket of her pajama top, she stepped into the hallway. Landon's door was closed, and it was dark downstairs. Dad and Mickey were always in bed downstairs before midnight.

She looked across the stair rail to the landing where the computer desk sat. They weren't supposed to use the computer without asking first, but she couldn't exactly ask about this. Tiptoeing, she stepped on a creaky board in the wood floor. She froze and stood like a statue, heart pounding. When she was sure the coast was clear, she eased into the chair and turned the computer on.

The computer made its start-up sound, and her heart nearly leapt through her skull. She scrambled to find the button that turned the sound off, then, while everything loaded, she stood stiff as a board, listening to see if the sound had woken Dad or Mickey up.

Almost three minutes ticked by on the clock, and the computer went into sleep mode. When she didn't hear any sounds downstairs, she eased onto the straight-back chair and clicked the mouse. She opened Google, and pressing one key at a time so they wouldn't make their usual clicking noise, she typed *e.p.t.* into the box.

One of the first entries that popped up matched the lettering on the stick she'd found. She clicked the link. There was a picture of the exact thing she'd found. She started reading. It said that the test was accurate 99 percent of the time, and that it could work before a woman even suspected she was pregnant . . . something about "as early as four days."

She thought back to the day she'd found the e.p.t. It was the day after Dad and Mickey got back from Salina—from their honeymoon. They'd gotten married on April 27. She remembered because it was the same day Seth turned thirteen. He'd flunked kindergarten so he was older than the other kids in their class.

Dad and Mickey came home the Monday after that. She counted on her fingers. Exactly four days.

She clicked a link that gave instructions for using e.p.t. There was some gross stuff about peeing on the stick. She looked down at the thing sticking out of her pocket. *Yuck.* She'd been touching it with her bare hands. Wrinkling her nose, she wiped her hands on her pajama pants before she touched the keyboard again.

She scrolled down the screen and read about how to read the little plus and minus signs in the window. She was right. The plus sign meant yes, you were pregnant. Her breath came faster. Mickey *had* to be pregnant.

What if Dad didn't know? A thought struck her: what if he did know, and that was why he and Mickey barely talked to each other anymore? She couldn't handle all the ideas and images that were coming into her head.

She heard a noise downstairs and froze. She checked to be sure the sound was turned off and slowly reached for the off button. The computer powered down and she sat there, staring into the darkness, listening for the sound she'd heard moments before. It never came.

Finally she tiptoed back to her room. But before she crawled into bed, she wrapped the e.p.t. in a tissue—a clean one, not the one with Mom's lipstick on it—and hid it in the back of her underwear drawer. She straightened the clothes in the drawer, separating her things from Harley's so nobody would have to dig on her side of the drawer.

When she finally crawled back into bed beside Harley, the clock said 1:12. But sleep wouldn't come, and she lay there, with her hand over her heart, feeling it beat so fast and so hard she was afraid it would burst through her skin.

He shot up a desperate query—words that composed a lament more than a prayer: <u>What have I done? Oh, Father in heaven, what have I done?</u>

Chapter Forty-one

Doug smelled supper the minute he opened the door. Spaghetti, if his nose was accurate at all.

"Is that you?" Mickey's voice drifted from the front of the house.

He hung his cap on the hook labeled with his name and walked through the kitchen. He stood in the doorway between the kitchen and living room, waiting for her to notice him.

She looked up from the book she was reading the little girls. Even Harley, from her perch on Sadie's lap, was enrapt with the story. At Mickey's silence they all glanced up and threw him an impatient "Hi, Daddy," as if he were an annoying intrusion.

"Hi to you, too," he said to whoever would listen.

Harley put her hands on either side of Mickey's face. "Read, Miss Mickey. Come on . . . read book."

"Wait a minute, sweetie." Mickey moved Harley's hands off her face and marked the page in the book with her hand. "Are you ready for dinner, Doug?"

He shook his head. "I'm not in for good. I just need to check the weather." He nodded toward the stairway and took the steps two at a time, hoping she wouldn't chide him for not taking his boots off.

But she only called after him, "There's spaghetti whenever you're ready. Let me know and I'll heat you up a plate."

"Okay, thanks," he hollered down. He turned on the computer and waited for it to boot up, composing a parts list for the local dealer in his mind. He should have ordered parts days ago, but he'd been trying to get caught up in the pressroom so he could use his vacation days for harvest. He couldn't afford to have the combine broken down for even a day if he was going to get the wheat in before the forecasted storms hit.

Finally the screen came to life, and he opened the browser. He posed clumsy fingers over the keyboard and tried to remember that new weather site he'd heard about. Hunt-and-peck style—the only way he knew to type—he keyed in the name. That didn't look right. He backed the delete key over the words to try another spelling. He hadn't typed four letters when an old URL from the history popped up in the address bar. He aimed for the M and got the space bar instead, backed up, and started to retype it. But when he looked up to check his spelling, he noticed an old address there again. He looked at it, then did a double take. What was this?

The first part of the address was *drugs*. But that wasn't the part that made him look twice. The words that followed *drugs* said *e.p.t.-pregnancy-test*.

Whoa. He must have mistyped something. He deleted and started to type in the weather site URL again, but something made him stop.

He opened up the drug/pregnancy page and an ad for one of those in-home pregnancy tests appeared on the screen. Kaye had used one of those each time she suspected she was pregnant. The memories hit him hard.

He started to scroll down the page, then looked behind him, half expecting to see Landon or Kayeleigh standing there with a million and one questions. But just then he heard them arguing downstairs, and Mickey in the background, shushing them, and still reading to the little girls.

He looked at the address again. He didn't have time for this. He needed to get off the computer and get a parts order placed and over-nighted. But something compelled him to pull down the browser's history and investigate further.

According to the history log, he was the first one to use the computer today. The most recent address before that was the pregnancy test site. He checked the date. June 18. Two days ago. He thought they had the pop-up blocker turned on, and security set so the kids wouldn't come across anything inappropriate. But sometimes stuff got through any-way. Or Mickey had turned off the parental controls. . . . A look at the rest of the history and the Google search history for that same day sent ice through his veins. Someone had purposefully typed in *e.p.t.,* then looked at half a dozen sites about pregnancy and pregnancy test kits.

He heard Mickey's laughter downstairs, heard the twins giggling as she acted out the Tickle Monster from the book.

His heart turned to lead. Mickey must suspect that she was preg— He couldn't let himself finish the thought. He tugged a rumpled hand-kerchief out of his back pocket and swabbed his forehead, fighting for breath, struggling to think straight.

Somehow he found the parts site and ordered what he needed, but he couldn't push the image of that larger-than-life purple and white plastic stick out of his mind.

For the millionth time in two months, he shot up a desperate query— words that composed a lament more than a prayer: *What have I done? Oh, Father in heaven, what have I done?*

He puttered around out in the shed, biding his time until he could be sure the kids were in bed. His belly protested with hunger pangs, but he ignored them. He had no right to even think about being hungry with such a weight pressing on him. On Mickey.

A new thought came over him. Maybe she wasn't actually pregnant. Maybe she'd just thought she was. Nothing he'd seen on the computer screen was about babies. It was all about the test itself. That had to be a good sign, right? He hadn't looked further back into the Internet history. That was only yesterday's search. Maybe there was more. He should have checked. If Mickey even suspected she was pregnant, it was serious. She was at least as crazy about kids as Kaye was, and he knew how Kaye had been every time she was a few days late.

They'd had more than one argument because she'd spent money on one of those stupid tests just because she ate too much pizza the night before and woke up sick. Those things weren't cheap, but Kaye always wanted to know at the first possible minute.

And the five times it had turned out positive she'd glowed with the news and found creative ways to announce it, then wanted to celebrate by making his favorite dinner, baking a cake, and making love again for good measure. He had loved it when she was carrying one of their babies.

He didn't even care about the razzing he got at work when one of the guys got wind that the DeVores were having *another* kid. Let 'em make fun. It didn't matter.

He and Kaye had decided when the twins were born that they didn't care what other people thought. They loved their kids. They'd always wanted a big family, both of them. And though money was scarce, they'd provided for their family plenty well.

He'd seen the articles in Kaye's parenting magazines that said it cost two hundred thousand dollars to raise a child to adulthood. Hogwash.

The food always stretched to feed the next mouth. Kaye had always breastfed the babies, so there was no formula to buy, and she'd kept a big vegetable garden that the kids took turns weeding. Shoot, they usually ended up with enough tomatoes and squash to share with the neighbors *and* the community pantry at the Clayburn Public Library. The kids handed their clothes down, and Kaye's bumper sticker—I BRAKE FOR GARAGE SALES—wasn't just for show. Her mother was generous at Christmas and birthdays. And the money Kaye made as a secretary at the school—what little was left over after they paid the daycare bill—filled in around the edges. Bottom line, the kids had never wanted for anything that was truly important.

He caught his breath. His children had never wanted because they had love. And parents who were crazy about each other. But if Mickey was pregnant—? How would the emptiness between them affect a child? He was afraid to imagine.

A shadow fell across the patch of light the yard lamp cast, and Doug looked up to see Mickey standing in the doorway.

"Do you want me to bring you out a plate? You must be starving."

His hands started trembling, and he shoved them in his pockets. "I'm okay," he lied.

"Are you sure? I don't mind heating you up a plate. It's spaghetti. Turned out pretty good if I do say so myself."

"I'm okay."

He didn't realize he'd snapped at her until her smile abruptly disappeared. She turned and started back for the house.

"Mickey!"

She turned around and stood in the open door, waiting. Her face was in shadow, but something about her demeanor made him think she was crying. *Oh, Father. Help me find the words.*

He took a step toward her, looked into her brimming eyes. "Mickey . . . are you pregnant?"

She reeled as if he'd struck her. "Wh-what?"

"Are you going to have a baby?"

She gave a humorless laugh. "I know what pregnant means."

"*Are* you?"

"No. No . . . of course not. Why would you even ask something like that?"

The relief he expected at her denial didn't come. Confusion clouded his mind. "But . . . I thought . . . I saw the search. On the computer."

She frowned. "What are you talking about?"

He rubbed a hand over his face, felt the grime and sweat bead under his calloused hands. "You didn't search—on the computer?"

"Search for what?"

He shook his head, trying to clear the cobwebs. He didn't think she was playing dumb. "When I ordered the parts—earlier tonight—there were several pages of Web sites in the history . . . sites about pregnancy tests . . . you know, those kits you can use to find out if you're pregnant?"

"I know what a pregnancy test is, Doug." She gave another dry laugh, and the sound pained him for reasons he couldn't put his finger on.

"So it wasn't you?"

She wagged her head. "No."

"Then who?"

She shrugged. "Are you sure it wasn't just an ad—one of those pop-up things that sometimes sneak through?"

"No. It was in the history. Several Web sites in a row. It looked like somebody was searching for information about pregnancy tests. I think e.p.t. was in the title of one page."

She nodded. "Yes, it's a brand name." She brought a hand to her mouth, and even in the dim circle of light the yard lamp cast, he could see her face turn ashen.

"What is it?"

"Oh, Doug, what if Kayeleigh—?"

"What?" He took another step toward her. He didn't like the look on her face. Surely she couldn't be thinking what her words implied.

"Kayeleigh was on the computer Sunday afternoon. She said she was looking up words from that library book she's reading. But you don't think . . . ?"

He narrowed his eyes at her. "What are you saying? Why would Kayeleigh be looking up stuff like that? Besides, this was from just a couple of days ago." He hadn't checked the history before that, but he intended to, the minute he got inside the house.

"Doug?" Mickey still looked stricken. "You don't think she . . . thinks she's pregnant?"

He reared back the way she had when he'd asked her if *she* was pregnant a few minutes ago. "Kayeleigh? You can't be serious? I don't think she's even got her period yet, has she? She's never even had a boyfriend. Why would you even *say* something like that?"

"Doug, I think Kayeleigh's a little more . . . experienced . . . than you might think."

"Experienced? What's that supposed to mean?" She was exaggerating.

"I told you about her being at Seth Berger's that day she ran off from Wren's."

"So?"

"She was in that house alone with Seth and his brother. His older brother."

He stared at her, knowing his mouth must be hanging open. But Mickey was talking crazy. Assuming things that simply could not be true. Seth was trouble, no doubt about that. But Mickey didn't know Kayeleigh. "You surely don't think they were—?" He couldn't finish the sentence. This was his little girl they were talking about. His innocent little girl. How could Mickey even think such disgusting things about her and that kid?

"You didn't see her with Seth, Doug. They were—all over each other."

He snorted. Funny that Mickey used the same words Harriet had used in reference to the two of them at the wedding dance that afternoon. "How exactly do you mean?"

"Seth's brother answered the door—"

"Ben?"

"Yes. Kayeleigh and Seth were in the basement—and I could see down the stairs . . . it was dark down there. When they came up, she looked . . . I guess *disheveled* is the best way to describe it. They stood there, right in front of me, and he had his arms around her waist and she was leaning back against him." She swallowed hard. "They looked pretty comfortable together that way."

"Oh, come on, Mickey."

Now it was her turn to stare at him open-mouthed. "You think I'm making that up?"

He took his cap off and slapped it against his knee. A little cloud of dust rose up like smoke in the glow from the yard light. "No. I'm not saying that. But . . . she's a *child*. I think you misunderstood what you saw."

"I assure you I did not. Is that—" She cut off her words and bent her head.

"What?"

She looked up and gazed at him beneath hooded eyes. "Is that what you would have said to Kayeleigh that day she caught us making out in my kitchen? That she misunderstood what she saw?"

The words were like a blow to his gut. He blew out a hard breath and kicked at a rusty nail on the shed's concrete floor. "That's different." But an image of Kayeleigh and the Berger kid dancing together at that wedding last spring kept nudging into his brain.

"I don't think so, Doug."

"You don't really think she—?"

"I don't know. But I think you need to talk with her."

He clenched and unclenched his fists at his side. "How can I do that? I don't want to put ideas in her head."

"Oh, Doug." She shook her head. "I'm afraid the ideas may already be there."

His eyes burned and his stomach did somersaults. "You don't honestly think Kayeleigh could be—*pregnant?*" He spit the word out, his voice breaking.

"I hope not. I hope it's just curiosity . . . the stuff she was searching online. But you need to talk to her. Before it becomes something else. Do you—do you want me to talk to her with you?"

"I don't want you to talk to her with me. I want *you* to talk to her." He mimicked the dry laugh she'd offered earlier.

She shook her head. "I don't think she much cares what I have to say. But I can help you with . . . the female stuff."

"Thank you." He let his shoulders slump, when what he really wanted to do was fall to his knees on the concrete. "Do you think we should wake her up?"

"Let's . . . wait. Do it first thing in the morning, okay?"

He nodded as tears clogged his throat. He'd thought he'd lived through the worst that life could possibly throw at him. But maybe there were worse things than losing your wife and daughter on Thanksgiving Day.

The realization
humbled him. Or
maybe ~~humiliated~~ was
~~the~~ better word.

Chapter Forty-two

Kayeleigh pulled the blankets around her and sought out the pleasant dream again. Another nudge threatened to ruin any chance of finishing it. "Stop it, Harley," she mumbled.

"Kayeleigh. Get up," a voice whispered.

No. It was Dad. *Go away. Go away. Don't ruin my dream.* Seth was there, holding her hand, looking at her like he thought she was the most beautiful girl in the world.

"Kayeleigh."

Go away! Too late.

It was gone. She couldn't even remember half of what had been playing out in the sweet world of slumberland.

What time was it anyway? She peeked out from the covers at the clock. Six o'clock? Rubbing her eyes, she tried to make Dad come into focus.

Mickey was standing beside him. Huh? That brought her fully awake. She sat up in bed and stared at them, her heart pounding. "What's wrong?"

"Maybe nothing," Dad said, his voice low. "But we need to talk to you."

"What'd I do?"

"Come downstairs and we'll talk. And don't wake Harley up."

She swung her legs over the side of the bed. What was the deal?

"I gotta pee first."

"Okay." Dad stood with one hand on the stair rail, Mickey right beside him. "But come right down then. And make it speedy. I've got to get in the field."

"What did I do?" She racked her brain, trying to think why she'd be in trouble. He'd said last night that they'd probably start harvesting today. It must be pretty serious for him to get her up before he went to the field. Probably some Mickey-the-Neatfreak thing. Maybe she left a piece of lint on the sofa. Or a crumb on the kitchen counter. Or maybe she didn't arrange the stuff on her shelf in alphabetical order.

She finished in the bathroom, washed her hands, splashed some cold water on her face, and plodded downstairs.

Dad and Mickey were sitting side by side at the kitchen table, looking like it was something a lot more serious than a piece of lint.

She sat down across from them, propped her elbows on the table, and hooked her bare feet around the chair legs. "What's wrong?"

✳ ❈ ✳

ayeleigh." Doug swallowed hard against a throat that felt like sandpaper. "We—*I* need to talk to you about something . . . ask you some questions."

Her eyes widened, and she sat up a little straighter on the chair. He didn't want to scare her or make any accusations that would cause her to feel she couldn't talk to him, but he needed to put his mind at ease. What Mickey said about Kayeleigh possibly being . . . *intimate* . . . with that Berger kid simply could not be true. Sitting here, looking into his daughter's sleep-crusted eyes, her tousled hair flying every which way around her angel face, he knew Mickey had to be wrong.

He felt Mickey's presence beside him. Their chairs were butted side by side across the table from Kayeleigh, but by unspoken agreement, they were both careful not to let their bodies touch at any point. He risked a glance at her. Mickey widened her eyes, a signal, he knew, that he should get on with it.

He glanced at the clock over the refrigerator. He didn't have time for this in the first place. The harvest crew he'd hired was probably fueling up already, and they'd have to wait on him if he didn't hustle. He took a deep breath and looked Kayeleigh in the eye. "I was ordering some parts on the computer last night and—I noticed that certain sites had been visited on the Internet." He shook his head and frowned. "Stuff kids really don't need to be looking at. You . . . you don't know anything about that, do you?

She opened her mouth to say something, but just as quickly clamped it shut. She leaned her forehead on the table, but the crooked part in her hair blazed pink.

He had his answer. "Why were you looking up that stuff, honey?"

She shook her head and mumbled something to the floor.

"Kayeleigh. Look at me."

After a long minute she lifted her head. Her face was crimson, her mouth screwed into an angry pout.

"Why were you searching those things on the Internet?" he asked again.

She glared at him, then turned slowly to Mickey. "Why don't you ask *her*?" She jabbed her chin in Mickey's direction, punctuating her words.

He looked to Mickey, questioning her with his eyes. She gave an almost imperceptible shrug. He and Mickey had gone up to the computer late last night and checked the history as far back as it went. They hadn't found anything else.

He turned back to Kayeleigh. "What do you mean by that?"

"Ask her!" she shouted. "She's the one you should be talking to. She's the one that had that stupid thing!"

Mickey leaned across the table. "Settle down, Kayeleigh. Tell us what you're talking about." She put a hand on Kayeleigh's arm. "What 'stupid thing'?"

Kayeleigh yanked her arm away, her eyes narrowed to slits. "You don't have to play dumb. You know what I'm talking about."

Doug scraped back his chair and grabbed her arm across the table. "You do not talk to Mickey that way, young lady!"

Eyes wild with fury, Kayeleigh sucked her cheeks in and worked her tongue. She spit a spray of saliva between them. Mickey gave a little yelp and reared back on her chair, but a bubbly drop of spittle landed on Doug's forearm, soaking into the sun-bleached hairs that peppered his leathery skin.

He recoiled, wiping his arm off on the front of his shirt and raising his arm high into the air in one smooth motion. He pushed off the table and brought the back of his hand down across Kayeleigh's mouth.

She gasped, and he felt sharp teeth behind the cushion of her lip. He pulled his hand away, smarting.

"Doug! Stop it!" Mickey's shrill plea came from beside him while he watched a thin trail of blood trickle slowly down Kayeleigh's chin.

Kayeleigh stood motionless, eyes round. Twin droplets of blood appeared beneath her lower lip, bubbling up the same way his own rage had.

"You hate me!" Kayeleigh screamed. "You *hate* me!"

He froze, a wool blanket of guilt wrapping itself around him. But he threw it off the way he threw off the quilts on a summer night when they couldn't afford to run the air conditioner.

The kid had it coming. Mouthy brat. He grabbed her arm and jerked her halfway across the table. "If you ever do that again—" The words came out in a spray of his own saliva. He licked his lips and started over, grinding out the words through clenched teeth. "If you *ever* do that again, I'll—"

"You'll what?" The sheer terror in her eyes changed rapidly to rage. She sucked the blood off her lip. Her teeth turned a ghoulish red. "Why don't you just kill me? You know you want to." But the minute the words were out, the defiance drained from her eyes, and suddenly she looked like his little girl again. His precious baby girl.

Her face crumpled, and she buried her head in the neckline of her pajama top. Tiny spots of blood soaked through where her mouth was. She collapsed into the chair, lay her head on the table, and began to sob.

He sucked in a breath, remorse hitting him as hard as he'd hit his daughter. *Oh, dear God . . .* What had he done? What was wrong with him?

"Doug?" There was a hint of horror in Mickey's voice, and he knew he must have become a stranger before her eyes just now. But Mickey wasn't his first concern right now. He had to make things right with Kayeleigh.

He leapt from his chair and went around the table to her. He tried to get her to stand up, but she was a limp dishrag. He knelt beside her chair and put an arm around her, pulling her against his chest. She didn't melt into his embrace the way she usually did, but fell limp against him, still hiding her face behind the collar of her pajamas.

"Kayeleigh. I'm sorry," he whispered. "Daddy never should have done that. Please forgive me." His stomach churned, and he was afraid he might be sick. But he kept his arms around her, gently shushing her as if she were three years old again, and she'd fallen off her tricycle.

He held her for several minutes until she calmed down and eased against him. He glanced at Mickey, who was still sitting across from them at the table, with her head in her hands. Her lips were moving silently as if she might be praying.

Finally he peeled Kayeleigh off of him, still keeping a hand on her knee. "I'm sorry, sweetie," he said again. "Will you forgive me?"

Kayeleigh gave a brief nod, but her hand went to her lip. She swiped her fingers across her mouth, then checked them for blood. Her lip wasn't bleeding anymore, but it was swollen.

Doug went to the kitchen for an ice cube. He wrapped it in a clean dishcloth and brought it back, handing it to her without a word.

"Mickey?"

She met his eyes, a dazed look in her own.

"I'm sorry for losing my temper, Mickey. That was inexcusable."

She stared at him, tight-lipped.

"Will you forgive me?"

"I forgive you," she whispered, but her tremulous voice made him doubt she was quite ready to wholly forgive what she'd witnessed.

He didn't blame her. What he'd done was unconscionable. But he couldn't just let things drop. "We still need to talk about this," he said, looking from Mickey to Kayeleigh and back.

He patted Kayeleigh's knee, wanting to reassure her that he had his temper under control now. With a glance back at Mickey, he forged ahead. "Kayeleigh, why do you think Mickey should know what that stuff on the Internet is about?" Without waiting for her to answer, he turned to Mickey. "You *don't* know, right?"

She shook her head. "No. I really don't, Kayeleigh." She glanced at Doug, asking permission with her eyes.

He nodded.

Mickey spoke quietly. "Just so we know we're talking about the same thing, what your dad and I saw was a search for information about a pregnancy test. Are you the one who was looking at those Web sites?"

Kayeleigh nodded.

"Were you just curious, honey?" Mickey leaned across the table, her voice soothing. "Or was there a reason you needed to know about pregnancy tests?"

Doug was relieved to have Mickey taking the lead. Why hadn't he thought to ask this way? Mickey was handling it like—like Kaye would have handled it. The realization humbled him. Or maybe *humiliated* was the better word.

"I found one of them . . . one of those tests," she mumbled, still refusing to look directly at him.

Relief flooded through him. She hadn't been looking for herself. *Praise God.* But that didn't explain—

"Where? Where did you find one?" Mickey coaxed.

"In the trash. In your room."

Doug looked to Mickey.

She shook her head, and Doug felt certain she was being honest.

"In the trash can in . . . the master bathroom?" Mickey pointed down the hall that led to the bedroom they shared.

Kayeleigh nodded. "Are you . . . are you going to have a baby?" She blurted the words as if they were hot coals on her tongue.

Mickey's eyes widened, and she started shaking her head. "No, Kayeleigh. I'm not. Is . . . is that what you thought?"

Kayeleigh tilted her head and eyed her. "Why did you have one of those tests, then?"

Doug stared at Kayeleigh. The test didn't belong to either of them? There was only one other possibility. He sank back into the chair, his legs suddenly turning to jelly. "When . . . when exactly did you find it?"

Kayeleigh shrugged. "That day you made us clean the house really good because she"—she nodded toward Mickey—"griped that it wasn't clean enough. It must have fallen out of the trash. It was kind of stuck in the corner in the back of the cabinet."

Mickey closed her eyes. "It must have been—" She cut off her sentence, apparently guessing the truth at the same moment he did.

The test had been *Kaye's.* Kaye must have thought she was pregnant.

She'd taken the test and thrown it away, but apparently it missed the trash can and nobody had bothered to clean the cupboard under the sink. Until Kayeleigh found it.

Had Kaye been pregnant? The thought left him stunned. Had she been planning, even on the Thanksgiving Day she died, some special way to break the news to him? She'd not wanted to kiss him that morning, telling him she thought she was coming down with the flu Rachel had. He'd always looked back and thought it was the carbon monoxide already working, but now he wondered.

"I . . . I still have it," Kayeleigh offered. "The test . . ."

Doug caught his breath. "You do? Where?"

"I'll get it."

He and Mickey nodded in unison, and Kayeleigh scooted her chair away from the table and padded up the stairs.

Doug watched her go and thought she moved like a ninety-year-old woman. A lump rose to his throat. Would his sweet daughter ever recover from this morning? Would she ever be able to forgive what he'd done?

His shoulders slumped as he realized that even if she could someday forgive him, she would never forget. As long as she lived, she would remember the day her daddy had hit her. Hit her hard enough to make her mouth bleed. He wanted to weep.

Mickey touched his arm with a feather stroke. "Doug?"

He struggled through the gloomy thoughts. "It must have been Kaye's? The test . . ."

She nodded. "That has to be it." She started to say something else, but they heard Kayeleigh on the stairs, and Mickey shook her head.

Kayeleigh appeared at the table with a tissue in her hand. She unfolded it to reveal the familiar e.p.t. device, identical to those Kaye had used on numerous occasions.

Kayeleigh held it out to him. "It has a plus sign on it, Daddy. That means . . . pregnant, doesn't it?"

He couldn't bring himself to look at it. He managed to nod. He had to remind himself to take a breath.

"Are you *sure* it's not yours?" Kayeleigh asked Mickey.

Mickey shot him a look of desperation.

Doug made a decision. She was almost thirteen. She deserved to know the truth. "No, honey. It . . . it must have been your mom's."

Comprehension came to Kayeleigh's eyes. "Mom was . . . ?"

Doug shook his head. "I don't know." He looked to Mickey, hoping she knew more than he did about this type of thing.

She shook her head and shrugged.

"If Mom was going to have a baby, she hadn't told me. We may never know, honey. I don't know if a plus sign is accurate . . . after this long. It might not mean anything. . . ."

"But what if Mom *was* going to have a baby?" Her voice broke on a sob.

He choked down the rock in his throat. "Then you have a little brother or sister in heaven." *Another* sister in heaven, he thought.

Mickey reached to put a hand on each of their arms. "I'm sorry."

He sat, stunned, unable to move, to even acknowledge her tender words.

Had those invisible, fatal fumes taken even more from him than he knew? Despite his and Kaye's decision that six was enough, despite the precautions they'd taken, had Kaye been pregnant with their seventh child that day? She hadn't said a word. Hadn't even mentioned she suspected as much.

Maybe Kaye had been suffering from morning sickness before the carbon monoxide snuffed out her life. And the life of their unborn child? It was too much to take in.

Who would this baby have been? Would this have been the brother Landon had always begged them for? Or another little angel like Harley? Or Rachel? Sweet Rachel . . .

He couldn't let his thoughts go there. Not now. It was too much.

Forcing himself to stand, he pulled Kayeleigh into a hug, and she let him, hugged him back. "You go get dressed now, okay?"

Tears spilled onto her cheeks. "Do I have to go to the daycare today? Please, Daddy. I don't want to go anywhere. I don't want to have to talk to anybody." Desperation was in her voice.

He looked to Mickey, feeling desperate himself.

"Listen," she said. "Why don't I call and see if I can get one of the college girls to cover for me today. I'll stay home with all the kids. It'd be nice if they could sleep in for once this summer."

Doug nodded, and his heart filled with gratitude. "Thanks," he mouthed to Mickey.

But Kayeleigh spoke the words aloud, her tone meek and earnest. "Thank you, Mickey."

He knew he needed to share some of the things he'd discovered with Mickey. Things that might not be easy for her to hear.

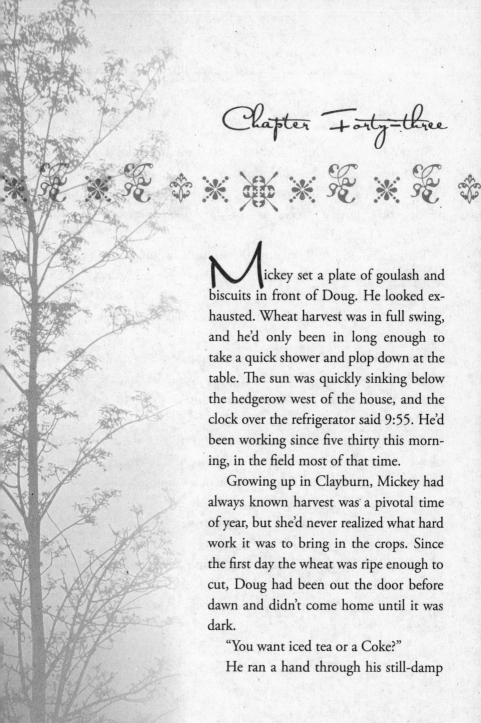

Chapter Forty-three

Mickey set a plate of goulash and biscuits in front of Doug. He looked exhausted. Wheat harvest was in full swing, and he'd only been in long enough to take a quick shower and plop down at the table. The sun was quickly sinking below the hedgerow west of the house, and the clock over the refrigerator said 9:55. He'd been working since five thirty this morning, in the field most of that time.

Growing up in Clayburn, Mickey had always known harvest was a pivotal time of year, but she'd never realized what hard work it was to bring in the crops. Since the first day the wheat was ripe enough to cut, Doug had been out the door before dawn and didn't come home until it was dark.

"You want iced tea or a Coke?"

He ran a hand through his still-damp

hair. "Tea, please. But I can get it." He started to push back his chair.

"Don't be silly. Stay put." She fixed his drink and brought it to the table, then went back to the sink.

"The kids are all in bed?"

She nodded.

They'd barely seen him for three days. If she hadn't taken them out to the field last night, he wouldn't have seen them at all yesterday. But she and the kids had stopped at Dairy Barn on their way home from the daycare and ordered chocolate malts for him and the crew.

"How's Kayeleigh?"

Dishrag still in hand, she turned from the sink and leaned the small of her back against the counter. "She seems okay. She really does. She asked about you."

He looked up and talked over a mouthful of goulash. "What do you mean?"

She twisted the dishrag. "When we got home from daycare, she asked when you'd be in. When I told her it would be late, she asked me to wake her up before you left the house tomorrow."

"You think something's wrong?"

"I asked her. She said no. I think she's just worried about you. I don't know—" Mickey hesitated, not sure if Doug was in the right frame of mind to discuss what had happened the other morning. But harvest or not, they couldn't just sweep things under the rug.

He took a swig of tea and looked up at her. "Go on . . . what were you going to say?"

"Kayeleigh seems like a different girl since . . . everything that happened. She's been really sweet to me." Her voice broke and she teared up. "I think she just wants reassurance that things are okay between you and her."

oug didn't trust his own voice, but he nodded. Mickey was right. He would be sure and wake Kayeleigh in the morning. He hoped her new demeanor meant she was handling everything okay. There was a lot for her to process—the terrible thing he'd done in striking her, then he and Mickey practically accusing her of being pregnant. And of course, their discovery about Kaye.

He still didn't know if it was true or not. Maybe they would never know. But he and Mickey had gone online and found numerous references to positive pregnancy results that remained readable many months or even years after the initial test.

Somehow, he felt certain in his heart that it *was* true. That Kaye had been expecting a baby. Knowing her, she'd probably had a plan up her sleeve to tell him in some clever, romantic way.

In spite of the harried pace and long hours of the harvest season, he'd had many hours riding the combine to think about everything that had happened. God had both touched his heart and broken him in those moments. He knew he needed to share some of the things he'd discovered with Mickey. Things that might not be easy for her to hear.

Maybe tonight was a good time to begin.

He finished eating and took his plate over to the sink. Mickey took it from him and put it in the dishwasher. Somehow, they'd become shy with each other, but he forced himself to look her in the eye. "Are you too tired to talk for a little bit?"

She lifted her brows in surprise. "No."

"Mind if we go out on the porch?"

"Sure." She switched off the light over the sink and followed him out front.

The air was still warm and crickets chirped a monotonous chorus. An inky blue sky formed a starry canopy over them, and something about that infinite sky put a lump in his throat. A portal to heaven.

Where Kaye and Rachel lived now. Where the answers to all his questions were hidden.

He eased onto the top step, elbows on his knees. Mickey sat beside him, leaning back against the round column that supported the porch roof.

She bent her head, waiting. How could he possibly say the things that were in his heart without hurting her? He opened his mouth to speak, but she held up a hand.

"Doug, I need to say something."

He waited, praying her words wouldn't make the things he had to say more difficult.

She shifted on the step, angling to face him. "When you . . . got so angry with Kayeleigh the other day, I realized that it wasn't really her you were angry with. It was me."

The pain etched on her face nearly killed him. He wasn't making excuses for his behavior, but he couldn't honestly argue with her conclusion.

She swallowed hard and went on. "I don't know how we . . . how you and I lost whatever there was between us once. I don't know why we haven't been able to"—her voice broke—"to find that again. I thought I could make a difference in spite of it . . . for the kids, if not for you. But if this . . . this anger is what I've done to you, what I've brought into your life, then I can't stay."

"No, Mickey. Please. It's not your fault. What I did—it's not your fault. Please don't ever think that."

"What am I supposed to think? I saw in Kayeleigh's eyes that she'd never seen you like this before. Not until I came along."

"But I can't blame you, Mickey. It's . . . when I lost Kaye, when I lost Rachel, I lost my way. I should have turned to God more than ever, and most of the time I thought I was. But . . . I've been praying a lot these last few days, and I realize that, in many ways, I turned my back on God."

Mickey nodded as though she'd recognized that all along.

"Since we found out about Kaye, about the baby—" He dropped his head. "I don't know . . . in some ways I feel like I've begun the grieving process all over again."

"And I wonder if you ever truly grieved in the first place. The way you needed to. I think I got in the way, Doug. It was too soon. I should have realized that. And did, I think. I just didn't want to admit it. To you, or to myself."

He nodded. She was probably right. In fact, her words sounded familiar. Maybe she'd said as much when he was courting her. Or maybe Wren's words—and Harriet's, and who-knew-who-else's—were coming into focus now. He should have listened. "I was in so much pain—emotional pain—when I first lost Kaye and Rachel. I don't think I allowed myself to think too deeply, even to remember what I'd had. How blessed I was. It hurt too much. That wasn't healthy. No matter how agonizing it was, I should have plowed through the pain. Instead . . ."

He looked at his boots, trying to find the right words. "Instead, I reached for you. And for a little while, I felt happy. You helped me forget how much I hurt. I just wanted something, anything that would take away the pain. You did that for me."

She looked at him with such hope in her eyes. But he couldn't lie to her again. He'd done too much of that already. "Mickey, I'm sorry. I didn't even realize what I was doing, but I used you. You were . . . almost like a drug for me. I just wanted the hurt to go away. I was just so desperate to be happy again. And for a little while you made me feel happy. But . . . I'm afraid I mistook happiness for love. I'm so sorry."

"And now—it's too late?"

He feared the ember of hope he saw in her eyes. Whatever he did, he could not fan it into flame. At a loss for words, he simply nodded.

She rubbed the frayed hem of her T-shirt. "I wish we could start all over. I wish there was some way to turn back the clock—But, of course, if that were possible, you'd turn it back to . . ." Her voice dropped to a whisper. "To Kaye."

He couldn't deny it. Nor could he look at the pain in this beautiful woman's face. He turned away, gazed to the east.

What had he done? *What had he done?*

Her lower lip quivered. "Do you want me to leave?"

"No! Oh, Mickey, no." He'd never thought she would leave him. Even when he told her the truth—that he didn't love her as he should, *couldn't* love her as long as he carried this terrible love for Kaye—he'd never expected that she might leave him.

"Doug, I know now that you never loved me . . . not in that way. Not the way I need you to. As much as it hurts, I understand that. I do. But how can I stay, knowing that?"

"I don't know." He shook his head, numb.

"If I leave . . ." She began to weep and covered her face with her hands. "What about the kids? I love them, *too*—" In the midst of her tears, she gave a little gasp, and he realized that with that small, three-letter word, she'd confessed that she still loved him.

Her shoulders shook and he wanted to hold her while she cried. But how could he? If he touched her, it would negate everything he needed to say. "I don't want you to leave, Mickey. I don't know if my kids could ever forgive me if I pushed you away. They love you."

He wished with all his might that he could go on, say the next logical words: *I love you, too.* But he couldn't. Confusion swirled around him like the swift eddies of the Smoky Hill in the spring thaw.

Finally he took a deep breath. "Mickey, I have nothing to offer you. Nothing. I'm a miserable, broken man, and I've caused you more pain than any woman deserves, let alone a woman as wonderful as you are. But . . . I'm asking you to stay. For the kids. They need you."

She sat with her head down, and he couldn't tell if she was angry or hurt, or simply numb . . . like he was.

"I promise you, Mickey, I'll be good to you. I will never, ever again lay a hand on one of the children, or God forbid, on you. I'm not a rich man, but you will never want for anything that's in my power to give you. But ... for now, I can't ... offer you love. Not the love you're wanting. That you expect."

"What choice do I have, Doug?" A splinter of bitterness crept into her voice. "I've rented my house out. I can't go to my brothers. I can't afford another place. You've left me no choice."

He tried to breathe through the boulder sitting on his chest. "If you hate me, I don't blame you. What I've done to you—the position I've put you in—it's reprehensible. But I'm asking you to stay. I'm begging you to stay."

"I don't hate you, Doug. What we did—you didn't force me to say, 'I do.' But if I stay, I-I can't share your bed."

Her words startled him. "No. Of course not. I'll ... move into Landon's room. You can have our—the master bedroom. And the bath."

"What will you tell the kids?"

"I don't know. We'll come up with something."

"*You'll* come up with something."

"I'm sorry. Of course." He dared to touch her arm. "Mickey, all I can hope for is that someday you'll forgive me. And that maybe ..." He'd been about to offer her hope that someday his wounds might heal, and he might be able to offer her some piece of himself, of his heart.

He shrugged and let his words trail off. He'd already made her too many idle promises. From this day forward, he vowed in his heart to offer her nothing less—or more—than kindness.

And the truth.

For his kids' sake, he was glad Mickey was part of their lives. But she deserved better.

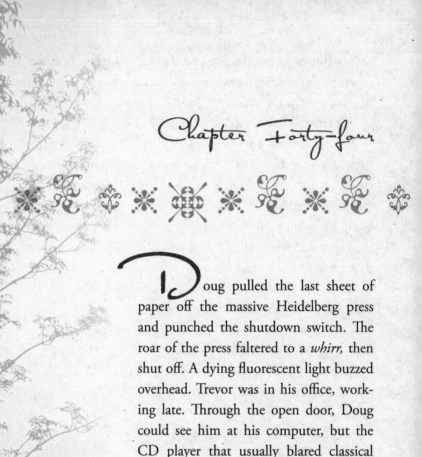

Chapter Forty-four

Doug pulled the last sheet of paper off the massive Heidelberg press and punched the shutdown switch. The roar of the press faltered to a *whirr,* then shut off. A dying fluorescent light buzzed overhead. Trevor was in his office, working late. Through the open door, Doug could see him at his computer, but the CD player that usually blared classical music was silent.

He untied his filthy apron and hung it by the back door. Grabbing a copy of this week's edition of the *Courier* to take home to Mickey, he gathered his lunch bag, flipped off the lights, and opened the back door to a blast of August heat.

"Doug?"

He turned to see Trevor standing in the doorway between his office and the pressroom.

"Hey, Trevor." He closed the door and

set his things on his desk beside a precariously stacked pile of school calendars. Enrollment was only a couple weeks off, and the district office had gotten the order for the calendar in late. "I was just finishing up. You need something?"

"I want to talk to you for a minute . . . if you have time." Trevor rubbed his hands together and looked at the floor, seeming reluctant to speak.

For a terrifying second Doug thought his boss—his friend—was going to let him go. Business had been on the slow side for the print shop, but that wasn't all that unusual for this time of year. Things would pick up once school started.

But when Trevor looked up, he was wearing an odd smile. "We just found out we're having another baby."

"Oh, man, that's great!" Doug closed the space between them and shook Trevor's hand, feeling genuinely happy for the man. "Congratulations, buddy."

"Yeah, thanks. I . . . we didn't exactly plan on having another one this soon."

Doug laughed. "Well, you've got to know I know how *that* feels." He waited for Trevor to laugh along.

Instead his friend's expression grew sober. "Man, we can barely handle Jenna. I don't know when the last time was either of us slept through the night. I thought babies were supposed to sleep all the time."

Doug stifled a laugh, then decided it might be just what the situation called for. "They start sleeping really well when they hit ten. About the same time they could finally be big help."

Trevor shook his head and let out a low whistle. "I don't know how you do it."

"You do it one day at a time." He punched Trevor in the arm. "One *kid* at a time."

"Was it as easy as you made it look when your kids were little? Last night Meg and I were doing the math—two cribs, two strollers, two highchairs, two—"

"Make that three of everything if you have twins. Like Kaye and me."

Trevor's eyes grew round. "Thanks a lot."

"Just a dose of reality." Doug laughed.

This time Trevor joined in. "So you're telling me we'll survive?"

Doug clapped a hand to Trevor's shoulder and held it there. "You'll not only survive, you'll thrive. That first baby's great, but she's just practice. When the others come along, that's when you really start to feel like a family."

"Whoa . . . whoa!" Trevor held up a hand and took a backward step. "We're thinking two is a very nice number. Two."

"Two's nice," Doug deadpanned. "Six is better." He thought of Rachel, and his heart welled with remembrance. And with love and pride.

"Don't let Meg hear you say that."

Doug laughed, then turned serious. "The thing is, Trevor, you do it together. I couldn't have done it alone . . . but then, I don't think Kaye could have, either. God knew what he was doing when he designed families."

"I know you're right on that point. The six kids' part, I'm not so sure about."

"I'd be up a creek without Mickey now. After I lost Kaye . . ." He shook his head. The truth was, for all the mistakes he made with Mickey, he didn't know how he ever would have gotten through without her. For sure, things would have been far rougher on the kids without her gentle touch on their lives.

"How are things going with you two? I know it was a struggle for a while. . . ."

"Still is some days. Most days, I guess. More for her than me, probably."

"Well, I'm praying for you."

"It's Mickey you ought to be praying for. To tell you the truth, I'm not sure how she's put up with me all this time. But she has. And she deserves a medal."

"I doubt she thinks she got the short end of the stick."

"Oh, she knows. She's a very intelligent woman." He raised an eyebrow and grinned. Then he immediately felt guilty for making light of what he'd said.

"You don't sound like you're kidding." Trevor's voice was tinged with worry.

He sighed. "I'm not, Trevor. I cheated Mickey out of a lot of things. Not intentionally, but I didn't think. Or if I did, I was only thinking of one person. And it wasn't Mickey."

More and more he was aware of how much Mickey had sacrificed to marry him. She'd never thrown it in his face or reminded him of all the dreams she'd thrown away. Dreams that would never be fulfilled—that big wedding with the white dress. Children of her own. Even the excitement of a long courtship and time to enjoy being engaged. All those things had been denied her because he'd fooled himself into thinking she would ease his pain.

And she did. It was good to have her laughter in his house. Even if it wasn't him that provoked it. For his kids' sake, he was glad Mickey was part of their lives. But she deserved better.

"But you're working things out?"

He wished he could honor the hope in Trevor's voice, but he couldn't look him in the eye. "Let's just say, we're making the best of it."

"You've been through some hard stuff. I know where you've been, man."

"I know you do."

"Maybe . . . maybe I should have been there for you more."

"You didn't have to say a word. Watching you—breathe, survive—helped me through those first days."

"But it's hard on a marriage. Even all these years"—Trevor swallowed hard—"after Amy and Trev, Meg still has to put up with the . . . aftermath."

Doug shook his head. He knew what Trevor was saying and hated that it was true for Mickey, too.

"Have you talked to Phil?"

"Pastor Phil?"

Trevor nodded.

"What do you mean?"

"He's a good counselor, Doug. If you haven't already talked to someone, I can't recommend it enough. He helped me get my head on straight."

"Your head is on straighter than any man I know."

Now it was Trevor's turn to laugh. But he quickly sobered. "Meg was a gift to me that I never expected. Yes, I went through hell and back to get where I am today. But to have Meg in my life . . ."

Doug winked. "And now *two* babies to boot . . ."

A look of revelation came over Trevor's face. "I guess it is a blessing, isn't it?"

"More than you'll ever know."

Ten minutes later Doug pulled out of the parking lot behind the print shop. But instead of heading toward home, he turned his truck toward Phil Grady's house.

All she could hope
for now was that
they might become
friends again.

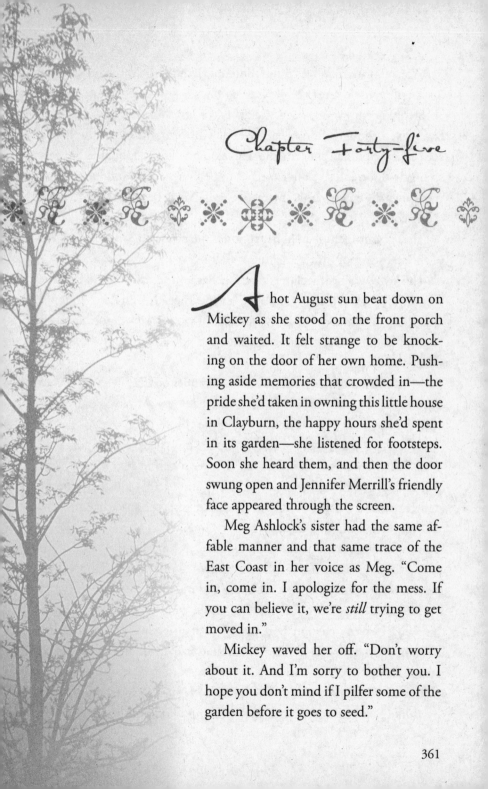

Chapter Forty-five

A hot August sun beat down on Mickey as she stood on the front porch and waited. It felt strange to be knocking on the door of her own home. Pushing aside memories that crowded in—the pride she'd taken in owning this little house in Clayburn, the happy hours she'd spent in its garden—she listened for footsteps. Soon she heard them, and then the door swung open and Jennifer Merrill's friendly face appeared through the screen.

Meg Ashlock's sister had the same affable manner and that same trace of the East Coast in her voice as Meg. "Come in, come in. I apologize for the mess. If you can believe it, we're *still* trying to get moved in."

Mickey waved her off. "Don't worry about it. And I'm sorry to bother you. I hope you don't mind if I pilfer some of the garden before it goes to seed."

"You're more than welcome." Smiling, Jennifer held the door wide. "It is *your* garden, after all."

Stepping into the house, Mickey felt a little like Alice in Wonderland. Even though she'd been here only three months ago, the house seemed smaller than she remembered. And not nearly as quaint. She felt strangely disoriented. She'd expected to be hit by regret and longing for the things she'd given up to marry Doug DeVore. But . . . those feelings didn't come.

That is, until Jennifer led her through the house and she stepped out of the sliding door into her garden.

The lawn was neatly clipped and the flagstone patio swept off, but it was obvious her renters were no gardeners. The shrubs were overgrown and leggy and the last of the summer flowers were in desperate need of deadheading. Weeds had crept into the flowerbeds, and the mulch needed replacing.

Mickey tried not to judge the young couple too harshly. They'd only been here for a few weeks, and they both had new jobs in Salina, along with getting settled in the house and in the community.

Still, it pained her to see the garden she'd lovingly tended for three years left to become a weed patch. It was sobering how quickly the plants had grown shabby and ragged. Without the constant, almost daily, attention she'd given it when she lived here, the space had become an overgrown tangle of weeds in a short time.

Even though she owned the house, and technically, the yard, it was hard to feel the same passion for the place now that she no longer lived here. Now that her life was with Doug and the kids.

Maybe that was how Doug felt about her. Technically, she was his wife, but the passion he'd once had for her had faded, and she despaired of him ever feeling a husband's love for her again. If he ever had.

Since he'd moved out of the bedroom and into Landon's room, they'd lived like polite strangers with each other. Sometimes she thought she would prefer the arguments they used to have. At least then she had some kind of relationship with him.

But true to his word, he had treated her with kindness, and though she sometimes worried that he was suffering from depression, she'd never once seen him lose his temper the way he had with Kayeleigh that day.

She was grateful he'd started meeting with Phil Grady twice a month. Doug never talked to her about those counseling sessions with Pastor Grady—or much else, for that matter—but lately, it seemed like he came home from those meetings in a good mood, at peace.

All she could hope for now was that they might become friends again. She was learning patience like she'd never known it before.

Sighing, she went around the side of the house and gathered a collection of flowerpots and flats from the trunk of her car.

She spent the next two hours digging up some of her favorite plants and flowers to transplant to Doug's place. She'd resigned herself to staying with him. For the kids' sake. And if that was where her life was going to be, she had to find something there that gave her pleasure. Besides the kids, of course.

She'd decided to start a new flower garden behind the farmhouse—on a smaller scale, at least for now. They couldn't really afford to buy all new plants, so today she dug up dianthus and gaura and phlox from her yard, and filled pots with several varieties of the sedums that thrived on the rocky hills she'd built against the corners of the fence.

It wasn't the best time of year for transplanting, but she kept collecting plants and loading them into the trunk and backseat of the car until she could barely get it closed. She had the whole weekend to get them into the ground. If even a few of the plants survived, she'd be content. Even here, in her protected garden, it had taken several tries to find the perfect spot for some of these specimens. But given a chance, their roots went down deep into the Coyote County clay and clung fast. Once they were established, even a Kansas prairie fire couldn't have kept them down. In fact, sometimes it seemed they flourished in adversity.

When she pulled into the driveway, it was almost suppertime. She tooted the horn and got out to open the trunk.

The kids spilled out of the house, all talking at once. "What did you get, Mickey? Hows come you're all muddy? What's for supper?"

"Come here, guys." In turn, she filled their little arms with pots. "Set everything in the backyard by the shed. We'll plant it tomorrow."

Landon and Kayeleigh grumbled, but not too loudly, she noticed. The garden would be great for the kids. It was something they could do together, and if they planted a few vegetables next spring, it would save some money on the grocery bill, too.

But the flowers came first. Her fingers itched at the thought. She hadn't realized how much she'd missed her garden.

She smiled at the image of Harley toddling through leafy rows of green, then cringed at a vision of the little squirt picking off all the flower buds before anything had a chance to bloom next spring. Oh, but wouldn't Harley have a grand time digging in the dirt? They all would.

Her heart swelled at the thought of her kids. If she and Doug had grown distant, his children had wormed their way into her heart until she could scarcely tell where she ended and they began.

Oh, she and Kayeleigh still had their moments, but she had a feeling even Kaye would have tangled with her headstrong oldest daughter.

Her kids. Mickey had begun to feel like an honest-to-goodness mother to Doug's precious children. And in that privilege, along with her work at the daycare, she felt God had given her purpose in life. Not in the way she'd always dreamed of. But she'd slowly come to accept that she may never understand why things had worked out the way they had. It wasn't a bad life. And most of the time, she felt genuinely happy.

Did she long for Doug to be her husband in more than name only? Every single night. She lay in bed and yearned to have his arms around her, his sweet words in her ear. She hoped God didn't get tired of her praying that Doug could learn to love her. And that perhaps, someday, they could have more than the polite friendship they shared now.

"Where do you want these empty pots, Mickey?" Landon stood in front of her, balancing a stack of terra-cotta pots. He would be as tall as she was by next summer if he grew as much as he had this year.

"Be careful with those, buddy. They're breakable."

Sometimes she had to push away dismal thoughts of the future. The twins would start school in the fall, and in another short year Kayeleigh would be in high school. Time was fleeting, and it was a little frightening to think about a day when the children wouldn't need her anymore. When she wouldn't have a reason to stay.

"Wow." Doug's voice broke through her thoughts. He stood, hands on hips, staring at the overflowing trunk. "Why didn't you borrow the pickup? You could have just brought the whole garden home."

She didn't think she was imagining the hint of a twinkle in his eyes. But she was almost afraid to respond, lest she break the spell and see that wary sadness creep back into his eyes.

Catching her breath, she decided to risk it. Working to keep a perfectly straight face, she gave a little nod. "I told them I'd be back for the rest tomorrow."

He froze in his tracks as if he might actually have bought her line. But she couldn't keep a straight face, and a split-second later, he was laughing at himself.

Reaching for a flat of flowers, he winked at her over the top of the twins' heads. "Good one, Mick."

For one enchanted moment, she dared to hope again.

If she resented
the life he'd trapped
her in, she never
showed it.

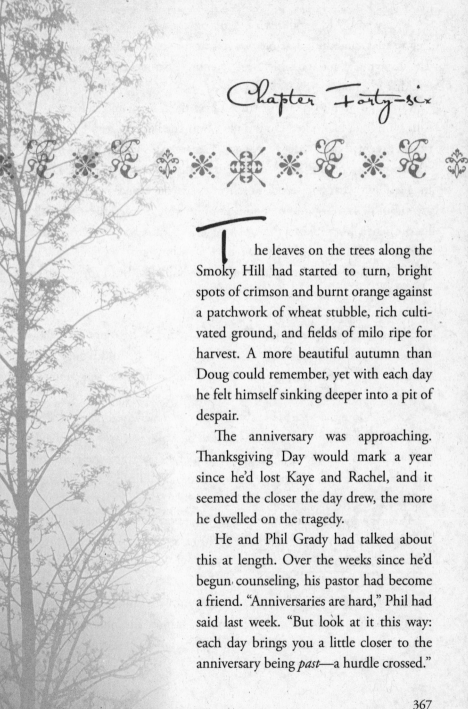

Chapter Forty-six

The leaves on the trees along the Smoky Hill had started to turn, bright spots of crimson and burnt orange against a patchwork of wheat stubble, rich cultivated ground, and fields of milo ripe for harvest. A more beautiful autumn than Doug could remember, yet with each day he felt himself sinking deeper into a pit of despair.

The anniversary was approaching. Thanksgiving Day would mark a year since he'd lost Kaye and Rachel, and it seemed the closer the day drew, the more he dwelled on the tragedy.

He and Phil Grady had talked about this at length. Over the weeks since he'd begun counseling, his pastor had become a friend. "Anniversaries are hard," Phil had said last week. "But look at it this way: each day brings you a little closer to the anniversary being *past*—a hurdle crossed."

It was probably good advice, but somehow he couldn't shake the feeling that something terrible was about to happen. Though how this Thanksgiving could possibly be any more horrible than the last, he couldn't imagine.

Over and over, alone in his truck or on the tractor, and in his prayer time with Phil, he'd asked God to take away the illogical fear. But sometimes it seemed the harder he prayed, the larger his fear loomed.

Most of his pastor's counseling had consisted of him allowing Doug to talk about what happened, to relive his marriage, agonize over his regrets. But this afternoon Phil had caught him off guard with a new tack. He'd opened his Bible to the book of Philippians and looked at him hard, not mincing words. "You've been in a long season of mourning, Doug, and that's been necessary and understandable. But I think you've come to a point where it's counterproductive for you to work so hard at mourning, dwell so much on what you've lost."

Phil read a passage, aloud, about not looking only to one's own interests, but also to the interests of others. "I think," he told Doug, "that it's time for you to start consciously moving away from self-centered thoughts. It's time to cultivate a servant's heart."

At first Doug had felt defensive. Wasn't that why he'd come to Phil for counseling in the first place—because he'd put everyone else's needs first and not taken the time to grieve properly? The kids, the farm, his job, Harriet, and then Mickey—they'd all kept him from doing the hard work of grieving.

Then the thought rang false inside him, and he acknowledged that it wasn't true. In his desperation to avoid his grief, he'd allowed himself to be distracted by all those things. But in recent months he hadn't put anyone but himself first. Not really.

Then Phil read the end of the passage: "Your attitude should be the same as that of Christ Jesus . . . who made himself nothing, taking the very nature of a servant . . . he humbled himself and became obedient to death—even death on a cross."

The words had soaked into him as if he were a thirsty sponge. And in that moment something happened inside him—and he was still trying to process it.

Phil had looked up from his worn Bible. "I'm going to give you an assignment, Doug. This week I want you to make a conscious effort to reach out to other people, to see where they might be hurting, where they could use help. Every time you start thinking about that anniversary, about Kaye and Rachel, I want you to stop and find something, some way—no matter how small—to serve someone else."

But here he was, not fifteen minutes out of his session with Phil, and he was already back to dwelling on that anniversary date, that fear.

He pulled into the garage, determined to take Phil's assignment seriously. Maybe one of the kids would need help with their homework. That was something Mickey usually did, since often he wasn't even home until it was almost bedtime for the kids.

Mickey. If he thought about it too hard, he would be eaten up with guilt over what he'd done to her.

He hung his jacket in the laundry room on the hook beneath his name. "I'm home," he announced, stepping into the kitchen.

"Daddy! Daddy's home!" The twins and Harley scrambled to be first for hugs. Landon was into shoulder punches these days. Doug was happy to oblige them all. He never grew tired of the welcome his children gave him.

"Where's Kayeleigh?"

Mickey was at the sink scrubbing a skillet. "She's spending the night with Rudi. I hope that was okay?"

He nodded. "Sure."

"You're early," she said. "Dinner won't be ready for a little bit."

"That's okay."

"You want something to drink?"

"I'll get it." He went to the refrigerator and grabbed a pitcher of iced tea.

"There's no sugar in that yet."

"I'm on it." He pulled the sugar canister from the cupboard and scooped a couple of spoonfuls of sugar into his glass. Mickey didn't like sugar in her tea.

"Sarah," Mickey said, "you and Sadie, come and dry these dishes, would you? I need to take the chicken out of the oven. Do you want a salad, Doug?"

He shook his head. "Not tonight, thanks." If she resented the life he'd trapped her in, she never showed it. They'd grown into a comfortable pattern with each other, talking only about the kids or household matters. Living separate lives in many ways.

Three Sundays a month they went to church together at Community Christian, and the first Sunday of each month Mickey had dinner in Salina with her brothers. She'd given up asking him to go with her a long time ago. He didn't know what she'd told her brothers and she didn't offer.

If there was a school activity for one of the kids, he went and she stayed home with the others. They rarely went to anything together, and if they did, the kids served as buffers. He didn't know what was said about them—about their marriage—around town, but he could imagine. He'd quit caring a long time ago.

But sometimes, like now, watching Mickey at the sink, laughing with the girls, he remembered those first days when he'd thought he was falling in love with her. When they'd taken the kids bowling or to the movies every Sunday afternoon, or sat out on her deck in town and talked.

In an odd way he wished those days back. Under different circumstances, of course, but sometimes he found himself daydreaming that he had only recently met Mickey. How different things might have been had he only given himself a chance to grieve Kaye before jumping into marriage again so quickly. Phil had told him, "In a way it was a compliment to Kaye that you wanted to get married again so soon. Kaye made marriage look like a good deal."

He understood what Phil was saying, but it didn't change the fact that he'd made a terrible mistake. And Mickey was paying the highest price for his mistake. How he wished he could change all that. The night he'd confessed to her that he didn't, *couldn't* love her the way she hoped, she'd led him to believe she still loved him. But a lot of water had passed under the bridge since then. They'd lived these separate existences for four months now. Yet it seemed like a lifetime. He didn't know how she felt about him anymore. And part of him was afraid to know.

An emotion swept over him—one he couldn't quite identify, except that it was a familiar feeling. He felt the way he'd felt as a boy when his parents dropped him off for a week at summer camp. *He was homesick.* Except the cure for homesickness had always been coming home. But he *was* home, and he had the worst case ever—with no idea how or where to find a remedy.

Sighing, he went through to the living room, looking for the newspaper. He rarely had time to read more than the headlines and the weather. Maybe he'd finish it while he waited for dinner.

Mickey's cat sat in front of the sofa, staring at him.

"What?" he said aloud, as if the cat might actually answer.

"What'd you say, Doug?" Mickey yelled from the kitchen.

"Nothing. I was talking to Sasha."

Mickey and the girls giggled at that.

He opened the paper and heard Phil's words in his head: *"Find some way—no matter how small—to serve someone else."* He looked through to the kitchen where Mickey was working, hustling between the stove and refrigerator and attending to Harley. She'd worked all day at the daycare, yet she came home and made dinner and cared for the kids. She did it all without complaining, cheerfully even. He did his best to help her on the nights he wasn't working late in the fields, but the truth was, she got the brunt of the housework and the childcare and—

"Ouch!"

Mickey's cry and the sound of the oven door slamming shut urged him from the sofa. "What happened?"

She stood at the sink, holding her hand under a stream of cold water. He could tell she was trying hard not to cry.

"What happened?"

She winced. "I burned myself . . . on that stupid oven."

He leaned over the sink. "Let me see . . ."

She held up her hand. An angry welt was already starting to blister on the back of her hand.

Without thinking he lifted her damp fingers to his lips and kissed them, the way he might have if she'd been one of the little girls. When he realized what he'd done, his face grew warm and he waited for her to pull her hand away.

But she didn't. Their eyes met and something—something that frightened him and thrilled him all at once—passed between them. It reminded him of that first time she'd brought the kids home from daycare because he was late, and she'd stayed to eat with them. Except this time there was no guilt for the stirrings inside him. This was his wife.

He inspected the wound. "Looks painful. You should keep water on it for a while." He reached for a clean dish towel. "Come here . . ."

Still holding her injured hand, he led her down the hall into the bathroom. He turned on the faucet and tested the temperature, then gently placed her hand under the slow stream of tepid water. She held her hand there while he rummaged in the medicine cabinet for something to put on the broken blister. After a minute of scanning labels and not comprehending anything he read, Mickey reached around him with her other hand.

"Here, try this." She shut the door to the cabinet.

As she held out the brown bottle of hydrogen peroxide, he caught her reflection in the mirror. She was watching him with bemused curiosity. "Um . . . didn't you used to be an EMT?" Her grin came into full bloom, her eyes alight with a sparkle he remembered from a long time ago.

He took the bottle from her, and uncapped it, feeling clumsy and inept. "Apparently I am seriously out of practice. Here . . . give me your hand."

Their eyes met again in the mirror, and her expression turned serious. "Thanks."

She looked away and he carefully patted her hand dry around the burn, then assessed the damage. "Well, I have good news and bad news."

"Oh?"

"The good news is, I think you'll live."

"Whew, that's a relief. And, um . . . the bad news?"

He held her hand over the sink and tipped the bottle. "This is gonna sting like crazy."

She winced in anticipation. "Oh . . . ouchie, owie . . . owie!" But the tremulous, unmistakable smile in her eyes let him hope that she was feeling something beyond the pain. That she was feeling the same stirrings as he was inside.

He blew across her hand in short little breaths, and for a reason he didn't quite comprehend, with every breath his spirits lifted. Higher and higher . . . until he thought he might float right up to the ceiling.

This was something
different, something
she couldn't quite put
her finger on. And
it worried her.

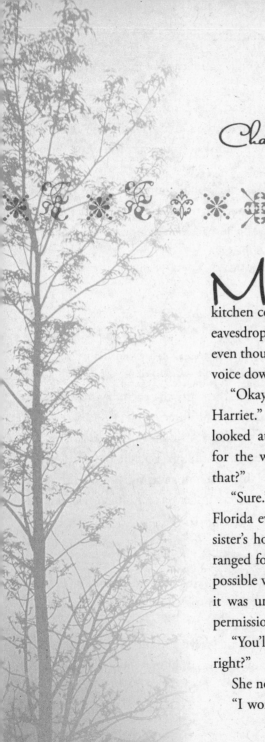

Chapter Forty-seven

Mickey wiped off perfectly clean kitchen counters, feeling a little guilty for eavesdropping on Doug's conversation—even though he made no effort to keep his voice down.

"Okay, sure. See you then. Thanks, Harriet." He hung up the phone and looked at her. "Harriet wants the kids for the whole weekend. You okay with that?"

"Sure." Kaye's mother came from Florida every few months, staying at her sister's house in Salina. Doug always arranged for her to see the kids as much as possible whenever she was in Kansas. But it was unusual for him to ask Mickey's permission about plans.

"You'll be with your brothers Sunday, right?"

She nodded. Something was up.

"I wondered . . ." He dipped his head

before looking her in the eye. "Would you have any interest in having me . . . come with you this time?"

Despite how well she and Doug had been getting along over the past few months, she'd long ago given up on the DeVore family ever blending with her extended family. She couldn't keep the surprise out of her voice. "I—I'd love it if you came."

He bit the corner of his lip. "Yes, but would your brothers love it?"

She grinned. "Probably not as much as I would. But I don't think they'll kick you out or anything." She hesitated for a minute. "Do I dare ask . . . why this sudden change of heart?"

He shrugged. "I've . . . been thinking."

"About?"

A faraway look came to his eyes. "A lot of things."

"Okay . . ." Thanksgiving, the anniversary of Kaye and Rachel's deaths, had been a turning point for her and Doug. Even before that, really. But after that anniversary passed, they somehow found their way back to the friendship they'd begun at the start, and each day she felt a tiny bit closer to him than she had the day before.

But for several days now, he'd seemed a little down—or *something*. Sometimes Harriet's visits sent him into a slump. But she didn't think that was what was bothering him this time. This was something different, something she couldn't quite put her finger on. And it worried her. "Is . . . is everything okay?"

He took a deep breath. "Mickey, I'd like to talk to you . . . about . . . some things."

She nodded and tried to smile, but a strange fear took hold of her, and a hundred possibilities—none of them pleasant—roamed through her mind, trying to take root.

"I told Harriet I'd bring the kids into town in time to have supper with her and Aunt Bess. How about I bring us home something to eat after I drop them off?"

"Sure." She forced a laugh. "You know me—I never turn down a chance to get out of the kitchen."

His shoulders lifted and he brightened. "Okay. I've got dinner covered." He glanced out the kitchen window. "Maybe we can eat outside?"

She followed his gaze to a perfect blue sky. "If it doesn't cool off too quick, that'd be lovely."

※ ※ ※

At six o'clock Mickey heard the garage door. Feeling strangely nervous, she ran to check her hair in the laundry room mirror. She so rarely spent time alone with Doug.

Oh, Father, please help this weekend to go well. Please help us just to enjoy each other, and to grow closer—to each other, and to You.

These little prayers throughout the day had become as natural to her as breathing. As Doug had continued to meet with Pastor Grady, he'd begun to pray with her and the kids. Not only at mealtimes, but before the kids went to bed each night. His were simple prayers, but they touched her deeply and compelled her to cultivate her own closer relationship with God.

Doug held up an Arby's bag. "I got your favorite. And the weather's perfect. It hit sixty-five this afternoon. I vote for that picnic."

"Okay." She grabbed bottles of water from the fridge and went for a jacket and the picnic blanket.

He spread it on the ground, and they ate in silence, enjoying the songbirds and the warmth of the fading sun on their backs.

"You have this place looking really nice, Mick," he said over a mouthful of roast beef.

Mickey followed his gaze around the corner of the backyard she'd claimed as her garden. A few things, the phlox and gaura, were just beginning to come up—enough that she could be sure at least some of her transplants had taken. But she knew it wasn't the plants themselves Doug was referring to.

Right now the framework of the garden was all that was visible: the hill of rocks she'd arranged for the sedum to climb, the arbor she hoped would someday burgeon with roses, the brick pathway Doug and the kids had helped her lay. Those were the only things the garden had to boast right now. And yet, viewed through the hope of spring, they had their own beauty.

"It'll be real pretty this summer," he said, as if he'd read her mind.

As the sun slunk below the horizon, a gentle breeze came through. Mickey shivered and pulled one corner of the picnic blanket over her legs.

"You cold?"

"A little. I'm fine."

"You want to go in?"

She shook her head. "I'm enjoying this."

"Hang on." He jumped up. "I'll be right back."

A minute later he came back with one of the old quilts they kept in the Suburban in case of a winter emergency—or a summer picnic. "Here." He stood behind her and she felt the quilt settle down around her shoulders.

"Mmm . . . that feels good. Thanks."

The sun disappeared, leaving a haze of pale blue in the west. In the distance crickets started a slow *chirrup chirrup chirrup.*

Doug cocked his head and listened for a minute. "It's still almost fifty degrees."

She wrinkled her brow. "How do you know that?"

"Crickets."

"Huh?"

"If you count the chirps, you'll know the temperature."

"No way."

Yesterday's Embers

"You didn't know that?"

"You're putting me on." All of a sudden she remembered the date on the calendar. "This is an April Fool's joke, right?"

He laughed. "No, I'm serious. You apparently don't read the *Farmer's Almanac.*"

"No, but I read *National Geographic,* and I sure don't remember ever hearing anything about crickets telling the temperature." She tilted her head like he had and listened. All she heard was one undulating drone. She narrowed her eyes. "Okay, I give. How do you count cricket chirps?"

"Listen again." He held up a finger and mouthed a count. *One, two, three, four, five . . .*

She nodded. Watching him count, she could sort of separate them out.

"Okay, now," he said. "You count to fourteen—silently, to yourself— and I'll count the chirps."

They locked eyes while she counted under her breath and he held up fingers for each chirp. ". . . six, seven, eight—"

She held up a hand when she hit fourteen. "Time's up."

"It's forty-eight degrees." He bobbed his head as if that settled it.

She shot him a skeptical look. "How did you get forty-eight degrees out of that?"

He wiggled his eyebrows. "You have to know the secret formula."

"And that would be?"

"Count the chirps in fourteen seconds and add forty."

She shed the quilt, jumped up, and ran over to the other side of the rose arbor where she'd nailed up a thermometer. "Forty-eight, on the money. That is so cool!"

He laughed and puffed out his chest.

She came back and sat cross-legged on the blanket.

"You want this?" He gestured to the quilt.

"Please." He shook it out and wrapped it back around her shoulders, making her think of the way he snugged Harley into her little hoodies.

She hated to spoil the moment, but her curiosity was getting the better of her. "You said you wanted to talk to me about something."

He looked thoughtful, and for a minute she was afraid he was going to say "never mind."

Instead, he got up and knelt in front of her on the blanket. Closing his eyes, as if he were about to dive into icy water, he reached for her hands.

She melted at the warmth of his touch.

For a full minute he sat that way, stroking her hands with his thumbs. She looked at him, wondering where this was going, and realized that he was struggling to control his emotions.

"Doug? What's wrong?"

He inhaled and breathed out her name. "This is going to sound a little funny . . . Mrs. DeVore." He grinned, suddenly seeming himself again. "But I wanted—I've wanted for a long time—to ask you to marry me."

She opened her mouth to speak, but words wouldn't come. Tears did, though, like a geyser. She fanned a hand in front of her face, trying to quell the sobs. She didn't know if she was crying from relief, or love, or sheer joy.

Doug moved to wrap her in his arms.

Except in her dreams, it had been nearly a year since he'd held her this way. But oh, it felt exactly the way she remembered.

He pulled back slightly and put a hand under her chin. "Hey, hey . . . that wasn't supposed to make you *cry*. What's wrong?"

"Oh, Doug." Now she laughed through her tears.

He held her and patted her back through the quilt. "You okay?" Genuine concern softened his voice.

She nodded. "I'm crying because I'm happy."

"You *sure*?"

She nodded again. "I've never been so sure about anything in my life."

He eased down on the blanket and pulled her beside him, squeezing her close. "I want to do it right this time, Mickey. I want you to have that big church wedding and that big white dress you always wanted."

His words touched her in a place so deep it was painful. But she shook her head. She knew what she wanted. And it wasn't the things he thought.

"Doug . . . oh, you're so sweet to offer that. A year ago I would have jumped all over that. But not anymore. I think the time has passed for that."

His arm dropped from her shoulder, and she realized he'd misunderstood.

She laughed softly and moved his arm back around her shoulder. "Hear me out. I want—I want the groom. Oh, do I ever want the groom."

She reached up and cradled his stubbled cheek in her palm. *Her husband.* The tears came again. "But I don't need all that other stuff anymore—the dress, the fancy wedding—I have what really matters. Everything that's truly important."

He turned his head until his lips touched her fingertips. "Is that a yes?"

She nodded, smiling until her face hurt.

"I love you, Michaela DeVore. I've been loving you for a while now. I don't know if you noticed."

"I was starting to suspect." She pulled away and drank in the boyish grin he gave her.

"The only thing I could ever want for now is—" She hesitated, feeling suddenly shy.

"What?" The longing in his eyes—still laced with a fair bit of mischief—told her that he was hoping she'd say exactly what she was about to say.

"As long as we're already married . . . ?"

He hung on her words. "Yes?"

"I'm lonely. At night. I miss . . . having you in my bed. Do you think we could . . . eventually . . . work our way back to that part of marriage?"

He drew back and narrowed his eyes. But he couldn't hide the gleam in them. "This isn't an April Fool's joke, is it?"

She mirrored his expression. "Would I joke about something like that?"

In answer, a thousand crickets began a cheerful *chirrup chirrup chirrup.*

Dear Reader

My husband jokes that we have been happily married for thirty years—and not so happily for the other four. There's a tiny bit of truth to his jesting. Marriage is an amazing institution and one of the greatest blessings in my own life, yet at times it has been the source of some of the greatest challenges I've ever faced. If you are married, have ever been married, or ever hope to be, somewhere along the journey, you probably have faced (or soon will) struggles similar to the ones Doug and Mickey confronted in *Yesterday's Embers*.

What did our Creator intend marriage to be? God has called many of us to marriage, and it is His plan that marriage should be a loving, fulfilling and profitable relationship. God said, "It is not good for the man to be alone. I will make a helper suitable for him" (Genesis 2:18). At least four times the Bible reminds us that "a man will leave his father and mother and be united to his wife, and the two will become one flesh."

But we live in a fallen world, and unfortunately, many marriages are reaping the consequences of sin and evil.

Perhaps, like Mickey and Doug, your marriage isn't all you hoped it would be. Maybe you even fear you made a mistake when you married your spouse. If so, your heart is probably aching. But here's the good news: Jesus Christ is in the business of healing wounded couples, joining men and women who have longed for a lifelong companion, and building lasting, happy marriages. Why not give God your wounded heart and the broken pieces of your relationship, and see if He won't do a miracle before your eyes?

It will take time. You might feel as though you are giving 110 percent while your spouse gives nothing. But many times in my life I've seen miracles occur when one partner in a marriage determines to trust God and love his or her spouse as they promised on their wedding day: for better or for worse, in sickness and in health, till death alone separates them.

Whether you long to be married and haven't met the right person yet, whether you're just starting out in marriage or have been married seventy-nine years like my husband's grandparents, whether your marriage is fabulous or failing, let today be the first day of a better marriage—and a better life—than you ever thought possible.

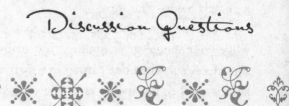

Discussion Questions

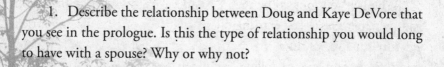

1. Describe the relationship between Doug and Kaye DeVore that you see in the prologue. Is this the type of relationship you would long to have with a spouse? Why or why not?

2. Doug arrives home from the funeral of his wife and daughter to the responsibility of being both father and mother, and to a "new normal"—one he does not want. If you've lost someone you love, what were your thoughts about going on without them? How would you advise Doug about coming to terms with his deep loss?

3. How does Doug perceive that people are treating him after the loss of his wife and daughter? How do you approach people who are grieving? What do you do and say? When have your well-thought-out words worked—and not worked? Explain the situation. Knowing how Doug feels, would you now do anything differently? If so, what?

4. In what ways was Doug like—and not like—Mickey's list for the man of her dreams in chapter 14? If you were Mickey, would you regret your decision to say yes to a "date" with this man? Why or why not? Do you think Kaye's mother has a valid point to her concerns? Why or why not?

5. Though they are both Christians, Doug and Mickey have grown up in very different denominations. What are some of the challenges they will face in marriage because of their different faith backgrounds? Have you ever dated or married someone of a different denomination? How did it affect your relationship, and how did you handle those differences?

6. What role did Mickey's brothers and their wives play in her life? How did her relationship with Doug change her ties to her family? If you are married, how has your relationship with your spouse changed the dynamics of your extended family? Talk about any challenges you've faced and the solutions you've discovered.

7. Why do you think Doug was drawn so quickly to Mickey even though his wife had only been gone a few short months? What were Doug's reasons for marrying again so soon after being widowed? Do you believe they were valid? Why or why not?

8. Why was Mickey attracted to Doug? How did she justify a relationship with a man who'd so recently lost his spouse? Read the following verses from the Bible and talk about how they might have applied (or not) to Doug and Mickey's situation: 1 Corinthians 7:1–9; Ecclesiastes 3:1–8; Ephesians 5:22–32. Did Doug and Mickey seek God's direction for whether and when they should marry? Why or why not?

9. What were Kayeleigh's responses to seeing the romantic interlude between her dad and "Miss Valdez" in chapter 24? Do you think they were justified? Why or why not? Were you surprised that Doug was second-guessing his proposal to Mickey? Why or why not? Have you ever second-guessed yourself on an important decision? Explain.

Discussion Questions

10.   Talk about Kayeleigh's relationship with Seth. Do you think she, as a twelve-year-old girl, is experiencing normal feelings toward him? What other things might be controlling her emotions and affections?

11.   How did you feel about the fact that Mickey got "stuck" with caring for Doug's children while he worked two jobs? How did this differ from her expectations of being married to Doug? How do you think you would respond in a similar situation? What compromises might they have made?

12.   In chapter 27 Mickey worries that Doug will compare her to Kaye. Have you ever compared yourself with someone else that you thought was "better" than you—and felt you couldn't compete? Explain the situation. Were your fears real—or unfounded? What did you choose to do about them?

13.   Do you think Mickey should have reorganized and redecorated the DeVore home? Talk about Doug's and the children's reactions. Were they justified? How might this have been handled differently to avoid the conflict that ensued?

14.   Do you think it was fair of Doug to share his thoughts and feelings with Mickey in chapter 43? Why or why not? Has anyone ever been brutally honest with you? How did you respond? How did your relationship with that person change?

15.   After almost giving up on ever recapturing the love they once felt for one another, what do you think was the turning point for Doug and Mickey to reconcile? Were their turning points different? Do you think one of them sacrificed more than the other toward reconciliation? If so, which one—and why? Have you ever been in a situation of conflict

where you felt like you were giving more than the other person toward the restoration of your relationship? Explain.

16. In chapter 45 how does Mickey's garden reflect, to her, the state of her love with Doug? If you were in Mickey's place, would you have stayed with Doug? Why or why not?

17. What did you think of the assignment Pastor Phil gave to Doug in chapter 46? In what way this week could you carry out the same assignment in your own life? Do you think it could make as great a difference as it made to Doug? Explain.

18. What did you think changed Doug's mind and heart in chapter 47? Did you expect this ending to the book? Why or why not?

About the Author

DEBORAH RANEY dreamed of writing a book since the summer she read all of Laura Ingalls Wilder's *Little House* books and discovered that a little Kansas farm girl could, indeed, grow up to be a writer. After a happy twenty-year detour as a stay-at-home wife and mom, Deb began her writing career. Her first novel, *A Vow to Cherish,* was awarded a Silver Angel from Excellence in Media, and inspired the acclaimed World Wide Pictures film of the same title. Since then her books have won the RITA Award, the HOLT Medallion, the National Readers' Choice Award, as well as being a two-time Christy Award finalist. Deb enjoys speaking and teaching at writers' conferences across the country. She and her husband, artist Ken Raney, make their home in their native Kansas and love the small-town life that is the setting for many of Deb's novels. The Raneys enjoy gardening, watching their teenage daughter's sports and music events, and traveling to visit three grown children and grandchildren who live much too far away.

Deborah loves hearing from her readers. To e-mail her or to learn more about her books, please visit www.deborahraney.com or write to Deborah in care of Howard Books, 3117 North 7th Street, West Monroe, Louisiana 71291.

Also available in the Clayburn series

Remember to Forget

What if you could start all over again? What if you had a chance to walk away from mistakes in your past and reinvent yourself? *Remember to Forget* is an unforgettable story of second chances that holds the promise of starting over, of creating a new life in God's care.

Leaving November

Eight years ago, Vienne Kenney moved away from Clayburn and all its gossip to pursue a law degree in California. But now she has failed the bar exam again. Is she destined to be stuck forever, a failure—just like her father—in this two-horse Kansas town?

HOWARD BOOKS
A Division of Simon & Schuster